AFTER THE RAINBOW

Yvonne Kalman

St. Martin's Press
New York

Library of Congress Cataloging-in-Publication Data

Kalman, Yvonne.
    After the rainbow / by Yvonne Kalman.
        p.   cm.
    ISBN 0-312-04957-9
    1. New Zealand—History—19th century—Fiction.   I. Title.
PR9639.3.K33A48   1990
823—dc20   90-37238
                                                               CIP

First published in Great Britain by Bantam Press

First U.S. Edition: November 1990
10 9 8 7 6 5 4 3 2 1

With Warm Affection for
Dorothy and James Sanders

AFTER THE RAINBOW

ONE

Daisy Morgan woke with a cold feeling of unease. In the first moment, when her eyes focused on the reflected sunlight that shimmered over the plaster roses on the ceiling, she remembered why.

Today Papa was marrying his mistress, Lisabeth Nye.

Last night she had fallen asleep hoping that something, anything, would happen to prevent it. A devastating storm perhaps. But, trudging to fling herself on to the brocade window-seat, she saw that it was a glorious made-to-order wedding day. Beyond the gardens the surf hush-hushed at the foot of the cliffs, birds carped in the orangery below her casement, while in the courtyard beyond the rose garden hoofs clicked against the cobblestones. A coarse male voice was saying: 'So Mistress Nye's about ter become respectable, hey? Not afore time, neither! 'Ere, did yer 'ear the riddle 'bout 'ow can yer tell the difference atween Mistress Nye an' a brick o' soap?' The voice lowered, mumbled, and was followed by Mrs Tenks's braying laugh. Daisy felt ill. Even the *servants* were cackling about Papa's marriage.

As Daisy reached to jerk the mullioned window closed, the wind lifted another sound across the plains to her, the multi-chorded bleating of thousands of merino sheep mustered down from the distant high country to the spider-webbing of sheep-pens around a huge red wool-shed which was down the slope behind the stables, at the back of the house. Rhys Morgan, the master of Mists of Heaven, might be marrying today and all his servants celebrating the fact, but the shearing (performed by gangs of itinerant workers) would stop for nothing.

The baaing sounded like laughter, too, thought Daisy as she snipped the lock shutting out the world.

Lisabeth Nye had been part of Daisy's life for years, and for most of that time Daisy had adored her. She was warm and generous with a sunny nature and a gift for amusing a lonely little girl, at first with stories about rabbits and kittens, and fairy folk who lived in the foxgloves that grew wild in the mountains Daisy could see from her window; then later nudging her towards works by Twain and Melville, though Daisy's pedestrian taste was avid for twopenny novelettes. It was then that the trouble began. Lisabeth persuaded Rhys that the child should go to school. She had a fine intelligent mind that needed (and deserved) training. Look at what she had achieved under Lisabeth's inexpert tutelage: she could devour a book in a single afternoon, name every country in the British Empire, execute five different types of embroidery and sing folk-songs in three languages.

Daisy was distraught; she didn't want to leave the home she loved, but Rhys and Lisabeth were firm. Rhys enrolled her in the Chapel Street School for Girls and arranged for her to board in town with Sir Kenneth and Lady Launcenolt, who had been Daisy's mother's godparents. It was on a visit to Benares, their Christchurch home, that Azura had met and married Rhys. Ever since she could speak Daisy had called them 'Kiki' and 'Aunt Bea', and whenever they got the opportunity they ruinously indulged this delightful child who reminded them so poignantly of their beloved long-dead Azura.

It was because they had never liked or approved of Lisabeth that Daisy now saw her illuminated in a different light. When Daisy explained that Lisabeth said it would be a sin to waste a clever mind like hers, Aunt Bea sniffed that Lisabeth should know all about sin, and when Daisy commented that Lisabeth blushed whenever someone called her 'Mistress Nye' Kiki laughed hugely and said if that wasn't an appropriate title, then he didn't know what was. Both hinted that Lisabeth wanted Daisy out of the way, but in her innocence Daisy didn't understand any of the veiled hints and comments. Not then.

It was three years ago on her fourteenth birthday that her eyes were irrevocably opened to the ugly truth. She was leaning against the hitching-rail outside Miss Newington's Pianoforte and Spinet Studio waiting for her friend Amy Thorne to finish her lesson (Amy's lesson always took longer than hers), and idly scanning the playbills that were pasted on the adjacent wall. There, among the advertisements for Christy's Minstrels, the Williams & Musgrove Opera posters and lurid posters advertising the arrival of Madame Cora, the world-famous hypnotiste, was a tatty grey pamphlet that Daisy would have passed by without reading but for the fact that her eye was caught by her father's name. Daisy tore it down and read it, and when Amy came skipping out to join her she found Daisy weeping over the rag of paper she had twisted in her gloved hands.

'This isn't true,' she blurted, thrusting it out. 'Papa isn't a wicked adult. He won't burn in hellfire. And Lisabeth—'

'Adulterer,' supplied the worldly Amy. 'But take no notice. Father has a theory that people are jealous of Mr Morgan because he's so wealthy and powerful. That's why they print these nasty pamphlets.'

'You mean, this isn't the only—'

'Heavens, no! There've been dozens. Ever since Lisabeth left her husband years and years ago there's been a terrible scandal. I thought you knew. These pamphlets sell at the Canfield Street market for a penny apiece, and every few months there's another . . .'

Daisy shivered in the chill wind. 'Lisabeth's not married.'

Amy was silent. Was that pity in her eyes? Daisy had seen that look before on the faces of her classmates, when she'd interrupted them giggling over some hastily concealed 'secret' in a corner of the school-yard. *A pamphlet*, guessed Daisy with a plummeting feeling of dread. She said stoutly: 'I *know* she's not married. Aunty Gwynne would have told me if she was! Aunty Gwynne and her husband adopted Lisabeth and Andrew when their mother died, and she's known them all of their lives. She'd know if Lisabeth had a husband. She'd have told me, wouldn't she?' But her voice faltered as she recalled Gwynne's eva-siveness when Daisy asked awkward questions, such as why didn't Papa ever tell her stories about Mamma like Aunt Bea did, and why did Lisabeth sleep in the room next to Papa's while Gwynne's, his sister's, room was in the servants' quarters out by the stables? (She was 'more comfortable' out there, she said, adding that Manx people believed white stone was unlucky, and a Manxwoman like herself could never sleep within the mansion's tall white walls. And Rhys never mentioned Azura 'because of grief'.)

Amy said: 'Is there any sign of your father yet? What time did he say he was meeting us? Just think, the Blue Room for afternoon tea! I'll make it the subject of my speech tomorrow.'

'It *is* true,' decided Daisy with sudden fierceness. 'Lisabeth *is* his "fancy piece" and that's why Papa never takes her out with him, why they always go separately to concerts and things. And that's why people stare and whisper, and why we never get invited anywhere . . . Because of *her*.' She glowered, thinking of the stories she'd heard about Sum-merlea where the Andruths entertained like royalty, and Lakeland West where the Westlakes held famous parties, and about the Martins' enor-mous picnic-days at Martinsfield.

What Daisy couldn't know was that Lisabeth, seeing that Daisy was being excluded from the district's society gatherings, sent her to school hoping that she would be insulated from hurt by a circle of genuine friends she'd make there. Instead her fellow-pupils were awed by Rhys Morgan's daughter, and the only one who befriended her was bold pushy Amy, the publican's daughter from the Golden Fleece, who, being motherless, too, felt an affinity for the lonely girl.

'I saw Lisabeth's husband once,' offered Amy. 'He's a hermit. He

9

used to be a schoolteacher but he lost his job over the scandal, they say. He gathers firewood along Sumner Beach like the Maori children do and ties it in bundles to sell in the market. He's tall and gowky, not handsome like Mr Morgan, and he wears newspapers under his jacket to keep warm, but they say that for all his miserly ways—'

'*They* say too much,' retorted Daisy, bright spots of pride flaming her cheeks. 'Here comes Papa now,' she added as Rhys Morgan's landau the colour of ox-blood turned into the street. 'I can't face him now, Amy. Tell him . . . tell him I had a headache and missed my lesson. I'm taking the steam-tram back to Benares, and I'm telling Aunt Bea all about—'

'No!' begged Amy in alarm. 'Please don't take on so, Daisy! You can't spoil our treat like this. It's your birthday! Please, Daisy, don't ruin everything!'

But it was already ruined. At the Blue Room, Rhys was his usual gracious charming self, but instead of responding with her customary delight Daisy noticed how their fellow-patrons cast overt glances in their direction. In the past she'd revelled in the attention her handsome father attracted, but now it sickened her. People were sniggering and gossiping about them, and it was all Lisabeth's fault.

And now Papa was about to *marry* her.

The door opened. She turned to see Gwynne Stafford hobbling in, every step reflected in a grimace that showed her dark-gummed dentures. 'The perfect day for a wedding!' she lilted in her sweet wavery voice. 'Oh, the perfect day! It whisks me right back to that wonderful day when your uncle Charles and I took our own—'

'I have a headache,' announced Daisy, wanting neither good cheer nor reminiscences about someone who had died an age ago.

'Oh dear . . . oh dear . . .' Because she spoke so tentatively, Gwynne often repeated herself. Massaging her arthritic wrists, she contemplated Daisy with a helpless frown.

Gwynne was twenty-five years older than her brother Rhys and nothing like him, being diminutive and round-shouldered with a great many plump chins that made her look much stouter than she really was. Her dull eyes were magnified by thick wire-rimmed spectacles – lorgnettes were a vanity, and she despised vanity – while her wispy grey hair was thrust up under a bulging house-cap cut from the same ugly mauve cloth as everything else she wore. People often commented on the difference between sister and brother without realizing what lay at the root of it: Rhys had led a charmed life of easy material success and enjoyable work that bore rewarding fruits, while Gwynne's life had been one of toil and frustration, of crushed hopes and ruined dreams. Life had taught Rhys to stride out confidently, head high, smiling, while Gwynne learned to shuffle slowly in an attitude of anticipated defeat.

Only in the last ten years had she tasted luxury, and the flavour made her uneasy. The rôle of a servant in her brother's house was more to her liking, so she devoted herself to looking after Daisy, a rôle that brought her frustration and was a constant irritant to Daisy, who detested fussing.

Genuine concern trembled in Gwynne's voice as she said: 'A headache? Oh dear. Was it from the sun yesterday? Have you a fever?'

Belatedly Daisy remembered Gwynne's repertoire of vile headache remedies: soda and rhubarb, nux vomica, sal volatile and the unspeakably nasty Guarana powder. Her mouth puckered in revulsion, and she moved away quickly saying, 'It's nothing severe. I'll be better soon!' as she hurried to slop cold water from the washstand ewer into the wide Willow Pattern basin. Before she could scoop it up to cool her face Gwynne was there pressing her hand, soft as a kid glove, over Daisy's forehead. 'Child, you're burning up! You're burning up. It was the sun. I'll fetch some Guarana—'

'No!' snapped Daisy, then swiftly: 'No, thank you, Aunty Gwynne. Truly, it's just excitement. I didn't sleep well.'

'It's too much sun. Dear Charles was the same. He would forget his hat, and he—'

Daisy stopped listening. She sloshed palmfuls of water on her face, gasping and feeling perceptibly better immediately. Dipping a square of clean cloth into the rose-coloured salt-pot, she scrubbed her teeth while Gwynne meandered through her reminiscences. When she had rinsed and spat she said: 'Has there been any word from Andrew yet?'

Gwynne sucked in her breath and shook her head. From behind the dressing-screen Daisy said: 'I hope he's there today. Oh, Aunty Gwynne, I hope it so much!' She was not exaggerating. The thought of seeing Andrew again was the only thing that sweetened this whole sour episode.

'I wouldn't get my hopes up, child. I wouldn't hope.'

'But he *must* come!' insisted Daisy as she wriggled into a green poplin day-dress, pushing her arms into the embroidered sleeves. 'Andrew is Lisabeth's brother. He wouldn't miss her wedding, would he? I mean, he's her only blood relative.'

'He's been away a long time,' ventured Gwynne doubtfully. 'A long, long time. I wouldn't get my hopes up, child.'

'Why wouldn't he come? Tell me, is there some reason I don't know about?' She noticed that Gwynne coloured and her eyes slid away. She persisted: 'Why doesn't Andrew come home? He's been qualified for four years now, and we need more doctors here in the province, especially osteopathic specialists like him. Doctor Meakings told me so himself.' Adjusting the skirt over her hips, she presented her back to Gwynne to be buttoned, asking over her shoulder: 'Have

Andrew and Lisabeth quarrelled? Is that why he stays in Europe?'

'What ideas you get in your head, Daisy!' Her voice sounded guilty. 'What notions you invent!'

I thought as much, mused Daisy, watching Gwynne in the pier-glass. *Andrew knows about Lisabeth's disgraceful behaviour, and that's why he's keeping his distance*. Then she caught sight of her grim scowling face and had to laugh aloud. 'You're right, Aunty Gwynne. I should take more care in the sun. Look at my freckled nose – I'll be taken for one of the McFallishes if I'm not careful. I do wish I looked more dramatically interesting. Do you think that Andrew will find me pretty?'

'That's vanity, dear, and Charles always said that vanity was—'

'A sin. I know. But I can't help worrying. Andrew won't think I'm a baby, will he? He'll be accustomed to sophisticated elegant women.'

'He'll be accustomed to *sick* women. Only sick women, dear.'

Daisy grimaced at her reflection. Even distorted it was a pretty face, wide of brow and pointed of chin with a pert nose, full pink lips and wide, almost staring blue eyes fringed with thick gold lashes, but Daisy noticed only the freckles, the too-wide mouth and the wispy fair hair. *Bland as baby food*, she thought. 'Yes,' she agreed gloomily. 'He'll be fascinated by sick women, and I'm disgustingly healthy.' She smiled. Just talking about Andrew had revived her spirits. 'I'm also disgustingly hungry. Do you know if Papa has come in for breakfast yet?'

Rhys's simply furnished room was empty, the Australian opossum-fur rug smoothed over the single-sized bed, sunlight lying in puddles on the polished floor. Daisy continued down the corridor past the banks of framed paintings – Lisabeth, who was artistically gifted, had gained modest recognition for her watercolours of local scenery – past the looming walnut dresser that used to terrify Daisy when she was little and had to walk down this dim passage alone, past the tall blue Chinese urns. Before she reached the suit of armour at the head of the stairs she hesitated, walked back a few paces and flung open the door to what had been Lisabeth's bedchamber.

It'll be their room now, thought Daisy, struggling with a tide of sick resentment as she gazed at the luxurious trappings, the enormous velvet canopied bed on its gold-carpeted platform, the marble fireplace with the fretted silver screen, the wheel-shaped chandelier and the wall of mirrors fitted so cunningly together that they effectively doubled the size of the room. The room had been empty for six months since Athol Nye's death, when Lisabeth's departure and the muffled quarrel that preceded it had given rise to wild hopes in Daisy's heart that the affair was over, but not so; Lisabeth had gone to pretend to be a respectable widow in town while the inquest ground on and the fresh scandal ran its course. Tonight she would be back, and the room was prepared for her, dusted and polished and swept, banked with a profusion of flowers – lilies and roses in great silver drums, freesias and orchids massed in the fireplace.

Just being there made Daisy feel squeamish and she had to fight down an impulse to slam the door and run. Instead she stepped into the room, thinking as she skirted around the heap of boxes and trunks that the scented lace-veiled air in here seemed to swirl with mysterious secrets. Hurrying to the dresser, Daisy's eyes searched for the place where Andrew's picture once stood. Was there an obvious gap? Would Lisabeth notice that the miniature had gone?

When she was less than halfway across the Persian rug she stopped. On the dresser in that very place was a beribboned gift-box, and propped against the box a plain white card with scalloped edges, boldly inscribed with Rhy's distinctive square lettering: 'WELCOME DEAREST LISABETH MY ONE TRUE WIFE – THIS TIME IT'S REAL.'

'No!' cried Daisy. 'That's all wrong! *Mamma* is his one true wife!' The words burst out of her in an agony of denial, but only when they echoed in the high gilded ceiling and bounced back to mock her did she realize that she had spoken aloud. Turning, she fled the room, letting the door swing to behind her.

Canterbury in the 1880s was blossoming into the fair and pleasant land that its founders had envisaged, an England born anew, unfettered by the confines of a crowded Homeland yet bound by those essential social conventions designed to keep the servant class firmly in their place and the gentry elevated in a position well above. Most of the wealthy station-owners called themselves 'English gentlemen', and lived up to the label as best they could, even going home for the hunting every few years and embarking on grand tours of Europe as if it was just across the Channel instead of three months away by steamship – and, oh, the honour if a presentation to the Queen could be included in their travels. While the lower classes idolized Victoria openly, the gentry restricted their admiration to simple proprietary gestures as if she was an intimate member of the family who happened to live across the world. A toast to her after dinner was in order and a single verse of 'God Save the Queen' to conclude a social evening. Nothing ostentatious.

Gwynne, who was lower-class to the soles of her home-made slippers, papered her bedroom with pictures of Victoria and Albert (as he was) and portraits of royal princes and princesses in sailor suits; while her brother Rhys, who was definitely upper-class, displayed a single Winterhalter print of young Victoria in his study. He was standing beside the picture now, his back to the door as he talked into the mouthpiece of the mansion's brand-new telephone.

Daisy saw him and paused, still chilled by the words on the card. He was saying: 'Me, too . . . And what about you – have you any regrets? You won't mind being married to a crusty old curmudgeon like me? Me? Of course not. It's been agony, dearest, having you yet not having you. . . .'

Anguish welled in Daisy's chest. If only Mamma hadn't died, none of this would be happening. Her father turned and saw her. She started with guilt, but he didn't realize she had overheard his murmured endearments, and wiggled his fingers at her, smiling the smile she loved. Wistfully she stood there, admiring his silver-bleached hair, his strong tanned features, unable to move away.

Rhys cupped his hand over the mouthpiece on the wall. 'Lisabeth wants to know if you'll please change your mind and be her attendant at the service. Go on, pet; it would mean so much to her. To both of us.'

Daisy shook her head with sudden violence. 'I can't,' she cried, and bolted.

'I do understand,' came Lisabeth's low sweet voice along the wires. 'I'm replacing her mother, and she's distressed. Be patient with her, Rhys. It's natural that she would resent me now.'

'She's resented you for far too long,' said Rhys. 'I've a mind to—'

'Patience, dearest,' counselled Lisabeth. 'Please, for me?'

'For you, anything,' he told her.

Gwynne was already at breakfast. She fixed Daisy with owlish scrutiny and asked after her headache in such a way that, though Daisy didn't feel hungry, she was obliged to shovel a scoop of braised mushrooms on to her plate and add a few ripples of bacon, then sit and force herself to eat. Anything was preferable to the threat of Guarana powder.

The feeling of unease was still with her, and by the time Rhys came in she was fidgeting with impatience. She watched him at the buffet, heaping his plate. He had been out riding, probably helping with the sheep, for he was dressed in his working clothes of twill jodhpurs tucked into tall burnished boots, a white shirt with a crisp wing-collar, silk cravat and a light tweed hacking-jacket. He was elated, smiling and talking as he selected eggs and tomatoes, kidneys and sausages. 'This is going to be the longest day of my life!' he declared as he brought his plate to the table. 'Such excitement, hey?'

Daisy felt like bursting into tears. 'Papa, this is our last meal together, just us,' she said, and her voice asked: *Oh, Papa, why?*

He turned from the chafing-dishes, a warm plate in his hands. 'You *will* welcome her back, won't you, Daisy? She's missed you.' His voice was deep and rough; years ago he almost lost his life in a plains fire which had left him with a hoarse voice and impaired lung capacity.

Daisy flushed. Welcoming Lisabeth was not part of her plans. 'I wish

14

we could welcome Andrew,' she said impulsively. 'Do you think he's arrived secretly, Papa, and will be waiting at the cathedral to surprise us?'

Rhys looked astonished. 'No, I don't think so.' Andrew's name rankled; it always did. Through all the scandals and gossip his criticism had been the shrillest, raised in furious indignation every time he received yet another pamphlet from New Zealand – sent, Rhys suspected, by the same person who wrote the vitriolic filth. If granted three wishes, Rhys would make one of them the ability to get his hands on the author. For years he had suspected his old enemy Thomas Fox and his daughter Leonie Gammerwoth, but Thomas was dead now and Leonie living with her Italian count in Bologna, and still the damned things kept coming, provoking yet more moralistic outbursts from young Andrew righteously pointing out their sins. Arrogant young whelp!

Daisy said: 'But Andrew will be so pleased that you and Lisabeth are getting married at last.' Intercepting another odd look from her father, she hastened on: 'I can't wait to see him again. The last time was the day when he rescued me. When I fell down the cliff. Do you remember that? He was so brave—'

'Andrew has never been afraid of anything,' agreed Rhys as he cut into a breaded sausage. Silently he added that it was a pity Andrew wasn't afraid to speak his mind.

As he ate he studied his daughter. She was so like her mother that it unnerved him, bringing to the surface all those half-buried regrets, how he'd never really loved Azura, actually hated her towards the end, and how her death filled him with guilt. By marrying her for all the wrong reasons he'd stolen away her chance for happiness. Daisy was the image of her now, and her headstrong passionate nature was Azura's all over again. Like her mother she'd rush out and grab life by the throat. He hoped, sadly, that Daisy would have a happier life. that she wouldn't be tripped up by her own impulses and crushed under the weight of her unfulfilled dreams.

But today was *his* day, and he wasn't going to taint it by encouraging blather about Andrew. 'How are the preparations going?' he asked Gwynne.

'Splendidly, splendidly. I need some help with the latest batch of wedding presents, though.'

'Daisy will help you.'

'But Mrs Hogg is bringing Amy out after breakfast and—'

'Amy.' Rhys frowned. Soon, he hoped, Amy's presence would be a thing of the past. He was grateful to Amy, of course – she'd kept Daisy from having a lonely childhood – but, now that he was quashing the gossips by marrying Lisabeth, Daisy no longer needed protection. She was free now to move out into society. 'I was thinking, pet, that Amy is a trifle mature to be a suitable companion for you.'

'She's only two years older than me, Papa.'

'But ten years older in experience, perhaps.' He saw her bewilderment and said gently: 'You two were overheard talking . . . indiscreetly . . . indelicately.' He glanced at Gwynne and cleared his throat.

Lisabeth Nye! thought Daisy.

At the Oxford Terrace art gallery, a few days earlier, Daisy and Amy had left Mrs Hogg admiring a collection of Egyptian vases and sneaked into the conservatory room where nude bronze statues were displayed.

'Tits, that's what they're called,' said Daisy. '*Poho* is their name in Maori. Kikorangi told me so.'

'They're so large,' ventured Amy nervously.

'Mine are bigger,' boasted Daisy. 'Mine are pink on the tips. Kikorangi's are dark brown. What colour are yours?'

'I'm not sure.'

'You've never *looked*? What about when you take a bath?'

'Mrs Hogg still makes me wear a nightgown when I bathe,' confessed Amy. The two girls stared at each other, then suddenly collapsed into a fit of giggling. Leaning on each other, still laughing, they staggered into the next room and almost bumped into Lisabeth who was hanging two of her watercolours for display. The cool look in her slanting green eyes told them she had heard every word.

'Please, Papa, you can't blame Amy for anything that's happened. She's a good friend, a dear friend and—'

'Perhaps living in that permissive hotel atmosphere has taught her too much of life too soon.'

'But, Papa, Mr Day is your closest friend, and his family have owned the Sumner Hotel for years!'

'It's not quite the same thing.' He smiled and, as he got up, kissed the top of her head where the centre parting ran. This problem would resolve itself, and soon. 'Never mind. Once Lisabeth has settled in she'll take you under her wing again. You've been allowed to run wild since school ended. Lisabeth will have you smartened up in no time.'

He spoke with satisfaction, a worrying problem settled. His conscience was nagged by his neglect of Daisy. She was no longer a child to go riding about, roaming freely and doing as she pleased. He understood nothing of the mysteries of young womanhood, and Gwynne . . . well, poor Gwynne tried her best. Lisabeth would know what to do. He would leave it all to Lisabeth.

To Daisy the reassurances sounded like threats. Under Lisabeth's wing were dreary hours spent squinting over needlepoint, endless afternoons of silence in the library and the hideous frustration of painting outings where Daisy transformed scene after scene into featureless mud-puddles. And the piano practice! Daisy shuddered.

16

TWO

'A PICTURE of a horse!' exclaimed Daisy. 'What an odd gift. It's not even in a silver frame. It can only be worth a few shillings at most.'

'My Charles always said it was the thought that counted,' sniffed Gwynne. 'He always—'

'There's something written on the back,' Amy interrupted. 'But you're right, Mrs Stafford. Father has a theory that one must never look a gift horse in the mouth.'

Daisy laughed. 'Very droll! This is a real horse. Silas and Charlotte Drake are presenting him. He's two years old and called Donegal. Fancy referring to themselves as "Silas and Charlotte," instead of the Hon. S. Drake, Esquire, and Mrs Drake. I know! They're those American people. Papa was helping Mr Drake get permits through Parliament for some factory or other he wants to build.'

'And wouldn't appreciate your telling people about it,' Gwynne pointed out, as she unwrapped a Waterford crystal jug. The day had hardly begun, and already she felt tired and irritable. A glass of tonic wine, or a sip of that new Cannabis Indica syrup, that's what she needed to soothe the aching in her wrists and calm the irritations to a pleasant blur.

'A beautiful horse, too,' murmured Daisy appreciatively.

Amy was oohing over a silver tray the size of a table-top, examining her reflection in its highly polished surface. Her face could be dismissed as plain, for it had a bony undernourished look, blue-white of complexion and with mean lips that belied her warm nature, but was saved from ugliness by her dark, almost black, thickly lashed eyes and fine arched eyebrows, and by her lustrous brown hair that she wore pulled back into a cascade of ringlets displaying her small pretty ears. Daisy envied this style but could not copy her because her ears jutted out unbecomingly, quite ruining the effect, so her hair was bunched into curls that hung, like spaniels' ears, on either side of her head.

17

The three worked in the music room, a long gallery near the dovecot that had originally been an open veranda. Daisy loved the view of the coast from here; it was especially beautiful today with the sky as dazzling as the ocean, a warm breeze stroking the long tussocky grass so that it lay like fur, and the fresh spring tendrils of Virginia creeper fingering the tall windows.

Daisy was surprised by the numbers of gifts, and Gwynne was gratified, for it meant that Rhys would not be snubbed on his wedding day. This was the first party Mists of Heaven had seen in many years, and she wanted it to be a success. It would be. People wouldn't send presents if they didn't intend to come. 'I hope we'll have enough food,' she fretted. 'I hope we'll have enough. Perhaps I should order another two dozen fowls roasted.'

'Oh, Mrs Stafford, you've enough food in the kitchens to feed Napoleon's army,' said Amy as she pulled sheafs of tissue away from an ornate branched structure of silver and gold. 'What is this?'

'An epergne. It's to hold sweets and chocolates.' Daisy was picking up the last package and reading the label. 'This one is from overseas. Paris, it says. I wonder who it's from?'

Amy set the epergne between two silver tea-pots and stood back to admire the effect. Now the trestle tables were laden so that scarcely a scrap of the cream damask tablecloths showed between the gifts. Silver and crystal, engraved wine-goblets and stacks of lace napery, towers of bone china so exquisitely fine that the girls could see their fingers through it when they held it up to the light. (Clearer than Mrs Stafford's spectacles, whispered Amy.) On the wall behind were hung two views of the southern Alps by the fashionable painter Hoyt, and between them a magnificent Landseer study of a stag at bay.

'If only Charles could see that,' sighed Gwynne, her eyes muddy pools behind her smudged lenses. 'He had such an appreciative eye for a good picture. Such a fine trained eye.'

Behind them Daisy gasped aloud, and when they turned it was to gasp, too. From the striped box within the wrappers Daisy was lifting a midnight-blue silk gown richly embossed all over with rows of glistening jet and tiny blue stones. In hushed awe she held it up to reveal the extravagantly ruched and decorated bustle and waterfall train.

'Is that Lisabeth's wedding gown?' asked Amy.

'Of course not. Of course not,' chided Gwynne. 'A widow must wear black, and Lisabeth is a respectable widow. If she wore this, the entire province would be scandalized!'

'Black on your wedding day. How dreary,' said Daisy, kicking Amy who was suddenly convulsed with giggles. Gwynne glared at them both, then swept the gown up in her arms and hobbled out of the door.

Respectable! thought Daisy bitterly, thinking that the province was already scandalized. She wished Amy would stop giggling. Stooping to bundle up the brown paper wrappings and wax-daubed string, she noticed a note in the box. Without thinking, she opened it and began to read. *It's from Andrew!* she realized at once. By then she knew that it was personal, but she was unable to stop herself.

Dear Sister,
Long ago I promised you that when I could afford it I would buy you a beautiful gown. Though my small hospital absorbs most of my income, I've set aside what I can to honour that promise. Please wear it on your wedding day, and know that I wish you every happiness. Nobody can condone the sins that have been committed, but perhaps this marriage will right some of the wrongs in the eyes of the world, if not in the eyes of God. I have not come to share your day because it would seem that I approve, and I have not the power to do that.

Your brother,
ANDREW

Daisy's eyes misted as disappointment crushed down on her like a rock. Up until now she had nursed the hope that Andrew would come home for the wedding, but now that hope was squashed, and the reason for it was confirmed. Andrew couldn't bring himself to come because of Lisabeth's immoral behaviour. It was all her fault.

'What's the matter?' asked Amy, frightened.

'He's not coming. He—'

Gwynne limped back in. Daisy tucked the note under a fold of the tablecloth. Gwynne stared at her flushed guilty face. 'That headache. That headache. Come with me. Sal volatile, I think—'

'No, I'll be all right. I'll walk outside. I . . .' Her throat spasmed.

'Not fresh air. Fresh air is bad for you at the best of times. A wee dose of sal volatile and a few drops of Cologne on a damp cloth pressed to—'

'No!' Daisy felt like screaming. Brushing off her aunt's solicitous hands, she dashed sobbing to the french doors and wrenched them open.

'Your hat, child! Your hat!' bleated Gwynne, but Daisy had gone.

By the time Amy had collected the hats and dashed across the freshly scythed croquet-lawn past the swan lake and Grecian-pillared summer-house Daisy was already marching along the cliff-path. Amy caught up to her at the highest point where a rustic wooden bench was provided for those who wished to sit and admire the view.

Around them was a breathtaking panorama, from the row of starched-white mountains that jammed the entire western horizon, across the sweep of plains and down to the two rocky headlands that jutted far into the Pacific Ocean. Behind them on this smaller promontory stood Mists of Heaven, its gabled roofs and mullioned windows visible far out to sea, while at the base of the much larger peninsular to the south spread the city of Christchurch, a red, green and grey clutter fogged by the smoke of countless chimneys. Between was a harbour, a mottled spread of turquoise veined with inky blue where the channels ran. Out across the harbour mouth, near the tiny settlement of Sumner, lay the treacherous Sumner Bar. Had Daisy been in a better mood, she would have paused to watch the sailing boats beyond the necklace of surf waiting to be guided across by Joseph Day the pilot, who even now was rowing out towards them.

Jamming her wide straw hat on, Daisy turned seawards to the stony track that undulated over and around the cliff-top contours, appearing and disappearing between low clumps of scrub until it was lost in the wild headland where huge monolithic stones stood like broken grey teeth against the blue maw of ocean and sky. Amy was afraid that Daisy would go that way; she hated the creepiness of that place, the way the wind sucked and whistled around the stones. In her opinion Gwynne and the Maoris were right: it was an evil place haunted by bad spirits.

'Do sit and rest, Daisy,' she begged.

'Andrew's definitely not coming.'

'Oh.'

'That letter . . . He's not coming, Amy, and I was so hoping he would.'

'It's not as if he ever actually promised . . . I mean—'

'You don't understand,' accused Daisy, ignoring the way Amy patted the seat beside her. Squaring her shoulders, she marched away down the inland path.

Amy followed meekly, hitching her skirt above her booted ankles. Beside the path glossy black *tuis* swayed on the flax stems as they dipped curving yellow beaks into the scarlet-throated flowers. Gulls whooped as they soared along the cliffs below, and the breeze tugged at Amy's straw hat. She paused to tighten the ribbons.

Ahead, the plains washed like a flood up the green swell of foothills. First were the rich river flats tucked up in a quilt of market gardens, vegetables, vines and berry fruits; then came the orchards of peaches, apricots, pears and cherries all sheltered by broad belts of valuable millable hardwood timber trees, protection from the bitter mountain winds; while beyond still further spread grain and grazing lands, thousands of acres of each. All of this and more belonged to Rhys Morgan. Because he had the foresight to diversify into exportable fruit and

20

vegetables, he had survived the slump of the past ten years when plummeting wool and wheat prices forced so many ranchers off their land. Rhys added several bankrupt farms to his spread and snapped up devalued Crown land in the foothills, cannily buying only the fertile valleys so that he could use the ridges and hills between for free. When he had finished he calculated that it would take him a week to walk the boundaries to his land.

Ratting through her mind for something comforting to say, Amy scrambled down the hill path behind her friend. She was secretly relieved; Daisy had talked of nothing but Andrew Stafford for weeks now, and it seemed pathetic that she was still mooning over someone she hadn't seen since she was a little girl. 'He'd probably be a disappointment anyway,' she offered as she grabbed at saplings to steady her descent. 'Father has a theory that we shouldn't look forward to anything too much because then the reality—'

'Oh, do be quiet about your father's theories!' And not another word was spoken until they reached the foot of the hill.

Here were a cluster of shabby cottages set in the oldest part of the orchards where Elephant Heart and Damson plum trees held stiff lichened branches aloft under their burden of millions of white blossoms. The air vibrated with the humming of bees, and above this sound rose a piping sweet refrain. The girls crept closer to the gooseberry hedge and peeped through into the yard of the nearest cottage. Years ago Gwynne and Charles Stafford had lived here with Andrew and Lisabeth, but now it was a retirement dwelling for old Birdie Nevin, Rhys's former housekeeper.

In the littered yard a ragged-looking woman was stoking up the beginnings of a fire under the outside clothes-copper.

'It's Siobhan,' whispered Amy, recognizing Birdie's daughter.

Her voice was haunting as she sang:

> 'Did you treat your Mary Anne to dulse and yellowman,
>   At the Ould Lammas Fair, at Ballycastle, O?

'She's having a baby, and she's not even married,' hissed Amy, her voice ripe with self-importance.

This was heady news – if it was true. 'Who told you that? Tommy Nevin, I suppose,' she said, her voice betraying the scorn she felt, for Amy adored Tom Nevin, old Birdie's son, and in Daisy's opinion he was not nearly good enough for her friend.

When Rhys Morgan began carving out his vast estate the Nevins were already here, as cockatoo, or squatter, farmers who were entitled to claim five acres of land wherever they chose. After Rhys almost lost his flocks – and his life – in a grassfire Sam Nevin had set, Rhys drove the Nevins out, torched their home and flung a few pounds' compensation in the dirt. Later, when Sam Nevin was killed in a goldfields disaster, Rhys relented, offered Birdie and her family a home, hired her as a housekeeper, Siobhan as a maidservant, and gave Tom work on the farm – a job he soon lost through insolence and disloyalty.

Daisy never mentioned that to Amy, but she hoped her friend would soon grow tired of flirting with Tommy, who hung around the Golden Fleece on his leaves from sea, hoping to catch a word with Amy or to pass her a love-note under Mrs Hogg's negligent gaze. Usually Daisy made some condescending (and jealous) remark when Amy sighed over Tom, and she never displayed interest in the Nevin family, but this was such riveting information that she was aghast. Siobhan having a baby! Through a gap in the thorny hedge she stared at the girl's shapeless figure.

Siobhan raised her head and reached up with slender arms to adjust the sloppy knot of dark hair at the base of her neck. She was olive-skinned and blue-eyed like her withered old mother, but startlingly beautiful except for a disfiguring burn-scar that corrugated one temple and dragged at her eyelid, half-closing that eye.

Suddenly Daisy realized that Siobhan was staring back at the hedge. 'Who's thut?' she demanded, picking up the fire-prod and advancing, scattering chickens around her scuffing wooden-soled shoes as she came.

Daisy plucked at Amy's sleeve. 'Let's run!' she urged and, turning, dashed away through the long grass. When she reached the Christchurch road she paused to look back, only to see Amy and Siobhan deep in conversation. With a shrug of disgust she began trudging up the hill towards the mansion's tall iron gates. As she walked her heart flooded with despair. She didn't want to go home, she didn't want any part of today. Now Andrew wasn't coming, and that was Lisabeth's fault, too. If only Papa would come to his senses and call the wedding off.

Amy and Siobhan were still talking, so Daisy walked on. By now it was late morning, and the sun blazed so hotly that Daisy's scalp was prickling with perspiration under her hat and her poplin gown was sticking to her back and arms. Her feet were sore, too, bruised through the inadequate soles of her slippers on the stones of the path, and she was wondering whether to sit in the shade of the nearest quince tree and wait for Amy, when a horse nickered behind her and Joseph Day's voice said: 'It's a hot morning for walk, Miss Morgan. Would you care to sit up behind me? I'll take Tahi slowly and won't let him jog.'

Daisy shook her head. 'I thought I saw your boat?'

'That was Alf. He's standing in for me today. I've more important work to do, being your father's best man.' He laughed, splitting his thick dark beard with a flash of white teeth. 'Ay, but it were a proud day for me when he asked.'

'Who else would he ask? You saved his life when he went fishing with Jock McFallish and that storm blew up. You risked your life for his, and he's never forgotten that.'

'Just part of my job.' He brushed the praise aside, for he had saved other lives in worse conditions. But to be asked to be Rhys Morgan's best man was an unexpected honour. Though he and Rhys shared a friendship going back twenty years, Joseph Day was not one of the 'gentry' nor did he belong to the posh clubs Rhys frequented, though he turned out for cricket when asked, if Rhys's team was short and needed a keen spin-bowler. No, he was one of the middle class, hard-working, fearless and decent, devoted to his wife Emma and their four young daughters, but with a particular soft spot in his heart for Daisy, whom he had known since babyhood.

He could see she was troubled, and thought he understood why. All these years she'd been Daddy's girl, riding out with him in public, sitting beside him in church, pouring his tea at the picnic lunches on cricket days. Daisy was about to be usurped. Smiling down at her tight face, he said: 'This is a grand day for your father, Daisy.'

'Is it?' Everybody seemed thrilled about it except her. Mists of Heaven was bubbling with an excitement which she alone couldn't share.

'It should be a grand day for you, too, lass,' he persisted gently. 'Be happy about this, hey? Lisabeth is a fine woman, and she loves your father. As for him . . . well, it wouldn't be an exaggeration to say that he's loved Lisabeth for as long as I can remember. He'd have married her twenty years ago if he could.'

'Twenty years?' repeated Daisy stupidly, thinking: *But that's way before he met Mamma! It can't be!*

'Yep,' he said, pushing his wideawake hat back so that dark curls tumbled over his tanned forehead. 'It's romantic, Daisy. That should appeal to you. Romantic, that's what this wedding is.' And without realizing what he'd told her he snapped the brim of his hat between thumb and forefinger in a cheery greeting and galloped away up the hill, stirring a trail of dust puffs as he urged Tahi forward.

Amy was humming light-heartedly. 'I didn't ask Siobhan about the baby – I didn't have the courage – but she told me that Tom is coming home in two weeks' time. I wasn't sure—' She stopped. Daisy was sitting on a dusty clump of tussock savagely ripping wiry stalks from the clump beside her. 'Daisy, stop that! Your hands are bleeding.'

Daisy stared at them in blank surprise. She said: 'I'll wash it off. I'll—' Standing up, she wandered off across the paddock. Her hands burned and her feet felt hot, too. 'I'm going swimming,' she called over her shoulder. 'I'm going up to the hillside dam.'

'You can't do that. Mr Morgan would skin you if—'

'I don't care what *Mr Morgan* does! I don't even care what he thinks any more! I'm hot and sticky and so angry I could explode. . . .'

Skipping to keep up, Amy said; 'Are you angry with me?'

'Not with you.'

'Are you sure? I know you don't like Tom much, but when you've a sweetheart of your own you'll understand how I feel.'

Nobody would want to be her sweetheart now. She had a sweetheart, Andrew – but what use was that when Papa and Lisabeth kept him away? She said: 'I'm angry with *him*.' They were standing in a circle of ancient apple trees where a charred sod chimney stood alone. 'He did this, you know. This was the Nevins' home, and he chased them away.'

Amy shivered. Apparently Tom's father had died cursing Rhys's name, and she'd heard Tom cursing it often enough himself, which always made her uncomfortable. Rhys was a fine, much admired man, and she hated hearing him reviled. But Tom must have his reasons, even though Amy didn't want to hear them. She said: 'Don't say things against your father, please, Daisy.'

'Whose side are you on?' challenged Daisy.

'Yours, of course.' In truth she was firmly on Rhys Morgan's side. His hospitality permitted her to stay at Mists of Heaven as Daisy's friend, and she revelled in the luxury of a life Daisy took for granted. To partake of exquisite meals, to gaze at the splendours of the house, to bathe in a marble tub were absolute heaven. When she shared Daisy's lace-canopied bed she never could sleep – it was impossible to relax in such softness – but lying awake in that rose-sprigged room was preferable to sleeping anywhere else. And if Rhys Morgan was displeased with her all this would stop.

'Please, Daisy, let's go home now,' she begged, but she might as well have been talking to herself.

THREE

THE HILLSIDE DAM was a solid felled tree-trunk, green with algae and grey with age, over which a silver waterfall bled to trickle away in a stony creek-bed. Behind the log a long deep pond had formed. A thicket of trees screened the glade from the road, while a padding of ferny undergrowth kept out the wind so that heat collected here as in a bowl and the surface was always as smooth and tight as skin, dark with reflections of the *ponga* palms that leaned over it. Animal tracks pocked the edges, for this was a watering-hole for sheep and cattle when they grazed the south paddock. It was a complete tiny world.

Daisy loved the silence and the solitude. She liked to sit on an old stump and watch the mirroring of clouds scudding by above. Sometimes fantails twittered around her with tails flirting, and she believed that if she reached out a hand she could touch their soft bodies. Wood-pigeons came, too, and bellbirds, to feed on the *kahikatea* berries.

People kept away. If one of the shepherds wanted a drink, he would go to Birdie's door. She was a good-hearted soul and always passed out a slab of champ or a slice of barmbrack along with the water-barrel dipper. In time Daisy came to regard this glade as hers. Here she felt at peace with the world.

Jeremy Drake knew nothing of Birdie Nevin's generous spirit. On his way to deliver the racehorse Donegal he had asked directions five times and doubled back twice. Now, tired and dusty, he was wishing his father had sent the Morgans a canteen of silver cutlery instead.

He rode the huge black stallion while leading his white mare Angel at trail the entire fifteen miles up the coast, while every step of the way Donegal pitched and danced and, skilled horseman though he was, Jeremy had to use every scrap of endurance to coax him so that he would arrive without the smallest abrasion around his mouth where he constantly reared against the bit.

So, close to his destination he paused to water the animals and to res
them before Donegal's ordeal of being introduced into a new stable. He
spotted the thread of stream by chance and followed it up the hillside
where he exchanged bridles for halters while the horses drank.

Donegal was still twitchy. 'Don't you fret,' murmured Jeremy,
stroking his velvet nose. 'You'll be well treated.' As he wiped away the
travel dust he schooled himself to show none of the distress he felt.
Parting with any horse meant a wrench; in Donegal's case it was acute.

Jeremy had been born twenty-four years earlier in Druid Hills on the
outskirts of Atlanta, the youngest son of a wealthy plantation-owner.
Silas Drake was an astute man who, sensing the trouble that was imminent, packed up his family and sold his property, moving north right
into Canada and arriving only a month before war between the States
broke out. Unable to settle, he moved across Canada buying and selling
property and increasing his wealth each time, until finally he came to
New Zealand, attracted by the stories he had heard of its quaint
'Englishness'. His children were grown and settled, scattered along the
way, all but Jeremy who was still at university in Vancouver. When his
studies were done Silas asked the boy to join him here at Georgia, his
already-thriving stud farm named for his home State. Jeremy had
arrived just nine weeks ago in charge of a consignment of prime
Kentucky bloodstock. Donegal was one of those.

And now Donegal was being given away. It indicated how influential
Rhys Morgan was that this stallion who had run several spectacular
successes at race meetings already could be given to him as a wedding
gift.

'We're keeping your mating rights, so I'll be seeing a lot of you, old
friend; there's consolation in that. I'll bring all your old girlfriends to
see you, and you can gripe about what a terrible time you had on the
voyage out, just as all the other colonists do.' He grinned and ducked as
Donegal rolled his eyes at him.

Jeremy was exhausted. Tethering both horses to graze in shade out of
sight of the road, he spread out the saddle-blanket and, pillowing his
head on the saddle, lay down to doze. In an hour or so he would groom
Donegal with a dandy brush, would wash, change his own clothes and
proceed to the house. He was wondering whether he should leave Angel
for a week or so to help Donegal settle in, when sleep overcame him.

'*Please*, Daisy, don't,' said Amy, though she obediently unbuttoned
Daisy's gown. 'Mrs Stafford will be wondering where we are. Isn't it
time to get ready?'

'We've four hours at least, and do stop flapping at me. You're worse
than Aunty Gwynne. She'd have a pink fit if she could see me,' she
chuckled, tugging off her gown and unlacing her camisole. 'When

26

she first went to live with Papa she made little draperies for the statues in the conservatory, and hid that naughty tobacco-jar with the picture of the shepherdess showing her knees. She said it wasn't fitting for a bachelor to have such things about. At that stage Papa had been married to Mamma and had me!' As she spoke she was overcome with a fresh surge of anguish as she remembered Joseph Day's words.

Amy watched, shocked, as Daisy shucked off her two petticoats and dropped them on to her dress. Unrolling her thigh-length stockings, she said; 'Kikurangi and the other Maori children swim like this, you know. It's much more comfortable than those horrible long-sleeved woollen things Aunty Gwynne makes me wear. Come on, Amy, I dare you to try it, too.'

'You're not . . . Daisy, you're *not!*'

But she was. Careless of Amy's incredulous gaze, Daisy untied the waist of her open-crotched pantalettes, let them drop, and stepped out of them, naked, into the water.

The coolness was balm to her sore feet, but by the time it reached her knees the coldness had a bite to it and at mid-thigh mark she was gasping aloud with little quavery yelps.

Jeremy woke, heard the repressed squeals and thought that children had intruded on his resting-place. He got up to chase them away, and as he pushed through the undergrowth caught a flash of something through the lacy foliage, an insinuation of pale limbs and loose butter-coloured hair. Moving to reach an opening with a clear view of the pond, he paused, holding his breath.

Daisy was standing with her back to him, dimpled buttocks resting on the water and her legs disappearing into wavery ripples below. She turned slightly, revealing the swell of a perfect-fruited breast, then in a single fluid motion dived forward, away from him. Foolishly he noticed that he had raised a hand to halt her.

She swam completely submerged, her body sinuous and elongated, until she reached the dam, when her head emerged with a slick toss for air and a twist of her slender shoulders, then back she came gliding beneath an undulating dappled wake.

When she stood up Jeremy realized that his breath had turned to a hard thing, sharp-edged, that dug into his ribs. An insect settled, unheeded, on his cheek. She was incredible. Absolutely unbelievable.

She was facing him. Water slid in a glossy sheen off every curve of her body, streaming down between her breasts and around the swell of her belly, down in rivulets over the wet patch of hair. Whooping with laughter, she raised her arms to the sky, shaking her head so that from the dripping threads of her long hair millions of beads of moisture flew outwards filling the shadowy glade with whirling points of light. It was magical, a—

Someone shrieked, shattering the tableau. The girl froze, her eyes cold with fright.

'Look!' screamed Amy, raising an unsteady hand towards Jeremy's hiding-place. 'Come out, quickly! Someone's spying on you.'

It was too late for him to bolt. The girl in the water crossed her arms over her breasts and subsided as if she was curtsying. The patch of hair floated and sank, the curve of her belly slipped from view, then waist and pale arms were swallowed, too, and all the time she fixed him with her enormous light-blue eyes. He bowed in response. For some reason he felt ridiculously happy.

'Go away!' clamoured Amy, hectoring him like a thrush scolding a cat. 'How dare you spy on us. How dare you!'

He realized he'd seen that one before, at the aptly named Golden Fleece hotel, where the beds were as cold and lumpy as the porridge and the prices as steep as the stairs. A couple of maids on their day off, reasoned Jeremy, immediately resolving to stop by the hotel again in the very near future. But what were they doing out here so far from town? Bowing again with elaborate courtesy, he left.

When his whistling had faded Daisy flew from the water, snatched up her garments and huddled behind a bush, pulling on her clothes, dragging them over the wet skin. Teeth clenching, she scrubbed at her hair with a wadded petticoat, then poked it all up under the crown of her hat.

'Did you recognize him?' fretted Amy, pacing the bank. 'If he wasn't anyone we know—'

'He might know us,' said Daisy unhappily. 'You know how it is with servants. You never really look at their faces, do you? Here, button me up quickly!'

'You're shivering,' observed Amy, obeying. 'What makes you think he was a servant? He didn't have a beard, and most servants have beards. He was awfully good-looking, didn't you think?'

'Good *at* looking.' *Damn his eyes*, she added silently. 'Of course he was a servant. Didn't you notice his rough clothes? He's one of the grooms, probably. Papa borrowed servants from half a dozen places for tonight, so that ours can have the evening off. Oh, dear Lord, I hope I never run into him again. I'll perish if I do.'

'If he's a groom, then you're safe. Just stay inside and he'll never get a chance to recognize you, will he?'

While Daisy hurried home for a hot bath, Lisabeth was stepping from the Sumner stagecoach, bearing a large cloth bag containing her wedding clothes. She attracted many curious stares. Used to the notoriety of being Rhys Morgan's fancy piece, she was surprised when instead of turning their backs some of the people smiled, tipped their hats and remarked on the fineness of the day.

28

Lisabeth hurried along the village's sandy main street and knocked on the door of a prim white cottage. Beside a stunted lemon tree within the garden railing stood an enormous anchor salvaged from one of the sand bar's many wrecks.

Emma Day answered the door to her friend. Three little girls with bows atop their heads crowded around her, while in the background a plump baby cooed in a wicker bassinet. 'Take the bag from Mrs Nye – carefully now, Ethel,' instructed her mother. 'Come in, Lisabeth and sit down.'

'It's your wedding!' chirped May, snuggling against her on the sofa, while four-year-old Josephine tried to climb into her lap.

'Will you have a baby like our Nina when you marry Mr Morgan?' asked Ethel solemnly.

'Girls, really,' protested their mother in her sweet voice. Lisabeth thought she sounded like a crow by comparison. 'Ethel, be a lamb and take the girls out to play. I'll call you in when it's time for tea.'

Lisabeth stood up. She paced three steps to the cradle and tickled Nina's bare toes, then walked two steps to the mantelpiece to examine the magnificent gold and silver cup won by Joe and Alf racing *Red Jacket*, the cutter they had built themselves, then walked another two steps to the lace-screened window.

'Wedding nerves?'

Lisabeth turned. 'Did you have doubts?'

'Dozens.' The two woman looked at each other. They were of an age, both past thirty; but, while Emma was plump and diminutive with a cosy air of fulfilment about her, Lisabeth was lean and upright with nervous hands and a restless expression in her green eyes. 'Yes, dozens of doubts,' repeated Emma. 'There were any number of gloom-dispensers who warned me against marrying Joe, me with my Irish boarding-school background, speaking French and playing the lute, widely read, with my passion for the classics, while Joe was a daredevil in those days with the sketchiest of educations.'

'You've managed splendidly together,' said Lisabeth, thinking that Emma, bless her, always took great pains to point out what a lady she was, how cultured and refined. 'It's not that. I've no doubts about Rhys.'

'Nor I about Joe,' insisted Emma. 'Did you know that there's been talk of making him a Special Constable for Sumner? He'll have his uniform, a penny-farthing bicycle to ride – and a *hundred pounds* a year. Just think of it! He'll be the most respected man in the community.'

Which would be important to Emma. Lisabeth congratulated her, then said: 'I pray we'll be blessed with children . . . I want to strengthen the family – *all* the family – and give Rhys the happiness he wants.'

'But *you're* what he wants.'

Lisabeth could have hugged her for saying that. Before she could speak there was a tap on the door. 'Mamma, Josephine's crying,' whispered serious-faced Ethel, a perfect miniature of her mother. 'She tore her pinafore on a nail and she's afraid you might be cross. I said you wouldn't 'cause it's only an *nax*ident.'

'Bring the girls in, and put the kettle on,' sighed Emma. To Lisabeth she said: 'Without that particular blessing you'd have a far more tranquil life, you know.'

'I'll take the blessing, please!' laughed Lisabeth.

Sir Kenneth and Lady Launcenolt raised a cheer as they clattered through the streets in their ancient black brougham. They were Christchurch characters, he still in his Raj uniform of tropical whites, pith helmet with streaming puggaree and ivory walking-cane – though he had been confined to a Bath chair for three years – and she with her air of colonial royalty, overdressed, gussied, powdered and imperious. Two elderly Indian servants rode up in front.

'Look at them all!' cried Sir Kenneth, waving his cane to point out the crowd outside Whelan's Furniture Emporium and in the process narrowly missing whacking Albert's scarlet turban. 'I haven't seen such rabble since the food-riots of Apatjodhpur when we had to close the grain stores, in 1854, or was it 1855? Leopold?'

'It were being 1855, sir,' intoned the second sepoy who managed the pair of plodding black horses.

Beatrice dipped her frothy parasol at the people crammed in the veranda shade of Brooke's Apothecary. She was reminded of an Indian funeral, a young man's funeral, when gawping thousands turned out to see the frightened young bride forced into suttee on the funeral pyre. There were parallels here, thought Beatrice, but the flames of gossip had died down and these throngs had come to see the fallen woman made respectable.

'I was talking to Hogamath the bookmaker – I mean, I was talking to someone who had been there,' he amended, catching a glance of steel. 'He says, apparently, that the odds are five to two against Rhys turning up. They're doing brisk business, apparently.'

'But not from you, of course, Kiki,' stated his wife. 'Personally I don't care whether Rhys marries that drab creature or not. All I want is for Daisy to come back and live with us at Benares. She needs us, Kiki; she needs what we can offer her now that she's ready to come out in society. Look how they've been snubbed all these years. Rhys kept saying that it didn't matter, that they were happy enough, but it's different now.'

'You just want Azura back again,' Kiki said gruffly, his gloved hand squeezing her gloved one. 'She's gone, Bea. Long gone.'

'Do you think I don't know that? Ah, Kiki, do you remember how she used to chase the peacocks across the lawn, how she laughed? Good

gracious, look at the rows of carriages. That cream one is the Martins',
isn't it? And the one with the gold fittings is Kippenburg the solicitor's.
And there's the Andruths' . . . The cathedral will be packed.' She
folded her parasol and lifted her chin. Long diamond ear-bobs swung on
either side of her age-creased neck. 'Of course they'd all come,' she said
grandly. 'Rich people are just as curious as the poor. It's all a circus for
them, too. Come, Kiki, Daisy has promised to save places for us beside
her.' And before Albert could scramble from his place to let down the
step she was fumbling with the latch to swing the door open.

There was truth in what she said. Because they had gossiped about them
so avidly and for so long, the townfolk had developed a proprietary
interest in Lisabeth and Rhys. Opinion was still divided over Athol
Nye's death; though the official inquest verdict stated death by mis-
adventure, many believed he'd been murdered.

Athol Nye had been a local character, too; stiff-legged and spare-
framed as a grey wading bird, he could often be seen pushing his
handcart of firewood bundles, dressed chickens, and eggs for sale.
Rumour had it that he subsisted entirely on a soup made of chicken feet
and sow thistle. Nobody had ever seen him spend money except on ferry
tickets, and that stopped when he found a cracked old river-punt submerged amongst the rushes. Manoeuvring it home, he patched it with
tar filched from a road gang and against Joseph Day's advice used it
from then on as his river-crossing, thus saving threepence per day. One
rainy gusty night when the river ran high, his precariously laden craft
swamped. Athol struggled in the freezing water but was weighted down
by the now-sodden newspapers tucked under his coat. His body washed
up on Sumner beach two days later. Maori children found the handcart
in shallow water near the Ferrymead wharf, but nobody saw the punt
again.

Public sympathy was aroused when it was revealed that he had left
over two thousand pounds – a fortune then – bequeathed to his wife.
Poor fellow, people said, doing without so that he could compete for her
against wealthy Rhys Morgan. Lisabeth was unimpressed. She knew that
Athol preferred grinding poverty to comfort, and she gave the money
and the barren Nye farmlet to the Maritime Widows' and Orphans'
Society. A sop to her conscience, the gossips said. Wasn't that proof that
it was blood money?

Most of the people who lined the square, however, were benignly
interested. The romance of the occasion was irresistible. Shop-girls and
tired matrons couldn't blame Lisabeth for abandoning spinsterish Athol
for the glamorous Rhys, and now that he was proving True Love by
marrying her . . . well, that was a Cinderella story to beat them all! If
Rhys was showing gallantry, Lisabeth was proving gumption, too.

Nobody was going to discard her like an outworn shoe. Good on her!

So they came to stare and to enjoy. They packed the roof of Ayres the hairdresser's, jammed the footpath outside Brooke's Apothecary, and were so thick in front of his jewellery store that Mr Urquhart called a policeman to stand guard at the entrance for fear that his plate-glass display-window might be broken in the crush. Pie-sellers and cake-vendors trilled to advertise their wares as they threaded through the throng.

Inside the cathedral Daisy could hear them over the sound of hushed organ music. By twisting her head and pretending to admire the nearby rose window she could sneak glances at the guests as they arrived. Most she knew by sight: the Westlake girls, identically dressed in pink, who tagged behind their parents; the Andruths, Maurice escorting his cousin from England, an insipid blonde who sweltered in her blue serge dress and coat; 'Baron' Windsor from White Clouds up the coast with his nephew Lowell, a silky-looking young man with sleeked-back hair; and just before the Launcenolts arrived *en procession* the Martin family swept up the aisle and into the pew opposite. Arabella sat on the end, back straight and not touching the pew-back like all the other ladies with bustles. Daisy stared at her, avidly taking in every detail from the rows of black piping around her hem and sleeves to the way her glorious russet hair was folded, petal upon petal, under her tiny black and white bonnet. She was longing to be eighteen like Amy so that she, too, could put her hair up and let her skirts down and wear a bustle. Arabella looked *gorgeous*.

She was still wistfully staring when Sir Kenneth's wicker Bath chair rolled down the aisle propelled by Albert, and Lady Launcenolt, a panting mass of frills and lace, plonked into the pew beside her. Arabella watched, caught Daisy's gaze and quite deliberately flicked two elegantly gloved fingers under her nose, turning away with a haughty sniff. Daisy crimsoned.

'Why is Mrs Stafford skulking in the porch?' asked Lady Launcenolt.

'It's . . . it's because she's Roman Catholic,' stammered Daisy. 'Amy is, too.'

'Hmph.' Beatrice surveyed Daisy critically, thinking that the wretched old Stafford woman was making a poor fist of dressing and grooming her angel. Her drab gown was of expensive enough material, but so old-fashioned, and by the looks of Daisy's hair she'd not seen curling-rags since the last wash. Hadn't they heard of heated tongs at Mists of Heaven? The child looked dreadful, and on a day like today, when the eyes of the whole province would be upon her. This was really too bad.

Rhys came in and stood, fidgeting, with his back to the congregation. Joseph Day murmured something to him. Looking at them both, Daisy felt a pang of impotent hatred. *So he's loved Lisabeth for twenty years, has he?* she raged silently. *What about Mamma? What about me?*

'What are you wearing to the party?' hissed Beatrice.

Her words fell into a hollow silence as abruptly the organ stopped. Before Daisy could reply there came a riffle of tremulous notes and a cheerful march began.

Rhys and Joe stepped forward into the blue and red sunlight that poured through the rose window. Turning, Rhys gazed down the aisle past the Bath chair, past the serried rows of guests, towards the far doors, where a tall caped figure in black appeared. She walked towards Rhys, head proud, smiling behind her jet-trimmed veil as if there was only one person in the world besides herself, and he burst into a smile of pure happiness as she approached. His face seemed lit from within. Seeing the love that flowed between them, Daisy felt alone and left out. She tunnelled her fingers through the lace froth at Beatrice's wrist, wishing that she could burrow her head against her kind soft bosom and sob her misery away.

Beatrice started at the touch of her. 'You're cold as charity! You're not well,' she breathed. Leaning across, she whispered to Kiki; then, right at the part of the service where the Bishop was asking if any man knew of just cause why Rhys and Lisabeth might not be joined together, she stood up and with Daisy firmly in tow marched back down the aisle.

Coming when it did, her interruption caused a minor sensation. Shocked silence flooded the cathedral. The Bishop faltered. Heads swivelled until the two had disappeared, when, with a harrumph of embarrassment, the Bishop resumed his reading.

In the shade of the doorway stood Amy, neatly attired in a bustled gown of peach-coloured cotton, with a brown bonnet and a choker of amber-coloured beads. Gwynne was beside her, deep in conversation with black-clad Mrs Hogg, Amy's plump and pretty but slow-witted chaperon. 'Whatever is the matter? Whatever is the matter?' clucked Gwynne.

Lady Launcenolt didn't lower herself to answer. Speaking to Gwynne as if she was a servant, she said: 'Kindly inform Sir Kenneth that I shall send the carriage back for him later.'

'But I'm not sick, truly.'

'You look terrible, child.' Beatrice patted Daisy's hand. She wore ostentatious diamond and ruby rings over her gloves. 'Can't you see how terrible she looks, Mrs Stafford? Look at her hair! She looks as if she's been dipped in a puddle!'

Daisy and Amy exchanged furtive glances. Amy began to choke but smothered it by saying: 'Please, Lady Launcenolt, may I come with you? I'm staying the night, and Mrs Hogg can fetch me tomorrow.'

Her lips tightened. She had never approved of Amy, either – a common scrap of a thing, though quiet and biddable enough. Nodding, she proceeded down the steps with such a commanding expression on her face that the crowd melted away before her as if she had been brandishing a sword. 'It's immaterial whether I hear the service or not,' she declared. 'At my age I have witnessed so many. Disasters, some of them, too. Just look at this mess; sixty thousand pounds spent and still we endure this wretched inconvenience!' she exclaimed, stabbing the ferrule of her parasol at the heap of stone slabs that blocked their way, for though the cathedral had been consecrated long ago it was still in the untidy process of being built.

While an urchin ran to summon Leopold and the carriage, she stood on the pavement, tulle-swathed hat tilted back as she surveyed the scaffold-encased steeple. 'On the day your father announced his intention to marry here we suffered an earthquake, and in the force of the disturbance an enormous chunk of stone tumbled from there right down on to the pavement.' She sighed. From her tone it was clear that nothing would give her greater satisfaction than to see another earthquake collapse the entire structure. Now, while the wedding was in progress.

Seated near the rear of the congregation, and only mildly interested in the proceedings, Jeremy Drake amused himself by polishing a crudely carved greenstone ornament that his spade had turned up when he was marking out extensions to the stable-yard. He raised his head when Lady Launcenolt surged down the aisle with a young woman in tow. Her head was bent, her face averted, but there was something about her that was instantly familiar. What, he couldn't say. Puzzling over it for a moment, he shrugged and went back to scuffing the dried soil out of the whorls in the talisman. He'd see her again, later.

Rhys and Lisabeth were unaware of Beatrice's diversion. They clasped hands. Hers was cold, rigid and shaking. Under that ridiculous black veil her face was bleached white, her eyes hazy with tears. She couldn't believe this was actually happening, yet through the roar of blood in her disbelieving ears she heard the Bishop pronounce them man and wife.

Rhys laughed aloud. Placing his hands on her shoulders, he drew her towards him for their first wedded kiss.

'No,' whispered Lisabeth. 'Not yet.' Stepping back a pace, she raised her hands to her throat and swiftly undid the three clasps that fastened the front of her cloak, then in one deft movement whipped it from her shoulders and cast it aside, raising her arms now clad in a simple taffeta gown of the palest silver grey, so pale that it soaked up all the colours from the stained-glass window, so pale that the congregation believed it at first to be white and gasped, thrilled by an apparent flouting of convention.

Rhys was profoundly moved. In casting off the black garment she had

34

shed the darkness of the past to emerge shimmering and new. With a warm swelling in his throat he stepped forward, fumbled with the veil and removed that, too, before sweeping her into his arms.

Jeremy's lips twitched with amusement. This was daring stuff for the buttoned-up colonials. No wonder the congregation buzzed. His sentimental mom would kick herself for not coming to the service; she'd have lapped up every intimate detail.

When the bridal couple moved to the vestry to sign the register Jeremy strolled outside. He felt hot and thirsty. Glancing across the throng to the post office clock, he decided he had time for a mug of ale and a nap before returning to the party at Mists of Heaven. The Golden Fleece was not far away; if the two serving girls had returned, he might enjoy an interesting afternoon.

FOUR

LADY LAUNCENOLT planned to spend a pleasant afternoon with the girls imbuing them with her fashion sense, but Gwynne was at the door, spectacles glinting, demanding that Daisy come home at once to attend the afternoon reception for the Maoris and servants.

Beatrice sighed, wondering how many more conventions Rhys was determined to flout. She had seen him educate his daughter in a most unseemly fashion, now marry his mistress (giving rise to scandal, not scotching it, Beatrice feared), and not content with thumbing his nose at society thus was insulting them by making them wait until this evening for the reception while he entertained all the riff-raff who lived on the fringes of Mists of Heaven. Yes, he was making it plain who came first in his priorities, and the most aggravating part was that nobody would snub him in turn by declining to attend. Tonight's party was the most eagerly awaited event of the decade, proving that Rhys Morgan could do as he pleased and be forgiven.

Not by me, thought Beatrice. Stiffly she said: 'There's no need for you to worry about her, Mrs Stafford. Daisy is perfectly—'

'I have instructions to fetch her,' insisted Gwynne sweetly. 'Rhys says it would be discourteous for her not to attend.'

'I see,' said Beatrice, trying to read Gwynne's expression through those thick lenses and wondering if Rhys had said any such thing. Gwynne might be dowdy and ineffectual, but where possession of Daisy was concerned she had a silent stubborn streak and, as Beatrice knew from experience, was quite capable of bending the truth to suit her own purposes.

Leaving Gwynne in the morning room, she mounted the stairs to the green and white bedroom which Daisy occupied far, far too seldom these days. Surrounded by straying tendrils of lace and ribbon, her lap heaped with an extravagance of artificial blossoms, Daisy was having her freshly washed hair crimped by Amy, who was expertly wielding the curling-tongs while the spirit-lamp hissed on the dresser beside her.

With another sigh Beatrice related her news, noting with satisfaction the dismayed looks on both girls' faces. 'You'll have to go, I'm afraid, but don't be too downcast. I'll bring everything with me and we'll fix your gown this evening, before the party,' she promised.

'Oh, Aunt Bea, thank you!' cried Daisy, rushing to give her a hug. Beatrice's arms ached. She was so like her mother, and Azura was the child that she and Sir Kenneth never had.

Gwynne led the way to the Mists of Heaven trap, where Tama, a gangly Maori lad, was amusing himself by whittling a stick to fill in time. She turned back as the girls climbed in, to say to Beatrice in an undertone: 'Not that I'll be going to the reception, of course. My Charles would spin in his grave if I did. He never trusted a one of these Maoris, never trusted one of them. Less than fifty years ago they were cannibals, you know! Savages, every one of them! My Charles said—'

'They are a proud and noble people,' responded Beatrice stiffly. Ignoring Gwynne's outstretched hand, she walked around her to greet Sir Kenneth, who was just arriving back from the service. 'You're late, Kiki! Where in the world have you been to take so long?'

Sir Kenneth glared at Leopold, who was beaming broadly. It was supposed to be a secret that they had detoured past Hogamath's where he had collected fifty guineas on a twenty-guinea bet and the sepoys had collected five shillings each on wagers their master had placed for them. That was a mistake; treat them like equals and they'd let you down every time. Holding the pouch of coins under his lap-rug, he said blandly: 'I was congratulating Rhys, dear. Lots of folk thought he wouldn't turn up, but I had not the slightest doubt about it.'

The Maori *pa*, or settlement, was the remains of what had been a thriving tribe which last century had occupied the entire headland with its fortified palisades and a great sweep of the shore with flourishing *kumara*, or sweet potato, gardens. The waters around here still teemed with schnapper, flounder, mullet, giant shrimp and crayfish, though the forests that rang with the songs of plump native pigeons had been felled and burned long ago. These Maoris had grown rich on the bounty of food, while additionally earning carved vessels and feather cloaks in payment for guiding parties from the North Island inland to where, high in the mountains, ran the sacred greenstone rivers.

'If not for we *pakeha*, or Europeans, there would be thousands of Maoris here now instead of just a few dozen,' Lisabeth explained as the four of them rode in a spring cart down the rough scrape of track towards the coast. 'If not for us, there would still be thickets of native timber here and giant *moa** with legs taller than a man, roaming the plains.'

*Huge flightless bird

37

'Why, Mrs Morgan? What did we do?' asked Amy. Daisy could have kicked her; she had to restrain herself whenever Amy simpered 'Mrs Morgan', which she was doing at every opportunity to gratify Lisabeth and Rhys. Daisy stared across the blistered sea, affecting boredom. It was lustrous, drowsy late afternoon.

'White men introduced muskets. Some of the tribes in the North Island armed themselves to the teeth with them, came down in canoes and virtually annihilated the local tribes. These few who remain are descendants of the fortunate ones who managed to escape the carnage by hiding in the bush.'

'My wife is presenting a paper to the Otago University on the subject,' said Rhys, taking off his top-hat so that he could duck his head under her ruffled parasol to kiss her. She smiled at him. A *possessive* smile, thought Daisy, her stomach knotting. Though she hated to watch, she couldn't seem to help herself.

'It's hardly *our* fault,' Daisy said suddenly. 'It sounds as if the Maoris were determined to kill each other anyway. What you're saying is like Doctor Meakings's argument that we *pakehas* killed off vast segments of the population by introducing diseases like measles and colds. How do we know that they wouldn't have developed equally dangerous diseases anyway? Doctor Meakings himself says that nobody knows what triggers these epidemics in different parts of the world. It's not fair to blame us.'

'Daisy!' interjected Rhys, shocked by her rude tone. 'Kindly mind your manners. Lisabeth was just explaining—'

'It's all right, dearest, honestly,' cooed Lisabeth, squeezing his hand in a proprietary way. 'Daisy is making a perfectly legitimate point. It's not entirely our fault, dear. Just partly. We are partly responsible for introducing such lethal weapons without weighing the consequences of placing them in naive and childlike hands.'

Daisy stared out at the headland, feigning deafness. It galled to be defended by Lisabeth.

Today the village was a cluster of four families and assorted relatives who lived crammed together in the three largest huts while their eccentric chieftain Hone Tainui lived separately with his wife in a dwelling Hone had rebuilt to copy a settler's house exact in detail down to a fowling piece above the mantelpiece, a toothless piano in one corner and even an outhouse down the path with a crescent moon in the door, a candle in a jar and squares of the *Lyttelton Times* speared on a nail. Ruins of other, abandoned huts sagged under blankets of creepers while chickens fluttered about as if blown by the wind and two pigs hurtled squealing into the fern as they approached.

'It's all right, pigs,' laughed Rhys. 'I've provided the meat for today's feast. Your bacon is safe for the moment.'

Passing Hone's white picket fence they followed the track to where, tucked against the looming cliffs of the headland, squatted a diminutive red and white church adjoining a graveyard and beside it a large thatched building with an open-gabled veranda, the arch of which was decorated with a broad strip of scarlet carvings depicting Maori mythology through grotesquely distorted human forms.

Lisabeth began to explain what they meant. She was flushed and happy, gabbling on in a fever of excitement; neither she nor Rhys had noticed that Daisy had said not one word in the past ten minutes. Rhys interrupted, warning them that Hone was ready to greet them. Stepping down, he left the ladies to follow as he called: 'Good day, John, my fine fellow. How excellent to see you again.'

'Congratulations, sir, and to your good lady,' replied Hone, showing tobacco-brown teeth. He was smartly, though ill-fittingly, dressed in a cast-off suit of Rhys's complete with plum-coloured brocade waistcoat, grey silk cravat and a brushed grey top-hat Rhys had given him one Christmas – an outfit that looked at odds with his elaborate indigo facial tattoos and his full and flattened Maori features.

Daisy took Hone's leathery hand for a formal greeting, but his young wife Isa grabbed Daisy's cheeks in her sweaty palms and gave her a *hongi*, or Maori kiss, pressing their noses together and inhaling deeply as she did so. Poor Isa was gussied out in purple serge and looked as hot as the English cousin in the cathedral, but twice as uncomfortable, trussed into a gown that was much too tight for her billowing figure. Daisy wondered if it was true that whenever Hone rode into town in his gig she shucked off her dress and corsets, tugged her hair loose of its snood and threw on a commodious 'Mother Hubbard' before racing barefoot to the house next door to flop on the floor for a gossip and a pipeful of Negro's Head with the other Maori women.

'You look beautiful,' Lisabeth said, thinking what a shame it was, when the native culture had such strengths, that they wanted to ape European ways. Had she said so to Hone, he would have been amazed, for what was better than to aspire to the customs of Queen Victoria – *Kuini Wikitoria* – whose face decorated every room in his house? Lisabeth had painted him once, posed in all his finery, then to make a point painted an identical portrait, this time clad in a *kiwi*-feather cloak with a *huia* plume in his hair, dangling greenstone pendant and ear-rings and holding a *mere*, a flattened greenstone club used in war. She thought it awesomely regal, but he offered no opinion, took both portraits and hung one in his parlour. The other, she heard later, was burned in the fireplace the moment he arrived home, for fear the others might see it and laugh.

Amy was saying: 'Isn't this exciting? The food smells delicious, doesn't it, Mrs Morgan?'

Wafting around them was the fragrance of barbecuing meats

mingling with the tang of *hangi** smoke. Despite her unhappy mood Daisy's mouth watered in anticipation, and she remembered that she had not eaten a bite since her skimpy breakfast. *Hangi* food was particularly delectable, the pork and *kumara* steamed together to a melting tenderness.

Hone said: 'We have pigeons and crayfish for you today, ladies; but first the entertainment, then we eat.'

The meeting-house was lined with people, the Maoris, extra relatives from Ferrymead together in the oppressive stifling heat with all the Mists of Heaven servants, stockmen, labourers and shepherds. The white faces all wore sour expressions; they were here because they'd been promised 'all the good ale they could sup', while the house servants looked particularly peeved, having heard that Jock McFallish and the other stock managers weren't here because they were invited to the big house-party. Why were they excluded? the others wondered. There was no snobbery as rigid as that practised by the servants.

Rhys knew how to defuse their discontent. As soon as he walked into the packed room he sensed the atmosphere and, raising his arms for silence, announced: 'Tomorrow you may all enjoy the day off, at my expense! Have a picnic, go to the race meeting at Addington or to the pleasure gardens. Do as you please and you'll each receive a full ten hours' wages for doing so!'

When the cheers died down Hone Tainui stepped on to the narrow stage, to be greeted by good-natured groans, for he was a lay preacher notorious for his endless repetitive sermons. He assured them he would keep his remarks brief, then went on at length, thanking Rhys for his gift to the settlement of two fine horses, a dozen sheep and a set of new hymnals for the church. He spoke in English to the end, when one of the young men leaped up to take his place and announced the song – an appropriate song, he said with a grin – called 'Ariki Morgana, e moe korua ko to waihine'.

Daisy understood and flushed scarlet, mortified by the knowing sniggers, for the words meant 'You and your wife are now one to sleep together', and people were laughing because they knew that Papa and Lisabeth had been 'one' for years. Even Hone was cawing with amusement, while Isa tittered beside him. Daisy seethed with humiliation. Looking at her father, she saw, incredibly, that he was grinning, too.

'What does it mean?' whispered Amy as they took their places on the wooden bench in front of the stage. Daisy was too miserable to reply. Amy's question reminded her that she had had such plans for today; it was supposed to be Andrew sitting beside her on this seat while she translated phrases of the Maori songs for him, impressing him with her

*Earth oven

40

knowledge. She glared at Lisabeth, who was answering Amy's question, and thought fiercely: *It's all her fault. Why did Papa marry her?* When, as if in reply, Rhys turned Lisabeth's bare hand over and placed a kiss in the palm, Daisy was scorched with anguish.

Lisabeth was having a marvellous time. She tapped her foot along with the songs, humming to herself, and when the *poi* dancers stood up, smoothing the *piu-piu*, or rolled flax skirts, they wore over their ordinary clothes, Lisabeth clapped her hands with delight. 'I do so love the *poi*. Watch closely, Amy. Notice how the women make those little balls whirl and snap on their strings in perfect time to the singing. It's so brilliantly clever . . . I don't know how they do it!'

I can do it as well as any of them, though Daisy smugly, comforting herself with the thought that she could beat Lisabeth at something, when from the stage Kikorangi brushed back her curtain of waist-length hair and beckoned, saying: 'Daisy! *Haere mai!* Come! You dance the *poi* with us, too, eh?'

Daisy jumped up, but was stunned when Rhys said with a frown: 'No, Daisy.'

'But I've been practising, Papa! I joined in everything at Rapata's wedding, and you didn't mind then.'

His frown deepened. That had been a private affair, just them and the Maoris. How could he explain that a young lady mustn't make an exhibition of herself in front of the hired help? Some were a rough lot and could easily get the wrong impression of her. He said shortly: 'No, Daisy, just no.'

Before she could protest he turned back to watch as the first tentative notes of the action song swelled to fill the room to the carved rafters. Sighing with contentment, Lisabeth leaned against him and whispered something tender in his ear.

Pointedly excluded, Daisy tried to swallow the hot hurtful lump that was pressing in her throat. *I won't cry, I won't*, she vowed, but the scalding pressure threatened to disgrace her. With head high and jaw determinedly rigid she stood up and tiptoed away outside into the blinding sunshine where she paused to take a great gulp of air into her constricted lungs. *I won't cry*, she repeated, taking several steps towards the sandhills, but despite her resolve her breath came ragged and that scorching hurt pressed insistently on her, and she trudged with slowing steps across the hot white sand. From the distance came a hollow whoosh of foam racing across the flat shore, and the sound, scratchy now, of the choir in the hall. She was quite alone.

Turning abruptly away from the ocean, she picked up her skirts and raced towards the little churchyard, her ankles slewing in the soft sand. The graveyard gate stood open, broken on tipsy hinges. Daisy raced through, past the rows of rotting wooden crosses, past the twin graves of

41

Hone's first two wives where wild blue lupins sprawled. Her feet pounded to the far corner near the church bell where a pine tree stood leaning inland, its branches combed up and over its crown by the prevailing wind. Here, bracketed by a single-granite plinth, lay Azura's grave beside that of Daisy's baby brother Darius.

I should have brought flowers, she thought, then guilt was pushed aside by the thought that *Papa* should have brought flowers; on today of all days Rhys should have put flowers on his dead wife's grave.

He didn't care about you and he doesn't care about me, thought Daisy, suddenly torn by the force of self-pity. Kneeling down, she brushed a drift of wind-blown grit from the dark red stone and realized when the plain inscription began to blur before her eyes that she was crying. Surrendering to unhappiness, she bowed her head and let the tears come.

It was surprisingly cool inside the tiny church. Jeremy gazed around the whitewashed interior with interest, studying the Maori carvings that rimmed the simple altar. Above this was the building's only real decoration. a window depicting Christ with a cluster of children, lambs and doves below a bannered legend: *Suffer them to come unto me.* A bronze plaque on the sill explained that the window had been donated in memory of Darius Rhys Kenneth Morgan, a name Jeremy had already seen on one of the gravestones. So the rich country squire had a tragedy in his background, did he? If Rhys Morgan had lost his only son, then Jeremy wondered why he was marrying someone who, though handsome enough in a spare, severe kind of way, looked almost too old to be of childbearing age.

The afternoon was proving to be a disappointment, especially after this morning's unexpected delight. Returning to the hotel in the hopes of seeing his water nymph again, he found the place shuttered, so decided to return to Mists of Heaven instead, where he had been offered a meal, a bath and the chance of a rest in the servants' quarters. He'd also been told about this little Maori village, and curiosity was strong in him; but the place was a let-down, too, and hardly worth the detour he'd made to reach it, though the meeting-house might repay a look another time when it wasn't being used.

His borrowed hack was tethered in a clump of trees nearby. Yawning, he strolled out into the sunshine, then wandered along in the slice of shade to where the flat shadow of the steeple flung its cross to the foot of the skeletal bell-tower a dozen yards away. Jeremy noticed that the bell-rope had been knotted so high that even an adult would be stretched to reach it, and guessed with a smile that the local imps had fun ringing it for mischief.

He also noticed something else. Beyond the rusty iron fence a woman crouched in grief over a tombstone, the one where the first Mrs Morgan lay buried. A friend? he wondered. A relative come to console her today, when she was being finally usurped from her place in Rhys Morgan's life?

Jeremy donned his shady-brimmed hat and stepped briskly out across the sandy wasteland towards the thicket. When he had mounted up he glanced back. The woman had not moved. Wheeling his horse's head around, Jeremy wondered who she was.

FIVE

BEFORE LEAVING FOR THE PARTY the Launcenolts dined on lobster at the Canterbury Hotel. Rhys had warned his old friend that supper would be delayed until midnight in deference to the Catholics' meatless Friday, which, as Beatrice pointed out, gave Kiki something else to grumble about while he ate his dinner.

'Don't know why we're going anyway,' he grumped. 'I don't feel like celebrating. Feel so useless – damned wheelchair – damned valvular heart disease.'

'Patience, patience,' counselled Beatrice, who was herself simmering with impatience to transform Daisy into a vision of loveliness.

'Damned doctors – what do they know? Perhaps we should go to London, hey, Bea? Go and see what the heart specialists think, hey?'

'Whatever you say.' Beatrice had been trying to get him aboard an English-bound steamer for two years. 'It's up to you, Kiki.'

When they came out the sky had darkened and a silver moon hid behind a lace curtain of cloud. Mists of Heaven was soon visible, for even miles away it was a spectacular sight with every window ablaze and the dome of the conservatory roof glowing. Lanterns illuminated the gateway, washed the trunks of the oaks along the curving driveway and flickered in the trimmed shrubberies. When they reached the top of the hill the moon slid into the open to glaze the black rippled ocean behind the mansion.

They were late; guests had been arriving for over two hours. Music and bubbling laughter frothed like champagne from open windows and spilled across the yellow lawn. Moths pirouetted in the bright doorways. Clutching her carpet bag of trimmings, Beatrice scrambled down, hooked her train to a button on her left sleeve and hurried straight in and upstairs, leaving the sepoys to manhandle Sir Kenneth and his chair out of the carriage.

*   *   *

Barricaded in the flower-bedecked bedchamber, Rhys and Lisabeth were still making love. They lay in the four-poster bed, limbs silkily entwined.

'I haven't stopped smiling all afternoon,' murmured Lisabeth. 'But we should go down. Really we should. People will be wondering—'

'We should do as we please,' Rhys corrected her, tracing a line around her nipple, then smothering her breast with his hand. What glory it was to make love to her completely after all the frustrating years of withdrawal. What delight to be alone with her again after this agonizing time apart. He said: 'And my pleasure is to be with you. Lisabeth, I've missed you. I've ached for you these past months . . . ay, and cursed you for your stubbornness in refusing to see me.'

Her smile was luxurious. 'I wanted you to be sure in your own mind that you really wanted me.'

'Sure? Feel this!' He took her hand. 'There! It's incredible how much I want you. Don't pull away. Aren't you impressed?'

'I'm impressed; but, Rhys, our guests are waiting.'

'Let them wait. Besides, I already know what everybody is going to talk about. Algie Martin will try to find out how much a pound our wool-clip is fetching, Sir Kenneth will talk about his history of the Indian Mutinies which he will never finish and how he should go to a specialist in London which he has no intention of doing, Andy Andruth will waffle on about how I should go back into politics, Reggie Westlake will bore me silly with his plans for the new wing he's building on Lakelands, 'Baron' Windsor will tell me how I should hound the Maoris off that land of theirs, and Nathan Berryman will—'

'Stop!' pleaded Lisabeth, laughing.

'And of course, when they think we're not noticing, they'll talk non-stop about us. Don't be afraid of them, Lisabeth. They will accept you in time. These wives, they do have positions to protect, you know.'

'Going to parties has never mattered to me. You know that. I'll look them right in the eye and talk about books they've never heard of.'

'I doubt if some of them can read.' He arranged strands of hair over her shoulders and admired the effect. 'That's why I'm afraid you won't like the Drakes, and I hope you will. I'm impressed with him even though he does think that books rot the brain. He's refreshingly honest and decent. Interested in things outside of himself, too, which is a pleasant change.'

'Such as?'

'Breeding.' Rhys laughed his low husky laugh. 'Speaking of which, I've six months of abstinence to make up.'

She pushed his hand away. 'Surely not all tonight?'

'No, but you'll not be safe around me for the next few weeks, I can promise you that.'

45

Pulling away, she teased: 'Then, I'll avoid you. I'll go for lots of long walks along the cliffs.'

'You'll be less safe there,' he said against her throat. 'Remember that day you came to talk to me and the rains started? Remember how you found me capering naked in the downpour? Remember how I stripped off all your wet clothes and laid you down on those rocks?'

'How could I forget?'

'You're blushing!' he noted in delight. Whispering, he added: 'Remember how I vowed I'd fill you full of babies and we'd spend the rest of our lives together in blissful domesticity?'

She traced a circle in his chest hair, the blond strands thickly peppered with grey. 'That worries me, darling. That was so many years ago. I may be too old to bear children.'

'Nonsense.' He captured her finger and nibbled its tip. 'I consulted Doctor Meakings and he says you've six good years in you yet. Perhaps longer—'

'You've talked about me as if I was a brood mare? Six good years in me? Rhys, how could—'

He laughed, stifling her protests with a kiss that silenced her and made her moan deep in her throat. Then, when she had relaxed, he propped himself up on one elbow and said: 'Mind you, he did remind me that we have no time to waste, so—'

She pushed away his daring, impudent, insistent fingers. 'People have been arriving for ages now. Can't you hear the crowd downstairs? We should go down and greet them.'

'Nonsense. They've come to eat my food and drink my wine and my whisky. We could stay here all evening and only a dozen of them would notice. However, if you'd rather go down there and *enjoy* yourself. . . .' His voice rose to a questioning note.

'Come here,' said Lisabeth, smiling. She had never been so happy in all her life.

Daisy was alone in her room, Amy having gone on an errand for Gwynne. When Beatrice entered she was seated at her bureau gazing into the embossed silver locket the Launcenolts had given her for her sixteenth birthday, containing a treasured picture of Azura at the same age. Daisy often wore it, they were pleased to notice.

'Let me look at her,' asked Beatrice taking it from Daisy's unexpectedly reluctant grip. Pressing the tiny spring, she gushed: 'She was a beautiful girl, an angel.' A pause. 'How nice! You've a miniature of your father in here, too.'

'That's Andrew.'

'Well, I've not got my lorgnette with me. Still, they are superficially alike, I suppose. People have commented. . . .' As she spoke she wondered if that was why the child was so besotted with Andrew. Women were supposed to be attracted to father-likenesses; certainly Kiki was growing more like dear Papa with every passing year. 'When did Andrew send you this, dear? I've not seen it before.'

Daisy panicked. She was not about to admit that she had stolen it and had cut it down to fit the locket, making it now impossible to replace. For six months she had gazed at Andrew's image, revered it, talked to it and slept with it under her pillow, feeding her mild infatuation until it became an obsession. She had not anticipated Aunt Bea wanting to look inside the locket and now she was terrified she might mention it to Lisabeth.

'It's a secret,' she stammered. 'I didn't want anybody to see it . . . but you, of course.' Swiftly changing the subject before Aunt Bea's questions could probe harder, she stood up and said: 'How is this? Did I pad out under my waist to make enough of a bustle? I used two petti-coats bundled up.' And she turned to display her back view.

'Splendid. And you've lengthened the skirt nicely with that sash I gave you. Now all we have to do is take the other sash and tie it around you so, to flatten your front and to make a splendid big bow over the bustled part. By the time we've added a few beads and ear-bobs and tucked the lacy pieces in your hair. . . . But you haven't put your hair up completely. Hasn't Amy finished it?'

'Aunty Gwynne made her take it down,' admitted Daisy.

Beatrice's majestic bosoms heaved. 'Did she now? Well—'

'I'm not *nearly* eighteen,' pleaded Daisy. 'I didn't want to quarrel with her, so Amy worked out this compromise, up at the back but with curls over my ears. And it *is* more becoming this way. Please,' she coaxed with a smile. 'I do have to humour her . . . and she didn't notice my hem-line, so we've scored a triumph there, haven't we?'

'Very well. And by the time she notices this it will be too late, won't it? You may not be nearly eighteen, but by the time I've finished with you you'll be the belle of the ball!'

To her Charles was such a fascinating subject that Gwynne could work his name into any conversation, no matter what the original topic. People who had met her before knew this; they made excuses and moved away when Gwynne joined their group. This did not deflate her because she took their excuses at face value. Besides, there were so many new people to meet who had never heard any of her reminiscences. This was a wonderful party.

Well into the evening Gwynne intercepted a trio of newcomers at the drawing-room door. Introducing herself as Mr Morgan's sister, she elicited that they were Silas and Charlotte Drake and their son Jeremy.

'We're late, I'm afraid,' boomed Silas in a harsh American twang that complemented his chunky florid face and barrel-shaped figure. He had enormous black eyebrows that twitched like live things when he spoke. 'My Charlotte would be late for the Day of Reckoning, wouldn't you, sugar plum? Then we had to visit our Donegal in the stables. Jeremy here is a bit worried that he's not settling.'

Charlotte laughed, showing a double row of small white teeth and a large pink tongue, looking for a moment like a killer whale when it opens its mouth. She was a plump dark woman with restless eyes and enough ostentatious jewels strung about her person to arouse Lady Launcenolt's envy. Gwynne thought her to be younger than her husband by thirty years or more and was shocked later to learn they were the same age. Her voice was as flat as a handclap. 'Miss Morgan doesn't want to hear about racehorses, do you, Miss Morgan?'

'She might do. Probably likes a flutter, do you, Miss Morgan?' And to her horror Silas nudged her in the ribs.

'Stafford. *Mrs* Stafford, my name is. As for racing, my dear husband Charles always said—'

'Mrs Stafford. Our mistake.' Her breath carried the scent of violets. 'Do you have any children, Mrs Stafford?'

'None. None. Charles and I adop—'

'Oh, you poor lamb! Silas and me, we raised eight – but he always was interested in breeding, weren't you, honey? All but young Jeremy here are married and living in Canada now.'

'We lived in Canada, too. My husband Charles had a particular desire to—'

'Really? Listen, Silas honey. I declare that's a polka I hear. These poor feet of mine have been longing for a polka since I don't know when.' Clinging to her husband's arm, she swept away.

Gwynne was left gasping, feeling that she had engaged in a wrestling match with something unseen.

'Mom often leaves folks stunned,' said Jeremy at her elbow. He was of medium height but muscular, impeccably dressed in a claret-coloured velvet jacket and silk shirt with one of the new high-pointed collars. His white tie was stuck with the biggest ruby pin Gwynne had ever seen. He had the kind of open face that looked as if he was capable of blushing, a look that belied his strong neck and jaw-line. His voice was thick and slow as sweet syrup as he said admiringly: 'She's a fine woman, don't you think so, Mrs Stafford?'

Gwynne didn't trust herself to reply, not even to say what Charles might have thought of that brash American woman. Canada, she said, but Gwynne wasn't fooled; she knew a Southern twang when she heard one. She was recovering, looking around for a fresh audience, when Jeremy suddenly grabbed her arm so hard that she squeaked.

'Who is that?'

'Young man, you hurt me!'

'I'm sorry. I didn't even realize. . . . Mrs Stafford, who is that? There, dancing past the palm tree beside the stage.'

'That, young man, is Mr McFallish, our head shepherd.'

'Not him. The young woman he was dancing with. Who is she?'

Nobody who would be interested in you, thought Gwynne as Daisy moved away and was lost amongst the dancers. Seeing that Jeremy was about to start after her, she grabbed his arm as tightly as he had seized hers and said: 'I've no idea who she is. Come and sit down here, young man. Let me tell you what Charles did in Canada.'

It was ten minutes before she permitted him to escape.

The young ladies clung in a nervous huddle in a fern-draped bower at one side of the room under the eye of a chaperon. Printed dance programmes were being compared. 'There, that's mine full!' declared Arabella Martin with a flourish of her gold pencil. 'I always fill my card right away so that if someone unattractive asks me to dance I can say I'm sorry but there are no spaces left.' She wore a cream brocade bustled gown and huge topaz ear-bobs the same colour as her close-set but magnificent eyes.

'That's tewwibly wicked,' lisped Hannah Westlake. 'Oh, I do hope someone asks me for the mazurka. Mr Tewwy the dance master has spent such a lot of time on that one.'

'I hope that Lowell Windsor asks *me* to dance,' said the blonde English cousin. 'When I was presented at Court there was a young man there in attendance who looked just like him.'

'Really?' piped Hannah's young sister, Sarah, who was anxious not to be left out. 'I overheard Father saying that Lowell Windsor was a nancy-boy. What does that mean?'

'Don't you know *anything*?' scoffed Hannah, who didn't know, either.

'Here comes Daisy,' hissed Arabella. 'And she has that common saloon-keeper's daughter with her.'

There was silence as Daisy and Amy stood in front of the bower. Daisy's glance scanned their faces. Only Arabella looked hostile, she noticed; all the others were guardedly curious. Amy hung back, her head twisted as she pretended to find something of interest on the other side of the room.

'You look very pretty, Sarah,' commented Daisy, aiming for the weakest link. Sarah flushed with pleasure and opened her mouth to reply, but Arabella trod on her foot.

'You look presentable, too, Miss Thorne,' Arabella said in the loud voice she reserved for cutting remarks. 'Real poplin, is it? Did one of your father's barmaids lend you her best dress?'

Amy started as if stabbed by a pin. Her pale face went even whiter. For a moment she said nothing, then a smile twisted her bony features as she remembered a piece of gossip from last summer, something not widely known, but scraps of information tended to wash into the Golden Fleece like flotsam into a sheltered beach. Last summer, the story went, Mr Martin had had to dismiss the young French chef he had imported at great expense for Martinsfield because he had been caught kissing Arabella in the herb garden.

Glancing at her friend, Daisy thought her smile was positively sinister. 'Amy, are you all—?' she began.

Cutting across her, Amy said slowly: 'Has your father hired himself a new cook, Miss Martin? And does this one share your *passion* for parsley and sage? Or, after Jacques, did Mr Martin decide to hire a woman cook instead?'

'It was André,' blurted Arabella. Then, realizing by Amy's expression what she had admitted, she drew a deep breath and said with elaborate dignity: 'Come, ladies, let's go and see if there is any fruit cup left.' And leaving Daisy and Amy standing there she swept away, the others automatically following like schoolchildren.

'Daisy, I *am* sorry,' muttered Amy miserably.

There was silence, then Daisy began to laugh. 'What a treat! What fun! The others are all afraid of Arabella, you know. None of them would dare. . . . Amy, you astonish me. You're so meek as a rule.'

'As a rule people aren't being nasty to us,' she replied simply.

Though Lisabeth had always professed not to mind being snubbed, tonight she was discovering that it was fun to be suddenly in a position of power, receiving compliments and having invitations thrust upon her, though she was confirming what she had long suspected: that the sheep-lords' wives were a covey of preening social climbers whose conversations were designed to impress each other. Even their tiresome anecdotes about the servants were a form of 'I'm superior'. Mrs Andruth sighed that her new ironing girl couldn't get the hang of using the pleating iron, a complaint Mrs Braithwaite trumped by saying that her second scullery-maid was breaking all of her fourth-best crockery. If their boasting was to be believed, Lisabeth calculated, then Mists of Heaven, the largest mansion on the plains, existed with a third of the household help most of the others employed.

Bored by this talk, she entertained herself by responding to invitations to the luncheons, musical matinées and drawing-room afternoons with the same reply: 'I shall have to consult my husband. Your invitation is flattering, *and* appreciated, but we could be busy on that day.' *Busy in the library reading something edifying*, she added silently.

So assured was she that, when introduced to the overbearingly confident Charlotte Drake, instead of being swamped by the woman Lisabeth was able to sail serenely into the conversation.

'Honey, I'm so thrilled to meet you,' gushed Charlotte. 'You are a very famous lady.' Seizing her arm, she drew her away from the menfolk.

'Famous?' Lisabeth was surprised but gratified. 'Do you like my paintings, then?'

'You paint, too?' The two women stared at each other for a moment, then Charlotte said, unabashed: 'You are a grand lady in this colony, did you know that? All these ladies here, they expected you to be dumped . . . you know, jilted in favour of someone new and younger. They all dismissed you as unimportant before, but now they respect you, honey! My, my, they do respect you. I've been watching the way they fawn over you and—'

'Hush, sugar,' warned Silas with an awkward glance at Rhys from under his quivering brows. 'You paint, do you, Mrs Morgan? Might we admire some of your work one day?'

Lisabeth was flabbergasted, but amused, too. Coming after a syrupy stream of compliments, this colourful woman's frankness was as startling – and refreshing – as a bucket of cold water doused over her, while the honesty in her own nature responded to the openness she'd been shown. She sensed that Charlotte was an outsider, too.

'You may appraise some of my work now,' she said, 'but whether you admire it is for you to choose. Come with me to the hall and I'll show you a few examples.'

Rhys took her arm, winking down at her, proud of the way she'd handled a potentially disastrous situation. 'She is a trifle obvious,' he apologized in a whisper.

'I like her,' Lisabeth decided. 'She's different.'

'Ay, she's that all right,' laughed Rhys.

Forty people could be seated in the dining-hall, but tonight the two long tables under the row of heraldic banners had been spread with a buffet for the two hundred guests who ebbed and flowed through the downstairs reception rooms. Here on starched napery the finest local produce was augmented by choice luxuries from abroad. Whole river salmon gleamed pink under aspic, saddles of venison were being carved into moist red petals by the Summerlea sub-chef, and a suckling pig, brown as toffee, rested between two enormous breadcrumbed hams. Pyramids of drumsticks wore neat paper frills, and bowls of savoury stews simmered over spirit-lamps.

Daisy was more interested in the dessert buffet where pies, trifles, fruit flans, brandy snaps and elaborate moulded desserts were arranged around a towering ice-sculpture of the mansion itself. 'Look, there's my room,' said Daisy, picking out the correct upstairs window. 'Mmm, this looks so good. I think I'll try everything. That dancing made me hungry, and in between I was running away from Jock McFallish. He's too shy to ask anyone else to dance and, oh, he's a trial! You'd think that fifteen years in the colony would have watered his Scots brogue, but it's thick as porridge still. He's terrible to dance with, too. My feet have been pounded to a pulp. I warn you, Amy, skip away if you see him headed in your direction.'

Amy was barely listening. She poked a port-wine jelly and moodily watched it wobble. 'That Arabella Martin is beastly,' she muttered. 'I heard her telling Hannah Westlake that my father was once bankrupted, and it's simply not true! And I heard that charming Andruth boy telling Arabella that she looked so beautiful in cream that she was like a perfect lily amongst the weeds. . . . She saw me listening and asked if weeds wear poplin dresses. Honestly! I'll wager that she hasn't got a silk camisole and silk pantalettes on like I have. She's all show and self-importance, that one.'

'Stay away from her, like I do,' suggested Daisy, dipping into a portion of strawberry fool. 'Mmm, this is heavenly. Try some, Amy. It's like sweetened clouds. It's—' She stopped, her spoon halfway to Amy's lips; she looked as if the breath had all been sucked out of her. 'Oh, Amy, do you see what I see?' she asked in a strange panicky voice.

Following her frightened gaze, Amy twisted her head. Joseph Day and his prim-looking wife were standing by the velvet-draped bay window, chatting to the Bishop, and to a familiar-looking young man. 'It can't be him,' Daisy's voice rose to a squeak. 'He was a groom, wasn't he? That *can't* be him.'

The young man turned his face very slightly, inclining it towards the Bishop. It was him all right, thought Daisy, giddiness squeezing her head. There was no mistaking those thickly lashed brown eyes and the boyish lick of brown hair that fell over his wide brow. His face glowed as he laughed at the Bishop's joke, and his teeth flashed white against his tanned skin. He was exquisite, noted Daisy dismally. Every bit as beautiful as she imagined Andrew to be; and rich, too, judging by his impeccably tailored clothes. And he'd seen her . . . he'd seen her. . . . It was too mortifying to contemplate.

At that moment Jeremy felt her eyes upon him. Turning his head, he glanced over and met her startled gaze. He might not have recognized her dry and dressed with her hair fluffed out, but her expression – stunned rabbit shot through with terror – was instantly familiar. Murmuring a hasty excuse to the others, he set off towards her just as Daisy dropped her spoon and dish and bolted for the door, darting a devious path between knots of guests. Heart beating as rapidly as her footsteps, she fled across the broad entrance-hall, brushing past Jock McFallish who was lighting his two-foot church-warden pipe, avoiding Maurice Andruth who stepped from a group to intercept her, deaf to Lisabeth's cry of 'Daisy! Come and meet—' She was aware of nothing but the need to escape.

Up the marble staircase she lurched in panic, cursing her restricted skirt that impeded her steps. Fear propelled her forward as it churned the breath in her cramped chest. He'd seen her, she knew he had. The evening was ruined – her *life* was ruined. All she could hope for was to bar herself in the sanctuary of her room and not come out until everybody had gone home. *Please God, let him be somebody's cousin from England out here on a very brief visit*, she implored silently. *Please, oh, please, don't let him find out who I am!*

At the top of the sweeping staircase she glanced back and saw in horror that he was following her, loping up the steps two and three at a time. And he was laughing, laughing as if chasing her was nothing but glorious sport, laughing as if he was confident of catching her, too.

That mustn't happen! Knowing that she had no hope of reaching her own room in time, she opened the first door she came to and slipped inside Rhys's room where she leaned on the door, her heart kicking in her throat.

Jeremy was chuckling to himself as he reached the landing. This was a rare piece of luck! His enchanting mermaid was *not* a figment of his imagination but she was a local lass, for only someone from the district would be dancing with the Mists of Heaven head shepherd. Perhaps she was a shepherdess herself. He'd be able to visit her on the plains when he came to the estate on business; he'd bring wine wrapped in a damp white towel and they'd drink it from each other's lips as they lay in the shade of a tree.

The hallway was empty. Jeremy checked to see if she was crouched on the far side of the dresser. He laughed aloud, a boyish gurgle of triumph. There was only one place she could be. Seizing the doorhandle, he flung the door open, only to gape in astonishment as the force of this action catapulted the object of his attentions from her hiding-place and sent her sprawling across the polished floor. 'Are you hurt?' he cried, rushing to help her up.

'It would be all the same if I was,' retorted Daisy.

Something in the recesses of his mind noticed that she spoke in too cultured a voice for a shepherdess, but Jeremy was so relieved that he ignored this warning. Scooping her up in his arms, he placed her on the adjacent bed and said: 'We can't be too careful, you know. A fall like that. . . . Who knows what injuries there might be? Let me check you over. . . .' And as he spoke he ran his hands lightly along her arms, then down, following the outline of her hips and thighs.

Enraged, Daisy pulled back and slapped him full force across the side

53

of the head. Strong and energetic, she could slap hard enough to make a recalcitrant horse snap to attention, and now in the slice of light from the open doorway she saw his expression suddenly grow sober.

He said, sounding genuinely rebuffed: 'I was only trying to be of service, ma'am.'

An American! she thought. Oh, thank goodness for that! Americans never stayed long in the colony. They were always on the way to some place on the way from some place else. She wriggled to get off the bed, but he pushed her back on to the fur spread and leaned over her so that he was gazing into her face. 'Let go of me,' she hissed. 'I warn you, let go of me or you'll regret it.'

'I'd regret it more if I did let you go,' Jeremy drawled, feeling the silky fur under his fingers and imagining what it would be like to be naked with her on this luxurious rug. The thought made him dizzy, and brought with it the realization that he had never felt such intense desire before. 'I've thought about you all day,' he confessed, stooping to brush his lips against her neck. 'I dreamed I saw a beautiful mermaid, and now to my delight I discover that she's real.'

Daisy's blood chilled. She stopped struggling and shivered. 'I don't know what you're talking about,' she said.

He laughed. 'I watched you dancing. You dance very prettily, but not as enchantingly as you swim.'

Tears surged up inside her, but she quelled them and said in a shaking voice: 'I don't know what you're talking about. Please let me go.' She would reach the safe haven of her room, bolt the door and never come out again. Never. She'd die there. She could die now.

'Don't deny that it was you,' he murmured, imprisoning her wrist as she swung to slap him again. 'And don't be angry. I've never seen anything half as beautiful as you were today.' As he spoke he leaned closer, his faintly Bourbon-scented breath fanning her cheek.

She opened her mouth to retort furiously and before she could draw breath he was kissing her, his mouth warm and moist and faintly Bourbon-tasting, too, moving slowly over hers. For a second she was too astonished to move – stillness he interpreted as acquiescence. Automatically his hand freed her wrist and moved down to cup the swell of her boned and laced bodice.

Almost choking with indignant disbelief, Daisy whacked him away, pushing herself backwards so violently that she fell on to the floor. Scrambling to her feet, she lurched towards the door.

He was there, intercepting her, not laughing this time but in earnest.

'I'll scream,' warned Daisy, pulling away from his touch.

'Don't,' he pleaded. 'Look, I noticed you weren't wearing any rings but, if you belong to someone, say so and I'll . . . I'll fight him. I'll challenge him to a duel. I'll—'

54

'You're insane,' Daisy informed him, but while her indignation was stoking to full-steam pitch there slipped into her mind the cold reminder that she had brought this situation squarely on to herself. If she had heeded Amy's protests, if she had listened to her own better judgement, she would never have taken that impulsive swim. Aunt Bea always stressed how important it was to keep a young man's respect; up until now Daisy has not quite understood because all the young men she knew treated her with a nervous apprehension. Now, bitterly, it was all too clear.

But the suspicion that this was entirely her fault made Daisy angrier still. 'Will you stop pestering me?' she cried, pushing past him and out the door on to the landing.

He followed. She would have gone towards her room, but he blocked her way so she turned the other way, towards the head of the stairway.

'Come back,' he urged. 'Come and talk to me.'

'I've nothing to say.' She shrugged off his hand, then swung around suddenly and screamed at him: 'Leave me alone! How dare you chase after me? How dare you speak to me so rudely, and molest me in my own home? It's insufferable! It's—'

He was looking at her oddly. She stopped, then was aware that a hush had decended on the cavernous entrance-hall and that from below dozens of faces were turned upward, all staring.

Jeremy's face was ashen. He was clearly as shocked as she. 'Your home?' he asked, lips white. 'But I thought you were a nobody, an employee, a—'

'So it was perfectly all right to treat me as badly as you did,' hissed Daisy. 'If that isn't the most contemptible—'

'Daisy!' bellowed her father.

'But that's our Jeremy!' said Silas. 'What can be going on?'

Rhys was already halfway up the stairs towards his daughter who, aghast, was biting her lip as she shrank against the banister-rail. He demanded: 'What are you doing, shrieking like a fishwife? This gentleman is a guest in our house!'

Disturbed that Rhys automatically blamed his daughter, Jeremy hastened to protest. 'I do apologize, sir. This is all my—'

'Daisy will apologize,' Rhys cut in. 'Her behaviour has been unacceptable all day, and now it is downright appalling. Well, Daisy? We're waiting!' Seizing her shoulders, he gave her a little shake.

This had to be the worst moment of her life. Dumbly she shook her head as hot tears stung her eyes. She was sure she was going to break down into weak sobs – and wasn't that Arabella watching smugly from the doorway – when Lisabeth suddenly appeared from behind Rhys and tucked her arm into his in a smiling proprietary gesture. 'Dear, this is a party, so let's have fun, shall we? I'm sure Daisy meant no harm.'

Hatred stiffened Daisy's backbone. To be defended by Lisabeth compounded her humiliation. She glared at her father with new defiance.

He was baffled. What was wrong with the girl? She used to adore Lisabeth, they were a family once, but what had gone wrong? On today of all days she could at least *try* to be pleasant instead of flaunting her distaste like a banner for all these people to see. In utter frustration he tightened his grip on Daisy's shoulders and shook her hard. 'Well?' he demanded.

'Sir!' pleaded Jeremy, horrified. 'I beg of you, sir, please don't blame your daughter. It was entirely my fault, and I bitterly regret any—'

'This is a family matter,' Rhys said. 'Go to your room, Daisy.'

Turning on his heel, he marched downstairs again. People turned their heads away quickly when they met his challenging gaze. Rhys was relieved that the band-music from the drawing-room drowned out this little rumpus, and only those immediately around the stairs had witnessed the quarrel. It was a party, and everybody should be laughing at a party.

'Come,' he said heartily to Silas and Charlotte. 'We have some excellent champagne on ice in the study. Very special, it is, and I'd appreciate your opinions on it. Let's celebrate!'

'I'm sorry about my son,' began Silas, his eyebrows clamped together as he frowned at Jeremy who was still standing, staring after Daisy.

'Nonsense. He's a young man . . . high spirits and all that,' Rhys assured him.

What about Daisy? thought Lisabeth.

SIX

Our first quarrel! thought Lisabeth in dismay. *And our marriage is less than nine hours old!* Worse, *she* had instigated the confrontation, coaxing Rhys away from his champagne to the butler's pantry where, instead of nudging him into a good mood with a few kisses, she had ridden straight over the irritation that was still rankling him, and had pleaded with him to make his peace with Daisy.

'No, certainly not!' he snapped, banging his hand against the shelves of pigeon-holes so that the laundry-lists and menus fluttered in their compartments.

She could have chewed her clumsy tongue. Rhys was the sweetest and most reasonable of men but when backed into a corner he became intractable. The too-direct approach seldom succeeded with him, and she knew it. She wheedled: 'Please, as a favour to me? Something is bothering Daisy . . . I've tried talking to her, but she just puts on her mulish face. She's unhappy, Rhys, and I want everyone to be happy today.'

'So do I. And I'm not about to tolerate her rudeness.'

Lisabeth sighed. Why was it that Rhys could bend over backwards to be fair with his shepherds, household staff or business associates, yet treated his daughter as if she had no rights of her own? With everyone else he was understanding to a fault. Gently she said: 'I know you pamper Daisy and you've a right to expect her gratitude, but she's not a pet, not something you *own*, Rhys. Won't you please see this from her point of view and—?'

'Great heavens, am I hearing you correctly?' He tried to laugh, but did not quite succeed. 'What nonsense, Lisabeth! You saw how she defied me when I ordered her to apologize.'

'But you didn't let her explain, dear. And young Mr Drake was trying to tell you—'

His blue eyes turned to cold grey, like the harbour when the sun goes behind a cloud. 'That will do, thank you, Lisabeth. I don't want to

57

listen to this nonsense. You are my wife, and I don't need you to instruct me in how to deal with my daughter.' Before she could protest he strode out of the dim, dusty room and banged the door behind him so hard that the rows of keys hanging behind it all jumped on their nails.

Lisabeth was aghast, but she checked herself from running after him. Three times since the wedding he had belittled different things she had said, dismissing them as 'nonsense'. Why? He used always to listen patiently to her views. Why the change?

Disquiet lay over her spirit. Was she to be just 'my wife', a possession like 'my daughter', something to be owned but never considered, respected or consulted? Is this what marriage meant, that she automatically had to obey and never disagree?

Sir Kenneth had once loved dancing. With his full spread of snowy whiskers and his rotund little figure he and his towering wife made quite a spectacle on the dance floor, but nobody who saw the joy on his face ever laughed at him. Now, with a heart condition that prevented undue exertion, he had to remain on the sidelines, hunched in his Bath chair, hungrily watching others enjoying themselves. His blood rose with the flash of bright skirts and the tap of supple shoes, and he nodded his head in time to the reels and mazurkas. Lady Launcenolt watched his face; his expression brought tears to her eyes. In an interval she came over to him smiling, bearing glasses of fruit cup.

Immediately he was his old self. 'Damned stuff! Whisky, that's what I need, not this old maid's drink.'

'It's delicious, Kiki. Go on, try it.'

Scowling, he ignored her and gave it to Albert to hold for him. 'Where's Daisy? I haven't seen her for half an hour.'

'I'll look for her soon. There's Doctor Meakings over by the new spinet. I think Rhys and Lisabeth are going to play it soon. Have you asked Doctor Meakings about going to London?'

'What do doctors know? I'd rather talk to Daisy.'

There was the nub of it, thought Beatrice. He was afraid that if he went he might never come back, and wouldn't see Daisy again. For all his scoffing at her devotion, he doted on Daisy more, though he'd never admit it.

The band struck up a rollicking schottische. Aggressively cheerful, Beatrice took both Kiki's hands in hers and swung them to the music, crouching over him and playing with him as if he was a baby. At first he resisted, then he submitted, and soon he was actually enjoying himself enough to laugh.

'My word, Kiki, we've shared some good times, haven't we?' she said when it was over.

*　　*　　*

You'll never guess who I've been talking to,' Amy whispered, though there was nobody in the room but them.

Daisy was picking listlessly at the fringe on her shawl. She shrugged. 'Not Tommy Nevin, I hope. If Papa catches him up here, he'll—'

'Of course not. He's still at sea,' Amy cut in, annoyed at being reminded that Tom was *persona non grata* at Mists of Heaven, a ban that was quite without justice. 'I told you that this morning. No, I've been talking to Jeremy Drake.'

'Splendid.'

'You know . . . that fellow who was by the dam this morning. I refused to talk to him at first, but he kept after me until I did.'

'He would.'

'Daisy, he's charming, truly he is. He was there quite by accident this morning, and he didn't mean to spy. He—'

'He's *abominable*!' Obviously Amy had missed the scene in the hall, which was fortunate; the fewer witnesses to her humiliation the better. One reason hatred still scorched through her was that Jeremy had been there to soak up every detail of her shame, the proof that Papa didn't love her and never had. Lisabeth, that's all he cared about. Wrenching her self-pity aside, she forced her mind back to Jeremy, his vile gloating. 'I wish I'd pushed him downstairs. Yes, that's what I should have done.'

'You don't mean that,' pleaded Amy. 'He said he got as big a fright as we did. You know that he's Silas Drake's son, don't you? The Westlake girls said he's "tewwibly wich", and you should see the way Arabella Martin is casting sheep's eyes at him. When he had finished talking to me she came over and demanded to know what he'd said.'

'You didn't tell her?'

'Of course not. How silly do you think I am? Arabella is smitten – I swear she is. When I left she was offering to fetch him a plate of trifle, as if she was a servant or something.'

'I'm not interested,' announced Daisy, to cover up the fact that she was. 'The only person I'm interested in is Andrew.'

'But Andrew's not here, and Mr Drake is. You know how I feel about Tom, but truly, Daisy, I'd dance with Jeremy Drake in a second if he asked me. Unfortunately he only wants to meet you.' There was a pause, then Amy said: 'Oh, well, I don't blame you. I'd not have the courage, either, to face him after what happened. I'd run and hide in my room, too, if I was in your shoes.'

'I'm not afraid of him!'

Amy turned away so that her expression was hidden. 'I'd be terrified. I'd be cowering in my room if—'

'I'm not and I'll prove it to you.' She picked up her osprey-feather fan and flicked it open, shrugging off the prospect of her father's wrath.

'Come on, Amy. Watch me – how do those Americans say it? – yes, watch me spit in his eye.'

At the foot of the stairs they joined in the throngs filing into the drawing-room where rows of chairs had been set out for the recital. Gwynne was seated in the front row with an empty chair on either side of her; while from a position on the end of another row Beatrice waved to the girls, but she had only one spare chair beside her.

'I don't want to sit down the front,' said Daisy. 'Let's go back there. Albert will fetch another chair to squeeze in the end of the row.' Which they did. Daisy was sitting between Beatrice and Kiki's Bath chair, while Amy sat on the other side.

The room filled up. Gwynne stood and turned to scan the rows, looking for the girls. Light caught on her pebble lenses, making her eyes flat and yellow. Not wanting to be seen, Daisy raised her fan, while Amy crouched lower in her seat so that the broad shoulders of the man in Canterbury Volunteers uniform blocked her from Gwynne's view. As soon as Gwynne sat down Daisy turned to whisper across Beatrice's lacy bosom to Amy, while Beatrice, secretly triumphant that Daisy had chosen her, ignored their conspiracy.

Daisy hissed to attract Amy's attention, then never spoke, for at that moment her eye was caught by Jeremy and Arabella at the end of the row. They looked strikingly handsome together, a couple, for while she was talking animatedly to him, fluttering her free hand as she spoke and placing it often on his arm, he seemed to be in a different world, not listening, like a husband who has heard it all before, thought Daisy. Jeremy was turning his head from side to side, his eyes restlessly roaming.

In the space of only a second Daisy wondered what he sought, guessed, and lifted her fan again to hide her face, when Jeremy saw her. A flash of light came into his dark eyes, his shoulders relaxed, and with a smile twisting the corners of his mouth he turned to the stage.

As the lights dimmed tall Lowell Windsor stepped on to the stage followed by the much shorter 'Baron' Windsor. Lowell was the sort of performer who attracts instant sympathy, being gangly and awkward to offset his striking prettiness, and as his uncle announced the songs he was blushing, beaming with a hopeful friendliness. 'Baron' – for he was never called anything else – was a slight neat man with thinning hair, a tiny moustache and clipped voice. He patted Lowell's shoulder, then sat down at the piano and began to play with a delicate touch. Astonished by his skill, Daisy wondered if he really was the ogre rumour had him to be, if it was true or a wicked invention that he drove his Australian blackmen like the devil, beating and underfeeding them.

The two kept glancing at each other, nodding as the rhythm or mood changed. Rapport between them enhanced the songs, and Lowell's throbbing tenor was so exquisite that 'The Ash Grove' brought tears of homesickness to many eyes.

The room was crowded, with people standing in a crush right around the seating. During the song Daisy became aware that someone stood close behind her; when she leaned back to applaud at the conclusion the person accidentally brushed her bare shoulder with his hand. She sat forward again at once, and he said: 'Please forgive me, Miss Morgan.' That warm thick voice was unmistakable.

Daisy's spine stiffened. The impertinence of it! And to say 'Please forgive me, Miss Morgan' in that way was obviously meant to cover everything: this morning, their confrontation and now this. He *was* optimistic, she would give him that.

Amy was giggling, her eyes scrunched up with repressed mirth. When Daisy glared at her she cupped her hands around her mouth and whispered: 'Go on, spit in his eye like you said you would.'

'Really, Miss Thorne,' Beatrice reprimanded her. 'You forget where you are!'

'So you're hiding here,' said Rhys, opening the bedchamber door to find Lisabeth with a stack of folded blouses in her hands.

'I'm not hiding.'

He noticed that she seemed tense. Prickled by guilt over their earlier quarrel, he tried to be cheerful, smooth it over. 'That "Baron" Windsor has no sense of decorum. Do you know that he tried to provoke a scene earlier? Reckons we pay our shearers too much, and that we should go along with his scheme of importing Negroes from Africa to do the work. Nobody would agree with him, of course, and he got quite nasty with me. Said this was my house so I should make them listen to his views. I said it was my wedding, too, and not the time or the place for business squabbles.' When Lisabeth did not respond he said: 'What's wrong? Are those matrons giving you a hard time? Do you recall how they used to mention morality and then make a great fuss of apologizing for their tactlessness? They can't do that now, can they?' He watched her place the stack neatly in an open trunk and tuck the edges in. 'I say, what is it, Lisabeth? Are you nervous about the recital? It's time to go on down now.'

'You go ahead, Rhys. You're much better than I am. Nobody will mind if you play alone.' She took another stack of clothes from an open drawer.

Missing the significance of what she was doing, he said: '*Has* somebody snubbed you? No? I'm glad of that. People will now have to accord you the respect you deserve.'

Except you, thought Lisabeth.

Giving her a proprietary kiss on the forehead, he chided: 'What is all this anyway? You've a maid now, so leave that. Carthew will unpack your things.'

This was the moment. Legs watery, she pressed her knees together to steady them and with every scrap of wavering courage said: 'I'm not unpacking. I'm packing. I'm going back to town, Rhys.'

'Oh?'

Sitting on the edge of the bed, she fiddled with a pink camisole ribbon. How could she do this properly? She dared not look at him, for everything about him was so indescribably precious to her, his sweet tired face, his tender blue eyes – the very prospect of leaving him tore at her, but she knew that she must do this, must say this so that there would never be any misunderstanding between them, ever again.

'I feel swamped here, Rhys. Getting married to you – it's been a mistake.'

'What nonsense is this, Lisabeth? How can you say such—?'

'There!' Now she could safely raise her eyes to his. '*That's* the reason, Rhys. Do you realize that in all the years I lived here as your housekeeper you never once said "What nonsense" to my opinions, yet four times today that's how you've dismissed me?'

'I don't understand.'

'Neither do I! In all those years I never felt owned by you. You listened. You respected me.'

'I respect you now. Ah, I see.' His lips tightened. 'This is about Daisy, isn't it? You're trying to force me—'

'No! Emphatically no! This is about *me*, Rhys. If being your wife means being your chattel, then I don't want that. I never did. I thought we'd be equals. . . .'

There was a silence as Rhys stared at the floor. Lisabeth gripped the ribbon so fiercely that she felt it rip. *Please don't be angry*, she prayed silently. *Please don't lose your temper and slam out of the room again. It's all over if you do.*

'You're serious, aren't you? You're really leaving?'

Her heart shrank to a cold little thing. 'I must.'

'But think of the advantages of being my wife. Financially—'

'I managed before, didn't I? With my paintings, my wages and the rent you paid for my fifty acres, I saved enough to buy that cottage in town, *and* furnish it, *and* buy a carriage and pair.'

'So that you could leave me?' His voice was bitter; her purchase of the cottage had long rankled between them. 'No, please forget I said that. I admire you for your independence, but dash it, Lisabeth, it frightens me. I want to provide for you, and—'

'And own me,' she said crisply. This was going to run in circles.

'I admit it, and I'm wrong,' he said unexpectedly. It was so unlike him that she gaped in astonishment, making him fluster and hurry to finish. 'I think I can see why you're upset. I've been patronizing, I suppose. Tell you what,' he said, sitting down and drawing her against him, kissing her neck just below the ear. 'How would you like still to be independent but be my wife, too? I'll continue to lease the land, you may sell your paintings and rent your town house, too, if you like, and I'll give you your housekeeper's wage as an allowance. But, be warned: you'll have to buy your own hats and gowns and books and painting things. It won't be easy for you.'

'It'll be marvellous!' She wound her arms around his neck, giving herself up to him with a sob. 'I do love you, Rhys. I didn't want to go – but I would have!'

'I'd have tried to stop you,' he warned, reaching for the covered buttons that marched the length of her spine. 'I hated these past six months. I never want to be without you again.'

She sighed, then gasped as she felt the coolness of his fingers on her skin. 'Rhys, what are you doing?'

'What do you think?'

'You're *terrible*!' She pushed at his head as he slid her gown from her shoulder, reaching down to taste a pink nipple. 'We can't do this *now*! People are waiting.'

'Lowell can sing another encore,' he said.

After the recital Rhys announced that there would be dancing 'until sunrise' and that tea was served in the conservatory for anyone who was weary of champagne. The moment he had stepped down from the stage Daisy leaped up as though stung and with Amy in tow sought refuge in the dining-room where servants were busy clearing away plates and cutlery. 'Don't speak to him,' she ordered Amy. 'I think he's despicable and I want nothing to do with him.' There was a depressed achey feeling in her chest which intensified as she spoke. If only Andrew were here. She'd enjoy herself then.

To her chagrin Jeremy didn't bother to pursue her. He waited until the girls emerged and detached himself from the group which included Maurice Andruth and Lowell Windsor, but when he approach he glanced briefly at Daisy's haughty expression and addressed his attentions to Amy instead. 'Miss Thorne, would you care to entrust your life to me? It's a waltz, I believe.'

'I'd be honoured,' said treacherous Amy.

Watching them dance away, a small cold regret entered Daisy's mind. If she'd smiled at Jeremy, he'd have asked her to partner him, and she could have accepted, have tripped and stamped hard on his foot.

If she'd accepted, she would be whirled around as Amy was now. She was simpering up at him, shameless with enjoyment, her plain face transformed. Daisy noticed how close he held her, how he murmured in her ear. Watching them laugh, Daisy felt more miserable still.

If only Andrew were here, she thought desperately.

When he had consumed several double shots of whisky Silas Drake reasoned that since Rhys Morgan's friendship was so important to him the chummy thing to do was dance with the fellow's sister. He heartily rejected Gwynne's refusal.

Gwynne hated dancing. Her feet hurt, and the loud music confused her; worse, she was mortified by the way her stout midriff clamped against his paunch as they waltzed. It wasn't decent to be bumping stomachs with a stranger, whatever the circumstances. Besides, his eyebrows repelled her. Charles had smooth tidy eyebrows.

Pleading fatigue, she begged to sit down.

Silas accompanied her to a couch where she patted the seat beside her, but before she could properly warm to the subject of dear Charles's appreciation of dancing Silas insisted on fetching a glass of fruit cup to alleviate her fatigue.

She settled back, anticipating a long chat about Charles. He sent a servant over with the drink.

When Lisabeth saw Daisy standing forlornly alone she nudged Rhys, pointing her out and hoping that Rhys wouldn't notice that, without anybody's permission, his daughter had hidden her ankles and shown the nape of her neck like the older girls. 'Doesn't she look pretty?'

'She looks . . . different,' said Rhys, uncomfortable. He recalled how briefly Azura had looked like that, how quickly she had become grossly fat.

'Ask her to dance. Go on,' prodded Lisabeth. She could see he didn't want to, but to please her he complied. Daisy, she noticed, accepted with equal reluctance.

They were awkward together, she light-footed and tentative, he stiff and measured. To distract himself he joked: 'I suppose you're breaking all the young men's hearts, hey?'

This, she realized, was an olive branch, to make up for when he had bellowed at her earlier. She said: 'They don't even notice me.'

'Of course they do! That young man – Jeremy Drake – he went out of his way earlier to assure me you weren't to be blamed. I must admit I was impressed by him. He's a fine young man and obviously thinks very highly of you.' She said nothing, so he continued clumsily: 'You're a little young yet, but when the time comes nothing would make me more pleased and proud than to see you married to someone like him.'

She was annoyed, stung into retorting airily: 'I've already decided who I'm going to marry!'

'Am I permitted to know him?'

'Andrew, of course.' She giggled at his perplexed expression, though the giggle was more nerves than amusement; already she was sorry she had spoken out.

'You don't mean Andrew *Stafford*?'

She nodded. His voice sounded deeper, darker, as though it was pressed flat by the weight of a threat, and he looked incredulous, dark-faced, almost angry. 'But you haven't seen Andrew for years – not since you were practically a baby. You've harboured some ridiculous notion because he saved your life. Those romantic fantasies aren't real, Daisy. It's silly to—'

Her mouth set in a stubborn line that matched any of his intractable expressions. In truth she was thrilled to arouse so strong a reaction in him. 'You may say what you please, but I've made up my mind,' she chirped, so blithely defiant that he wanted to shake her again. 'I think about Andrew all the time, and I write notes to pop in with Aunty Gwynne's letters. I know he'll come back to New Zealand soon, and when he does he'll see me all grown up. Wait and see, Papa – it'll be all my dreams come true!'

And all my nightmares, thought Rhys. *My God, Lisabeth, what shall we do?*

Seeing them standing at one side of the dance-floor, Lisabeth glided over. 'You look a picture together!' she exclaimed. 'Did you enjoy the dance?'

Hearing the satisfied note in Lisabeth's voice, Daisy realized that Papa had only asked her to dance because Lisabeth had pushed him into it. Turning abruptly, she hurried away.

'What *is* the matter with her?' puzzled Lisabeth.

'She wants to marry Andrew. Yes, I'm serious.'

'Oh, I *see*. She's disappointed because he didn't come home. Don't look so gloomy, Rhys, *please*. This thing with Daisy. It's just a childish infatuation.'

'I doubt it. I'd like to think so, but I doubt it.'

Then, you'll have to tell her, thought Lisabeth, not daring to say it aloud. She could see how distressed he was. 'It'll be all right. You'll see,' she said.

He doubted that, too.

It was inevitable, she supposed. Just when she was beginning to enjoy herself again the music signalled 'change partners', she curtsied to thank old Reginald Westlake, turned to the next gentleman in the line and found herself staring into Jeremy Drake's pleased face.

Before she could escape he grabbed her in a hold too insistent to be polite and whirled her out of the double row of dancers so that the two of them swayed alone in the centre of the floor.

Daisy was furious; she could feel the disapproving stares from black-clad chaperons who sat together like crows on a fence. 'Let me go at once!' she hissed. 'Only engaged couples are permitted to break the ring. We'll be *talked about.*'

'We could announce our engagement,' he offered.

'That will never happen,' she retorted.

'Pity,' he said, maddeningly refusing to rise to her bait. 'I was looking forward to it.' Lord, but she was beautiful!

Sensing that he was laughing at her, she struggled and tried to kick his shins but was hampered by her extra-long skirt. Enraged by his smile, she said: 'If you don't let go of me at once, I'll . . . I'll. . . .'

'You'll what?'

Daisy was glaring past his shoulder, temper plainly stamped on her face, when she noticed Arabella who stood with Maurice Andruth at the edge of the ring. Maurice was looking at Arabella, his pudgy face wistful with adoration, but she was staring at the dancers, through the gaps between the dancers, at Daisy and Jeremy – and she looked unhappy. Meeting her gaze, Daisy hastily adjusted her face into a pleasant expression, then smiled as if she was having a simply wonderful time. It was gratifying to see Arabella's dismay deepen.

'You'll what?' repeated Jeremy, whirling her around.

'Oh, nothing. You won't let me go anyway, unless I cause a scene, and if I do that Papa will descend like a gannet on a herring, so. . . .'

He dared breathe, thankful that she had settled as he had hoped. The last moments had been more nervous than harnessing an unbroken colt. Dear Lord, but she was beautiful! His heart was a sharp-edged hard mass that hammered bruisingly on his ribs, and all he could think of was how she had looked in that pool. To touch her silk-clad waist evoked powerful reminders of how golden and smooth her body had been under the slick of sunlit water. Dancing with her, holding her, became an agonizingly sensual experience. It was all he could do to refrain from crushing her body hard against his.

A manful effort was needed to say casually: 'You dance very gracefully, Miss Morgan.'

How unoriginal! they both thought, with equal scorn.

With a dazzling smile directed past his shoulder, and in a voice that could chip ice, she said: 'I believe you mentioned that before.'

'Look, Daisy, I am sorry. Truly I am, for all that's happened. Is there any way I can make it up to you?'

'That is a very tempting offer,' she said, still with the smile and cold voice – an effect, Jeremy thought, that was like clear sunshine on a frosty morning.

'I'll tell you what,' he said rapidly, for the music was bouncing to its close. 'I'll even the score for you, shall I? Tomorrow at the same time if you and Miss Thorne go down to the dam you can surprise *me* taking a swim. There, how's that for an idea? What do you say, huh?'

'But that's outrageous! It would only make things worse!' she blurted, then it occurred to her that he was pointing out what a ludicrous situation he was in, and through no fault of his own. Seeing the mischief in his eyes, she began to laugh.

Gwynne was disturbed by what she saw. Daisy was being much too familiar with that young man . . . and what had she done to her dress and her hair? If she wasn't so tired, and her feet didn't ache so, she'd march over to that young lady and deliver a piece of her mind. Sighing, she unobtrusively rubbed her ankles together. A tablespoon or two of that soothing syrup was what she needed. She would have to fetch it herself; Carthew was at the staff party, and Gwynne wouldn't let one of these nosy borrowed flibbertigibbets go poking around in her bedside bureau.

Daisy and the Drake lad were still deep in conversation. She hoped they weren't developing a friendship. Imagine if a romance blossomed between them! Gwynne shuddered. If that happened, Charlotte Drake and that husband of hers would be at Mists of Heaven every other minute on some pretext or other. Life would be unendurable.

I'll write to Andrew again, she decided. Daisy needed someone like Andrew, someone older, educated, someone a woman could really look up to. Yes, someone like her Charles.

Under the fronds of towering potted palms in the conservatory two middle-aged maids in White Clouds uniforms poured coffee and tea into Royal Doulton cups and offered milk and cream with a selection of grated sugars, some flavoured with vanilla, some with cinnamon. On the trestle table beside them tiered cake-plates were heaped with petits fours, fruit tartlets and crisp brandy snaps stuffed with whipped cream.

'I couldn't eat a bite,' declared Daisy, spearing a thin slice of lemon to float in her tea.

'Not even a nibble, a kiss perhaps?' teased Jeremy.

'Kisses are for afternoon tea,' explained Daisy before she realized what he meant. She blushed, snapping open her fan and screening the lower part of her face.

In all his twenty-four years Jeremy had never been so enchanted. When he accosted her on the stairs he'd expected her to be a brazen creature, a serving wench dressed up to decorate some widower's arm for the evening, but now he was positive that her nude swim was not a wanton act but a natural bubbling-over of high spirits. If everybody was judged by what they did when they thought they were safely alone, then the world would be a harsh place, he reasoned.

'Might I ask your father for permission to come calling on you?' he asked, stirring the cream into his coffee with unwarranted concentration. When she didn't reply he glanced up to see that she was frowning and biting her lip. 'What is it?'

'I don't know how to put this, but I'm sort of engaged.'

'*Sort of?*'

'Well, it's like this,' she began. What was wrong? In her heart she was Andrew's. She loved him, she thought about him all the spare quiet moments she had, and in her imagination their inevitable betrothal was a solid real thing, yet to bring it out like this in front of Jeremy seemed to shrink it, fade it. Suddenly it looked like a wispy hope instead of a fact. She forged on as best she could, saying: 'Lisabeth has a brother called Andrew, who is a doctor. He isn't here at the moment.' She passed that off as artlessly as if he had just stepped out of the room. 'But when he comes back . . . which I hope will be soon. . . .'

'When he comes back, then we'll see,' said Jeremy with more confidence than he felt. He smiled, but from then on the evening turned grey.

When Amy had finished tying her hair up in curling-rags she helped Daisy tie hers. 'Let me do it for you. You tie such lumpy knots.'

Daisy fiddled with her locket-clasp, then sprung it open and stared at the picture, trying with all her might to summon up a clear image of what Andrew was really like.

Peeping over her shoulder, Amy said: 'Mr Drake asked me about him. He wanted to know if you were really engaged.'

'I hope you told him I was.' Their eyes met in the pier-glass.

'Well, I told him that you probably would be when Andrew, Doctor Stafford, arrive back from Europe. He seemed surprised to hear that he was so far away, but I told him you expected him back in a year or so. That's true, isn't it? He promised to be back for your eighteenth birthday, so—'

'Why did you tell him anything?' Daisy jerked the last curling-ribbon out of Amy's grasp and began to wind the hair around it herself.

'But you were getting on so well with him—'

'I was.' Daisy felt helpless. The whole evening things kept sliding out from underneath her; and now, even though she had everything her own way, she was left with a depressing sense of loss. She said: 'What else did our inquisitive Mr Drake want to know.'

'Nothing really.' Amy shucked off her slippers and swung her legs up into the big bed, settling back on the fluffy pillows with a gurgle of contentment. 'Do you realize it's almost five o'clock in the morning,' she said, pulling up the lace bedspread and snuggling down between the cool cotton sheets. *What bliss*, she thought, deciding not to tell Daisy any more, especially not about how Jeremy asked how long Andrew had been away and when she told him eleven years – or was it twelve? – he laughed so hard that she was frightened he was going to choke himself. There was no point in telling Daisy that; it would only upset her, and Amy hated it when Daisy was upset.

SEVEN

IT WAS UNLUCKY TIMING, Lisabeth reflected later. If Moiroa, the Maori laundrywoman, had found the letter ten minutes earlier, the incident would not have erupted. Lisabeth would have had time to read Andrew's letter and thrust it into the fire under the boiling copper. It would have been ashes by the time Rhys arrived. As it was, she was standing in the doorway of the steam-filled wash-house watching Rhys as he clattered into the cobblestone yard on his bay mare Mazurka. Tama, the scrawny brown stable-boy, darted out to catch the reins as he dismounted.

'Is the shearing almost done?' called Lisabeth. 'We haven't heard a sound all day. The wind is blowing onshore.' Thank heavens, too, she added silently, for when there was a strong breeze across from the vast shearing-yards it wafted not only the bleating but also the powerful odour of thousands of massed sheep and brought the accompanying swarms of flies, too.

'It's a good clip, and they're not through yet.' Rhys helped himself to a dipperful of water from the shaded barrel and, removing his wide hat and neckerchief, tipped a second dipperful over the back of his neck. Straightening, he grinned. 'That's better. We're breathing dust down there. Our merinos are doing splendidly. Some of the fleeces are weighing in at six pounds. Five is a good average. We have to have the very best to compete with the Australian sheep stations in the European markets, but I'm confident that our Mists of Heaven clip will bring top prices again.' He grabbed her by the waist and swung her around. He was dirty and smelt sheepy, but she didn't mind because she wore an old print dress with a damp canvas apron over the top. When he set her down he said: 'I won't see you until much later this evening. I'm off to talk to Silas Drake about this freezing works we're setting up together. We're riding out to look at possible sites.'

'You're not going like that?' she asked, wrinkling her nose.

'I'm going to bathe and change.' Groping at her playfully, he added in a theatrical whisper: 'Will you come up and scrub my back?'

She laughed, and as she shoved him away was aware that Moiroa was standing close by, waiting to talk to her, her smooth dark face impassive. It was impossible to know what Moiroa was thinking.

'Yes, Moiroa?' Lisabeth hoped the Maori woman hadn't heard, nor noticed the way Rhys had fumbled under her apron.

'Here, Miz Morgan,' said Moiroa in her expressionless voice. 'This were in the cloth.' She thrust a folded note at Lisabeth and turned back to feed a billow of linen into the bubbling lye-scented water.

'You're wicked,' scolded Lisabeth, stepping outside. 'How can you expect the servants to respect me when—' She broke off.

'Who's it from?' asked Rhys. When she didn't reply but continued to scan the note with eyes that were filled with dismay he stepped around so that he could read over her shoulder.

It was too late to hide it. Dumbly she handed it over.

Rhy's face contorted. 'The impudent young bastard,' he muttered, crumpling the note in his fist as he strode towards the house.

Lisabeth caught up to him when he paused to lever his boots off on the jack. 'Please don't be angry with him, Rhys.'

'I'm furious.' He glared at her. 'I tell you, Lisabeth, I've had enough of that young whelp's moralizing. We're *married* now!'

'Hush,' she warned, for Tama was feeding carrots to Mazurka only a few yards away, but watching them with huge round eyes.

In the library Rhys flung Andrew's note on the map table and strode to the window where he glared out at the rose garden. Gwynne and Daisy were pruning roses there. Both wore wide straw hats and thick protective gloves. A little Maori girl held a basket for the trimmings. Rhys said: 'At least you didn't see that note on our wedding day.'

'Yes,' said Lisabeth, then added: 'Rhys, can't you try harder not to mind what Andrew thinks?'

'He's my son, dammit. Of course I mind! And when we get these high-minded moralistic preachings – dammit, of course I mind.'

'But he doesn't know he's your son. If he did, it would be different, I'm sure. Oh, Rhys, we should have told him the truth long ago, before he went away. All these years between have made it so much worse.'

Rhys rounded on her. 'How could I tell him? The only time he spoke to me was to shriek abuse and to hurl punches in my direction. Hardly the atmosphere to break such news to him. And since he's been away he's adopted such a preachy priggish tone that I'm damned if I want to tell him.'

'It's not the sort of thing you can explain in a letter,' agreed Lisabeth, smoothing out the note. 'Let's hope he comes home for a visit soon, so all this can be brought out in the open. I do long for a reconciliation between you two. You are the two people I love most in the world, and it seems so wrong that he's far across the globe and not here with you, where he belongs by rights.' She paused and moved over to lean her face on his shoulder. 'Rhys, no matter what Doctor Meakings says, it's possible that I am past childbearing. We may never have a son together, which leaves only Andrew to—'

'I'd rather have no son than one who hates me, Lisabeth.' His heart shrank away from her words. All his prayers were directed towards his longing for a son from Lisabeth. His punishment for years of stolen moments had been the frustration of knowing that none of their lovemaking could be complete. His soul had ached for fulfilment. Surely it wasn't too late.

'He won't hate you, Rhys.'

'Yes, he will. He's so judgemental that it frightens me. Ironic, isn't it? All my power, wealth and strength is as nothing because I'm helpless to change his opinion of me.'

'When you explain, he'll understand. Heavens, Rhys, you were so young when you had that affair with Mamma. She was bored and lonely, and her marriage with Mr Rennie had proved to be a ghastly mistake. I know that Andrew will be understanding.' But even as she spoke the paper in her hand with its burden of bitter words seemed to mock her.

'*You* didn't understand,' Rhys reminded her. 'You hated me for years because of it. Lisabeth, I dread this whole thing. It's bad enough to anticipate Andrew's contempt, but what will Daisy think? What will she say when she finds out her father—?'

'Hush. Don't distress yourself.' Lisabeth cursed the note and cursed Andrew for sending it.

There was an empty silence. Both stood watching the group in the rose garden. Daisy was laughing at something Gwynne had said. This sight saddened Lisabeth, who had been unable to make Daisy laugh or even smile. She had been extremely cool towards Lisabeth in the several days since the wedding and had taken it with bad grace when Rhys declined the invitation from Benares for her to stay with the Launcenolts. Looking at her now, Lisabeth suddenly wondered whether Daisy had read the note when she unpacked the gown, and afterwards had tucked it amongst the folds of the tablecloth where Moiroa found it. Come to think of it, the lass had looked ill at ease when Lisabeth asked where the wrappings had gone, in case a letter or card had been overlooked. Yes, she must have read it, and that would explain her hostile attitude. She'd be blaming Lisabeth for the fact that Andrew hadn't come home to New Zealand.

Lisabeth resolved right then that she would embark on a campaign to lure him back. She would bombard him with letters, invitations and

expressions of devotion and affection. If there was any brotherly sentiment there under his cloak of disapproval, he would respond.

She slid her arm through Rhys's and nuzzled his shoulder.

'Please don't borrow trouble, Rhys. As for that nonsense about wanting to marry Andrew – she was just distressed because he wasn't at the
party. She'll be delighted when she finds out the truth. Give her credit for
some understanding. She has a warm nature underneath that stubbornness of hers. Perhaps we should encourage young men around here
more – Lowell Windsor, the Andruth lad, and Jeremy Drake. He seems
keen on her.'

Rhys fidgeted; he felt uneasy. This problem was assuming the dimen-
sions of an avalanche that threatened to sweep down and demolish
everything he cared about. 'You're wasting your time with Lowell
Windsor.'

'Why? He seems a fine lad. His family have estates in Devon and—'

Rhys laughed. 'Forget him.'

'Gwynne says . . . she says we should find Daisy a perfect young man,
just like Charles.'

'Like Charles?' Rhys really laughed at that. He laughed, thumping
his riding-crop against his thigh until he doubled over, then laughed
until his voice wore away to a scrape, bracing himself on the sill with
both hands. Gwynne looked around, her spectacles owlish, her skin
dappled like feathers in the speckled shade of her straw brim. The sight
of her made Rhys gasp helplessly. 'Like Charles? Pity help us all!'

Three weeks after Christmas, Jeremy rode to Mists of Heaven on his
white mare Angel with two jittery mares at trail. He had ridden through
the cool of early morning, would stay with them all day, help with the
mating in the afternoon when they had rested, then would dine with the
Morgans before riding home in the cool twilight.

This was his fourth visit to the station with Georgia brood mares, and
there would be several more visits before the season was finished.
During this spring–summer racing season Donegal had proved to be
such a master of the racetrack that Silas Drake regretted his generous
impulse, and in the hopes of siring an equally fine winner was putting
all his stable of mares to him in turn. Another stallion like Donegal
would fetch a fortune in America, he thought, while Jeremy thought
that another stallion like him would be magnificent to own, to race and
to be proud of. This season Donegal had already won over two thousand
guineas – which caused friction between Silas and Rhys, because Rhys
insisted Silas keep all the first season's winnings, while Silas, wanting
the money, felt obliged to refuse – at first, at least. 'The thrill of watching him flash across the turf is enough for me,' Rhys assured his friend.

On each of these visits Jeremy saw Daisy, and he had seen her at the
races twice, too, looking fragile and misty and beautiful. Each time he

73

saw her his chest seemed to solidify so that it took an effort to drag his breath through the mass of longing.

On each of his visits he ignored her. He was always polite, offering a 'Good morning, Miss Morgan', but he never looked at her face and he resisted the temptation to ask whether her fiancé was coming home soon. She would guess that he was teasing her then. His parents never failed to enquire about Daisy. 'How are you getting on with that honey of a child?' Charlotte asked. 'She's on ice, Mom,' he would reply. His father, being a blunt man with a passionate interest in breeding, was more direct. 'She's the one for you. Spirited, good blood, strong breeding hips, and all her father's gumption. You'd get sons out of her that any man could be proud of.' Jeremy knew that these remarks reflected a lingering disappointment that he wasn't as tall or as broad as Silas's other sons, that unlike his brothers he'd lost more boyhood scraps than he'd won. The remarks made Jeremy squirm.

Adjoining the wool-shed a special enclosure was built for the mating of these racehorses, screened with high brush fences so that the animals couldn't hurt themselves or be seen by delicate feminine eyes which were not supposed to view the coarser aspects of life. The wool-shed was deemed far enough away from the house to be out of earshot, but on this day Amy and Daisy were walking across a nearby meadow armed with fashion magazines lent by Beatrice and a basket of peaches picked from the orchard, in search of quiet shade to spread their rug. Under a huge elm Amy had set down the ginger-ale crock and Daisy was unpacking glasses when an unearthly sound, a cross between a scream and a roar, made them stare at each other in fright.

'It's at the wool-shed,' whispered Amy.

'Let's go and see what it is.'

'No! I mean . . . we don't know what it could be.'

'It couldn't be anything that would hurt us, that's for sure,' said Daisy briskly. 'It's probably just a sick cow, or—' She broke off as the sound came again, swelling around them, making the tiny hairs on their arms rise and their scalps prickle eerily.

'It's scary,' muttered Amy. 'I feel like I do in an electrical storm. All tingly. I say, Lowell said the "Baron" was planning to import mountain lions to shoot for sport. You don't suppose—'

'No. Papa told him he'd be hounded out of the colony if he tried anything like that. It's a sick cow, for sure. Let's go and see if it needs attention.'

This was one of the least attractive aspects of Daisy's personality, reflected Amy glumly as she followed. Though she had never seen Daisy take medicine without an almighty fuss, Daisy was inordinately interested in the diseases and treatment of others, and, unless chased away by Rhys or Jock McFallish, watched animals being doctored as if it was interesting entertainment instead of a gruesome repulsive spectacle. As they scurried across the meadow Daisy was speculating what might be the matter: the cow couldn't be hoven or choking, it was making too much noise. Was it cast with a damaged leg? As they drew closer to the shed she doubted that it was a cow at all. More likely it was a horse.

Then, in a lull between these unearthly sounds, Jeremy's voice carried clearly. 'That didn't work. She's trying to kick him away. Here, buddy, you hold him while I tighten those hobbles. We might need to bail her to keep her still. Easy there, boy. Easy.'

'Let's go away,' begged Amy. She didn't know what was going on beyond that high brush wall, but she didn't want to know, either. She tugged at Daisy, who was trying to peep through slivers of cracks in the fence.

Turning, her face alight with determined curiosity, Daisy pointed to a window high on the red-painted wool-shed wall. On the inside it was thickly encrusted with spider-webs that would screen them, Daisy calculated, like a lace curtain through which she could peer unseen. 'Come on, up there!' she mouthed.

Shaking her head, Amy hissed a protest. She didn't want to go into the gloomy sheep-smelling shed. 'We'll be caught!' she warned as they scrambled over the greasy railings. 'Your father will forbid me to visit,' she wailed as their feet pattered across the smooth timber floor. 'Daisy, *please*,' she bleated as they scampered up the open steps past the pegs holding rope and cutters and branding-irons and leather harnesses. 'Daisy, you're *impossible*!' she fretted, when, oblivious of the huge black spider that lumbered to safety only inches from her face, Daisy squatted at the window, immediately absorbed in what was happening below. Amy kept well back; spiders terrified her almost as much as the prospect of being caught.

Jeremy was tightening the straps that linked the mare's forelegs to its hind legs, while Tama the stable-boy held Donegal on a long rope attached to the horse's halter. Both horses were very excited, the mare tossing her head, rolling her eyes so that the whites showed, and kicking out with hind legs constantly, so that Jeremy swore at her while he struggled with the strap-buckles. Donegal was prancing and kicking, too, whinnying and snorting, then suddenly tearing loose with that terrible roaring shriek as he reared up, flailing with his front hoofs. Daisy sucked in her breath, and her eyes widened as she suddenly noticed the stallion's *thing*. It was enormous, black and glossy as he was but red on the end as if it was hurt. A *raho*, that's what it was. Kikorangi called Tama a *raho* once, a *raho i te hoiho*, a horse's thing; inexplicably he was flattered by what to Daisy seemed a grubby insult. She had never seen a *raho* stretched to this unbelievable size before.

Finished adjusting the hobbles, Jeremy took the rope from Tama and led Donegal up to the mare. The stallion pawed at her with his front hoofs that Daisy now saw were bandaged, as were the first ten inches or so of the mare's tail. He staggered forward on his rear hoofs, his forelegs drumming on the mare's back. Jeremy reached underneath Donegal's belly, but Daisy could not see what he was doing. She noticed only that the mare suddenly became more agitated, twisting her head and jawing against her bridle until her black mouth was white with foam, trying to dislodge the stallion who now was biting her neck, at the base of her mane. Daisy was horrified for the poor mare, but it lasted only a minute or so, then Donegal half-staggered, half-fell back to four feet and, with tail switching with indignation, the mare skittered away.

'That was a good one, Tama,' said Jeremy. 'The cold water now, please,' and Tama picked up a bucket from the corner, dousing the contents around the base of the mare's tail.

'It's all work, isn't it, boy?' joked Jeremy, reaching in his pocket for sugar lumps and placing two flat on his palm for Donegal's soft-padded lips to pick up. He was affectionately rubbing his nose when a flutter of movement at the corner of his vision made him glance upwards.

She was turning away from the window. He didn't see her face but he knew who she was; some instinct stirred unerringly in him whenever he heard her footsteps, heard her humming a snatch of song or saw her parasol float by above a hedge. He smiled. So she was spying on him in turn, was she?

Suddenly it occurred to him that she was the girl Lady Launcenolt had hustled out of the cathedral in the middle of the service, and also the woman he had seen grieving in the churchyard later that day. He did not understand why he knew these things. He just did.

Summer was dying. The days rose reluctantly and retired earlier, and while they shone blue and golden on the autumn landscape there was a fierce chill in the air and a threat of frost in the brisk wind. The plains were pure gold, spread before brown foothills, while beyond the mountains were lowering their white skirts and drawing shawls of snow cloud about their satiny shoulders. When Daisy woke one morning and opened her casement window she saw that the house was shrouded in mist. She could see the swan lake and a faint outline of the arched wooden bridge to the island in its centre, but nothing of the trees beyond or of the headland. The surf sounded muffled.

'Mists of Heaven,' mused Lisabeth at her own window where she stood brushing her hair. '*Rangi Pokekohu*. The Maoris say that the *kehua*, the goblins, live amongst the mountain peaks and when the mists come down they play their magic flutes to lure travellers up through the mists of heaven. They say it's where departed souls wait for their partners to join them.'

Rhys kissed her neck. Bending to the mirror to adjust the pin in his cravat, he said: 'Don't let Gwynne hear you talk like that.'

'But it's true.'

'I know, but her befuddled head is stuffed with enough superstition already. If she heard that legend, she'd reckon that Charles was waiting for her and she'd pack her swag and toddle off to look for him.'

'I wonder . . .,' mused Lisabeth. 'You know, Charles was such a lazy selfish old sod that I think she prefers him out of the way. I think she was ashamed of him when he was alive, and now. . . .'

'He's certainly acquired amazing virtues since he died. Who'd have imagined that a scruffy uncultured reprobate would develop into a paragon after death? It's a miracle! We should write to the Vatican and see about having him canonized,' joked Rhys.

'Or deified!' She brushed her hair upwards and began pinning it into place with long corrugated hair-clips. 'It's funny, I know, but perhaps we shouldn't mock her. She's built Charles up so much in her mind that now she genuinely believes he *was* wonderful. Mrs Hogg encourages her, mind you. She sits with her needlepoint, and Gwynne knits socks, and for hours at a time they talk of nothing but Charles. I don't know how Mrs Hogg endures it.'

'If Charles appeared at the door exactly as he was in life, Gwynne probably would shoo him away. She'd never recognize him,' agreed Rhys. 'But I blame all this tonic wine she drinks. I saw the grocer's accounts once when you were away – before the wedding – and naturally I asked Tenks about the huge figure for tonic wine. He swore she was the only one who partook of it.'

'It's harmless, Rhys.'

'Is it? I wonder. Gwynne seems very . . . vague at times. But what about you? Are you taking those tonics Doctor Meakings prescribed?'

'Yes, Rhys. Of course I am.' Her voice sounded sad. 'But don't get your hopes up. It'd be a shame to pin all your hopes—'

He hugged her. His embrace was hearty, intended to be reassuring, but the nervous quiver lingered under Lisabeth's heart all day. She remembered all the plaintive things Gwynne had said about being barren. What a bitter irony it would be if she was to prove barren, too.

Still, she kept trying. Following Doctor Meakings's orders, she fortified herself with syrups and pills that tightened her bowels and turned her urine alarmingly dark. She tried with Andrew, too, writing him open loving letters that urged him to come home. To Daisy she was unfailingly pleasant, even when she felt like screaming at the implacably neutral response she received. She felt as though she was trying to batter her way out of an elastic-sided bag; no sooner had she made some headway than the walls sprang back on her again.

*   *   *

'You must have done *something* to upset him,' said Amy one day. Jeremy had arrived before lunch to visit Donegal, then after lunch Lisabeth took him out to the headland to show him a likely place to dig for Maori artefacts. She squinted as she watched them go off together, Jeremy in his rough farm clothes with a pick and shovel over his shoulder. 'He was absolutely *smitten* with you. Absolutely smitten! Yet these days he takes no notice of you at all! Did you see how he yawned and studied the pattern on his bread-and-butter plate when you were talking about the Caledonian Sports Day? You must have done something to discourage him,' she persisted. 'If you ask me—'

'I'm not asking you!' retorted Daisy, marching off along the cliff-path so that Amy had to run to catch up.

It was a glorious day, ripe and warm, a remnant of the summer gone. In the distance a reaper and binder was chugging through the swaths of golden wheat, while from all around rose the insistent autumn song of cicadas, a high rasping buzz that droned day and night, ceaselessly, at this time of year. Daisy often wondered if they knew the snow was coming and this was their protest. She loved these mellow days, but today she felt unhappy, sick at heart. It was ludicrous, she told herself impatiently. Every time Jeremy Drake came to the house she was left with this dissatisfied let-down feeling of being cheated. There was no sense to it. He had asked to call on her, she had refused, and ever since he had been unfailingly polite. Why, then, did she feel like bursting into idiotic tears every time she left his presence?

'Any girl in the district would be delighted to have him,' Amy continued relentlessly. 'If I wasn't so involved with my Tom, I'd not hesitate a moment—'

'Oh, do be quiet,' snapped Daisy.

As they followed the track down to where it joined the road the ground shook beneath their feet, and presently a gigantic steam engine appeared from between the rows of cabbage trees that lined the road. Huffing as it bumped along on its huge iron wheels, it was towing four trailers of bagged wheat to the Morgan flour mills on the outskirts of town. Three children ran shrieking alongside, their arms flapping like seagulls' wings.

'Bother,' said Amy when she saw the children. 'I hope they don't decide to go up to the dam. I was looking forward to a long *cosy* chat with Tom. Those brats would ruin everything.'

'If you ask *me*, you never come to visit me any more,' observed Daisy, nailing part of the reason for her gnawing dissatisfaction. Amy had changed. She was so smug, so swollen with her Tom, that it seemed she was brooding on an important secret that excluded Daisy. It would be different if Daisy could boast about Andrew in turn, but Andrew's letters were the same colourless infrequent epistles they had always been, utterly lacking in romantic encouragement. 'Oh, yes!' Daisy over-rode Amy's denial. 'You come out on the pretext of visiting but all you want to do is huddle with Tom while I have to amuse myself nearby playing gooseberry! I tell you, Amy, this is getting tedious.'

Amy looked stricken. 'But you told me you didn't mind! Oh, please, Daisy, it's only while Tom is ashore.'

'Why can't he see you at the hotel?'

She swung along in silence for a moment, hands thrust into the sleeves of her cream cloth coat, her thin face chapped and pink as it always was once the weather cooled. 'Father won't make him welcome there,' she admitted miserably. 'And he's told Mrs Hogg that I'm not permitted to talk to him. Oh, Daisy, I'd *die* without my Tom!' As she spoke she clutched Daisy's sleeve and stared into her eyes, her own huge and glossy with fear. Her fervour startled Daisy.

'But why doesn't he like Tom?'

'How do I know?' But she looked away, and Daisy guessed she was hiding something. 'Father is jealous of Tom because he's so successful. Father has been stuck in that one little hotel for years and years, while Tom proclaims openly that he has prospects and ambitions. Father has a theory that Tom is all bluff and bluster, but it's not true! Already Tom is prospering. Every time he comes home from one of his voyages he brings crates and crates of goods to sell – all sorts of things – and he fetches such good prices for them that he's bought two cottages already. Not outright, of course, but he's paid a little on account and the rent money is paying off the balance. Father's jealous, so he theorizes that Tom isn't honest. Can you imagine that?' Her face was tight with scorn. 'Father would like me to marry someone like Maurice Andruth. He keeps on at me that I should set my cap at him while I've the chance, but I don't want to marry a toff, someone whose family will look down their noses at me. I'm marrying Tom because I feel comfortable with him. He's right for me.'

Daisy was silent. Maurice Andruth would never look at lower-class Amy Thorne. At the party only old men and Jock McFallish wrote on her card, and Jeremy probably asked her out of kindness, or not knowing who she was. There was no point railing over the unfairness of it; that was the way society was. Then the significance of Amy's words struck home. 'You mean you're going to *marry* Tom Nevin against your father's wishes?'

Amy nodded.

'But you can't do that, can you? I mean, you can't just—'

'Why not?' Amy challenged, her face tight.

Daisy had no answer. It was fun to flout convention by not wearing a hat or gloves, or to eat two helpings of something delicious at a dinner-party when custom decreed that one helping only was polite. Her nude swim had been uncharacteristic, though, a wild gesture of desperate rebellion against her father, but to disobey him openly the way Amy planned to defy her father seemed wrong. Though Daisy was shocked, however, she couldn't explain why.

'It's not as if *Father* was marrying Tom. He'll come round to the idea later,' added Amy reasonably. 'I say, I do hope that Tom is back from his business in town. I told him I'd be here at four o'clock, and it can't be three yet.'

A dog was howling in the Nevins' yard. It was a mournful chilling sound. Amy hurried towards the cottage, but Daisy, after a glance at the dismal hut and its bleak surroundings, walked quickly away up the hill.

Birdie Nevin was a chatty woman. By the time Amy had freed herself Daisy was already disappearing into the thicket at the dam.

The dog's howling unnerved Daisy. Even at this distance the high-pitched haunting wail seemed to follow her. Shuddering, she pushed through the underbrush, her boots scuffing the drifts of dead leaves. When she heard the voices she was right there, almost in the glade itself, so close that she could feel the anger emanating from Tom Nevin as he struggled with his sister, so close that she could see the hatred in Siobhan's face.

He was clutching a sack, and she was trying to pull it away from him. She was crying, punching and clawing at him with thin white hands, ineffectually, for he was a tall bulky man who repelled her with ease. Under her tight ragged dress her stomach was grotesquely bloated. So she hadn't had the baby yet, thought Daisy in astonishment. She seemed to have been pregnant for ever, poor wretch. Noticing her black gown was torn right down one side of the bodice, with the hem muddy and drooping, Daisy wondered why, if Tom Nevin was so successful, he didn't clothe his family better.

His back to her, he wrestled to tie a cord around the mouth of the sack. Over Siobhan's moans and thumps as she punched his shoulders Daisy heard him say: 'I'll show you what hoppens to fotherless babbies. It'll hoppen to yours, unless you see sense and tull me who's being the fother, I promise you thot!'

'Don't cull them!' sobbed Siobhan, tangled hair falling over her scar-puckered eye. 'Don't cull them, Tommy! Ah, but you're being a cruel busstard.'

Kill what? wondered Daisy as Tom said: 'There's but one busstard here and it's being the one you're currying. Sure, I never thought I'd see a suster of mine dersgraced in soch a dersgustin' foshion.' His broad freckled face scowled as he tightened the knot and, ignoring Siobhan's frantically clawing hands, tossed the sack into the centre of the pond, where it splashed and immediately sank.

Siobhan screamed high in anguish. The sound was so exactly like the dog's that in a scalp-tingling moment of horror Daisy knew what the sack contained. *Puppies*! Tom had taken the distressed dog's litter away to drown, and was threatening Siobhan's baby with the same fate. Before she could move, Amy's voice called out, questioning, as she emerged from another path into the clearing.

The change in Tom was instantaneous. His face creased into a pleasant grin as he became good-looking in an impudent boyish way, the aggressive stance of his shoulders relaxed and he stepped forward in his slightly swaggering sailor's gait to meet Amy. Behind him Siobhan collapsed sobbing to the ground.

Amy looked at her in alarm. 'Tom, what's the matter? Are you still trying to find out who the father is?'

'I'm nut harming her. . . . Ut's for her own soul, you understand,' said Tom sincerely. 'Uf she told me there'd be a wudding for sure, und then a good Catholic babby, not a busstard. See uf you can talk sense to her, like—' He noticed Amy's startled expression and turned to see what she was gaping at.

Daisy was up to her waist, fully clothed, in the pond, groping with her booted feet for the bulging sack. Her legs were numb, and the icy water gripped her with a hold that froze right through to her bones.

'What are you doing?' cried Amy.

Daisy looked at her without seeing her. Taking a deep breath, for courage as much as for air, she plunged down into the water, reaching forward into the black depths with both hands. When she straightened after a few seconds, she was carrying the wriggling, squeaking sack.

EIGHT

'SO THIS IS WHERE the fortifications ran, all around the lip of this crater,' mused Jeremy. 'And the Maoris from the plains below retreated here whenever enemies swept down from the north. They must have been a warlike bunch, those early tribes.'

'If we Europeans hadn't colonized this country, then they'd probably have ended up wiping each other out completely,' said Lisabeth. A bluebottle buzzed around her face, and when she raised her hand to waft it away she was lifted from within by a wave of giddiness. 'My, but the sun is hot,' she remarked.

'It's a grand day,' agreed Jeremy, pushing his hat back on his brow and dabbing the sweat from his forehead with a large red handkerchief. Bracing himself, he swung his pick, slicing it into the solid layer of turf, before taking up his spade to lift the loose sods away. 'I think I've found something,' he announced, squatting to poke at the packed earth with a small hand-trowel. 'I hope it's not another piece of thigh-bone.'

'I've found quite a few little things here,' Lisabeth said. Gracious, she did feel odd! 'I found a *tiki*,* and several adzes, and a whole collection of bone fish-hooks. I offered them to Hone Tainui, and he didn't seem interested, so I sold them on his behalf to a collector from Stockholm. He was more interested in shrunken heads, but. . . .'

'Shrunken heads?' prompted Jeremy, unearthing a dirt-encrusted object about the size of a shoulder-blade.

She took several deep breaths. 'It was because of the intricate tattooing. Maoris used to cut off the heads of enemy slain in battle, and smoke-dry. . . .' Her voice faltered.

He glanced up at her. Obviously this gruesome topic was making her queasy. 'What do you think this is?' The dirt was solid as mortar, so he rubbed and chipped at it with care. 'It seems to be greenstone.'

* greenstone pendant

She went to sit down, and the world tipped sideways, causing her to poof' in surprise. Recovering at once, she said: 'Jeremy, that's a *mere*, a greenstone club. It's a magnificent find. You *do* have the luck of the devil, don't you?'

'It's damaged.' He rubbed the indented edges.

'It's supposed to be that shape.' She grasped its stubby handle. 'Look, a swift thrust sideways, like this, could lift the top off a skull as neatly as a knife cracks the top from an egg. Let's go and wash it, to see if it's perfect. Oh, Jeremy, what a find!'

Perfect it was. After sluicing it off in the horse-trough outside the stables Jeremy held it up to the light. The sun glowed through the translucent blade illuminating the mottled veins, showing up the whorls, like tattooing, that decorated the smooth surface just above the handle. When Jeremy jabbed and lunged to see how a warrior would have felt with this weapon in his hand, the sharp edges glinted, whipping in the sunlight.

'It suits you.' Lisabeth leaned on the railing, applauding.

'But it belongs to Mr Tainui. I'll ask to buy it, but I'll be disappointed in him if he sells. This is too beautiful to part with. A stranger wouldn't—' He saw her face. 'What's wrong, Mrs Morgan?'

'It's Daisy. What can have happened?' Pulling herself upright, she hurried towards the bedraggled figure who was limping up the drive.

Daisy was freezing. Water dribbled behind her, her boots squelched and her skirts were plastered to her numb legs. Her dripping hair hung in rags around her shoulders.

Amy tagged beside her. 'You're wrong to be so harsh. Tom wasn't being cruel. Puppies and kittens *have* to be drowned. It's the only sensible thing. Father has a theory that if they were left to breed they'd overrun the world in the space of a couple of years.' Daisy didn't reply. Amy said: 'Please don't give me away at least. Father would lock me in my room if he knew about me and Tom, so please don't say anything. If you ever need me to do anything for you, then I will, without question, only please do this one thing!'

Daisy grimaced. She shook her head wordlessly when Lisabeth asked what happened, and in the end it was Amy who answered reluctantly: 'She jumped in, Mrs Morgan. Siobhan was drowning some puppies, and she rescued them.'

'Oh.' That sounded like Daisy. 'But why aren't you wearing your cloak, at least? It's no use bundled in your arms, Daisy. Here, put it around you. Don't worry about it getting—'

Clutching the bunched material to her chest, Daisy shook her head. 'It's a puppy,' she stammered, her jaw jamming on the words.

'The others are back with their mother,' explained Amy. 'But this one didn't want . . . it isn't as strong as the others. Daisy thought that we might be able to give it some warm milk and make a bed for it by the kitchen stove until it gets better.'

The pup was breathing, but only just. Its skin looked as blue as Daisy's. 'I don't hold out much hope for it,' said Lisabeth frankly. 'As for you, you'll be down with pneumonia by tomorrow, I shouldn't wonder. Here, give the pup to Tama and come upstairs. I'll have Carthew fill you a nice hot bath.' She reached out kindly and placed a hand on Daisy's cheek. 'Gracious, child, you're *icy*!'

'I . . . I'll look after the p-p-puppy first,' Daisy managed to say.

'Daisy, please. You're in no state—' Lisabeth broke off helplessly. The girl was impossible at times. Feeling far from well herself, she didn't want to argue.

It was Jeremy who intervened. Stepping forward, he took the bundle before Daisy could protest. Looking into its cold wizened face, he said: 'I've had some experience in this direction. Rescued a litter from a snow bank, once. I'll try to get some milk into the little chap.'

'E-Excalibur,' Daisy said over her shoulder as Lisabeth led her away. 'Excalibur of the l-l-lake.' But he didn't seem to have heard her. Through the haze of biting cold her numbed brain assimilated the fact that, although Jeremy had taken the pup, he had not so much as glanced at her. All his interest was focused on the animal. Hampered by her freezing wet skirts, Daisy stumbled, lurched forward and painfully wrenched her ankle. She would have fallen, but Lisabeth and Amy were both instantly there to steady her. Jeremy was not even looking in her direction.

'You look better now,' observed Lisabeth. 'There's colour back in your cheeks. My, but you did give me a start when I saw—'

'Has Amy gone home?'

'Yes. Now, don't go running off again. Doctor Meakings will be here soon,' she called after her.

The puppy was in the kitchen, dozing in a basket beside the stove where Mrs Tenks, the stringy Cornish cook, was stirring a pot of sauce on the coal range. She told Daisy how Jeremy had massaged the wee body with a warmed cloth and had coaxed him to drink milk and honey. 'Look, 'e even popped a water-bottle under 'is blanket. Got a right fetching way with 'im, that Mr Drake 'as.'

Daisy placed a hand on Excalibur's tiny body. His whiskers tickled against her thumb, and his heart pattered faintly under her palm. 'I should thank Mr Drake,' she said.

'If you can catch 'im.' Mrs Tenks was a pessimist. ' 'E left some two minutes since. You'll never catch 'im now.'

He was adjusting the girth-straps on Angel's saddle when she came skimming across the cobblestones on slippered feet to pause, panting, in front of him. 'I thought I'd missed you.'

He glanced up. His face wore its habitual expression, pleasant but not quite a smile as if the thoughts behind it were consistently agreeable. Then he bent his head to finish his task, not bothering to reply.

Daisy fumed with frustration. She wanted to share what had happened down at the dam, how she'd challenged Tom Nevin, told him that these pups he was drowning were already promised to the Mists of Heaven rabbiters, and how Siobhan, terrified, had nodded a dumb agreement when she asked her to back up the story. It was a lie, but could be true because the pups looked like Jack Russell crosses and would be small enough to ferret rabbits out of their burrows. Proud of her quick thinking and her daring, she wanted approval and admiration from Jeremy.

She was not going to get anything. The wind ruffled his hair as he straightened. 'It's late,' he remarked, looking up at the darkening sky, at the gold-rimmed mountains and dusk-shrouded foothills. 'It's cold out here, Miss Morgan. You should be inside.'

'I wanted to thank you,' she said heavily.

'Thank me? Oh, the pup already did that,' he said with a grin, indicating a damp patch on one knee of his jodhpurs. 'Well, Miss Morgan. . . .' And he gathered up the reins in one hand.

Disappointment flooded her, sour and sharp as brine. He was not going to offer her praise, good wishes nor even a simple 'How are you?' She couldn't bear it. To her dismay she heard herself say: 'Why do you dislike me so much?'

'Pardon?' he asked, though he had heard. When she flushed and bit her lip he felt sorry for her and said: 'I don't dislike you. I don't dislike anybody.' *Except perhaps Doctor Stafford*, he added to himself.

She was standing very close to him, and he could smell the flowery fragrance of whatever she had used on her skin and hair when she bathed. Her freshly dried hair was tied back loosely into a glossy knot. For a moment he tantalized himself by leaning slightly towards her and inclining his head a fraction as if he was about to kiss her. He expected her to jump away, but to his surprise she stood very still staring at the mountains. He could see the peaks reflected in her eyes, and knew without doubt that he could kiss her now if he wanted. She might slap him afterwards to save face, but he was certain she would respond, and enjoy it, too.

'Goodbye, then,' he said, swinging up into the saddle. As he wheeled Angel's head around he smiled down into her perplexed face. 'Have beautiful dreams,' he said, then galloped away.

Beautiful dreams? I hate him, Daisy brooded as she trudged back to the house. Forgetting her wrenched ankle, she kicked out at a loose stone only to squeak with pain when her foot felt the impact. Limping, she hurried inside.

In shape Doctor Meakings reminded Daisy of the skittles she had played with as a child, being bald and round-headed with a thick neck and narrow shoulders that sloped down to meet the bulge of his ample figure. His clothes were always too tight, as if his tailor skimped or he shopped in a mood of optimism, and he always smiled, his teeth lurking below an enormous pair of ginger mutton-chop whiskers that reached around his ears like the arms of spectacles.

'A chill?' he boomed, thermometer, tongue-depressor and stethoscope at the ready. Doctor Meakings was a great believer in inspiring confidence with props whether they were needed or not, and his black bag bulged with a collection that fascinated Daisy: devices for measuring blood-pressure, for trimming ingrown nails and for peering into eyes and ears, douche bags and syringes, the thickest book she had ever seen, called *A Short Diagnosis*, and a strange doll with half a head and with the legs and arms cut off like stumps. Some society ladies refused, or their husbands refused, to permit intimate examinations, but on this doll they could point to the appropriate place and describe their own symptoms for him. Once when his back was turned Daisy couldn't resist rummaging in the bag, and before he could stop her she had pulled out the doll which she promptly named 'Poor Clara'. Though that was twelve years ago, Daisy had never forgotten his discomfiture. 'How is Poor Clara today?' she asked.

His face went pink, but he ignored her, speaking to Lisabeth in his usual stuffy fashion. 'It is a chill, with only slight danger. Might I recommend a poultice of steaming towels? It's the latest treatment recommended – very highly, too – by the *Boston Medical Journal*. The whole body is enshrouded and the lungs cleansed while all effects of the chill are dissipated. Most efficacious.'

'Thank you, but I think not,' decided Lisabeth, wondering how often he read the medical journals. Nine years ago when Rhys was pulled half-drowning from his capsized boat off the Sumner Bar, Doctor Meakings had recommended his steaming towels as 'the very latest thing'. She said: 'If you've finished, I'd appreciate a private word, Doctor. I doubt if it's anything serious, but since you're here. . . .'

Rhys rode home exhausted after a gruelling afternoon's negotiations with Silas Drake, two solicitors, three accountants and two representatives from the Smithfield market in London. He had left the meeting without reaching a firm decision and hoped the ride home would clear his head, but one of his upper molars began to torment him on the way, and he completed the ride in agony, every scrap of his concentration

ccupied with trying to absorb the jolting of Mazurka's hoofs, for each
olt struck like a hammer-blow inside his skull.

He paused in pain at the gates, and fixed his eyes and his mind on the
ouse. Sometimes if he thought of other things it eased a toothache,
nd nothing made his heart swell like the sight of this house. He had
uilt it for Lisabeth, intending to bring her to it as his bride, and every
tone of it had been placed with her in mind. It was the most magnifi-
ent thing he had ever created, all in love as a gift for her. Though it had
een an age before she claimed it, the waiting now seemed worth while,
ich in fulfilment, the future ripe with the promise of continued happi-
ess. He gazed at the walls that glowed with the last of the sunset, faint
old as the lit windows, and from beyond the house came the evening
ounds he loved, the hollow notes of doves settling in for the night, the
cuffle of hoofs in the stables, a voice raised in laughter, and overlaying
verything the contented sigh of the ocean. Nobody could be happier
han he was right now, he thought. Even his toothache had subsided.

In the library he picked up the greenstone *mere* with little interest, for
e was used to finding Maori artefacts lying about the house. As he
eplaced it on the table his tooth suddenly scoured his jaw, making him
atch his breath. Hastily he poured himself a tumbler of brandy and
willed some around the afflicted area.

'That's better,' he said to Lisabeth, who sidled in with an expression
f repressed excitement. 'Yes, it's my tooth again. No, there's no need
o scold. This time I promise I'll visit the surgeon.'

'You always do promise. Every time.' She rang the bell to summon
Carthew to fetch some belladonna for the pain. 'How was your
meeting? Have you finalized your plans?'

No other man he knew discussed all aspects of business with a
woman – or would admit to it – but Rhys had always found Lisabeth to
e a sympathetic audience, a useful sounding-board. Nursing his
brandy, he sat in a wing-chair opposite her, and she leaned forward, her
ace luminous with interest. He said: 'I don't mind telling you that I've
got cold feet about the whole idea. It's an enormous gamble, so much
hat my other commercial ventures will look puny by comparison. But
t's such an exciting idea, Lisabeth. The men from Smithfield assured us
t was viable – that experimental load of frozen meat in the *Dunedin*
rrived so sweet that it was impossible to distinguish between it and
reshly slaughtered English lamb. They say that the hungry markets of
he whole of Europe will open to our onslaught. The idea has stupen-
lous possibilities. Silas already has details of cross-breed sheep that have
been bred in England especially for the quality of their meat without
osing their wool-growing potential, and he's enormously excited about
he idea of trying different breeds here. I don't mind admitting his
nthusiasm is infectious. The thought of making maximum use of the

land instead of growing just wool and then being faced with the loathsome job of slaughtering thousands of old sheep because they're of nfurther use – why, that could be a thing of the past.'

'But?' she asked, taking his hand.

He patted it absently and swilled more brandy around his mouth 'It's a frightening gamble. Enormous risks. I'll have to mortgage every thing I own, and if the venture fails I could lose everything.'

'Everything?'

'Well, perhaps not. I'd manage to keep this house, I think. I say, you don't seem particularly perturbed by the prospect.'

'I'm not.' Standing in front of him, she twined her hands around thback of his neck, her fingers playing in his coarse blond hair. 'You takyour risks, Rhys. You'll always regret it if you don't. Only. . . .' Shsmiled, tasting her news, holding it on her tongue in delicious anticipation. 'Only, be sure to put enough money by to support me and thbaby.'

'Of course I—' He broke off, staring incredulously into her smiling face. 'Do you mean—?' He was almost too afraid to spit it out, afraid hhad misheard.

She nodded. 'I knew something was amiss, but I thought it was thseasonable weather making me queasy. Doctor Meakings confirmed it Rhys. It's true! There'll be a baby here by Christmas!'

He whooped then, his tired voice cracking, and laughed aloud isheer joy. Flinging his arms wide, he gathered her to him and pressed hiface into her belly, kissing her and laughing over and over. She coulfeel the warmth of his mouth right through to her skin. 'I could eat you! I could devour you!' he cried.

'Rhys – no,' she said, pleased, but remembering she had rung for thmaid. 'Carthew might come in and—' As she spoke she swung her heatowards the doorway.

Daisy stood there, her mouth open. As soon as Lisabeth lookearound Daisy uttered a sob and dashed away.

'I rather suspect we might have shocked her,' confessed Lisabeth.

'A baby?' gasped Amy. 'But they're so *old*! I didn't think it wapossible. . . .'

'It must be,' snapped Daisy. She resented the attention Lisabeth wagetting – anybody would think she had an advanced disease the way the household had to pivot around her comforts now – and was thoroughly bored with the whole subject. Even Aunt Bea talked of nothing else – though she plainly thought it all rather disgraceful – and Aunty Gwynne had already knitted enough bootees to clad a centipede. 'One good thing about it, though: Andrew is certain to come home now. He'll be here for my birthday, I know he will.'

The girls were sitting on a sunny veranda while Daisy nursed Excalibur on her lap, feeding him milk and honey from an orphan lambs' feeding-bottle. He looked less like a little piglet now; his eyes were fully open, and he looked up at her adoringly while he drank. Tiny pearls of milk clung to the whiskers around his mouth, and his tongue was pink as a petal when he licked them off. With a fingertip she stroked his faintly wrinkled brow and the ears that were like scraps of velvet. 'He soothes my soul in this time of trial,' Daisy declared loftily.

'Time of trial?' repeated unsympathetic Amy. 'But it'll be great fun to have a baby around the place.'

Long ago Amy had tried to point out to Daisy that her dreams were based on fantasy and likely to disappoint her, but that sensible warning went the same way as anything else Daisy thought unpalatable: she simply didn't listen. Her philosophy was simple: if you want something desperately enough and you focus all your heart and mind on that something, then you will attain it. Rhys had told her that years ago when she was studying for an examination. She didn't particularly care whether she passed, but for a few days followed the advice as an experiment and, pure as magic, the examination was flown past. The philosophy always worked, so naturally she expected it to work on Andrew, too. She longed for him, therefore eventually he would come to her.

So confident was she that it came as no surprise when one morning at breakfast Lisabeth announced: 'Tenks brought a letter home from town late last night. It's exciting news – I thought I'd read it to you and Daisy together, Gwynne.'

'It's from Andrew!' squealed Daisy, dropping her knife with a clatter. 'Andrew is coming home!'

'How did you know?' For a terrible moment Lisabeth wondered whether Daisy could hear her and Rhys together in their room. Perish the thought!

She explained how, and Lisabeth said unfortunately it was true, which was why one must be scrupulously careful when choosing what to want. Picking up the letter, she read: ' '' Dearest Sister, I am bringing you felicitous news. Very soon we shall be with you because on the thirtieth of next month we embark for Port Lyttelton in *Argus*, a fine and swift vessel, we are told.'' '

'He'll be here in six weeks, or perhaps less!' Daisy hugged Gwynne, almost upsetting her tea-cup. 'I knew it, Aunty Gwynne! I *knew* he'd be here for my birthday party!'

'There's more,' said Lisabeth in an odd voice. 'Please listen, Daisy. ''You will have deduced from the 'we' that I am not alone. Two weeks ago I took a wife, one Jane Bellford, a curate's daughter from Reigate. She is delicate in health but iron in spirit, and we hope that the climate

in Canterbury will be beneficial to her. Jane sends her love and
looking forward to meeting you all, especially Daisy whom she alread
regards as a dear friend. Jane hopes to engage in missionary wor
amongst the Maoris when—'' '

'A friend?' choked Daisy. 'A *friend*? Never!'

'Daisy!' from Gwynne. She was bemused. Her dear boy marriec
What momentous news!

'She sounds perfect for him,' ventured Lisabeth.

To Daisy that was the final insult. A mealy-mouthed, frail, piou
curate's daughter was 'perfect' and *she* was not! 'You haven't even me
her!' she cried, flinging down her damask napkin. 'As for myself, I hop
I never do meet her! I hope something happens, and she *never gets here*
I hope she *dies*!'

'Daisy!' From Lisabeth this time. She wished Rhys was here. She fe.
helpless, whereas Rhys could humour Daisy with a few cheerful word
'Please, dear. . . . It's not as if—'

But Daisy was gone, the door reverberating behind her.

'Read me the letter again,' implored Gwynne. 'Such a lovely lette
Charles always wrote a fine letter, too, you know. He had—'

Hastily Lisabeth began to read.

To Rhys the news came as hope and relief. This meant an end to thos
ridiculous notions Daisy had been harbouring. It also meant tha
Andrew's own attitudes might soften. Once married himself, he migh
become less judgemental towards others, hoped Rhys. When Lisabet
told him that Daisy was moping he was concerned, wanting her to shar
in the household's happiness.

'Let's involve her in the preparations for her birthday party,' h
suggested. 'Invite some of the young people over for lunch one da
soon. That pretty Martin girl, the Westlakes, and young Jeremy. I wisl
she'd notice him. Fine young man, that.'

Lisabeth agreed. 'Daisy needs intellectual stimulation, too,' she said
'She's not done anything thought-provoking since she passed he
Advanced Proficiency Certificate, last year. I wonder if she'd like to g
to university?'

'University? A girl go to university?'

'And why not?'

'Why not indeed?'Rhys agreed, unable to think of a reason. He said
'I'd rather she noticed Jeremy, though.'

'Or Lowell,' said Lisabeth. 'He's cultured and well read, and he like
Daisy, too. Did I tell you that he wrote a poem for her on Bonfire Night
It was beautiful, too, but he spoiled the effect by looking at Jerem
while he read it out. He was probably too shy to look at Daisy.'

'Probably.' Rhys laughed. He laughed a lot these days.

'Why is that funny?' Lisabeth wanted to know. 'I think Lowell is sweet.'

'He's sweet all right. Tell you what. The Stratford troupe are doing *Macbeth* on Friday night. Let's take Daisy, shall we? Have dinner some-here first, hire a box, have fun. What do you say?'

'I say you're a marvellous man,' she declared, leaning over to kiss his eek.

Daisy didn't want to think about university, she was uninterested in her arty and lack-lustre about the luncheon. She felt so left out that she ouldn't see how everybody was bending over backwards to include her, to umour her and please her. Amy was now secretly betrothed to Tom and ll of plans to elope in the spring. 'My life is blighted,' she told Excalibur. Everybody has someone to love except me. How could Andrew abandon he like this?'

Excalibur whimpered and striped her cheek with his tongue.

Even Jeremy exacerbated her wounds. After the luncheon when they ere saddling up for a ride to the beach he manoeuvred his horse close to ers and asked what she wanted for her birthday.

She raised her chin and stared at the skim of crazed ice on the lake. Two hite swans glided between the shards. All through luncheon he had whis-ered in Arabella's ear, ignoring her, and now he offered her crumbs of ttention. 'Nothing,' she informed him. 'Second best is not good enough or me.'

Stung, he rode in closer, boxing her against the fence until his thigh ressed hard against her woollen riding-skirt. 'I've been wondering. . . . his Andrew has a great deal in common with Mrs Stafford's "dear Charles". . . . In that he looks immeasurably better from a safe distance, I nean. I suspect his absence has bestowed wonderful qualities on him that e simply doesn't possess, just as Mrs Stafford has—'

'You are quite wrong! And impertinent, too! How dare you . . . how are you. . . .'

'How dare I make frank observations?' Without looking she could see hat infuriating smile of his and she was angrily aware of his muscled thigh gainst hers. 'Tell you what. I'll wager you a pair of gloves that this famous Andrew Stafford is no better than a milksop in person. We'll take a poll of ix honest people for their opinions, and *you* may name them. Is it a vager?'

Her eyes were hard and tight, then they softened as she decided how to ure his arrogance. 'Done!' she decided, thrusting out a black gloved and. 'And if he *isn't* a milksop, then you can eat the same pair of gloves, nd I'll watch you choke on your words.'

Lowell's silky eyebrows pinnacled. 'A milksop?' he asked in sleek tones. 'Who is a milksop?'

'Nobody at all,' Daisy declared.

'Oh, do tell! I've been accused of being one so often that I have an innate sympathy with a fellow-accusee!' And he winked at Jeremy.

Daisy laughed. She laughed because she was feeling better than she had done all day, she laughed because Arabella had witnessed Jeremy bailing her up and whispering to her and was now riding up from the stables looking as sour as last week's milk, and she laughed because she liked Lowell. Everything about him was silky: his shiny skin, his satin clothes, his easy charm. She smiled at him, but he didn't see her; he was watching Jeremy, and he looked sad.

NINE

THE WINTER HAD BEEN MILD with only a few flurries of soft flakes that melted as soon as they touched the ground, but on the afternoon before Daisy's eighteenth birthday the sky darkened and the temperature plummeted so low that Excalibur huddled shivering when she tried to play with him, whining to be allowed back inside. That night it snowed. Daisy woke to see the headland smothered in marshmallowy coating and the sky a heavy grey that promised more.

My party might be cancelled, she thought, looking at the distant Christchurch road which was scored with fresh wheel-marks. *If it snows again, nobody will be able to get here.*

She was closing the ice-crazed window again when she noticed three ships beyond the bar, their funnel-smoke tall and straight as masts in the still air. Was one of those *Argus*? she wondered. It was due a week ago and still hadn't arrived.

As she dressed she kept glancing at her new birthday gown which Miss Hopkins the dressmaker had delivered two days before. In an effort to rouse her enthusiasm Lisabeth permitted her absolute free choice, so with Amy's assistance and much referring to Beatrice's *Paris Modes* magazines she settled on a pale blue sateen with darker blue lace trimming, ruched at the shoulders and hips with a narrow hobbled skirt and an extravagant waterfall bustle cascading down to a scalloped train. With it she planned to wear her mother's necklace of gold and sapphires and the matching sapphire ear-bobs. From Aunt Bea she borrowed gold combs set with blue stones to scoop her hair up into cascades of curls. 'You're a picture,' Beatrice fussed approvingly. 'Like a bride – something borrowed, something blue.' She could not fathom why Daisy blushed and looked guilty, having no idea that Daisy planned to be radiant and beautiful at her party in order to overwhelm Andrew and make him bitterly sorry that she was out of his reach. Daisy was naïve; she saw neither danger nor wickedness in this plan. All she knew was that Andrew should have waited for her and he didn't, and she was determined to point this out to him as forcefully as her feminine wiles would permit.

Replacing the dust-cloth over her gown, she skimmed down the stairs and along to the kitchen where five people were already working: Mrs Tenks, who was arguing with the borrowed young Irish cook from White Clouds, two scullery maids recruited from Summerlea, and Birdie Nevin, here because Gwynne insisted they hire her to make the pastries and tarts for which she was famous. 'The ones at the wedding tasted like plaster,' she said. 'And, as Charles always said, Birdie Nevin's pastry would make the angels sigh.'

Mrs Tenks swung around when Daisy came in. She lowered the wooden spurdle she had been waving threateningly at the Irish cook and said: 'I fear that this will all be for nowt, Miss Morgan. It's s'posed to snow later, according to Mr Tenks. An' if there's one thing a Cornishman knows it's when snow be imminent.'

'Whuch us being one thung more thun a Cornishmun's woife knows!' said the Irish cook in a pert voice that wiped the self-satisfied smile from Mrs Tenks's broad pink face.

As long as Andrew comes, I won't mind, thought Daisy, amused by the red-headed young Irish lass. Was Ireland entirely peopled by copper-topped freckled-faced beings? she wondered, liking the girl's saucy manner. All the Mists of Heaven servants were in awe of Mrs Tenks, who wielded absolute power in the household. This girl seemed almost contemptuous of her.

Daisy went to see what she was doing. In a copper bowl egg white had been whisked to peaks like snow drifts and the girl was dipping out spoonfuls of the meringue and placing them on metal trays. 'Ut's snowmen I be making,' she said when Daisy asked. 'One bug dab is for the body, like, and thun a wee dab goes on for the hud, wuth a swirl of sweet cream for a moffler round hus nuck.'

'Very pretty,' approved Daisy.'How clever you are!' And the girl flushed with pleasure.

'A waste of time, if yer ask me,' complained Mrs Tenks. 'All this work 'ere ter do, an' she fiddles and frippers 'er time away.' She glared at Daisy, who was laughing. 'It'll snow and all this will go to waste. Nobody will come.'

'Then, *we* won't go hungry, will we?' said Daisy, scooping Excalibur from his bed-prison, a deep willow hamper which he was chewing to rope. He was now roly-poly but elongated of face with a tufty liver-and-white blotched coat – one patch tilted like a beret over a coal-bright eye – and with a curved switching tail that drummed the ground whenever he plonked down to catch his breath. Nuzzling him, she gurgled: 'Wish me a happy birthday, then, boy!'

'Yer barthday, us ut?' Birdie asked, blinking her little yellow eyes as she whacked the rolling-pin down on the cushion of dough. Flour dusted the fine sandy hairs on her forearms where the flesh flopped like heavy pink sleeves. Birdie was as big-bosomed as Gwynne and as fat as Lady Launcenolt, but hers was a lardy stoutness solid as poverty while Gwynne and Beatrice had an airy lightness about their bulk that put Daisy in mind of cream puffs.

'My eighteenth,' said Daisy. She was nervous of all the Nevins. 'Papa has invited a hundred guests, and the Chinese merchant from Nugent Street is putting on a fireworks display after supper to entertain us.'

'If it's not snowing,' said Mrs Tenks.

'Gud wishes to you, then,' said Birdie, wiping her floury hands on her floury apron. 'Cud be the babby's barthday an' all. Inny munnut now, I'm picking, and I'm picking that it cud be twuns an' all, too.'

At first Daisy felt illogically indignant, not because Birdie was quite unaffected by the disgrace Siobhan had invited on to the family but at the thought of her producing her infant, even if it was twins, on what she regarded as *her* birthday. Immediately she was ashamed of her uncharitable thoughts and said: 'Please tell her that I wish her well. I'm sure we all do.'

As she left with Excalibur for his morning romp she could hear Mrs Tenks – who had never had children – muttering about what a dire and risky business childbirth was.

Excalibur was intrigued by the snow, growling at it and making snapping, yapping leaps to catch the gobs of snow she shook off tree branches for him. They had been down to the gates and were on their way back when Tenks and the landau arrived, rattling across the barred cattle-stop and up the drive. Daisy stood still; her arms and legs lost their strength. 'Andrew!' she whispered. 'The ship's in! He's here already!'

Tenks slowed. She saw that the carriage was empty. ''E weren't on board, miss!' shouted Tenks above Excalibur's ferocious barking (which failed to impress the horses). 'I've a letter 'ere for Mr Morgan, to explain why 'e ain't coming.'

'It's Andrew's wife,' said Rhys, reading as the women clustered around his chair. 'She became extremely ill on the first leg of the journey with some fever that had already killed several of the oldest and the youngest on board. Andrew obviously fears for her life. He had the ship put them both ashore at Cape Town in the hopes that she might recuperate on solid ground, but he says that none of the others who contracted the illness survived.' He glanced up at their faces. 'I won't read the letter aloud. The details are distressing. . . . But here at the end he writes: "I ask that you offer your prayers for Jane, though I fear you may be too late." '

Daisy felt hollow inside. 'What if Andrew contracts the disease, too? He could die, and we'd never see him again.'

'Vaguely possible,' conceded Rhys, who did not wish to alarm Gwynne or Lisabeth – especially Lisabeth – so kept back the instruction that whoever read the letter was to burn it and scour their hands thoroughly afterwards. 'But not likely. I'll see if we can communicate with Cape Town, though I wouldn't hold out hope about that, either.'

'We'll cancel the party,' offered Daisy.

'We'll do no such thing,' said Lisabeth, talking brightly to hide her own fears, for her heart was wallowing like a sinking ship. Glancing at Rhys, she saw that his face was ashen; he stared at the paper in his fist and she knew what he was thinking: that Andrew might die without a reconciliation ever being made. To him as much as to Daisy she said, 'Andrew will be all right. He's a doctor, remember? Right now he'll be—'

'He could be *dead*!' wailed Daisy.

'Nonsense,' said Lisabeth sharply. 'Behave yourself, Daisy, and remember that you have guests arriving soon, and it is your duty to see that they enjoy themselves.' She spoke far more coldly than she had ever done before, to reprimand herself as much as to remind the others, for her own heart was still floundering in terror. *Andrew mustn't die!* she prayed.

Daisy gasped, stung by Lisabeth's harshness. Fleeing to her room with Excalibur, she flung herself on her bed and stared at the ceiling, not seeing the white roses or noticing the puppy when he whined and nuzzled at her face. Over and over she thought: *I wished Jane was dead. I wanted something to prevent her from coming here, so I said I wished she'd die. Now Andrew might die, too.*

'Dear girl, you look exquisite!' cried Lady Launcenolt as she swept into the hallway, a perfumed heap of furs and lace and trailing ribbons. 'What a pretty dress, dear! But why the long face?'

'Aunt Bea, is it possible to kill someone just by wishing them dead?' muttered Daisy in a low voice.

'What a strange question! Yes, it is possible, but Kiki would know more about it. You need to have knowledge of black magic, to put a hex on them or something. When he was on the bench in India he came across several interesting cases. Why? Are we going to play answer-or-forfeit later on? What fun! Here he is; I'll ask him.' She raised her voice. 'Kiki—'

'No! It's all right, Aunt Bea. Truly.'

Albert pushed the Bath chair into the hall. Kiki was smiling broadly, his whiskers fanning out around his jaws in silky ruffles. 'Happy birthday lass!' he boomed. 'You don't look a day over forty, does she, Bea?'

It was the same joke every year, and she knew already that the square box he produced from the folds of his lap-rug would contain an ornate and far-too-expensive piece of jewellery. 'Go on, open it. It'll match those other gew-gaws. It had better! Mr Urquhart made those for your mother. It's amazing. After all these years he remembered our order to the exact detail.'

'Sapphire forget-me-nots! How appropriate!' exclaimed Jeremy, coming inside in a flurry of snow to see her fastening the bracelet around her wrist while Beatrice and Kiki admired the effect. He was carrying a flat oblong box which he slipped into her free hand. 'Gloves,' he murmured. 'I thought I'd come prepared.'

'Would you like them boiled or fried?' she had rehearsed the retort so often that it popped out automatically.

'Not so fast. I want to meet him first.' He looked at her; she seemed so confused, so suddenly distressed that the Launcenolts were staring at her, too. 'Daisy, what's wrong?' he asked urgently.

'Nothing's wrong!' she said gaily, recovering. 'Andrew isn't going to be here. He's . . . he's been delayed. Naturally we're all very disappointed. Do come on through. We've only a small gathering so far, but Papa said it's inevitable that people would be discouraged by the weather. Still, you people are here, and that's the main thing.' She smiled at Lowell, who strolled over when he saw them enter the drawing-room. 'Lowell, would you please offer Lady Launcenolt some punch or some hot negus? Lisabeth thought that negus would be appropriate for this evening, what with the snow, and. . . .' She prattled on, her wide smile stretching her face until it felt numb, not noticing how they stared at her. 'Enjoy yourselves, everybody, do! It's going to be a lovely party! Such fun!'

Rhys was in the study celebrating with Silas the signing of their contract jointly to build a freezing works when Sir Kenneth was wheeled in. Rhys took another crystal flute from the rack and wrapped the champagne-bottle in a white napkin as he drew it, dripping, from the ice-bucket. 'We've a lot to drink tonight,' he told Sir Kenneth. 'Everything's good in the world, hey, Kiki?'

'If you say so, then it must be true,' said Sir Kenneth, nodding to Albert to leave. He swung his gaze back to Rhys. There was something odd about him, too, this evening. He was over-hearty, over-bright, so solicitous of his guests' comfort that it made Kiki feel almost uncomfortable. Rhys was usually a relaxed affable host who put guests at their ease by example.

It wasn't until later that he realized what it was. Rhys was acting cheerful because he was, simply, acting.

* * *

97

In the kitchen the borrowed Irish cook was trying to shoo Tom Nevin outside. She had told him no, Birdie wasn't there, she was serving negus in the morning room; and no, he couldn't have anything to eat or drink; and no, she certainly wouldn't risk her job by smuggling a note to Amy.

Tom smiled at her. He was big and handsome, and he had a persuasive way of not raising his voice, not getting riled, but quietly kidding her along. Colleen gave him a ham bone; she found a thick glass goblet and poured him a good half-pint of negus from the potful that was warming on the slowest part of the stove; and finally, after more quiet persuasion, she thrust the note into her cleavage and exchanged her dishwater-stained apron for a clean one. 'But out you go,' she insisted, pushing his shoulders and slapping his hand when he reached around to grab her. 'Faith! Ut's my job you'll be losin' me!' she squawked when he scooped up a handful of cream cakes from the carefully arranged pyramid. Shoving him out the door, she began to arrange them again, giggling as she did so.

When he had finished gnawing shreds from the bone Tom flung it in an arc towards the stable-yard where, if his memory still held true, the house-dogs were kennelled. After three seconds' wait came a crash followed by a cacophony of shrill barks and growls.

Within three minutes the huge front door swung open and a figure stood in the oblong of hall light. Through the swirling snow it was impossible to tell who it was, but Tom imagined it to be Rhys and loathing seeped like cold through his bones. *One day you'll regret the way you treated us Nevins,* he vowed silently. He watched, sucking at his warmed wine, until the door closed again.

The goblet was heavy in his hand. He'd planned to take it as a souvenir, but on a wild impulse, spurred by that freezing hatred, he drained the glass in one deep swallow and drawing back his arm he lobbed it high and far into the whirling mist, laughing mirthlessly as it exploded with a surprisingly loud noise on the mansion roof.

'An excellent year, excellent,' approved the 'Baron', who had sauntered into the study uninvited and lifted up the bottle so he could read the label. 'What's the occasion for this celebration?' When Rhys, annoyed, didn't reply he said: 'Come now, surely you're not still toasting your wife's fecundity! There's many a slip, you know. Many a slip. Wait until she produces the goods, old boy! That's my advice.'

Rhys lowered his head, feeling anger pressing up in his chest. This man's smoothness, his satiny way of belittling everything had goaded him many times before into an outburst, and he was determined not to be provoked again. Knowing it would delight the 'Baron' if he snapped back at him, Rhys controlled his irritation and was silent.

The 'Baron' filled himself a flute, held it up to admire the effervescence and the pure golden colour, and said: 'I cannot drink if I do not know what we are celebrating.'

'Don't drink, then,' muttered Silas, who heartily disliked the fellow, too; but Sir Kenneth, deaf enough to miss the subtleties, was thinking all this was some kind of a ritual joke and said: 'It's a toast to the freezing works, of course. The Morgan–Drake meat-exporting business! They turned the first sod on the site today and ordered their first refrigerated vessel, and by this time next year they'll be in business!'

'This is good news,' said the 'Baron', who looked at everything in terms of his own interests. 'We ran a herd of two thousand old ewes off the cliffs last month because we hadn't been able to get them in lamb. This time next year we'll be able to sell them to you instead, and at a good profit! Well done, gentlemen!' He raised his glass, sipped, and studied the bubbles again, his neat features thoughtful. 'A touch too much acid, I'd have thought. Not enough lime in the soil—'

At that moment they were interrupted by the crash as Tom's negus-goblet shattered on the tiles above their heads.

'What's that?' asked Silas.

'What was what?' asked Sir Kenneth.

'It's outside,' Rhys decided. 'First a crash in the stable-yard, and now this. Listen to those dogs. I think someone's trying to cause trouble, gentlemen. We'd best put a stop to it.' And he ushered the others ahead of him, wheeling Sir Kenneth out himself.

There was no need for any fuss, it was probably one of the shepherds' children causing mischief or even Ah Low clumping around while he set the fireworks display, but Rhys was glad to seize on this as an excuse to disband the huddle in the study. He still harboured a nervous insecurity about the hugeness of the project, and the last thing he needed was the negative comments from the 'Baron'.

At the party Daisy, already feeling wretched about Andrew and his wife, was gloomily watching Jeremy paying outrageous attention to Arabella. She sat on a sofa between him and Maurice Andruth, dancing with them in turn and flirting coyly with both. Maurice looked as miserable as Daisy felt.

'It's her red hair,' explained Amy. They were watching a game in which Jeremy and Arabella galloped the length of the room holding hands and with an apple held between their foreheads. Arabella's close-set eyes had been crossed the whole time. Around them couples were retrieving apples that had rolled across the floor. 'Her red hair makes her attractive. She told that cousin of Maurice's that Jeremy had a passion for titan-haired ladies.'

'Titian,' corrected Daisy. All she could think of was that Andrew could be lying somewhere ill, or even dead, and she had wished it on him.

'Jeremy Drake wants shooting,' said Amy loyally. 'It's your birthday and he's paid not a speck of attention to you. I've half a mind to tell him—'

'You'll do no such thing. What do I care what he does? I'm having a lovely time. Lowell has asked to come and visit on Wednesday, and Maurice Andruth has invited me to Summerlea to admire his new music-box. You turn the handle and it plays amazing tunes, he says. It's one of the new sort that—'

They were interrupted by Paul Trotter from the Volunteer Mounted Rifles who came to ask Daisy to dance, but when he saw the unguarded misery on her face asked Amy instead. They were about to step on to the floor when the young Irish cook, pink-faced with panic, grabbed Amy's arm. 'It's a noot, miss. A noot,' she hissed.

Poor Paul looked confused. Daisy tapped him on the shoulder and smiled. 'I'll dance with you instead, Paul,' she offered hastily.

He swung her around, his sword clanking against his thigh. She smiled again, a dazzling smile. They had taken only a few steps together when they bumped into Jeremy Drake who had, as Daisy guessed, been on his way to ask her to dance. Pretending not to see him, she kept her eyes and her dazzling smile fixed on Paul's face.

Befitting her condition, Lisabeth remained in the parlour. 'Like a queen bee,' said Gwynne. This was her idea. Charles had never approved of ladies in that delicate state showing themselves in public.

The other ladies were happy to buzz around her. Her news astounded them. To fall pregnant at her age and so soon after the wedding! The cynical amongst them eyed her figure in a calculating way and wondered if she really was expecting a baby. The more charitable wondered if all those vicious rumours over the years had been true after all. If she had been Rhys Morgan's mistress, then surely she would have produced at least one child during that time. There could have been abortions, of course, but they all knew how dangerous abortions were. In the case of an unwanted pregnancy the woman would simply disappear for six or eight months, but nobody could recall Lisabeth going away for that period of time. This was frankly mystifying.

Charlotte Drake was delighted. She squealed: 'Oh, honey, what marvellous news! I'm fit to bust with joy for you. Got any cravings, honey?' she cooed as she tucked an extra cushion behind Lisabeth's back and fetched a hassock for her feet. 'I had the most terrible cravings for fried chicken and grits. Stuffed myself like a hog, I did, the entire time.'

'I can't manage anything fried,' said Lisabeth faintly.

'You look pale, honey. Here, sniff this. It'll keep the heaves at bay.' And she unstoppered a tiny porcelain bottle.

Lisabeth sniffed. The lemony scent was soothing and cool; she felt better at once.

'Keep it,' said Charlotte. 'Why suffer the heaves if you don't have to?'

'What a horrible woman,' grumped Gwynne later. 'So coarse and vulgar. My Charles liked women to be ladies. He'd have said—'

'I like her very much,' said Lisabeth.

Amy squeaked in pretended fright when Tom loomed out of the shadows and into the snow-flecked lamplight where she stood silhouetted against the kitchen window. Seizing her wrist, he drew her after him to a sheltered spot against the chimney where the bricks were warmed by the fire within. Enjoying her struggles and muffled protests, he began to kiss her hungrily.

He pulled away, grinning down at her. 'Surpraised?' he drawled.

'Surprised?' She flailed at his powerful shoulders. 'Thomas, you're wicked!'

'Ah, but you love my wuckedness! Go on, you do that!'

She did; his daring excited her. There was a *Romeo and Juliet* quality about their romance that gave it spice and piquancy. Tom could have anybody – she'd often heard the barmaids giggling and sighing over him – but she knew that he wanted only her, and this gave her a special feeling of being cherished. She protested: 'But this is so risky. Mrs Hogg is not a dozen yards away, sipping sherry in the butler's pantry with Mrs Tenks. I managed to slip past, but what if they see me on the way back? What can I tell them?'

'Tull her you're with your lover,' he said, grinning as he rubbed her arms and shoulders, then, very lightly, passed his square corded hands over her breasts, a gesture that made her shiver with the anticipation of promised delights. That was another thing about Tom: he was scrupulously moral, treating her like something precious, worth waiting for. He whispered: 'I'll be your lover very soon. . . . I can't wait, luss, and thut's the truth. One more voyage, then ut's you und me, for keeps.'

She clung to him, murmuring that he must leave, yet tightening her grip on him. She wished that she could stroll into the party on his arm – wouldn't heads turn then! – but the fact that Rhys had banned him from the property made this even more exciting. 'Mrs Thomas Nevin,' she sighed. 'I can't wait, either.'

'Whut's thus "Thomas"?'

'It sounds elegant. Thomas Nevin. . . . Don't you think so?'

'Elegant! Tom's my name, und don't you forgut it. I'm not one of them poncey toffs in there and don't you forgut that, neither.' His voice softened. 'Cheer up, gull. Rhys Morgan started off wuth nuthin', too, und before we're done we'll have those toffs doffing their huts to us, won't we? We'll buy and sull a dozen of thum. Thut's a promise.'

Amy nodded. She loved the way Tom always included her, said 'we' instead of 'I'. He made her feel important to him. She said: 'I know you will, Tom. You're the cleverest man in the province. I have such faith—'

'Hush!' warned Tom, suddenly alert, his face turned towards the door, senses sharp. 'Quick, unside with yer!'

'What's wrong?' Staring past him into the cold whiteness, she could see nothing. The dogs had started up barking with a peculiar intense stridency, but that could simply mean that they had been startled by one of the guests walking past to the stables to check on his horse. On these snowy nights the dogs spooked easily. 'What do you think—?'

'Do as I tull yer. Unside, quick,' repeated Tom urgently as he propelled her towards the kitchen door. Protesting, reluctant, she obeyed, her freezing slippered feet stumbling on the cobblestones as he shoved her roughly along. Almost cramming her into the door, he jerked it shut behind her.

Not a moment too soon. She was leaning on the door to catch her breath in the sudden heat of the kitchen when pandemonium erupted outside. There was shouting, loud and ugly, several male voices bellowing over each other with Tom's the loudest and angriest of all, a scuffling and thumping so hard on the door that Amy jumped away from it in fright, and overlaying the noise and intermittently drowning it a flurry of ferocious barking.

Keeping close to the wall, she peeped through the window but could see nothing of the fracas outside, only two dogs snarling at the edge of the light-pool, their ears flattened and shoulder fur raised, crested with a froth of snow.

'Leave me be, you scummy busstards!' shouted Tom as more dull thumps shook the door. Amy clutched at her necklace, fearful but cheering him on. Her Tom was strong enough to fight off half a dozen men.

The noise had disturbed the rest of the house, coming as it did in an interval between the mazurka and a game of pass-the-parcel. Already a crowd spilled down the steps and into the driveway. The snow had stopped, and in the clear darkness laughing faces were illuminated by high-swinging lanterns. Daisy was there, tagging behind Rhys who strode ahead of the others, his boots sinking into the quilt of soft snow.

'Who is it, man?' he called.

'As you thought, sir, it's young Nevin,' replied Mr Tenks just through the door which concealed Amy from their view. 'He's here to cause trouble, as you suspected. He was forcing the kitchen door when we seized him.'

'But, Papa, he may only be—' began Daisy, a hand tentatively on her father's arm. *Amy!* she thought in horror. *He's come to find Amy.*

Tom Nevin himself interrupted her. With a furious shrug of his broad shoulders he flung off the hands that restrained him and snatched up his plaid cap from where it had been knocked into the snow in the scuffle. 'How dare yer lay so motch as a funger on me!' he bellowed, though from the red mashed look of his face they'd done more than that, thought Daisy.

'This property is out of bounds to you, and well you know it.' Rhys's voice was as chilly as the air into which his vaporized breath plumed.

'But Papa . . .,' said Daisy. Where *was* Amy? she wondered.

'Us thut so?' sneered Tom, forging a single threatening stride towards Rhys before the three men seized and restrained him again. 'I come up here ter fetch hulp fer me susster, an' I'm sut upon by the dogs. I've uvry right ter fetch me own mother an' no busstard's about ter stop me. I *sput* on you an' yer hired thogs!'

And he spat.

Daisy and the others gasped. Many of those assembled quite expected to see murder done right then and there, Mr Morgan looked so ferocious, while Tom Nevin would have lunged for his throat if the men had relaxed their grip for an instant. Three of them were straining to hold him back, and the dogs knew to keep well back from the force of his lashing boots. As Arabella whispered later, there was something fatally powerful about Tom Nevin. Even held down like that he looked as if he was master of the situation. Lowell Windsor, watching from the doorway, would have agreed. As he chewed his tender lower lip he reflected that there was something oddly thrilling about a man who was not afraid of anything.

Rhys stared at the young man. It had been a long time since he had been dismissed, and that had been over a trivial matter, more for the fact that he had proved himself untrustworthy than for the specific misdemeanour itself. He'd feared the lad was proving to be cast in his father's treacherous mould, and now, looking at the contorted face and the hatred in Tom's eyes, Rhys felt a prickle of recognition. This could just as easily have been Sam Nevin hurling abuse at him, exactly as he had that night almost twenty years ago when Rhys had evicted Sam, Birdie and their young family and had torched their cottage behind them. He wondered how much hostility reached back from that night, but decided not to remind Tom how well deserved the eviction had been. Why rake over the dead ashes?

Forcing a note of calm into his voice, Rhys said: 'I accept your explanation.'

'Oh, yer do?' sneered Tom. 'How kind of yer.' And he aimed another kick in the direction of the dogs.

'Put him off the property before I change my mind,' Rhys ordered shortly.

'I'll be buck!' shouted Tom. 'Yer may nut be sorry enough to apologize to me now, but you'll be sorry thun, I promise you thut!'

Rhys showed no sign of having heard. Turning on his heel, he walked inside. The party guests fell in behind him – all but Lowell Windsor who lingered to watch as, struggling and cursing, Tom was roughly manhandled off towards the gate.

'What a dreadful young man,' shuddered Lady Launcenolt.

'You thought so? I admired his spunk, myself,' commented Charlotte Drake, hoisting her ostentatious fur wrap closer around her bejewelled shoulders.

'Is he someone you know, dear?' asked Martha Westlake of Daisy, but Daisy fled, her eyes scanning the room for Amy.

Mrs Hogg had found her first, cowering against the wall in the kitchen, silent tears oozing down her cheeks as she listened to the shouts and curses as Tom was being jostled away. They didn't need to *hurt* him, she thought.

When Mrs Hogg entered the room Amy was relieved to see her. 'I want to go home,' she wept.

Mrs Hogg was confused. She could hear the commotion outside but had missed the significance of it because she and Mrs Tenks had been indulging in a surreptitious glass of Canary wine in the butler's pantry and had been unaware of the earlier exodus of guests. 'What's happened? What's happened?' she said, confused and guilty, thinking Amy had come to the kitchen in search of her. 'Are you ill, child?'

'I want to go home,' repeated Amy, and deaf to Mrs Hogg's coaxing questions she refused to say more.

Daisy met them in the corridor. 'We're going home,' announced Amy, pushing past.

Daisy followed, and when Mrs Hogg was collecting the coats from amongst the heap in the cloakroom she tugged at Amy's arm. 'Please! You can't go now. I was hoping—'

'I hate your father and I hate this party. We're going now, and I'm never coming back to this house again. Never!'

Aghast, Daisy protested: 'I tried my best, Amy. Believe me, I tried to speak up for Tom, but it was useless. Oh, please stay. Don't take your resentment out on me.'

Amy shook her head stiffly. She was perilously close to breaking down completely and terrified she might. As it was, she could fob Mrs Hogg off with the excuse of a headache or, better still, a vague hint about feminine malaise which would stop the woman's questions instantly. 'I know you tried. It's your father I can't forgive. His men punched and kicked Thomas – Tom – and they even set the dogs on him. I can't forgive your father for that.'

'They thought he was a burglar,' explained Daisy, but Amy scorched her with a withering look of disbelief as she snatched her coat from Mrs Hogg and marched out into the darkness, thrusting her arms into the sleeves as she went. Daisy watched helplessly. There was nothing more she could say in front of Mrs Hogg – the woman was simple but not completely stupid, and Daisy dared not say anything that might arouse a stirring of suspicion in her mind.

But she had to stop Amy somehow. If her friend carried out the threat of never returning, that effectively meant the end of their friendship, for Daisy was not permitted to visit the Golden Fleece. Her heart raced in a panic. This, too, was her fault.

Standing in the doorway, she hugged her upper arms against the cold as she peered towards the stables where Amy and Mrs Hogg would have gone to fetch their coachman. Now the sky was as clear as a summer night with every star sharp and bright against the velvet blackness. Daisy shivered, thinking that this was a day of disasters. First the alarming news about Andrew, then a party that failed to spark any happiness in her and now, worst of all, her only real friend was storming out of her life. Justifiably, too.

Fluttering towards her came the light of a pair of weak carriage-lamps accompanied by the rattle of iron-shod wheels over the worn stones. Daisy hurried forward, hoping to intercept the carriage, but the Thornes' coachman had his cap down and collar up against the cold and didn't see her. He cracked the whip smartly over the horses' padded backs, increasing their pace to a brisk trot so that the shuttered coach came lurching at Daisy with sudden speed. As she reached the drive it blurred past her with a creak of sagging springs while a whirr of wheels churned up a spray of frozen slush, flinging it all over her as if it had been sluiced from a bucket.

Gasping, she turned towards the lighted doorway to survey the damage to her beautiful gown. She was covered from hem to waist with mud, and her bodice was splodged, and from the cold wetness on her face and throat she guessed that no part of her had escaped.

Still in shock, she heard her name called and, looking up, she saw the last person she wanted right now. Jeremy Drake.

TEN

'Daisy, wait!' His footsteps clattered down the steps behind her.

She hurried forward, her dress tight as a mermaid's tail, hampering her steps. Already her slippers were soaked.

'I want to talk to you!'

She could imagine *how* he wanted to talk. 'What's delayed Doctor Stafford in Cape Town? Nothing trivial, I hope!' And how he'd laugh when he saw the ruins of her gown. Well, it *was* her fault for standing so close to the driveway, but she didn't need to have him point it out to her. Hitching up her sodden skirts, she forced herself to go faster, flitting into the screen of shrubbery where drifts of snow draped the branches, formless and grey as the laundry Birdie Nevin hung on the bushes around her cottage. She couldn't feel her feet.

'Where are you going?' called Jeremy, lengthening his stride. He guessed where she was headed, to the sanctuary of old Mrs Stafford's rooms at the far end of the servants' annexe. If she reached the entrance first, she'd bolt inside, slam the door against him and he'd never be able to talk to her.

As he ran he cursed himself for leaving things so long. He'd given Daisy time to adjust to the idea that her precious Doctor Stafford had – thank goodness – got himself married, and this evening after he'd made her jealous for a while he'd planned to make the first real move towards her. But something had gone badly wrong. There was an atmosphere at the big house tonight, something in the air that was putting everyone on edge, himself included.

At the corner of the building he caught her by the shoulder, but she twisted free with a sob and went pelting on. He caught her again, this time seizing her upper arm and jerking so that she spun around and slapped up against him.

She glared at him, her breath dragging out of her. His jacket front rubbed against her muddy gown. *You'll be filthy*, she thought. *It serves you right for pursuing me. Now your clothes will be ruined, too.* But it was a hard empty thought with no satisfaction in it.

He misunderstood, of course, and was overwhelmed that she stood so quietly in the circle of his arms. 'You're freezing!' he said in wonder, and placed his hands on her shoulder-blades, gently hugging her against him. In the darkness at his shoulder he couldn't see her grim face.

'Something's the matter, isn't it? Something's really wrong. Daisy, you can talk to me. I am your friend, you know. You can trust me.'

Mention of the word 'friend' touched the tenderest part of Daisy's distress. For a few seconds she had allowed herself to enjoy the sensation of being in his arms, but now, afraid she was going to cry, she wrenched away from him so suddenly that she broke his grasp on her. Headlong she ran, dashing in a flurry of sliding footsteps to where a light shone in the window beside Gwynne's door.

She never reached that sanctuary. A few yards short of the doorway she skidded on the snowy path and when she tried to regain her balance by flailing her arms she over-corrected and her feet slid forward from under her. From behind her she heard Jeremy's shout as he dashed to catch her, but he was too late. With a dull popping sound she landed full on her right arm and crumpled it awkwardly beneath her.

'Are you all right?'

'Of course I am!' She was furious – how careless! – and anticipated teasing laughter from him. What a fool she was making of herself! But when she tried to push herself up to a sitting position her arm didn't want to work.

'Let me help you.' He could see that something was amiss – what, he wasn't sure – and when he tugged her arm to pull her up she screamed at the unexpected violence of the pain.

'Great Lord,' whispered Jeremy, seeing now that Daisy's wrist and hand hung at an odd angle.

'She's broken her arm,' said Lowell, materializing as he had a habit of doing. 'I heard her scream,' he explained. 'I wasn't snooping. . . . I say, I'll go and fetch Mr Morgan, shall I?'

Jeremy picked Daisy up with extreme care, making sure that the injured arm lay across her body. She stifled a moan when he took her weight. Her wrist and forearm shrilled like a whistle with pain, and she bit her lip against it.

As he climbed the steps she realized how this would look, how Arabella and the others would gloat when they staggered in covered in filth. In five minutes her reputation would be in worse tatters than her clothes. She plucked at his lapel with her free hand. 'The kitchen . . . go that way, please.'

But the front doorway was already crammed with people, and more spilled out. Rhys strode to meet them, Lisabeth, Aunty Gwynne, Aunt Bea, the Andruths and the Martins, Arabella, Maurice . . . she tried to focus . . . she tried to keep her eyes open, but the pain reached up and squeezed her body in a grip like a vice, squeezing out all her feelings, squeezing her thoughts until she fainted.

This could be serious, thought Rhys, studying the place where a piece of broken bone was jutting through the skin, and cursing the fact that Doctor Meakings wasn't here this evening. Or that Andrew wasn't, for that matter. Wasn't he a specialist in this sort of thing?

Lisabeth finished cutting away the sleeve. She waved Gwynne away as she jostled close with smelling salts. 'No, thank you, dear. We don't want Daisy coming round. The pain will be excruciating.'

Rhys said: 'This looks bad.' They all glanced at each other. Compound fractures were notoriously difficult to set properly, and if this was not urgently and competently treated Daisy could lose the arm altogether.

Beatrice was at the wall telephone, whirring the handle, listening, jiggling the handpiece-rest and whirring the handle again. 'There's still no response at all,' she reported. 'It could be the snow. It's falling again, too.'

Rhys felt like screaming. Sir Kenneth said suddenly: 'Please permit us to help. We can take Daisy to the Doctor's. Harold lives practically across the road from us, as you know.'

'We were talking to him earlier, about the snow, and he said he wasn't going out this evening, didn't he, Kiki?' put in Beatrice.

Jeremy was the only other person in the study. He had placed Daisy on the chaise-longue, helped bind a tourniquet to her arm and then gone to stand beside the open fire, keeping silent lest he be asked to leave the room. He was thinking how odd it was that only the Launcenolts seemed able to make decisions, while the others were in obvious shock. Now he was prompted to say: 'Mr Morgan, it would be best to take her to town. The snow could close in and cut you off from the outside world, whereas Daisy could be in need of daily care. Is there somewhere she could stay in town? Perhaps—'

'With us, of course. She could stay with us!' It had been in Beatrice's mind to suggest this when she first began trying to stir the wretched telephone into life.

'Mmm,' said Rhys, frowning, and Sir Kenneth said: 'It's the obvious solution, old chap. Let's get some blankets now and. . . .'

Gwynne listened to this with mounting disbelief. All day she had been in an agony of worry over dear Andrew and his poor sick bride, and now to have Daisy lying hideously injured and unconscious was more than she could cope with, but this was too much! Would this scheming woman stop at nothing to get Daisy away from Mists of Heaven? Charles wouldn't be surprised at this, she thought. Charles saw through her from the start, how she was prissy-sweet to anyone important but sneered at the Staffords behind their backs, calling them grubby immigrants. Her voice shaking, Gwynne cried: 'This is Daisy's home, and it's where she belongs! Being a ''lady'' doesn't give you the right to help yourself to her, you know, and as for—'

'Gwynne, please!' interrupted Rhys. 'Yes, Kiki, I think that's what we must do. I'll ring for carriages and—'

'Ours is already out the front,' Beatrice told him. 'We were about to leave anyway because Kiki was tired. His heart. . . .' She faltered, wondering what effect this excitement might have on him, but then rallied as she remembered that it was physical exertion and physical stress that he needed to avoid.

'You take her, then. We'll follow as soon as we can,' said Rhys. 'Gwynne, could you please see to the guests? Make sure they—'

'No,' said Gwynne. Her jaw was set mulishly. 'I'm coming with you.'

'I'll stay,' offered Lisabeth. The strain of the day was beginning to tell on her, too, and she watched wearily as Daisy was carried out to the carriage.

Rhys paused to have a quiet moment with her while he waited for the carriage to be brought around. Cupping her face in both his hands, he kissed her lips tenderly. 'Take care of yourself, and of our child,' he said.

She smiled up at him, thinking how much younger he seemed these days. His pride in the baby was ridiculous – you'd think nobody had ever fathered a child before – and so touching that even the servants commented. Yes, it would be good to have a baby in the house, but that was still a long way off, and all sorts of things (please God, no) could go wrong. Gently she said: 'Take care of Daisy, dearest. Make sure Doctor Meakings looks after her well. I've my doubts about him. . . . If only Andrew were here. We need him now – he's a specialist in such things. Wouldn't it have been good if he was here to look after his own sister?'

Rhy's face darkened, and a shiver went through Lisabeth as she thought: *He is terrified about Andrew, too. He does care!* She said: 'He'll be all right, dearest. I know it in my bones that he's safe.'

Her confidence assured him. 'Let's hope so,' he said.

In his haste to harness the horses the coachman had not thought to fasten the padded side-curtains on the windows, so while they rolled down the drive Rhys busied himself unbuckling the straps and unrolling the curtains to exclude the piercing draughts. He was leaning past Gwynne to fix the second set in place when they drew level with the Nevin cottage, brightly lit behind the fringe of bare fruit trees.

He whistled between his teeth and rang the bell to stop the carriage.

'That's Doctor Meakings's gig, I'd swear it,' he said, wresting the door open. 'What would he be doing here?' He frowned, trying to scratch up Tom Nevin's words, and by the time the carriage had rolled to a halt he remembered. A few seconds later Birdie's dogs set up a shrill barking to greet him, all the puppies joining in with their mother's voice.

The cottage stank, Rhys noticed in disgust as he took a breath of the fetid air into lungs cleansed by the sharp night atmosphere. Foul-smelling refuse was piled into a pail near the door, and Rhys wouldn't have been surprised to see a rat scurry across the littered floor. He'd heard that Birdie was slatternly, but not until now had he believed it because in all her years of housekeeping for him she'd kept the mansion immaculate and the servants on their toes.

Tom was sprawled in a chair in front of the fire. Rhys noticed that it was an expensive chair, upholstered in silk tapestry by the look of it, and that on the mantelpiece were a collection of china figurines and two brass and porcelain lamps, fit to grace the most luxurious parlour. As Tom turned his head Rhys saw, by their light, that his face was puffy and purpling from the beating he had been given.

Rhys said: 'Where's Doctor Meakings? We need him urgently.'

'Get out of thus house thus munnut,' said Tom, equally brusque. 'You've not been asked un, so get out.'

'Is he with your mother? Is Birdie ill?' asked Rhys, but at that moment a velvet curtain billowed and Birdie pushed through the doorway with a bundle in her arms. She looked as if she was crying, and was still wearing the apron she had donned hours ago to serve guests at the party. Thrusting the bundle into Tom's arms, she said: 'I'll tend to thum soon, but first. . . .' She gulped. 'I fear we've lost her, Tom. We've lost our lovely gull.'

'There, now, Ma,' said Tom gruffly. His face softened as he looked down at the tiny swaddled baby. Rhys noticed another wrapped bundle lying in a nest of satin cushions beyond the fireplace.

Birdie dabbed her eyes with her apron hem, then saw Rhys. 'Musster Morgan! Whut brungs you here, then, sir?'

'He came to offer help,' lied Tom. 'But he's just leaving.'

'I came to find the Doctor,' repeated Rhys, cursing the fact that the Launcenolts had hurried ahead with Daisy in their carriage. All this panic and he was right here next door! He said: 'I'm sorry if you've troubles, Birdie, and if there's anything we can do—'

'He's sorry,' said Tom quietly, rocking the baby in his arms. 'He came without his bully-boys to show just how sorry he us. Ay, I cud make you real sorry, Musster Morgan.'

Rhys felt a thrill of fear tickle his spine and for a second he wondered if he would get safely from the property. Forcing a thin smile, he pushed through the curtain (it was greasy, he noticed) and into the bedroom beyond.

Here again was the bizarre combination of filth and luxury, and the walls were plastered, like Gwynne's, with a profusion of pictures of the royal family and garish crucifixes. On the bed, under a soiled sateen bedspread, lay Siobhan, so hollow-cheeked and sallow that but for the disfiguring scar Rhys wouldn't have recognized her.

'I'm afraid I've done all I can,' said Doctor Meakings, who was bending over to repack his bag. Then he straightened and saw he was talking to Rhys. 'What in the devil are you doing here? Ah, I *see*!' He placed one finger alongside his nose. 'In that case, I'm doubly sorry, sir. She was a pretty lass, very sad, but we've saved the babies, and a fine—'

'Don't be ridiculous!' snapped Rhys.

'Wouldn't be the first time,' chirped the doctor without remorse. '*Droit de seigneur* and all that. You'd be surprised which of our pillars of society indulge in a little "overlording". Heh, heh!' He raised his voice as the curtain billowed to admit Tom, then Birdie. 'There's not much time, I'm afraid. Young man, you should fetch that priest, and without delay.'

'He wouldn't come,' admitted Tom. Seeing the naked hurt and shame in his eyes, Rhys felt compassion, a compassion that was snuffed out as engorged rage replaced that brief flicker. 'The busstard wouldn't come!'

Birdie crossed herself. Her nails were black with dirt.

'Can I do anything?' offered Rhys. 'I have to take the Doctor away now, to tend to Daisy, but if I can help in any way—'

'You've done enough,' spat Tom. 'One of your scummy men done this to her. Or maybe ut's even you who—'

Without hesitating Birdie hauled back and cuffed Tom across the ear. She had to stand on tip-toe to reach, but she whacked him so hard that he gulped back the rest of what he had been going to say. Birdie followed Rhys outside. 'Excuse my Tom,' she said stiffly. 'He's a foine lad, truly he is, but thus business with his susster. . . . Ut's dustressed hum terrible, loike. Always doted on her, he has. . . . He wus loike a father to her ufter Sam died.'

In the carriage Gwynne listened with mounting distress. 'If the priest wouldn't come, then he's judged her, Rhys. That means that poor girl won't have a proper Christian burial. Oh, Rhys, that would kill poor Birdie.'

They were following the Doctor's gig along the gas-lit Christchurch streets. Rhys was weary of the subject of the Nevins, but he knew that his sister regarded them as her pet charity, and that she and Birdie were unlikely but firm friends. He patted her hand and said: 'She'll be buried in the churchyard, with all your wretched papal palavering. I'll see to it. I'll take a bottle of the best Irish whiskey to Father O'Flynn and we'll have a wee chat about that new convent the Church is building at Fendalton, and maybe, just maybe, the subject of Siobhan's burial will come up when I'm considering the size of Mists of Heaven's contribution. That could fix it – what do you think, Gwynne?'

'That'll do nicely,' beamed Gwynne. She looked so old in the brief slaps of lamplight that it wrung his heart. 'Bless you, Rhys, bless you. Charles always said that you had a true Christian soul. He said—'

'Never mind. You know that Charles was always too fulsome in his praise, especially of me,' said Rhys drily, but he smiled. He knew that this was his sister's apology for the way she had behaved earlier. 'I'll fix it for Birdie, but you be nice to the Launcenolts, d'you hear me?' There was silence. 'Unless you'd rather wait in the carriage?'

'I'd be nice to the devil himself, for you, Rhys,' she said.

ELEVEN

'Y OUR MOTHER named you "Vashti", of course. Such a pretty name
. . Indian of course. It means "thread of life".'

'Mamma had imaginative taste,' mused Daisy. 'Vashti has so much
more style to it than Daisy. Daisy is so plain.'

'Your father preferred it,' Beatrice said. She stood behind Daisy
brushing her damp hair, lifting the long strands so that they glistened in
the sunlight as they dried. They were in a sunny corner of the garden
surrounded by the yellows and pinks of early spring. Daffodils and
jonquils crowded thickly along the edges of the mossy lawn, while
beyond a crimson-flowered hedge the River Avon slid past, dark and
silent. Excalibur, exhausted from chasing ducks and barking at the
peacocks, dozed under the trailing sweet green fronds of a weeping
willow.

'I love it here, and I love hearing about Mamma,' sighed Daisy. 'It
makes it almost worthwhile breaking my arm!' She glanced down at her
lap where, on a cushion, her wrist rested, bulky with the bandages that
held the splints in place. 'I'm especially pleased that you make Amy
welcome. I know that you don't really like her much and Kiki calls her
"a Thorne in his side", but she is my dearest friend and I was so afraid
the other night that I'd never see her again.'

'As long as you're happy, dear.' But she wished Daisy would agree to
invite other young ladies to the house – that vivacious Arabella Martin
with the russet hair, or the Westlake girls. All her hints, however, had so
far been in vain.

'You're getting tired, Aunt Bea. Let me brush *your* hair now. I love
it – it's as soft and springy as sheep's wool.' She stretched up for the
brush which Beatrice was holding out of reach, but subsided with a
chuckle as Albert approached. 'Albert disapproves of me,' she whispered. 'He stares at me with his huge cloudy eyes, and I know he thinks
I'm silly.'

113

'Kindly be excusing me, ma'am,' said Albert, who heard what Daisy said and was offended. He inclined his scarlet-turbaned head. 'But there is coming a gentleman for to see Miss Morgan.'

'Jeremy! Oh, good! He's bringing me those books of his mother's. *Scarlet Sunsets* – doesn't that sound riveting?'

'Azura loved romantic novelettes, too,' said Beatrice. She wondered why Albert was standing there, but when he raised a hand tentatively towards his head she understood and laughed. 'Don't be so fussy, Albert. Not with Mr Drake. He won't faint if he sees Miss Morgan with her hair down.'

He's seen a lot more than that, thought Daisy.

The accident had turned Jeremy into a friend, and a delightful one. For weeks he had been every day to see her, to cheer her up and make the days pass swiftly. His visits were a treat she looked forward to.

Today he was teasing Excalibur as he pretended to, then didn't, throw a twig. Excalibur growled, tugging at it, then when it finally was thrown he was after it at once, barrelling across the lawn, his legs a blur. Daisy clapped in delight. 'He adores you, but you are so mean to tease him!' she chided.

'And I adore you. Marry me, Daisy,' he said matter-of-factly.

'Now you're teasing me!' she retorted, but her heart was pounding jerkily, overcome by the suddenness of what he had said. She looked down into her lap and noticed that her good hand was trembling. Marry him! Why, out of the blue, would he say such a thing? And why couldn't she think of a single sensible word in reply?

He had noticed the effect of his words. 'Daisy, you must know that I care for you.'

'And I care for you, too,' she said quickly while she cast about desperately for a dignified rejection, kind words that wouldn't wound or offend. She tried to get up, but he captured her hand in his and was leaning over her, his face so close that she was gazing right into his dark eager eyes. The effect was pleasant but dangerous, too; not knowing what he would say or do next unnerved her.

He raised one hand and with his fingertips traced the planes of her face. She wanted to tell him to stop, to tell him that this whole conversation must cease, right now, but there was a slow delectable thrill in his touch that paralysed her. When his fingers trailed over her lips it tickled in an exciting way, and she felt her lips part under his touch.

He smiled. 'Daisy,' he said happily and bent to kiss her.

She held her breath for a long time, then inhaled and was full of the scent of him, warm skin, the spicy tang of soap – and horses. His mouth was gentle, neither dry nor moist but wholesome and somehow perfect, as natural and right as if she had pressed one of her own hands to her lips, and yet when he sighed and increased the pressure, pulling her body against his, it was as if she had drifted from calm waters into a strong mysterious current and she felt unfamiliar stirrings and a panicky sensation, fear of the unknown.

'Daisy,' he said against her neck, not happily this time but with a sound like pain. His fingers were tangled in her loose, still damp hair, and she smelt and tasted of springtime. He felt that he was in heaven.

'No, please, no,' she managed, pushing him away. He obeyed immediately, and she was aware of stirrings of disappointment.

'What's the matter? I'm not offending you, am I? After all' – and he smiled impishly – 'Mrs Tenks says that kisses are perfectly appropriate for the afternoon.' He laughed aloud when she smiled in response. 'Oh, it's going to be marvellous! We'll be married in late summer, and Father is giving us a house in town, while your father says we can have five hundred acres of his best racehorse-grazing country to build a—'

'Wait a minute!' cried Daisy, alarmed. 'I've not been consulted, and you've discussed this with Papa—'

'And Mrs Morgan. They both think it's a splendid idea, and have given us their blessing.'

Daisy felt hot angry tears stabbing at her eyelids. So Papa and Lisabeth thought it would be a great idea to have her married off and out of the way, did they? How very convenient for them not to have her, an unwanted reminder of Papa's unfortunate first marriage, around the place while they started their own new family. Rage choked in her throat, and she could hardly see Jeremy as she said wildly: 'Well, they're not packing me off like spare baggage. They needn't think they can!'

'It's not like that at all!'

'Yes, it is! You don't understand.'

'Don't I?' He stood up and took a couple of steps towards the river. Excalibur followed, lunging to gnaw at his boots. 'Let me see if I've got this straight, Daisy. I've been here several dozen times in the past six weeks, and on every occasion you've made it clear that you're pleased to see me. We've become close. Very close. Would you agree?'

'Yes, I would,' she whispered. Her emotions were a turmoil. She wished that Jeremy would stop staring at her in that angry accusing way and go back to being her friend. 'Jeremy, I know you think I've been flirting with you, leading you on, but—'

'Haven't you?' he demanded, and she thought he was going to grab her shoulders and shake her.

'Tea-time!' called Lady Launcenolt, emerging from the french doors pushing a laden trolley before her. 'Time for tea, and Miss Thorne has just arrived. We're really spoiled for company today, aren't we, Daisy?'

'*Spoiled* is the exact word,' muttered Jeremy grimly, but he was his usual gallant self, jumping up to help with the tea-trolley. He went to meet Amy and he complimented her on her new blue and white bustled gown, making her twirl with her blue ruffled parasol so they could all admire her.

'I won't see any of you for a few weeks,' he announced as he accepted a cream horn from the silver tray. 'I'm going on a trip. An expedition into the mountains.'

'At this time of year?' queried Lady Launcenolt.

'Father has a bee in his bonnet about raising wild pigs, and cross-breeding them with domestic pigs to make a hardier strain, more suited to New Zealand conditions, less disease-prone than the imported varieties. He's organized an expedition to capture a hundred or so piglets.' He spoke to Lady Launcenolt.

'You'll have to be very careful. Sows with young are ferocious creatures,' said Daisy.

'That'll make it more of an adventure, won't it?' But still he didn't look at her.

'Papa knows about wild pigs,' said Daisy, still trying to 'be friends' again. 'He had to kill lots when he first began here. They attack the sheep – they're worse than lions or wolves for that, or so "Baron" Windsor says, but that's his argument for wanting to import wild game. There's lots of wild pigs in the hills around White Clouds. Jock McFallish said that one huge boar was tracked all the way from our place right up to White Clouds's north boundary. I say, do be careful, won't you?'

He smiled at her then. It was impossible to resist the appeal in her voice, and he couldn't blame her; he *had* been clumsy. 'I'll talk to you again when I get back,' he said. 'Will you promise to think about it?'

Daisy nodded. Beatrice studied her topaz-and-diamond ring, and Amy stared with open curiosity. When Beatrice was showing Jeremy out, Amy demanded: 'Think about what?'

'You're not the only one who receives proposals,' Daisy told her airily.

'Isn't it romantic, Lady Launcenolt?' gushed Amy, greeting her with the news.

'Jeremy isn't romantic,' protested Daisy. 'He's only a friend, and I wish he hadn't ruined everything.' She picked up *Scarlet Sunsets* and riffled through its pages. 'This is what I want. Real thrilling romance. I want my dream lover to come boldly into my life and sweep me off my feet!'

Amy sighed extravagantly, but Beatrice prickled, irritated by Amy and by the fact that Daisy chose to confide in the girl first, rather than in her. 'Real life isn't like that at all,' she warned. 'Real life is his parents and your parents and his friends and your friends all getting on well together, and organizing the house and keeping an appointments

116

calendar and watching his health and making him take sulphur and belladonna when he coughs, and counting the silver every evening before the servants go off duty . . . *and* always making him feel important. That's what real life is!'

'Oh, Lady Launcenolt, that does sound dull!' said Amy.

'Not for me. I'm going to have excitement, Aunt Bea.'

'*That* sounds like a prescription for disaster, young lady,' said Beatrice. Though she spoke sternly, she did think that Daisy was only teasing her. Jeremy Drake was such a lovely lad. What young lady in her right mind would refuse him?

The next afternoon when Daisy and Beatrice were sitting in that same sheltered corner poring over the intricacies of a jig-saw puzzle of Buckingham Palace, Albert sidled out again and again informed them that a gentleman had arrived to see Miss Morgan.

Jeremy. Her heart fluttered and sank. Ever since he left yesterday she had been agonizing over what he said, over how he kissed her. It was as if he proposed to two people, one of whom warmed to the idea at once, because he was such fun, so lovely and she so utterly adored his company, while the other person saw only that this was a convenient way for Papa and Lisabeth to rid themselves of her.

On his wedding day Daisy knew she would lose her papa but she hadn't expected it to be so total a loss. While recovering at Benares she hoped that Rhys would come alone to visit, giving them a chance to recapture the old days, which was why she stayed there and refused all attempts to coax her home; but no, always Lisabeth was with him 'because she needs the air', and the visits became ordeals for Daisy who with her broken arm was virtually ignored while Lisabeth (who looked to Daisy as healthy as a sow) was fussed over and cosseted. The subject of every conversation, it seemed, was babies, except once when Amy with pretended innocence remarked how her own mother had died giving birth to her and it was her father's theory that her mother had tried to have her first child much too late, at a dangerous age in fact. 'She wasn't a young woman at all,' Amy said. 'She was almost as old as you are, Mrs Morgan.'

Which killed that conversation stone dead.

The thought that her father was behind the proposal – 'Nothing would give me greater pleasure than to see you marry a young man like Jeremy Drake' – blighted the sensuality Jeremy's kiss had stirred in her. He had awakened her. Alerted her to the possibilities in life. Provided the fertile base for her fantasies from *Scarlet Sunsets* to proliferate. After she had read it through last night she had lain awake for hours remembering how it had felt when he kissed her. A strumming tingled her whole body as she recalled the feeling when he trailed his fingertips over her skin.

But what could she say to him now? She didn't want to marry him; that would be too ordinary, too predictable, too *ordained* by her father.

'I don't know what to tell him,' she pleaded to Beatrice.

'If you are pleasing, miss. The gentleman he is not being Mr Drake,' smirked Albert.

'Not Jeremy? Then, who . . .?'

Daisy glanced back at the house. She tried to speak, but faltered. Her breath caught in her throat as the french doors opened and Andrew Stafford stepped into the garden.

She knew at once who he was. Anybody else, glimpsing him as she had done, half-seen through the small panes of glass, might have mistaken him for Rhys, but as she told Amy later: 'It was like that part of the story where Chloe Longsworth sees Nigel Heppelwhite across the lawn at the garden-party. I recognized him *instantly*, even before he came outside. Oh, Amy, it was more thrilling than any novelette!'

'He's like Mr Morgan, isn't he?' said Amy, proud of her part in the drama. Andrew had arrived unannounced in *Raymond W. Boyd* several days before and had been suffering so acutely from sea-sickness that he had put himself up at the Golden Fleece to recuperate. Seeing his name in the guest-register, Amy approached him in the dining-room one lunch-time and pleaded with him to visit Daisy here. He seemed delighted at the idea. As she spoke to him, Amy was intrigued by his likeness to Rhys: the square jawline, high cheekbones, their height and the habit they both had of holding the head on one side while they listened – these things, Amy guessed, were the secret of his attraction to her friend. And he and Daisy were alike, too, with butter-coloured hair and a widow's peak on their forehead; though, come to think of it, Mr Morgan shared those similarities, too.

'Papa and Andrew are nothing alike,' snapped Daisy. 'How can you say that? Papa is an outdoors man, and Andrew is an intellectual, yes, a cultured intellectual!'

Amy kept silent, though she wondered what Mr Morgan was if not cultured and intellectual with his library full of books and tickets to all the operas and musical evenings that ever came to Canterbury. *Like does indeed attract like*, she thought.

'He's so . . . tender,' Daisy mused aloud. 'He wanted to know everything that Doctor Meakings had said and done, and he wants to be there when the bandages come off in three weeks. Do you know – he thought I would have forgotten him after all this time, that he would be like one of those great-uncles one writes to but cannot remember at all. And he still pictured me as a little girl. *That* astonished him, I'm pleased to say. Do you know, Amy, it has been a stroke of absolute providence, breaking these bones. Here I am, close to Andrew and not having to share him with anybody at Mists of Heaven. It's paradise!'

118

'Do you mean he hasn't been out there yet?'

'Of course! He goes out there every day, but Papa isn't home, and it *is* his house; but, if you ask me, Andrew is just using that as an excuse to be here by me. Oh, Amy, I'm so *happy*!'

'So you like him as much as you thought you would?'

'As much? Oh, more, Amy. A hundred, thousand times more.'

Amy shook her head. 'I don't understand what you see in him,' she said with aggravating frankness. 'He's so old, and so . . . quiet, and he never seems to be looking at you when he speaks to you, but his mind and his thoughts always seem to be off in the distance somewhere.'

At another time Daisy would have tossed off an angry retort but she was eager that her friend understood. 'He's suffered in a romantic way,' she explained earnestly. 'He's not really old, not much past thirty anyway, and he's quiet because he's thoughtful. I feel wonderful with him, Amy. I know *instinctively* that he's my dream lover.'

Amy was unconvinced. 'I think you've talked yourself into this. You've mooned over Andrew for so many years that now he's here all you can see is the ideal you've built up in your own mind. Open your eyes, Daisy, please! Jeremy Drake is a far better—'

'That's quite enough!' Daisy's eyes snapped dangerously, the pale blue darkening to a cold grey. 'That's as bad as suggesting that he reminds me of Papa. I *insist* that he and Papa are *nothing* alike. *Jeremy* is more like Papa, which is probably why Papa approves of him. Andrew is like me. Don't smile like that, Amy; I'm deadly serious. I understand Andrew. I feel right with him, as if we belong together in some predestined way. With him I have this marvellous sensation of all my dreams coming true.'

'If you say so,' said Amy doubtfully.

'I love him, Amy,' she confided in a low voice that shook with fervour. 'And do you know what? I think he loves me, too.'

'Really? Just like in *Scarlet Sunsets?*' enquired Amy innocently, knowing how avidly Daisy had devoured the story.

'Oh, yes! Exactly,' she sighed.

'Kiki, it was so romantic,' gushed Beatrice. 'Do you recall the day Rhys first saw Azura, on the lawn with the peacocks strolling about? Remember how he was instantly smitten? Well, Kiki, seeing these two together brought it all back to me.'

'This is very different, Bea.'

'Is it?' She paused with a smile, a sheaf of daffodils in one hand and a half-arranged vase in front of her on the mantelpiece. Placing another stem, she said: 'Daisy is so like her mother that sometimes I almost sense Azura there, simmering below the surface.'

'I do wish you wouldn't talk such drivel.' Sir Kenneth placed a black pawn to queen four then wheeled himself around to the other end of the marble table to contemplate white's position. Picking up a folded copy of the *India Gazette*, he lunged to swat Excalibur away from his feet. 'Look, would you please keep that dratted dog out in the garden? It persists in worrying my shoe-buckles, but when it gets carried away it nips at my ankles. It seems to know that I can't give it the healthy kick it deserves.'

In response to his complaint Albert materialized and scooped up the struggling puppy, bearing him off down the corridor. Sir Kenneth stared after them, grumbling: 'I swear that those damned sepoys hear every word spoken in this house.'

'It's us,' explained Bea, choosing to ignore his bad temper. 'As we get older we get deafer and we speak more loudly.'

'What? I'm not deaf! As to your ecstasy, Bea, I'd not get too excited over that Stafford fellow. Never did like him much. No backbone. Insipid piece of goods, if you ask me. Turns tail at the first sign of trouble, if I recall.'

'He did run away, true, but he was only a schoolboy then. He's grown-up now, and a trained doctor. Besides, Daisy adores him and that's what matters. Beauty is in the eye of the beholder, and what *you* call insipid Daisy calls pale and interesting.'

'Pale and *un*interesting,' snorted Sir Kenneth. 'What's happened to that Mr Drake? Now, he's a real man. Plenty of ooomph to him. He's the fellow for our Daisy. Always got a smile and a funny story. Did I tell you his story about the elephant that couldn't—?'

'Not now, thank you, Kiki,' said Bea, wondering if Albert was hovering near by.

'He's the one for her. She doesn't want a widower,' he said, conveniently forgetting that he himself had been a widower when he married Beatrice. 'Widowers are too stuffy, too set in their ways.'

She smiled. 'Oh, I agree! But you know Daisy. She'll make up her own mind,' she said.

When Rhys came home after the first week of the pig-hunting expedition he was weary and heartily sick of his fellow-man, as he told Lisabeth. 'Specifically, young Lowell Windsor,' he added. 'He never should have been included in the group. Already he's causing trouble. Gave some of the young Maori lads brandy to drink and made improper suggestions.'

'Have you got *women* with you?' said Lisabeth, astonished.

Silently cursing his careless tongue, Rhys asked after her health. Had she been looking after herself properly? Was she well? No headaches or fainting fits?

She blushed, delighted with his attention. They were so happy together that she couldn't believe it at times. She said lovingly: 'You do go on, Rhys! You're as inquisitive as Andrew! And, you'll be pleased to know, he's given me a clean bill of health and says I should have no difficulty with the birth, either.'

'Andrew? When did he arrive?'

She told him, and added that he had been visiting Daisy, too, and said her arm was healing perfectly. To Rhys this was the last straw after a tiring and tiresome journey home.

'Don't be upset,' said Lisabeth. 'Daisy's so bored there by herself, and we can't be visiting her every minute. From all accounts she and Andrew are getting on splendidly.' She walked ahead of him into the morning room where Gwynne was working on her tapestry beside the fire. Lisabeth kept her voice low and said: 'I'm glad Daisy and Andrew are friends. It'll make it all easier for you. . . .' She paused, then said: 'When you have that talk with him.'

Gwynne adjusted the portable screen which sheltered her face from the fire's heat. 'Isn't he a fine young man? I do wish Charles was here to see him and to hear him talk about his hospital. Charles always impressed on Andrew the importance of keeping up with his studies, and he was certainly proved right. Yes, Charles was certainly right.'

Rhys knotted his fists in frustration, recalling how he had flung money in disgust at Charles to pay for the boy's education because the selfish old fool kept Andrew at home to labour in his lettuce fields.

Lisabeth read his face and said quickly: 'Andrew is delighted about the baby, Rhys. He's so nice. It's been a tonic to see him. He's old, though, and this business of losing his wife has knocked him. . . . He seems dazed somehow, defeated. It would be wonderful if you could talk to him soon.'

Rhys barely heard her pleading. Fuming, he wondered what young Jeremy had been doing. He was expecting other news, expecting to hear that Jeremy's proposal had been accepted by Daisy. He'd seemed confident when he reported back to Rhys. 'It came as a bit of a surprise, sir, but I insisted that she think it over, and when I return I know she'll say "yes". I just know she will!'

Rhys wished he could feel so complacent. He wished he could feel enthusiastic about what must be done. At heart he wished he could go back to the hunting party. Catching wild piglets was fraught with danger but was infinitely preferable to facing an old adversary and telling him he was your son.

Avoiding Lisabeth's eye, he said: 'I'll arrange to meet with Andrew in a few days. . . . Next week some time. Silas and I have left the hunting because we have to go south to take a look at the *Dunedin* and to watch her being loaded. We're leaving tomorrow afternoon, after I've set the burn in those hills around the orchard valley.'

'You're not burning them yourself? You're not burning them yourself?' fretted Gwynne. 'Rhys, lad, I wish you'd leave that task to others.'

Rhys kissed the top of her mauve house-cap. 'All these years and to you I'm still a little boy who can't be trusted with a tinder-box. It's a wonder you let me light my own cigars!'

Lisabeth said nothing. She guessed he'd tackle any task in preference to the one he dreaded most.

Meanwhile others were forming their own opinions of Andrew Stafford.

'Look at this!' said Horace Thorne, plonking an empty brandy-bottle down on the desk where Mrs Hogg sat writing a letter to her sister in New South Wales. 'Look! That's the second one the chambermaids have found in his room since he got here. It's no wonder he looks like one of death's angels.'

Mrs Hogg puzzled over how a death's angel might look. Then she said tentatively: 'Amy says Doctor Stafford is a perfect gentleman.'

'How would *she* know?' he asked resentfully. 'When has any sort of a gentleman come calling on her? Anyway, it's not for her to decide. Keep her away from him, d'you hear me?'

She rolled her eyes heavenwards. 'I cannot avoid some contact, Mr Thorne. Doctor Stafford *is* Mrs Morgan's brother. You haven't forgotten that, have you?' She smirked; that made a difference, and she could see it. Horace Thorne was an excellent employer, and really she had no complaints, but his ambitions for Amy were tiresome at times, as was this phobia, this obsession that she was secretly meeting a man. As if Amy would do such a thing. And how could she, under Mrs Hogg's sharp gaze? The notion was ridiculous.

TWELVE

On the day Rhys cut short his hunting excursion, Andrew was hiring a carriage to take Daisy and Beatrice for a drive around the city. 'This is my first outing since the accident, and with Andrew I feel as if it's my first outing ever. Does that make sense to you?'

Beatrice smiled indulgently but she said; 'Dear, you will take things cautiously, won't you? You won't rush headlong into anything. . . . You've only known Andrew a few hours.'

'A few hours? Gracious, it seems forever. I've *always* known Andrew, Aunt Bea, somewhere in my heart, and even when he was telling us all about his wife last night that didn't distress me in the least; it seemed right and proper that his first wife was a good pure woman, who was above being sullied by the coarse and rough aspects of life. That's so romantic, isn't it, Aunt Bea?'

'It doesn't sound like the stuff of good pioneering stock,' said Beatrice tartly, and when she repeated the conversation to Sir Kenneth a few minutes later he roared and slapped his knees in delight. 'I'll wager you a pair of gold ear-bobs that she wouldn't let the coarse rough Doctor sully her precious purity. Loathed sex! Kept the poor wretch at a respectful distance. Romantic, hey? That's a joke! She'd be the kind of woman who ends up getting herself strangled.'

'Kiki, really! Daisy wondered if *she* was pure and good, too.'

'Let's hope not, for her sake,' guffawed Kiki. 'Make her husband's life a misery if she was, hey?'

Beatrice left, offended. The trouble with Kiki was he'd been on the magistrates' bench far too long. Years of rubbing along the seamy parts of life had blunted his sensitivity.

When the carriage arrived Amy was sitting in it. 'I persuaded Mrs Hogg that Doctor Stafford was practically family and, since Father was away at the brewery, here I am!' She whispered to Daisy as she climbed into the

high seat: 'If only Tom was here, it would be perfect. But he's still away
It seems forever. . . .'

'You go without me,' decided Beatrice. 'I've three sacks of summe
bulbs to put in, and if they don't get planted—'

'Would you like us to stay and help you?'

'No, Andrew, please!' chided Daisy. 'I've been so looking forward t
today. I even broke my rule about bothering God over trivialities an
prayed for a fine day. We *must* go!'

'Of course you must,' agreed Beatrice.

Daisy sat beside Andrew, hugging his arm with her good hand. The
other was suspended in a loop of silk scarf. Andrew looked down int
her glowing face in a fog of numb happiness. This girl was a complete
surprise to him, as transparent as the wind and as forceful, unlike an
women he'd met in Europe, nothing like Jane who offered the prospec
of layers and layers of interesting discoveries but who closed, no
opened, herself on their wedding day. Daisy was already open, warm
with sunny approval, flattering in the total rapt attention she paid him
If she wasn't Rhys Morgan's daughter, then he might believe that he
loved her.

Today! thought Daisy, seething with excitement. Andrew hadn't
kissed her yet, but today would be perfect! He'd not told her how he felt
about her, but today he would! It didn't matter that she and Andrew
had met only a few times. What did Aunt Bea know of love? Amy said
she first saw Tom standing on the street corner outside Whelan's Furniture Emporium; she slowed to glance at him unobtrusively, but he
suddenly turned, knocked the packages out of her hands, and when he
picked them up for her that was it. As quickly as that they were in love.

'It's a perfect day for driving,' Amy said, wishing that Tom was here
to share it. The sky was washed with the blue of spring, and because it
had rained in the night the roadside shrubberies and thickets of coppery
ferns glittered in the sunshine.

They drove at a lazy pace through the town's wide muddy streets, past
rows of shops all huddled behind imposing facades and deep verandas,
past the creamy stone Provincial Council buildings and on to the grey
walls of King's College where they paused for a minute at the arched
gateway to look in. Dozens of boys in severe black and white uniforms
were filing out into the quadrangle for break. Andrew said: 'The place
hasn't changed a jot. The trees are taller, that's all. They've probably
got the same old fossils as masters, too.'

'Mr Nye was one of your masters, wasn't he?' asked Daisy.

'Yes,' said Andrew. Something in his tone warned her not to go on.
She had heard that tone before, when she began to talk about Papa and
Lisabeth's wedding.

Next came the tall wooden walls that surrounded the Pleasure Gardens where on summer nights music and the smell of tantalizing food drifted through the air, where there was laughter and excited chatter, where there were boat rides and coconut shies, wheels of fortune and gypsy fortune-tellers, greasy poles and slippery pigs, and at the centre near the organ-grinder and his monkey a carousel with exquisite carved painted horses and a canopy decorated with every colour of the rainbow. Here the nobs of society jostled elbows with the labourers and house-maids, for anybody with a few pence to jingle in their fob came flocking on summer evenings.

Today it was shuttered and looked forlorn. 'We'll come back when it's open, won't we?' pleaded Daisy.

'I won't be able to,' said Amy mysteriously. Her plans were ripening to fruition, and she resented not being able to get Daisy aside to tell her of the latest exciting developments.

'Why not?' asked Andrew.

'I may not be here,' said Amy, wincing with pain when Daisy gave her a warning kick on the ankle. She wasn't playing the game, thought Daisy in irritation. Hadn't Daisy wasted hours and hours in boredom so that Amy and Tommy Nevin could be alone? She'd always kept right out of things; but, now that it was Amy's turn to play gooseberry, instead of feigning deafness she was chipping into the conversation at every chance. And now Amy had put on a sour face for Andrew and her to look at.

'Let's stop here, shall we?' Daisy suggested. 'Let's walk in the park.' She looked at Amy.

'I'll stay here,' Amy said with obvious reluctance. 'My ankle hurts,' she added.

'Really? What is wrong with it, Miss Thorne?'

'Nothing,' said Daisy hastily. 'She just hates walking, don't you, Amy?'

Once under the trees, their feet crunching on the gravel path, Daisy clung to Andrew's arm so that she was leaning against him. Her nerves were strung so tightly that she felt any moment they would snap and she would be soaring free in a kind of giddy bliss. 'Isn't this romantic?' she breathed.

'I suppose so.'

'I mean all this! The stillness of this place – it's like an enchanted glade, isn't it? And see how the river shines in the sun? It looks like a strand of pure gold, doesn't it?'

'Yes. Yes, it does.'

Tugging on his arm so that he stopped and turned to face her, Daisy smiled up into his languid green eyes. She whispered: 'And if you stand very still and very quietly you can hear the ocean far, far in the distance. There! Can you hear it?'

He was looking down into her intense face. 'Do you know what I most regret? I regret being away all these years and not knowing you.'

She looked as if he had given her a present, her skin pink with pleasure, her eyes dancing. 'Oh, so do I! But it doesn't matter now, does it? We're together at last, and the past is forgotten.'

'Is it?' He was not sure what she meant.

'Oh, not the part where you rescued me from the cliff. I'll never forget how brave you were, and that I owe my life to you just as Papa owes his to Mr Day; but all the rest – the waiting for you to come home, the writing love-letters to you and never posting them, the nights of dreaming about you—'

'Daisy!' He was astounded. 'Daisy, please—'

She stopped only to draw breath. She was swept away by the wonder of being alone with him at last, out of sight even of Amy and the coach and the coachman. It was daring and intimate and very, very exciting, too exciting to be wasted. She had to tell him now. This was the moment to declare their love.

'All these years I've thought of you and waited for you to come home. I knew, I *instinctively* knew that it would be like this.' While she spoke her fingers were restlessly plucking and patting at his sleeve. She ached for him to put his arms around her, but for some reason he seemed thunderstruck, as if this moment was too marvellous to be believed. 'It's true, it's all true,' she assured him. 'Look!' And with one trembling hand she fidgeted with the catch of her locket. 'Look at that. See? I even carry your picture with me everywhere I go. Oh, Andrew. . . .' Her eyes moistened with tears. 'Oh, Andrew, I've loved you all my life. You do love me, too, don't you?'

He was bemused, he was captivated. What was there to say? Of course he loved her. He adored her. Who could fail to be moved by such enchantment? When she blindly reached her free hand up to pull his face down to hers he responded swiftly to her touch, crushing her in his arms – though mindful of her injuries – and kissing her eager mouth.

He pulled away almost at once, burned by the sudden realization of what he was doing. 'This is wrong,' he said hoarsely. 'Daisy, forgive me, please.'

'Forgive you?' Her lips still tingled. The kiss may have been brief, but there was a hunger and a passion in it that aroused all her senses. 'Forgive you?' She laughed giddily. 'There's nothing to forgive! This isn't wrong, Andrew. It's—'

'Yes, it is!' He grabbed her shoulders, as much to keep her distant as to emphasize what he was saying. 'It's totally wrong.'

'Because of your wife?'

He shook his head, suddenly struck by remorse. He was supposed to be in mourning, yet apart from answering Daisy's questions the previus evening he hadn't spared a thought for poor Jane since arriving in New Zealand. Horrified and ashamed, he stammered: 'Everything is wrong, Daisy. This. Us being alone together. Talking of love. This . . . intimacy.'

'But you do love me?' The shame in his eyes frightened her. Andrew, tell me you love me, *please!*'

'I can't,' he said unhappily. 'Daisy, please try to understand. I had no idea that you – Daisy, don't cry, please!'

She couldn't stop herself. Tears welled in her eyes, and she kept taring at him, making him witness her pain.

It was more than he could endure. 'Of course I love you; but, Daisy, his *is* wrong. There's your father. . . . I've not even spoken to him yet, and. . . .' His mind dried up at the thought of Rhys and the interview he was dreading. At night when his nerves were fired with brandy he rehearsed what he'd say, how he'd tell Rhys that he wasn't taking back one word of the accusations he'd made over the years. Rhys had dragged Lisabeth's mortal soul through the slime and, while marriage made things right for now, the past could never be erased.

'Oh, *Papa!*' Daisy was saying with relief. She might have expected Andrew to fuss over details. Then the import of his statement swept through her, and she remembered that Beatrice had reassured her that young men always speak to the father before offering a proposal. A proposal! 'That means you intend to ask if you can marry me, doesn't it? Oh, Andrew! Oh, Andrew! I'm alight with joy!'

'It may not turn out the way you expect. Your father and I have a few old scores to settle, and he might not like the idea of—'

'He'll love it!' Her eyes were luminous, her lips parted, and she closed her eyes. 'He already knows that I want to marry you, so he won't refuse. I promise you that.' Guiltily she thought of Jeremy: how she was supposed to be considering his proposal, too. A stab of regret ruptured her happiness, but she thought: *I can't accept everyone, and Andrew needs me more than Jeremy ever could.*

How had this happened? Andrew wondered, dazed. One minute they were strolling innocently down a path and the next, without a shred of intent, he was engaged. It was impossible to restrain her; she was nuggling like a puppy against him, her face warm on his shirt-front and the crown of her green silk bonnet bumping on his chin.

He stroked her back, curiously unmoved by her naïve sensuality. She was a luxury, a beautiful, expensive, out-of-reach luxury suddenly placed in his arms. Nobody had ever adored him before; Jane had permitted him to court her and then allowed him to marry her. He had not been longed for or dreamed about or passionately wanted the way Daisy seemed to want him.

'This is all very unexpected,' he said hoarsely, his voice sounding so

like Rhys's that it startled her. 'We mustn't rush, Daisy. I need time t
adjust, and I don't know how—' He stopped. Somehow he must fin
the words to tell Rhys. 'And there's the mourning. I have to abide by th
proper moral conventions. I'm a very conservative man, Daisy.'

I'm a hypocrite, he thought dismally. Recalling the hostil
judgemental letters he had sent Lisabeth, he was scorched with shame
*I'm no better than them myself! Jane's been dead only a few weeks, an
already. . . .*

'You're a perfect, lovely, wonderful man!' insisted Daisy. She tugge
at his arm. 'Let's go out to Sumner beach and walk along the sea-fron
This is the most glorious day, Andrew, and I wish it would never end.

With Andrew in the centre with a girl on each arm they sauntered pa
the rock groins that were thrusting out from shore to enclose a tid
swimming-pool. 'It's to make us safe from sharks,' explained Daisy
skipping along breathlessly. 'A man's hand washed up near here an
though it was placed by someone who was trying to fake his own death
people at first blamed sharks, so with all the uproar it was decided th
something must be done, and this is it.'

'Must you be so gruesome?' shuddered Amy.

'It's a fascinating story,' said Andrew.

They strolled past a row of pastel-coloured bathing machines, sma
huts on wheels that could be rolled right into the water enabling th
neck-to-knee-clad bathers to emerge and submerge without showing
glimpse of naked ankle or the outline of shrouded limbs.

On past the hotel, past the masts from which signals were hung to te
ships the condition of the bar, whether the tide was running in or ou
and how safe it was for smaller craft to pass over unassisted. Joseph Da
was talking to someone nearby. 'It's *Constable* Day now,' Daisy tol
Andrew before they stopped to say hello. 'Doesn't he look grand in h
uniform?'

At the end of the beach they turned to walk back. Daisy tugged a
Andrew's arm as she paused, catching her breath in a gulp. 'Look!' sh
whispered.

Far to the north, over the ocean but with one end almost touching th
coast, arched a shimmering perfect rainbow. As they watched, it move
very slowly west until it was spanning the coast, then further west aga
over a period of perhaps two or three minutes until the ocean was f
behind it.

'Why do they do that?' marvelled Daisy. 'I often watch them fro
the music-room windows when the weather is right, and they drift i
from the ocean like clouds until they seem to come to rest in the mou
tains. Always they begin at sea and always they travel inland, and the
they slowly melt against the sky. Every time it's the same.'

'There's an ancient Maori legend about that rainbow. He came to New Zealand in one of the canoes of the Great Fleet and landed up the coast there, then made his way inland to one of the mountains where he now lives.'

'That's a beautiful story,' said Amy.

'I remember hearing it from Lisabeth once,' said Daisy.

'The mountain has a name. Let me see if I can remember it. *Tapu . . . Tupu . . .* Yes! *Tupuae o Uenuku*, which means "Footsteps of the Rainbow". It's an odd-looking mountain, with a jagged top like a crown, and at the foot of it is a pretty little timber town all surrounded by forests. Or it used to be. I hear it's pretty much milled out, and there's been a gold rush to the area since I lived there.'

'Lived there?'

'That was long ago, Daisy. Long ago when I was young.' He sounded sad.

'You're still young.' Daisy hugged his arm, looking up at his face which was already dear and familiar to her. 'There's so much I don't know about you,' she said. So much to learn, and her whole life in which to learn it. As she gazed at the fading rainbow she felt that her happiness was complete.

THIRTEEN

It HAD BEEN SO LONG since he had sat on a horse that Andrew could feel every joint in his hips and legs protesting at the unfamiliar strain. *I'll not be able to walk tomorrow*, he thought wryly.

His farm hack was jogging along the tussock-covered plain at the foot of a long high ridge. Behind the horse, bouncing and tumbling at the end of a long rope, dragged a tight blazing bundle of burning tar and straw. Wherever it brushed the ground, dry tussock-stems flared alight. The wind caught the flames and combed them upwards so that the fire went lapping up the slope with a bright ragged edge.

Andrew had also forgotten how beautiful this part of the world was. Mountains, still draped to their toes in snow, stood shoulder to shoulder along the entire horizon like a frieze painted on the blank blue sky. The plains unrolled to the north and south and east, sagging and swelling, cracked by gullies and streams, all the same rich yellow of a baked piecrust.

Rhys was riding ahead with a team of dogs which fanned out over the slopes in search of stray sheep that may have been missed by the muster, though only an occasional rabbit started up and dashed away, alerted by the clamour of barking.

Andrew winced as he adjusted his position in the saddle. *Damn Rhys Morgan*, he thought. This was not how he had planned to spend the day.

When he had arrived at Mists of Heaven in a hired trap just after breakfast Rhys had greeted him with a mixture of warmth and brusqueness. 'You can come and help me,' he said, dispatching Tama to find a set of old clothes. 'We have to torch as much territory as we can while these perfect weather conditions hold.'

Andrew protested. He'd hoped to make his peace and broach the subject of Daisy, then be back at Benares where they expected him for luncheon, but Rhys curtly dismissed his hesitant objections that he had 'things' to discuss and he really didn't see how he could be of much help—

'We can talk all you want when we boil the billy,' Rhys said.

If it hadn't been for Andrew's nervousness, he might have noticed that Rhys was equally uneasy.

Rhys was standing at the library window when Andrew arrived. From behind the lace curtains he watched his son step down and hand the reins to Tama, flipping him a halfpenny for his trouble and dismissing his eager thanks with a word Rhys could not hear.

My son, he thought, probing the words as a tongue probes a toothache. *My son, home at last*.

His emotions were curiously flat. As he waited for Andrew to be shown in he reflected that he had never been able to warm to Andrew as a lad, never liked him as a young man. He wondered how much of that was natural distaste, for all through their earlier association he'd believed that Mary was already pregnant with Andrew when they embarked on their brief affair. Andrew had been a reminder of an episode in Rhys's life that he preferred to forget.

Even after Lisabeth told him the truth he wondered sometimes whether Mary had concocted that story to take revenge on him for abandoning her. At times when he lay awake he wondered if he was really Andrew's father. Was Andrew's birth really so premature? How would it be possible, he wondered, for him to know Andrew for all these years and not realize, not instinctively recognize his own flesh and blood?

When Andrew stepped down from the trap all these doubts dissolved. The sunlight polished Andrew's hair and illuminated his features, so that, in the moment when Andrew took off his hat before stepping on to the porch to greet Lisabeth, Rhys saw himself of twenty years ago. The physical resemblance was undeniable.

All these years he had half-hoped Lisabeth was wrong. Now he knew she was right.

Unlocking the glass-fronted cabinet with a key from his fob-chain, he poured himself a double measure of whisky and downed it with a gulp, relocked the cabinet and busied himself by unwrapping and preparing a cigar. His hands shook, yet he felt nothing. When Andrew came in he was poring over a detailed map of the south-west corner of the estate.

'Welcome!' he said, and swallowed. 'Welcome . . . son.' Then, hurrying on, he said: 'I'm afraid you've caught us at a busy time.'

Andrew said: 'Not much has changed. I remember you as always being busy.'

Rhys laughed, too heartily. Lisabeth was hovering at Andrew's elbow wearing a smile that was at the same time anxious and encouraging. It was a nightmare. What was he expected to do?

131

Rolling up the map, he slid it into a chart-case and clipped the top shut. 'Let's be on our way,' he said. 'Come on, Andrew. I could do with your help.'

'But, darling, surely . . .,' began Lisabeth in dismay.

He bent swiftly to kiss her. 'Take care of yourself. Rest quietly, hey? We'll be back later this afternoon.'

Before she could protest further, he hustled Andrew away.

Every spring a vast part of Mists of Heaven had to be seared by fire so that from the ashes fresh young herbage would regenerate. Sheep couldn't eat the tough old stems, but when the tussock was tender and new they thrived on it. At this time of the year all the sheep were mustered for lambing on the low paddocks while the hills were fired. In a couple of months, at Christmas-time, shearing would begin and then the sheep could be drafted back into the hills where the new pastures would sustain them until autumn. Provided, of course, that there wasn't a drought, or floods, or unseasonal snow.

Proper management was a never-ending tussle, Rhys explained to Andrew as they rode out to the south-west foothills. Food and water supplies had to be kept constant, which meant always planning ahead and trying to anticipate the weather conditions. Keeping vast flocks like these alive was a skill on its own, but at Mists of Heaven they prided themselves on producing superior animals with the finest wool, the tenderest meat.

'All our shepherds are trained in animal husbandry – and are paid accordingly,' Rhys explained as they rode past a milling, bleating herd of ewes and lambs. 'A few years ago we were losing up to ten per cent of lambs at the docking and castrating time. It was a puzzle to me. The McFallishes never lost many, but herds under the care of other shepherds were always badly decimated. Finally we realized that the untrained fellows were using clumsy cutting methods and were not applying Stockholm tar carefully to even the smallest scratch. The lambs were getting listless and dying. Even strong healthy lambs.'

'Blood poisoning,' Andrew said knowledgeably.

'Exactly. Back in those days the shepherds were a queer lonely lot, some of them half-mad with boredom in their isolated huts. We changed all that. Now they live in pairs in better conditions and are trained to notice the first symptoms of every disease that has ever plagued us. Foot rot, nasal bot, ergot staggers, lung worms – our men can spot and treat them all. And, of course, if any sheep dies, it is opened up immediately to ascertain the cause.'

'What about prevention? Do you dose the flocks with anything?' Andrew was interested; holidaying on a farm in Scotland, he had often assisted with sick sheep and cattle.

132

'We dip them after shearing, of course, but otherwise only give them salt-licks and from time to time smear their noses with whale oil if flies are bothersome. Foot rot is the nastiest problem we deal with because it causes pain and it is contagious, but because our land is well drained and usually dry we've been lucky there. "Baron" Windsor, at White Clouds, has huge tracts of swampy land on his property, and he's constantly plagued with it. I saw a whole herd limping there once. No, we're fortunate here.'

'You've worked hard, too,' allowed Andrew, adding: 'I imagine that stock-control – breeding – has quite a rôle to play in a successful operation like this.'

'Definitely. At every mustering-time we cull out a good fifteen per cent of the flock, and of course none but the best breeding stock ever grow old. We imported two hundred pedigreed ewes from Spain a few years back – merinos originated in Spain, as you know – and from them we've developed a fine breeding stock which we cross with Leicesters. They produce beautiful soft wool with an extra-long staple, and the meat makes splendid eating.'

'I hear you've been showing some of your animals and winning prizes at agricultural shows,' said Andrew, deciding to try to steer the conversation around to the topic he wanted to discuss. 'Daisy tells me—'

At the mention of Daisy's name Rhys's face hardened. He seemed to stop listening. One moment he was all attentiveness and the next he was spurring Mazurka forward, opening up a figurative as well as a literal distance between them.

I have to tell him, thought Rhys, angry at himself for his cowardice. As they rode on he found himself remembering the first day he had ever travelled over this property, how enchanted he had been with the richness of the place, the obviously fertile soil, the proliferation of life-giving streams and springs, the clumps of shelter-trees in hollows and gullies and the amazing profusion of bird life. This was all his, he had thought in wonder, his and his sons' and their sons'. *His son.*

I'll have to say something soon, he thought. *I should have told him in a letter*. Yes, a letter. That would have been easy. This was going to be the most difficult thing he ever had to do.

At noon they stopped to eat near a shepherd's hut. These dwellings dotted the property and were so inconspicuous that Andrew would have ridden past without seeing this one. Like the others it was cut into a knoll for summer coolness and winter warmth, the roof made of iron covered with sod over which tussock had grown. All that was visible to the casual passer-by was a length of chimney-pipe protruding from the crown and a low doorway like an igloo's, with a corrugated-iron door.

'We won't go in,' said Rhys. 'It hasn't been used for months and will

133

be swarming with ravenous fleas.' While Andrew gingerly eased himself out of the saddle, Rhys was already scrounging firewood from a stack beside the dog-kennels and setting a fire under a rusty iron tripod. 'The tea and food are in my saddlebags,' Rhys said as he fumbled with a lucifer and a handful of dry tussock shreds. On the ground was a slopping billy, filled back at the stream where they stopped to dismantle the torch and to water the thirsty horses.

Obediently Andrew brought the bundles swathed in tea-cloths but was too exhausted to open them. Instead he lay down, tilting his too-big borrowed wideawake hat forward to shelter his eyes, and through the slice of shade he watched Rhys expertly swing the billy and coax it quickly to boiling with an artfully stacked fire.

'Maximum heat with minimum wood,' said Rhys.

He's nervous, realized Andrew suddenly. *He's as edgy around me as I am around him. But why?*

Andrew knew why he was fidgety. He was still tainted by the hangover that he had woken with after a skimpy fitful sleep, interrupted by long patches where he mulled over the day's extraordinary events. Daisy loved him! Who could have predicted such an amazing thing? At nine o'clock the very notion was incredible, at ten it still seemed far-fetched, and at eleven ludicrous and a little frightening. By midnight he wondered if he was hallucinating, then suddenly his focus sharpened around 1 a.m. and he realized that it was right and proper that Daisy should choose him, and it was his right to declare himself. Nobody, least of all Rhys Morgan, could stand in his way. He was Andrew Stafford after all, a gifted doctor, esteemed, respected, *eminently* respected in his field of diagnostic work. There was nothing at all remarkable about a beautiful, socially prominent and wealthy girl like Daisy Morgan wanting to marry him. The fact that he had little to offer her was quite beside the point.

Boldly he rehearsed how he would approach Rhys and not request but demand Daisy's hand. He'd tell him! Unfortunately, all the grand phrases that flipped so easily from his mind then completely escaped him now, for some reason. All he could remember was the thumping on the walls of his room and the angry abuse as voices shouted at him to be quiet. He'd thought of the perfect words to put Rhys in his place; but now, when he needed those words and the courage to go with them, his mind was empty.

Rhys was throwing a handful of dried tea-leaves into the bubbling billy. His expression was grim. Above him the sky was curdled black and blue, billowing with gigantic bruises. It was cold now that smoke was blocking out the sun's warmth. Andrew was aware of the mountains, glacial with low-draped snow. He wished he was back at Benares, strolling in the garden with Daisy, admiring the swans on the Avon and the trails of weeping willow.

Now, his brain urged him. *Do it now.*

He stood up. 'Sir,' he said. 'You may not be aware of it, but I've visited Daisy several times since I arrived in Christchurch.'

'You've no business to,' said Rhys. He was stirring the billy with a stick.

'I beg your pardon?'

'You've no business to visit Daisy,' repeated Rhys. Unhooking the billy, he poured dark brown tea into two mugs. Tea-leaves floated on the dusty surface.

'But, sir, she was chaperoned,' stammered Andrew. This turn of events rocked him. Of course it was not proper to call on a young woman without her father's consent but, damn it all, this was *Daisy*. He'd known her since she was in her cradle.

'Chaperoned? That froth-brained woman couldn't chaperon a covey of nuns,' snorted Rhys.

Andrew sat down on the bare ground and picked up the bundle Rhys shoved at him, unwrapping it absently. His head throbbed; the sight of the wedges of cheese and thickly buttered bread offended his stomach. Covering them with an edge of the cloth, he took a mouthful of scalding tea instead. When he felt better he said: 'I went to see Daisy when I heard about her injuries, and she asked me to call on her again. You, sir, were not at home, so there was no way of securing your permission.'

Rhys grunted. He was chewing hungrily.

Andrew continued, gathering courage. 'The fact is, sir, that I came out this morning to talk to you about Daisy. I wish to marry her, and—'

'No!' choked Rhys.

'No?' asked Andrew. 'Why not? Daisy—'

'No, never, absolutely not!' roared Rhys in his harsh voice. 'You've been home five minutes and you're sniffing around Daisy. Got an eye on her money no doubt!'

Andrew's scalding tea spilled over his thigh. He hardly felt it. 'Sir!' he hissed, aghast. 'Money is of absolutely no consideration to me at all!'

'So I understand,' sneered Rhys. 'You've been qualified for four years now and still have nothing to show for yourself. What do you do? Give your services free?'

'Often, yes,' said Andrew. 'Poor people get sick, too, you know. I've no desire to be a society doctor and treat imaginary aches and fevers caused by over-indulgence. But Daisy understands my views and she says—'

The mention of Daisy's name inflamed Rhys to ignition point. 'I said "*No*" already!' he shouted, his face contorting. His voice was so loud that the dogs came running from where they rested by the stream; they yelped and barked in a frantic chorus.

Andrew waited while Rhys ordered them back. Then in a tone of deliberate and contrasting politeness he said: 'Sir, you must give me a reason for your attitude.'

'A reason? You want a reason?' countered Rhys.

Andrew nodded. He could think of several reasons. Rhys had never forgiven him for his part in the accidental drowning of his young son Darius all those years ago. Rhys doted on Daisy, his cosseted, indulged only child and he feared that Andrew would be unsuitable as a husband. Or perhaps—

'She's marrying someone else,' Rhys said abruptly.

Andrew gaped at him in disbelief. 'Then, why didn't he say so? Sir, I must tell you that all this is Daisy's idea. I didn't declare myself to her; she proposed to me. If there was this ''someone else'' you mention, why didn't she say so?'

Rhys jumped to his feet, too angry to sit still. The arrogant young whelp! Why didn't he accept a plain blunt rejection? Why did he have to challenge every little detail? He couldn't marry Daisy anyway, so why wouldn't he leave it alone?

He walked over to the fire and squatted in front of it, knotting and unknotting his fists. How could he tell him now? The very prospect made him feel ill.

Andrew was struggling to understand. Certainly he had expected some opposition, but not as fierce or as illogical as this. Why was Rhys so hostile? If Lisabeth was fit to be his wife, surely Lisabeth's brother couldn't be so unsuitable for his daughter?

Carefully choosing his words, he said: 'I can sympathize if you feel animosity towards me because of comments I've made in the past, but surely, sir, you do understand that my sister's well-being is extremely important to me, and when I tried to dissuade her in what God and society would deem to be immoral conduct I was not judging her or you but—'

'For heaven's sake shut up your blathering!' Rhys blurted, wheeling around so suddenly that Andrew flinched.

'I fail to see that explaining myself—'

'Shut up! You always were a sanctimonious prig.' His voice was scratched and raw, but immediately he spoke he saw the tight closed look on Andrew's face and regretted the outburst. Standing up, he turned his back and stared at the mountains and their wide black base of scorched foothills where smoke wisped from the ridges. 'The fact is,' he said wearily, still with his back turned. 'The fact is that you can't ever marry Daisy. I'm your father, Andrew. She's your sister. That's probably why you feel attracted to each other.'

There was a silence. Andrew stared incredulously at the other man's back. He waited. Rhys waited.

'Is that all?' Andrew said at last. 'You're going to tell me that and expect me to believe it, just like that?'

'Why not?' shrugged Rhys. 'It's the truth.'

Andrew snorted. 'You'll stop at nothing, will you? First you throw my poverty up as a barrier, then you lie to me about Daisy already being engaged to someone else, and when that doesn't work, either, you offer an even more ludicrous excuse.'

'It's the truth.' Rhys turned and looked at him. It took real effort, but he forced himself to gaze directly into his son's eyes.

The contact sparked recognition, and horror. Gaping up into the older man's face Andrew felt a void open under his heart. It couldn't be the truth – it *couldn't*.

But in that moment he knew it was.

FOURTEEN

'How?' Andrew asked in a stiff chill voice.

'How do you think? You're a doctor,' snapped Rhys; then, checking himself, he shrugged unhappily. 'I was twenty at the time. A boy. Just a boy. I went to visit Gwynne and Charles. They lived in the bush, on a little farm. Isolated, it was. Your mother lived on the next place. She was lonely. Miserable. . . .' He faltered, then continued. 'We became . . . friends for a little while, then I went away. I didn't know about you.'

'Another lie,' challenged Andrew.

'The truth. When I did learn of your existence, I never suspected. . . . How could I? You were born prematurely . . . very prematurely, and I thought . . . I assumed . . . I just didn't want to think about it. It was only a few years ago that Lisabeth told me. Believe me, I. . . .' He stopped.

Andrew was no longer listening. *Dear God!* he thought in horror. Twisting around, he bent his head as a flood of sour bile rose in his throat. Helpless to stop himself, he retched weakly as loathing and disgust churned out of him. For a while he stayed there heaving on hands and knees, then crawled away, his body shaking like an empty paper bag. He groped for a handkerchief to wipe his mouth, then realized he was in borrowed clothes and had none, so tugged off the neck bandana and scrubbed his mouth with that instead. He felt indescribably filthy. For the rest of his life, whenever he smelt smoke-impregnated cloth he would remember this moment and recoil in disgust.

'Are you all right?' asked Rhys.

Andrew pushed himself to his feet. The sky swung crazily around his head, then settled on its horizons. Andrew sucked in a deep breath. The pounding inside his skull intensified.

'You utter bastard,' he gasped. 'You immoral putrid bastard. How dare you call me a sanctimonious prig after what you've done? You've soiled Lisabeth's name, dragging her through your slime, and now you

138

have the gall to tell me you soiled my mother, too. Worse than that, you probably *killed* her.'

'I say, easy on,' warned Rhys.

Andrew's voice rose. 'I'll tell you what I *do* know about my mother. She died frightened and poor and alone, and when I was born she'd been a widow for months. Yes, that I do know – Gwynne and Charles both told me that. She was a *widow*; so, if she was good enough to satisfy your despicable appetites, why wasn't she good enough to be made an honest woman of? Ah! I suppose you thought *she* had designs on your money! Yes, I suppose that's why I've been kept in the dark all this while. No doubt you're terrified I'll be after your money, too. If you acknowledge me as your son, I could pester you for a handout. That's why I was never told the truth.'

Struggling to control his anger, Rhys said: 'I didn't know, I swear. Can't I even convince you by—?'

'Don't even try!' Andrew's lip curled. 'All those years at King's College when you paid for my education. Don't try to tell me you didn't know. Hell, but you disgust me! You're a rutting dog, that's what you are. The gutter is where you—'

He was so crazed with rage that he didn't see the punch coming. When Rhys's control snapped and he swung out – to shut Andrew up as much as anything – Andrew was leaning aggressively towards him, his eyes glazed with hostility. The fist hit him squarely on the chin.

He was lifted completely off his feet and fell sprawling on to his back. He was astonished more than hurt; but as soon as that initial blank numbness faded the rage came seeping back, and when he scrambled to his feet it was with murder in his heart. Propelling himself at Rhys, he dashed out with bunched fists, flailing with every ounce of pent-up frustration.

Rhys tried only half-heartedly to defend himself. He was instantly sorry that he had knocked Andrew down. The lad couldn't be blamed for his violent reaction. It was understandable that without all the facts he would leap quickly to such damning conclusions. When he'd calmed down they would be able to sit down together and talk the whole thing out, then hopefully walk away as friends. That was Rhys's thought as Andrew staggered to his feet.

Before he could utter one conciliatory sentiment Andrew was battering him. 'Stop!' Rhys cried, fending off the blows with crossed forearms, a posture intended to signal that he was not wanting to fight.

Andrew ignored him. He may not have had Rhys's packed muscular strength or his solid frame, but Andrew had one insurmountable advantage: thorough knowledge of the human body. He placed three blows with unerring accuracy, the first to the groin – *that* with grim satisfaction – then as Rhys crumpled forward Andrew chopped an edge of the hand to his Adam's apple, then swiftly another chop to the side of the neck.

Rhys sagged without a sound. Bending over him, Andrew paused only to check his pulse; then, dusting his hands together, he marched over to his horse and jerked the reins free from where they were tied to a clump of tussock.

Without looking back he galloped away.

He was still seething when he tossed the reins to Tama and clattered up the steps. Lisabeth was in the drawing-room hem-stitching a delicate white garment. She smiled when she saw him.

'Look, do admire this for me,' she said, holding it up. The garment had a tiny pin-tucked bodice and a disproportionately long skirt trimmed with three rows of inset lace and more pin-tucks. 'Aren't I clever?' she said happily. 'Oh, Andrew, I'm so excited about the baby and so pleased that you'll be here to—' Glancing at him again, she saw his expression. 'Why, darling, what is it?'

'Look at you, all dirty,' said Gwynne. Even though he had been grown-up and away for a dozen years Gwynne still thought of him as the little boy she had raised from an orphan baby. She scolded: 'Look at you, those dirty clothes in here. And those boots! Charles never came inside with—'

'What is it?' whispered Lisabeth urgently.

She knows what 'it' is, thought Andrew. *Look at the guilty expression in her eyes. She knows.*

Lisabeth stood up and placed her hands protectively over her stomach. In a queer voice she said: 'Gwynne, dear, would you please excuse us?'

Gwynne frowned, squinting from one to the other through her ugly pebble lenses. 'There's been trouble, hasn't there? There's been trouble,' she said. 'The fire! Rhys is caught up in the fire again. Ever since the last time when he almost died he's had that weakness in his lungs, you know. You can tell me, lad. You can tell me if—'

'It's all right, Aunty Gwynne. There's been no accident, truly. I just need to talk to Lisabeth alone.'

'We'll go out into the garden,' suggested Lisabeth.

'I'll leave, I'll leave.' Gwynne put her knitting aside. 'I do know when I'm not wanted. I do know. . . .' Huffing and mumbling, she left the room, her mauve train twitching behind her.

'Oh dear! We've offended her,' said Lisabeth, smiling wryly at her brother. His expression stopped her.

'Well?' he said.

Lisabeth shook her head. She looked frightened.

'Why wasn't I told?'

'Oh, Andrew, please don't be angry.'

140

'Don't be *angry*?' He was incredulous. 'Do you know what's happened? Daisy has *proposed* to me. She's fallen in love with me, for
heaven's sake. Have you any idea what this is going to do to her?'

'Andrew, please.' She clutched at his sleeve, her face white. 'Please
don't say anything to Daisy. Rhys is so worried about what she might
think of him. He paces the floor at night—'

'He *should* worry, too! He has every reason to, just as Daisy has every
right to know the truth. Lisabeth, how could you get yourself involved
with a man like him?'

'He's a wonderful man,' Lisabeth flared. 'He's kind and good and fun
to be with. Really, Andrew, just because of what's in the dead past you
mustn't judge him so harshly.'

His lips twitched. Seeing his cold unforgiving expression, Lisabeth
knew how he must have looked when he penned the critical letters to
her. His eyebrows would have been drawn together *so*, and his lips would
have pursed sternly as he wrote that she must abandon her life of sin. For
a moment it seemed that he could not speak, but then he said sarcas-
tically: 'Yes, I should forget the dead past, shouldn't I? I should forget
that my mother – *our* mother – was seduced and abandoned, abandoned to die broken-hearted. I should forget that Daisy and I have both
been kept in ignorance of the facts so that what now looks like a cruel
trick has been perpetrated on us both. I should forget that the only reason I've been kept uninformed is that His Majesty Rhys Morgan is
worried about what his daughter will think of him. Good grief, Lisabeth!
No wonder the whole province laughed at those scurrilous pamphlets
about us. We must be the joke of the century!'

Bright spots of colour stood out in her cheeks. 'I don't blame you
for being angry,' she whispered. 'Only, darling, please try not to
judge. Nobody in the history of the world has ever led a blameless life.
Even Jesus Himself made mistakes, and it was He who urged us to judge
not. Please try to forgive Rhys. It will be so sad for all of us if you
can't.'

For a moment Andrew was swayed by her impassioned plea, then he
reminded himself that she was only begging in order to protect Rhys. She
was as guilty as he in this.

'Why?' he demanded. 'Why wasn't I told? Why didn't the bastard
acknowledge me? Why didn't you insist on it?'

'For a long time he didn't know. And then he thought it best to tell
you face to face. This unfortunate business about Daisy – it wouldn't
have happened if Rhys had been here when you arrived. He planned all
along to tell you as soon as he saw you again.' Her green eyes filled with
tears; she looked old and harried and unspeakably sad. 'Please promise
you won't tell Daisy. Rhys intends to tell her, but you had to know first. I
insisted on that. Please, darling. You must appreciate how difficult it's

going to be . . . what it's going to cost him. You're angry and upset. It wouldn't be right to fling it at her when—'

Cutting in abruptly, Andrew said: '*You* knew, Lisabeth. You must have known all along. Why didn't you tell me?'

She swallowed. 'I knew, but I was afraid. Terrified. I loved you so much. Aunty Gwynne and Uncle Charles adopted us, but you were mine. I looked after you, fed you, bathed you. Aunty Gwynne used to complain that I never let anybody else near. I was afraid, right from the beginning, that if Rhys knew he was your father he would claim you and snatch you away. Then, later, I never told because I hated him for what he'd done to Mamma.'

'He was barely starting then,' Andrew said nastily. 'Look at what he's done since, to you and me and to Daisy.'

Lisabeth flinched. 'Rhys has never done one single unkind deed to anybody in all the time I've—'

'Save it,' snapped Andrew in disgust. 'Save it for Daisy. She might believe you. You say you hated him, Lisabeth. I want you to know that your hatred is nothing, *nothing* compared to how *I* feel.'

'But I was wrong,' pleaded Lisabeth. He turned to go, but she hurried after him, agitated. 'I was quite wrong, Andrew, and you are, too. Believe me, Rhys has never—'

He wasn't listening. With one gesture of contempt he flung the door open and with another he banged it shut behind him.

As the door swung shut Andrew glanced back. Lisabeth was crying, her cheeks slick with tears, hands spread over her swollen stomach.

With the reverberating slam echoing in his head Andrew thought: *I may never see her again. That child she is carrying is another of my brothers or sisters, and I may never see it.* He wanted to open the door again and rush to embrace Lisabeth, urge her to take care, tell her that he loved her, but with his hand already twisting the door-knob he was halted by the sour realization that if he rushed to console her she would immediately use his weakness as a lever to plead Rhys's cause again.

As he stumbled from the passageway Gwynne came hobbling across the hall's marble floor, her face pinched with worry. 'Andrew, what is it? What is it? Something *has* happened to Rhys, hasn't it?'

'No,' Andrew told her shortly. The very name *Rhys* aggravated his sour anger.

Her arthritic claws clutched at his jacket. 'I *know* something terrible has happened. It's the dizziness. It always tells me, always. This morning when you and Rhys left I had such a dizzy feeling – such a dizzy ominous feeling. Your Uncle Charles always said I knew when something terrible was about to happen. You can tell me, Andrew. You can tell me.'

'Well, your dizziness is wrong this time,' Andrew told her, amused in spite of his urge to brush off her clinging hands and hurry away from this

142

place. 'I'd say that dizziness is caused by a surfeit of those tonic wines you've been dosing yourself with.' He paused, suddenly aware of how much he loved her. Silly old thing with her head addled by superstitions and her adoration of that lazy, grasping old bastard Charles – yes, he loved her. Grasping her shoulders, he smiled down into her puckered owlish face, permitting himself a moment of tenderness.

'If it wasn't for you, Lisabeth and I would have been brought up in a workhouse, wouldn't we?' he said. 'You insisted on taking us in when Mamma died, me a baby and Lisabeth a young girl. We owe you—'

'No, dear, not me,' she said positively. 'It was your Uncle Charles who insisted that we give you a home. He was the one who—'

Andrew laughed; he knew better. 'If you say so,' he said, giving her a hug, his eyes welling with sentimental tears. He'd likely never see her again, either. Turning swiftly, he left the house.

A sense of loss and isolation lay heavily in his heart as he drove back towards town. In the space of a few hours he had lost all his family and the dazzling young woman who had fallen in love with him. Even when he had stood in the hot South African sun at his wife's graveside he had not felt as alone and bereft as he did right now.

When Lisabeth heard the racketing of hoofs in the drive she started up out of her chair in relief. 'That's Rhys now,' she told Gwynne sharply, for the older woman's bleating about 'trouble' had frayed her nerves to snapping-point. 'I told you he was all right.'

But it was Carthew who came pattering along the corridor, her small dark eyes glinting with the drama of the occasion. 'It's young Mr Drake! And there's been an accident!' she reported.

Lisabeth closed the door to shield Gwynne from this news. Automatically she placed her hands over her stomach, feeling ill with apprehension.

He was in the library, standing with his back to the door. When he turned she gasped, for the side of his face was an oozing grazed mass, one eye purpled and swollen as a tropical fruit, his nose spread and puffed, the nostrils bloody slits.

Seeing her horror, he tried to smile, the effort making him wince with pain. 'It's not as bad as it looks, Mrs Morgan.'

'Not as bad . . .?' To Carthew she said: 'Fetch me a bowl of water and some bandage, and the dark blue bottle marked "Calendula", please. Quickly.' To Jeremy: 'Did you fall from your horse?'

He shook his head, grimacing. 'I don't wish to impose, but I'm not feeling very bright. Could I please trouble you for a glass of brandy?'

'Of course. Of course.' She was confused, trying to sort things out in her mind. Jeremy hadn't been with Rhys. Jeremy was supposed to be still

143

on the wild-pig expedition. 'This accident, it's nothing to do with Rhys, is it?' she said, handing him a stemmed glass.

'Nothing whatsoever.'

'Oh, thank goodness for that.' She sat down abruptly and rested her forehead in her hands. Looking up again, she said: 'I'm sorry. Please forgive me, only . . . Rhys is late. He was supposed to be back hours ago because he arranged to meet your father in town. They were catching the evening train to Dunedin, and your father has telephoned. . . .' She was shaking now, with the force of her accumulated worry.

'I'll go and look for him at once.' Jeremy set the glass on the mantelpiece.

'No . . . no! I mean, yes, please, would you? Only, let me bathe your face first, while you drink your brandy. Carthew can ask Tama to saddle up a fresh horse for you.'

While she dabbed the tinctured water on his punctured face he told her what had happened. Lowell Windsor had died this morning, horribly, after being gored by a wild boar. When Jeremy and one of the Aboriginal stockmen rode into White Clouds with the body 'Baron' Windsor met them in a shrieking fit of uncontrolled rage. 'He took the news very badly – as if it was all my fault. Before I could finish describing what had happened he punched me in the face, knocking me down, then lashed into my face and body with his boots and riding-crop. There were about a dozen blackfellows standing around in the field where this took place, and none tried to help; they all just cowered away, cringing, while I struggled to escape. Still, he might have killed me, so I'm lucky just to have bruises and cuts.'

'Are you in much pain?'

He saw the concern on her face and was immediately guilty. In her condition she should be protected from unsavoury matters like this ugly brawl. He was glad he'd kept back a few details: how Lowell had walked calmly right into the path of the charging boar as if he welcomed death; how 'Baron' Windsor had wept and howled as if he was receiving, not inflicting, the pain. It was as if a wife or mistress had died, not his nephew from England.

'In pain?' repeated Jeremy. 'It's not much of a pleasure to laugh, Mrs Morgan, I can tell you that.'

While Gwynne aggravated Lisabeth with her repetitious bleatings about Rhys, back at Benares an anxious Daisy was waiting for Andrew. She pleaded with Beatrice to delay luncheon (a celebration luncheon), and when finally it was served at two o'clock she fled from the table, too upset to eat.

'First she ruins a perfectly good cutlet by making it wait an hour, then she won't taste it!' grumbled Sir Kenneth, irascibility covering his concern.

'She's in love,' sighed Beatrice as Daisy paced along the gravel path. 'Look, Excalibur is romping at her heels and snapping at the hem of her gown, but she's too upset to notice.'

Daisy was still restless, still fretful, when Amy arrived at afternoon-tea time. 'You cheer her up,' advised Beatrice, taking a wedge of apple cake and leaving the two girls together in the morning room. She strolled out to find Kiki, secretly worried by Andrew's failure to arrive. Was he really a 'bolter' as Kiki maintained? Was he jilting poor Daisy?

Daisy had never felt less like welcoming her friend, and responded irritably when, as soon as they were alone, Amy seized her hands and hissed: 'It's so exciting! The time has come at last.'

'What time?' Daisy pulled her hands free. For her it was past time; Andrew should have been here five hours ago.

'My elopement! I'm going to burst, I'm so happy! Tom came back, and he passed me a note and he whispered: "Ut's Sutterday, me darlin'." ' She giggled, her dark eyes alight, her bony face flushed and almost pretty. 'He's organized everything, and it will be so romantic. There'll be a priest, and flowers, and Tom's even paid for a slap-up dinner in one of the back rooms of the Duke of Wellington hotel. The proprietors are new there and don't know Father, so there'll be no tales told. We're to have oysters and roast beef, sherry trifle *and* a bottle of real champagne. I can't wait! Are you going to pour the tea or are we going to sit here and look at the cosy? All this excitement is giving me a raging thirst. I say, Daisy, don't look like that, *please*. I'd ask you to the wedding if I could, truly, and I'm heartbroken that you're missing it. I'd love to have my dearest friend in all the world with me at the big moment and afterwards when we'll celebrate, but who would bring you to the likes of Tommy Nevin's wedding?' She plucked the embroidered cosy from the tea-pot and began pouring into the blue china cups, her voice hardening to a sharp edge as she continued: 'Mind you, I've been looked down on all my life, one way and another, so I'm used to it, but it won't be for much longer, you can mark that on the slate! People in this province will be looking up to Tom Nevin soon. . . .' Handing Daisy a cup, she poured one for herself, giggling: 'We're even having a honeymoon! Imagine that! Tom is taking me up north with a load of goods he has to sell. Valuable things he doesn't want to trust in others' care. He's conscientious like that, Tom is. The town we're off to is inland, so we have to travel in a bullock wagon. Tom says it'll be rough, and I'll feel exactly like the contents of a butter-churn by the time we get there, from all the jolting, but—' She stopped, shocked. 'Daisy, you're *crying*.'

Tears brimmed in her eyes, her lower lip trembled, while in her quaking hands the cup slopped and shook. Amy took it from her. 'Daisy, what is it?' she whispered. 'Have I upset you by telling—?'

'*No!*' It was less a word than a choking sound. 'I'm pleased for you,

Amy, truly. I know you love Tommy and this is what you want. It's . . . it's Andrew! He promised to go out and talk to Papa this morning and to be back by lunch-time, but he . . . he. . . .'

Amy inhaled a crumb of coffee biscuit and coughed as she gasped: 'I'm sorry . . . I'm so sorry, Daisy!' When she had recovered from her spluttering fit she poked two fingers down into the pink gown's modest neckline and from her cleavage withdrew a rolled paper tube. 'Doctor Stafford gave me this. I'm so sorry, Daisy, but he gave it to me earlier this afternoon – he followed me out into the back garden when I went out to toss a skittle for the dog to fetch – and he made me promise to give it to you. I don't understand. Lady Launcenolt hasn't stopped him coming here, has she?'

'Shush,' said Daisy, reading. The note was brief, she had scanned it in half a minute, read it a second time more slowly, then gazed up at Amy. 'This doesn't make any sense at all! Here, see if you can understand it.'

Amy read aloud, but in a low tone. ' ''Dearest Daisy, I regret to say that matters between us have become irredeemably complicated. I am unable to explain the situation, but your father will acquaint you with all the details if you ask him. I am leaving today, and do not plan to return. Please understand that this development is not of my making. You and I are innocent victims in an irrevocable tragedy. Your servant, Andrew.'' ' She frowned, staring at the neatly penned signature. 'What a peculiar letter. What do you suppose he means?'

'Let's ask him,' Daisy decided. 'Where is your carriage?'

'Outside. But we can't go haring after him in that. Mrs Hogg is sitting there with her crochet.'

'Then, I'll lure her inside . . . tell her that Lady Launcenolt wants to know if she'll take tea.'

'She may be simple but she'd never believe that,' retorted Amy. 'I'll tell you what. . . . I'll go back to the hotel now, find out what I can, and then you telephone me in an hour.'

It was all bad news. When Daisy rang Amy reported that Andrew had left the hotel in the early afternoon, and nobody knew where he had gone.

Jock McFallish and Jeremy found Rhys at once, drawn by the racket of his dogs who were grouped around him. He was alive but unconscious.

'He can't have fallen from his horse,' wondered Jeremy. Mazurka was nearby, tethered to a clump of tussock. Leaning over Rhys, he examined his face, which was unmarked apart from the dribble of bloody saliva that trickled from one corner of his mouth. He shook his head, baffled. This was a day of violence, and he was sickened by it. 'Let's get him back home. The doctor can worry about what happened,' he said.

When Gwynne rushed out to see them lowering a slumped and

146

apparently lifeless Rhys from his horse she threw her mauve apron over her face and screamed herself rigid. 'I knew it, I knew it!' she wailed.

'He's nae dead, missus,' explained Jock to Lisabeth who was grasping the door-frame for support. 'The master's alaive as I am.'

'We think it could be his throat,' Jeremy said to Lisabeth as they laid him on a chaise-longue in the morning room. She was weeping as she undid his boots, a gesture that moved him in its intimacy. Love was a palpable thing between those two fine people, and often when they looked at each other Jeremy felt he was intruding on a private moment. Avoiding her eyes, he said: 'There was some blood around his mouth, but he doesn't seem to be cut, and his breathing sounds odd – constricted in some way. There it is, that wheezing noise.'

'He never should have gone to burn off, he never should have gone to burn off,' muttered Gwynne. 'It's this house, you know. It brings bad luck to everyone who lives in it! Never build a house from white stone, young man! It's fit only for gravestones!'

'Please, Mrs Stafford. . . .' Jeremy caught the stricken look on Lisabeth's face.

'He must have fallen from his horse,' she said. 'It must have happened after Andrew left. They quarrelled, and Andrew came back here alone. This must have happened after that.'

Andrew? Andrew Stafford? I should have expected this, he thought. Slowly he said: 'Yes, that's what it must have been.'

'If only Andrew were still here,' she fretted. 'Andrew would know at once what was wrong with Rhys.'

'He probably would,' said Jeremy.

Carthew tapped at the door. 'Excuse me, ma'am, but Doctor Meakings is on his way now.'

'I asked you to call Doctor Stafford. At the Golden Fleece.'

'Excuse me, ma'am, but he's not there. So I called Doctor Meakings instead.'

Jeremy's mind was seething. He knew, or guessed, what might have happened out on the plains. Trying to sound casual, he asked: 'How long has Doctor Stafford been in town?'

'Long enough . . . long enough for this disaster to overtake us all,' blurted Lisabeth, stroking her husband's soot-striped face. She was crying hard now. 'Oh, Rhys, oh, Rhys, why did we let it come to this?'

Come to what? wondered Jeremy.

She raised her bleak face. 'Jeremy, please, would you go to see Daisy, and tell her about this? And would you see if you can find Andrew?'

'I most certainly shall,' he assured her.

FIFTEEN

'THIS IS incredible!' said Daisy, getting up from the parlour sofa and walking across the room to a waist-high display-table where she stood absently stroking the dome of the miniature Taj Mahal, an alabaster model that had been presented in recognition of Sir Kenneth's twenty-five years on the Bench. She looked ludicrously sensual, as if she was fondling a single perfect breast. Despite his frustration with her, despite his anger, he was strongly aroused by what she was doing.

She was unaware of any sexual overtones in her actions. 'This is impossible of you, Jeremy! I'm sorry to hear about Lowell – that's terrible news – and I'm sorry you fell off your horse and hurt your face, and I'm even sorry that Papa is ill, but I'm not going out to Mists of Heaven with you to see him, and I'm not going to answer any of those insulting questions about Andrew. Jeremy, you simply don't know what's been happening here.'

She spoke in a hard flat voice. From the moment he arrived and she had to smother her disappointment that it was him and not Andrew, she had felt like shrieking aloud. Her life was ruined. Andrew had abandoned her, and the worst of it was that she had no idea, either, what had been happening.

She could guess, she could surmise all right. Papa was anxious to marry her off to Jeremy. *He's delighted, Daisy. Mrs Morgan is thrilled, too. He's giving us five hundred acres of his best grazing-land.* Papa had always disliked Andrew, and wouldn't welcome the thought of him as a son-in-law when he had already given his blessing to his business partner's son. Oh, yes, it was easy to picture what had happened between Papa and Andrew, how Papa had sent him packing. *It serves him right*, she thought. *It serves him right if he is ill now. An attack of conscience, perhaps!*

'Andrew must have been there when it happened,' Jeremy was saying. 'He was out in the hills with your father, and when Jock McFallish and I found him your father was lying injured on the ground. Mrs Morgan thinks he fell from his horse, and I've let her think that, but it's not how it happened at all. His horse was tethered.'

'It might have kicked him,' she said, both hands cupping the alabaster dome. 'Or he suffered from smoke inhalation. He almost lost his life in a fire once, and ever since then—'

'It wasn't either of those things,' he said, crossing his legs. She was driving him crazy with what she was doing. 'He was hit, Daisy. Struck. Not by the horse; it was too far away. Someone beat him, Daisy. Hit him in the throat and left him lying there. He could have died if we hadn't found him.' He paused. 'Please, Daisy. Tell me where Doctor Stafford went, and why he ran away.'

'Ran away?' She flung around to face him, and he could see that the logic of his implications hit her on a raw nerve. 'You're *accusing* Andrew, aren't you? You're saying that he hit Papa and left him lying injured. Well, you've no right to suggest such a monstrous thing! Get out of here, Jeremy! Get out and don't come back! I never want to see you again. I never. . . .'

Before she could finish he was confronting her, grabbing her shoulders to shake her. She struck out at him, her soft blows stinging his tender face and ribs, goading his anger. Crushing her hands in his, he pinned them behind her back so that her body arched into his. His penis lay hard against the swell of her belly, but he made no effort to pull away to protect her feminine modesty – the decent thing to do – nor did he care that his face was bruised and ugly, nor that there was indignation and fear in her eyes. If she was going to scream at him like a fishwife, then he'd damned swell treat her like one.

Without a word he covered her mouth with his and kissed her savagely, forcing her mouth open and shoving his tongue against hers. Her body spasmed with shock, small sips of breath hissed through her nostrils and with one foot she kicked at his ankles. He laughed in his throat and relaxed his grip on her, gentling his mouth so that it moved with luxurious softness now. She shivered; her breath flowed out of her, and her mouth responded to his. Only when he was satisfied that their kissing was equal did he let go, and then his leaving of her was in an abrupt movement that had her sagging and fumbling hastily for a chair-back to support herself. Pausing only to read her expression, he turned, still without a word, and was gone.

Above the whisper of a brush of rain on the roof she heard the front door bang. Through the blurred window she saw him hurry to the gate, Excalibur yapping behind him. 'Jeremy!' she called, but he did not hear. She rapped on the glass, but he was gone.

Sinking to the window-seat, she leaned her forehead to the cold pane, staring gloomily after him. She told herself that she wanted him to come back and explain what he had meant. It couldn't be true, what he said about Andrew. He was a doctor, dedicated to healing people, not to hurting them. Besides, though it was disloyal to Andrew to think it, Papa was much stronger and fitter, and had there been a fight it would be Andrew lying unconscious on the ground. No, there must be some other explanation.

And Jeremy must have come here hoping to sow doubts in her mind against Andrew. If he was driven to such depths, then he must love her with an overwhelming passion. She hugged herself, reliving the pressure of his body against hers, feeling a pleasurable warm restlessness at the pit of her belly. Why was it that Jeremy stirred her, excited her and infuriated her so strongly when she knew so positively that Andrew was the right one for her? And why, when she was so sure of him, had Andrew deserted her?

The slithering wetness on the window echoed her self-pity. Looking out at the empty garden, she felt a vast emptiness widen inside her. Why had he gone without at least talking to her? And where had he gone to? His summary rejection and Jeremy's abrupt departure combined to make her feel mean and unworthy.

The wind was rising now. She had hunched here so long that her face was numb; her eyes ached with cold as she gazed out at the watery sky where the wind was scraping great gobs of dirty scum away to show the blue beneath. Sunlight shone weakly on the distant foothills and, while Daisy watched, a rainbow materialized out of the grey, poising in a perfect arch above the hills.

Daisy stirred, scratching the upper edge of her bandage where the skin was itching. She needed no reminders of Andrew, she decided, turning away. He'd been talking about rainbows on the last afternoon, talking about the legend of the rainbow, the mountain and the pretty town that lay beneath it. Of course! She turned back, staring at the rainbow again. That was the answer. In the footsteps of the rainbow. That's where Andrew had gone.

The Duke of Wellington hotel stood bare and peeling at an intersection of two wide muddy streets. Daisy stood on the tarred pavement opposite and studied it doubtfully. Hitched to the rail outside several horses switched their tails against early flies, while in the adjacent street a man on a ladder was working with paint-pot and brush to freshen the hotel's scarlet name-board. Nearby stood a high-laden wagon with two draught horses between the propped shafts.

She paused, uncertain, wondering if she was too late, for there was no sign of the ox-cart Amy had described.

Rightness of purpose tightened her grip on her valise and on Excalibur's lead. There was no turning back now. In a few hours Kiki and Aunt Bea would return from Mists of Heaven and find her note. She quailed to think of the lies she'd written, of the excuses she'd made to get out of going to visit Papa, but smothered her guilty pangs with the reassurance that when she returned with Andrew they would see her happiness and understand.

Perhaps Albert had found the note already and was prising it open to read it. He'd be capable of that. Left at Benares to look after her, he'd tagged at her side until she insisted that she wanted to rest, whereupon he retreated to the service yard below her window to busy himself by polishing Sir Kenneth's already spotless boots. As he worked he sang the undulating moaning songs of his home village in Uttar Pradesh, and as he sang he dreamed of the life he had once known but never would again. It had been easy for Daisy to pack a few items of clothing into her carpet bag, don her warmest clothes and stoutest boots, and on the way out to collect Excalibur's plaited lead from the hat-rack inside the front door. He was, as usual, lurking inside the privet hedge, from where he could rush out to bark at passers-by.

Daisy tugged at his lead. 'Come on, boy. We'll ask how long they've been gone,' she said, as picking her way between the puddles of yesterday's rain she crossed to the potholed pavement opposite. Hesitating, she stared at the laden wagon.

The man on the ladder was whistling. When she looked up he winked at her. 'Foine lookin' beast yer got there, miss!'

'Excuse me, please,' she said. 'But do you happen to be acquainted with the owner of this wagon?'

'Oi?'

'Excuse me, but do you happen—?' She stopped, then said: 'Whose wagon is this?'

'Oi dunno,' he said, applying a slick line of paint to the huge W. 'Some feller just got wed, oi think.'

'Thank you! Oh, thank you!' Without lingering Daisy opened an iron gate and slipped into the alley that ran between the hotel and a shuttered-up Government Stores building next door. A back room, Amy had said. Daisy hoped it was one of the downstairs ones.

The alley stank so strongly of warm urine that Daisy hitched her skirts higher from the ground, awkwardly managing her bag with one hand and dragging at Excalibur, who preferred to linger and sniff, with the other.

After a short distance the alley opened on to a littered square yard, half of which was fenced off to enclose a pen where an enormous sow lay blissfully sunbathing. Excalibur growled, dashing towards the pen and barking when the lead jerked him up short. A door flapped open and a middle-aged woman in a long white pinafore and white mob-cap emerged with a bucketful of vegetable scraps. The sow was already up and squealing, but the woman stopped, raked Daisy with a haughty look and demanded to know what she wanted.

'Mr and Mrs Nevin,' blurted Daisy. 'I'm seeking the whereabouts of Mr and—'

''Eard you first time. Go in that way, will do. Third door to yer right. 'Oller loud if yer can't find 'em.' She called out as Daisy mounted the rickety steps: 'Yer can't take 'im in there. Guv'nor would 'ave a fit. 'Itch 'im ter the rail there.'

'It's Daisy!' cried Amy in surprise. Wriggling from Tom's embrace, she jumped up from the sofa and hastily buttoned up the front of her white satin blouse. 'Tom, it's Daisy, come to our wedding celebration. Go on, let her in.'

'Just hush and maybe she'll go away,' suggested Tom. He held out his arms to her. 'Come back here, wife. We've only got thus room for a few wee munnuts. Let's not waste unny of ut.'

'She's a *guest*. Every wedding needs guests,' Amy told him. Her hair smoothed into place, she opened the door.

'Hello,' said Daisy, venturing in timidly and seeing Tom's scowling face. She wasn't welcome, she could see that. 'Congratulations, Tom. Is that the right thing to say? Or should it be "Felicitations"?'

'Whut about "Gudbye"? That ud sound foine,' muttered Tom.

'Oh, please, Tom!' Amy rushed to tuck her arm through Daisy's, and the two women faced him, Amy appealing, Daisy grim but frightened.

'Whut brings you here?' Tom wanted to know.

'I brought you a wedding present.' Placing her bag on a chair, she produced a cut-glass bowl which she had purchased on the way over. It was still wrapped in the newspaper the shopkeeper had put around it.

Amy was delighted. 'A gift! Oh, Tom, that sets the seal on the day, a gift from my dearest friend. Sit down, Daisy. Tom will pour you a glass of champagne. Here, Daisy, have some sherry trifle. We ate all the oysters, but there's some roast beef left if you want. I'm so glad you're here. A guest makes everything proper and respectable somehow.'

'Ay, ut's respectable now, all right!' grumbled Tom, thrusting a glass at Daisy. 'Sup ut down quickly, not to waste the bubbles,' he instructed.

Daisy raised the foaming glass to her lips. The champagne had a yeasty smell, and the bubbles tingled against her mouth, reminding her of the sensation Jeremy's fingertips had aroused when he stroked her lips. She gulped, coughed, and set the glass down while she groped for her handkerchief. When her throat relaxed sufficiently for her to speak she said: 'Are you two travelling north now?'

'Cud be.' He tucked his thumbs into his lapels and rocked back on his heels. Already he looked the image of a prosperous businessman in his three-piece worsted suit, linen shirt with starched collar and cuffs and a blue silk tie that looped through a triple gold ring at his throat. Across his chest stretched a gold watch-chain thick as his thumb, and when he raised a hand to pat his macassared russet-coloured hair Daisy saw a wide gold ring gleaming on his finger. Tucked against him with an arm looped about his waist, Amy looked like a fragile dark bird, poised ready to trill with happiness.

'Are you going far? To that Rainbow place, the town at the foot of the mountain?'

'To Shakerville? Yes, we are, aren't we, Tom?' Amy craned her neck to smile up at him.

'Then, please take me with you!' burst out Daisy. She hadn't meant to ask boldly like that, so she hurried on to explain. 'It's Andrew. . . . He's gone, and I know he's gone there. None of the shipping offices has seen him, and he's nowhere around town, so I *know* that's where he must be! The way he talked about it to us. . . . Please take me with you. I have to find him.'

'Of course we will. Won't we, Tom?'

Jealousy flared in Tom's mind. These Morgans acted as if they owned the entire province and everyone in it, and here was his wife meekly agreeing to the outrageous suggestion that Daisy insinuate herself on their honeymoon and thus ruin everything. That thought had not even occurred to Amy, nor had her husband's wishes.

He said: 'Uf Doctor Stafford wunts to be left in peace, thun nobody hus any business chasing after hum.'

'You don't understand.' pleaded Daisy.

'I understund ull right. Thut I do! You thunk thut the entire world shud do whut you wunt, just because you're Daisy Morgan.'

'Please, it's not like that at all! Andrew went to ask Papa if he could marry me, and Papa quarrelled with him and sent him away. That's why he's left in a hurry. That's why I must find him and talk to him.'

Tom felt a flicker of interest. Quarrels often led to full-scale damaging feuds.

'I've helped you, Tommy Nevin,' continued Daisy heatedly now. 'Cast your mind back to all those countless times you met Amy at the old dam. You'd not have had one of those meetings if I hadn't helped. It's the least you can do to help me now.'

'She is right, Tom,' murmured Amy.

Tom never conceded a point easily; to do so would be to abrogate some of his power. 'Thus us rudiculous! Muster Morgan wull have the entire province out looking for hus precious daughter come tomorrow!'

'He can't. He's been hurt,' began Daisy, then stopped when she saw naked interest in Tom's eyes. She already felt guilty about refusing to go out to Mists of Heaven to see Papa when from what Doctor Meakings

153

told them last night he was quite unpleasantly, though not seriously injured. Her guilt had deepened when Aunt Bea interpreted it as minor triumph that Daisy preferred to remain at Benares. The treacher of what she was doing was going to hurt everybody, even dearest Kik and Aunt Bea. *I'll think about that later,* she resolved. For the moment all that mattered was Andrew; she must get to him as swiftly as she could. She said: 'If people are looking for me, they'll be searching fo Amy, too. I assumed you'd made provision to be out of sight, and that' why I came to you. Besides, nobody will miss me until at least tomorrow night. I left a note to say I was staying at your cousins' place Amy, and not to worry if I was late home.'

Tom frowned. In theory he'd be damned if he'd move a finger to help Rhys Morgan's daughter, but was clear that to refuse her would be helping Rhys Morgan himself. The arrogant bastard would be beside himself if he knew what was happening now. For years now Tom had dreamed of how he'd place a boot on the back of Rhys Morgan's neck and grind his face into the mud. Here before him could be that opportunity.

'You cun come with us,' he said slowly.

'There's one more thing . . .,' Daisy told him.

'That bloddy dog? Fust river we come to. . . .'

'He's only teasing,' whispered Amy. 'Ooh, this is going to be fun!'

SIXTEEN

DAISY WOKE NEXT MORNING to the sound of birds heckling Excalibur. She crawled out from under the wagon, clutching a rough blanket to cover the underwear she'd worn to bed. Amy was crouching on a flat stone at the creek splashing water on to her face. There was no sign of Tom.

'Isn't it a lovely day?' called Amy. 'I feel marvellous!'

'I'm aching all over,' complained Daisy. 'All that jolting in the hot sun yesterday, and sleeping on the ground. . . .' She wriggled into yesterday's dress – elegant pale blue and navy figured wool, with a high fashionable bustle – then presented her back so that Amy could do up the dozens of covered buttons. Glancing at the shabby skirt and cast-off man's jacket Amy was wearing, she said: 'Why are you dressed like that? You look as scruffy as Siobhan!' She laughed, then glimpsing Amy's expression added hastily: 'God rest her soul.'

'They're old things Tom found,' said Amy, piqued about Daisy's complaints – the latest in a string that began an hour after they left the outskirts of Christchurch and could throw off their long concealing shawls. *Tom* should complain: he'd given up his bed to Daisy. She said: 'I don't mind wearing them because I've got my pretty satin blouse underneath, and it's lovely next to my skin, real luxury.'

Amy began doing up the buttons. 'I'm dressed like this because Tom and I are supposed to be simple travellers and if anybody sees us they'll think nothing of it.' She giggled. 'It's great fun, too. I feel as if I'm playing a real-life game of charades.'

'And I feel as if my body is fracturing into a hundred pieces,' groaned Daisy as she plucked the curling-rags from her hair and began to drag her hair-brush through the tangle. 'You'll have to help me dress my hair. I can't do a thing without a proper mirror.'

Tom arrived back at the camp with a large writhing eel which Amy admired and Daisy shuddered away from. With the creature flapping from one hand he inspected the fire Amy had built. Excalibur danced around him, yelping with excitement.

'Good. Thut's perfect, luss.'

'I watched you last night, and copied everything you did,' said Amy, flushing with pleasure.

'Yer look grund, too. Yer should huve been a jupsy's wife. Ut suits yer.'

'Stop teasing me, Tom,'she said, swatting him playfully. 'And kill that poor thing quickly. Don't torment it like that.'

He dispatched it with a swift blow of a stick, but before skinning it and cutting it into pieces he glanced up at Daisy who was wincing in disgust. *She lives on a sheep station!* he thought in astonishment. *Has she never been exposed to the harsh realities of life?* In sarcastic tones he said: 'Und where are you off to, foine lady? Und who styled yer har so prutty?'

Daisy said: 'I think you're cruel, bringing that poor . . . poor *thing* to show us and killing it like that. I suppose you think it's great sport! Well, it's not!'

'Sport? It's no soch thung. Thus, Muss Morgan is your bruckfast!'

'Breakfast?'

He laughed at her horrified expression. 'Where do you thunk lumb chops come frum? Und beef? Und pork? Ut's a cruel world, Muss Morgan.' Picking up the stick, he added: 'Und keep thut dog out of my way!'

Daisy ate nothing. While Tom watched, grinning, she fed her entire portion, chunk by chunk to Excalibur, then cuddled him on her lap, crooning to him while Tom and Amy harnessed the horses. Excalibur ran alongside the wagon for the first part of the journey, as the horses strained up and over the ridge-saddle where another valley opened up before them. Tom sang Irish ballads, with Amy hugging his arm and joining in the chorus of the ones she knew. Daisy sat stiff and aloof, watching Excalibur running and darting, sniffing off after rabbits.

It was still cool as they descended into the valley floor past twisted blackened trunks of trees consumed in a long-ago fire. Then their pace picked up. A panting and exhausted Excalibur was allowed to ride again and, as the sun climbed above the rim of hills and the temperature increased, even Tom's singing stopped. Daisy unfurled her parasol, but before she could open it Tom told her sharply to put it away. She hesitated. He snatched it off her and flung it back under the tarpaulin.

'Copy me. Cover your head with your shawl,' suggested Amy. 'If you have that fancy parasol up, someone could see you from miles away.'

'But there's nobody here,' protested Daisy.

Tom laughed.

156

Daisy's lip quivered. She reached down to pat Excalibur, for her own comfort rather than for his. Her stomach was rattling so loudly that she was grateful that the creaking of the wagon wheels covered the noise. She had never felt hunger before, nor could she recall such a miserable state of physical discomfort. Under the bandage her skin itched ferociously, her back ached, her arm ached, and as the sun glared hotly down her head throbbed and her insides churned. Craning her neck, she glanced around towards the mountains. Often on a hot day just a glimpse of their glacial whiteness could make her feel refreshed. Today there was no solace; the mountains were covered with soupy-looking cloud. High in the peaks it was raining.

Tom gave Amy the reins to hold while he lit his pipe, and when he took them back from her he said: 'Hello. There's someone up ahead. Look, up on thut hullside.' To Daisy he said: 'Hide yourself. Gut under the tarpaulin, und don't move. Quuckly now.'

Through cracked dry lips Daisy said: 'I'll do no such thing.'

'Please, Daisy,' begged Amy. 'Tom's right. Whoever that is, they'll be sure to come down and talk to us, and all they need to do is glance at you and they'll know that something's not right. Why would a wealthy young lady be keeping company with two gypsies? Then, when they hear that the whole province is looking for you, they'll know right away that it was you. So please do as Tom asks. It's best for all of us.'

'Uf yer don't hop to ut I'll throw you under,' added Tom.

Tossing him a haughty glare, Daisy lifted a corner of the cover and burrowed underneath, crouching on hands and knees in the suffocating heat. She squawked when Tom slapped the tarpaulin back into place and managed to swipe her heftily at the same time. With his guffaws ringing in her ears she crouched there in the hot green darkness, fuming.

It was as well that she did hide. The two men were rabbiters who, eager for company, scrambled down the bank to intercept the wagon. Daisy could hear the clanking of their traps, the snarling of their dogs as they noticed Excalibur, and she could smell their particular odour, sharp and putrid, of sun-baked rabbit-hides.

For what seemed an hour she hunched in hideous discomfort while the dogs yapped and Tom exchanged leisurely shouted gossip with them. They were hungry for the chance to grumble about their stingy employer who was cheating them out of the going rate for skins and wild pig's tails, and keen to talk about the accident that had occurred not far off, where the poncey young visitor from England had been gored by a boar. Something weird about the whole thing, they thought. The boss had gone crazy when he heard the news. Laid into his blackfellows with a stock-whip and had to be restrained.

'Ut wasn't anything to do with Muster Rhys Morgan by any chance?'

asked Tom, and on being told that, no, he lived on the spread next door and wasn't involved Tom replied laconically that that was a real pity. 'I hear he's a roight busstard,' said Tom, to which the rabbiters replied that Rhys Morgan was a great boss, generous and fair, and they wished they were working for him instead of slaving for 'bloody "Baron" Windsor'.

Which was not what Tom wanted to hear. Scowling, he clucked up the horses, and presently Amy poked Daisy's ankle to let her know it was safe to emerge.

'That was fun,' said Amy, 'But whew! I could scarcely draw breath. And the *flies*! They don't need a parasol with that cloud buzzing around their heads.'

Daisy couldn't reply. The brightness hit her like a blow that she winced away from, shutting her eyes quickly. Giddiness swamped her.

Amy grabbed her arm to steady her on the seat. 'Tom! Look at Daisy! She's not well!'

'She'll be ull right,' remarked Tom, flicking the reins over the horses' sweat-sheened backs.

'You didn't even look at her. She almost fell. . . . Look at how white she is.'

'Ut's only a wee touch of the sun, I tull you. She'll be better soon, sure an' all she wull.'

She felt as if her body was a fragile jar being shaken by every jolt and the jar was half-full of a vile stinking liquid that sloshed about inside her. Her mouth tasted of metal polish, and her eyes hurt so much that the ache in her injured arm was lost in the dozens of other aches that plagued her.

Tom sang, and when he wasn't singing he boasted of the brewery he planned to own one day. 'We'll be in the money thun, luss, and all the nobs loike Muster Morgan, they'll be doffing their huts to us thun!'

In a pig's eye, thought Daisy, too wretched to speak.

Amy's eyes were glowing as she contemplated the future. With her head on Tom's shoulder she said: 'You'll succeed, too, Tom. Father has a theory that no matter how little money the average man has in his purse he'll always scrape up some of it for ale.'

Papa says that drink is the ruin of the country, thought Daisy, and the thought of Papa brought hot tears to her eyes. She'd give anything now to be back in her flowery bedroom in the cool sheets; she'd even swallow Aunty Gwynne's headache remedies without flinching.

Amy's hand wormed through the folds in her skirt to squeeze Daisy's fingers. Daisy was too miserable to respond. She thirsted for coolness, for darkness and for quiet.

At noon they paused in an ugly brown valley, treeless as the past

several had been, with a shingly stream so meagre that Tom had to
shovel out a hollow so that the horses could slurp their fill. Daisy drank a
few sips of scalding black tea, but couldn't eat. She averted her eyes as
Tom tore hunks from a charred wheel of hard damper bread and wolfed
them down.

Amy tagged after her husband when he returned to the stream swinging his enamel mug. Glancing back to where Daisy shrank into the
wagon's shade, she said: 'She is ill, Tom. She needs laudanum. I've
never seen her like that before.'

'I haven't got laudanum, Amy!' His voice rose in irritation. In his
voice was a plain warning that the subject was closed. He scooped up a
mugful of water and drank it down with satisfaction. 'Ah, Adam's ale.
I'm tulling you, luss, if I cun brew an ale thut tastes but half as grand us
thus tastes now, thun we'll huv our fortunes assured.'

'Oh, Tom, you're so clever. . . .'

He bent to kiss her. 'Wait untul we're alone an' I'll show you just how
cluvver I cun be,' he promised.

In the late afternoon they climbed a slow winding road up to the crest
of a ridge, making painful progress because Tom had frequently to
climb down and clear scatterings of boulders from the road. The silence
seemed to smother them like a blanket. There was no sign of life, no
friendly flashing rabbits' tails, not even the rustle of birds starting up.
Amy glanced up at the sky and shuddered.

'Look at the colour of those clouds over the mountains. I'd say we're
in for a storm. What do you think, Tom? Daisy?'

'Lut's hope nut,' said Tom.

Daisy stirred, opening her eyes with difficulty. She was unable to look
up at the sky. 'I feel so sick. . . . Please take me home.'

Tom laughed. 'By all thut's lovely, thut's a tempting offer.'

'I'll ask Papa to pay you for your trouble.'

'Your dear papa wud huv me arrested und tossed unter gaol.'

'He would, too,' agreed Amy. 'Please, Daisy, we can't go back. It's
impossible.'

'I wish I could die,' groaned Daisy, weak hot tears oozing from under
her eyelids.

'Ah, but thut's a tempting idea, too, und all.'

'Tom!'

They were quiet after that, rocking together as the wagon jolted up
and over another low saddle. Each was occupied with different
thoughts. Amy was wondering how she could make the peace between
her husband and her best friend, Daisy was struggling with her aches
and giddiness, and Tom's mind was seething with hostile thoughts
against the Morgans. The mention of Rhys had stimulated his hatred
afresh, and as he flapped the reins he wondered how he might best take

159

his revenge. Perhaps he could lock Daisy up in an isolated cottage an then ask a ransom for her. Perhaps he could send word to Rhys that h daughter had died. Somehow, somehow there must be a way to mak these arrogant Morgans suffer. Look at this whining bitch! Foisted he self on them, she did, ruined his honeymoon, and with not one word apology nor one shred of gratitude.

'Tom!' cried Amy, breaking into his glowerings as she hugged h arm and pointed down into this next valley. About a mile away, close the rim of hills and deep in their shadows, was a tiny cottage with a oblong of light at the doorway and a stream of smoke, all spangled wit sparks, pouring from the corrugated-iron chimney.

'Ut'll be a prospector's hut,' said Tom, scratching in his leathe pouch for tobacco for his pipe. 'Here, luss, full thus for me.'

'But, Tom, they might have laudanum. Daisy needs medicine. She' really ill.'

Tom sighed. 'She'll be fine when we get to Shakerville. I'm nut goin out of my way, I tull you. Sooner we get there—'

'Then, I will!' cried Amy suddenly. Before he could stop her, she ha scrambled over Daisy and was down on the ground on the other side o the wagon. Without a backward glance she was gone, her rough boo slithering over the rocky ground, a rattle of gravel bouncing down th slope ahead of her.

'Come back!' roared Tom, his teeth gritted in frustration. Draggin on the reins, he snapped at Daisy: 'Look ut whut trouble you've cause now.'

Daisy was white and shaking. Hands clenching the seat, she watche Amy slither down a steep place. If she heard Tom, she gave no sign.

He studied her in disgust. For weeks he'd planned this honeymoo trip. It was to be a romantic adventure, just he and Amy meanderin along, singing and laughing together, with frequent interludes wher ever a shady glade or inviting stream suggested a picturesque setting fo lovemaking. Lovemaking! That was the bitterest joke of all. After th long sweet tension of their secret engagement, when Amy alway slapped his hands away if he tried for anything more than a kiss, he' been in exquisite agonies of anticipation looking forward to the wed ding feast in their intimate little room. What delicious plans he had what ecstasies they would enjoy naked in bed in each other's arms, bu no sooner had he slipped the first dozen buttons on her blouse whe sour Miss High-and-mighty arrived to wreck everything with he demands. They'd now been married a full day and a half, and he'd no so much as caressed one of his wife's nipples. Nor would he, by the loo of things while this miserable baggage was hanging around their necks

'Uf I had my way I'd dump you right here und let you walk the rest o the way,' Tom told her. When she made no reply but haughtily to rais her head a further inch he said roughly: 'You might look ut me whun I'm talking to yer.'

'Looking at you would scarcely improve my disposition,' Daisy told him. 'I'm only here because there is no other way of getting to Shakerville.'

'You're nut too ull ter talk, I notuss,' sneered Tom.

'I'm too ill to be badgered,' she told him. 'Please leave me alone.' She swallowed. 'And please put that smelly pipe out. The fumes are nauseating.'

Leaning over, he deliberately sucked in a mouthful of smoke and blew it in her face. Laughing, he watched her fumble her way down from the wagon, her tight skirt impeding her movements. As she landed she tripped and fell to her hands and knees. Excalibur barked to be lifted down, too.

'Shut op thut noise,' said Tom, reaching to cuff the dog.

'Leave him alone,' cried Daisy, straightening awkwardly.

Tom cuffed him, a sharp clip to the side of the head that set up a frantic shrieking of pain. Daisy grabbed her dog, hugged his rigid quivering body, but because he was howling in her ear at an unbearable pitch was forced to set him down. Immediately he fled to a safe distance where he hunched, whimpering, behind a rock.

At the foot of the slope Amy heard the noise and paused to look back, before turning and hurrying on again.

'You've no right to touch him,' said Daisy.

Leaning back against the covered packing-cases, Tom surveyed her from head to foot as she picked dirt and gravel from the palms of her hands. Who did she think she was, telling him what he had a right to do or not to do? This wasn't Mists of Heaven here, by hell it wasn't. This was Tom Nevin's wagon, and he had every damned right to do exactly as he damned well pleased. He'd humble her. By all that was lovely, he'd see her grovelling.

'You're nut so ladylike us yer protund ter be,' he said.

She raised her chin in that haughty gesture that irritated him beyond endurance. Before he was aware of what he was doing he had knocked the dottle out of his pipe, set his pipe down on the seat and was on the ground facing her. She glanced up into his face and then looked away. She wasn't scared of him; she was too wretchedly ill to be scared of anything.

'A *lady* wudn't take off her clothes und go swummin' un a public place,' said Tom softly.

Daisy stopped breathing. She stared at the yellowish grey rain-clouds that were cramming the sky like mattress stuffing. Amy must have told him. How else would he know?

Tom's voice was like cream. 'A *lady* wudn't flaunt hersulf to unnybody who wus passing by.'

161

Daisy took a step away. He was right there beside her. She took another, edging towards the slope, and he matched her step for step.

'A *lady* behaves un a respuctable munner,' he whispered.

She felt sickened right through. She knew that if she glanced up at him he would be smiling at her with the same gloating air that permeated his voice. When he stepped in front of her she turned away and began edging backwards until she found herself bumped against the wooden side of the wagon.

'Aha! Gut you!' chuckled Tom, slapping one hand down on either side of her. He leaned over her. His breath smelt of tobacco smoke. No part of him was touching her, yet he boxed her in completely with his bulky frame.

Staring at his plaid shirt-front, she tried to ignore him. Through the throbbing giddiness she fastened on to the hope that if she showed no reaction he would soon weary of this sport and leave her alone. Soon, please, she prayed, as the stale sweaty odour of his unwashed body assailed her.

'Well, foine lady?'

Because she couldn't move without touching him, she kept perfectly still. His shirt was torn around the buttons, and she noticed that the buttons were clumsily sewn on in different-coloured threads, blue and yellow and green, though the shirt was black and red. Again she marvelled at Amy's choice of a husband. Hard-working sober and well-to-do he may be, but he'd always be a coarse peasant underneath and all the macassar oil and Cologne and expensive suits and soft leather boots and brushed top-hats would never be able to disguise that fact. His crudeness would always be there, plain as the halfpenny-sized freckles on his thick forearms.

'Well, Muss Morgan, whut else does a foine lady gut up to out un the countrysoide whun there's nobuddy about?'

She shivered, blinking. Her face was very white, like translucent parchment paper. 'Amy will be back soon,' she said.

'Nut fer ages,' he purred, twisting his head and noticing that Amy was still a hundred yards or so short of the cottage. 'She'll be a good while yut. Now, you tull me, Muss Morgan. Whut ulse do yer do fer fun? Whut ulse besides flaunt yersulf and unterfere un other folk's business?'

He really hates me, thought Daisy in dull surprise. *I knew he resented my being here, but he actually loathes me*. This revelation came as a genuine shock; while it was perfectly reasonable for her to harbour feelings of distaste towards Tom, she had assumed all along that underneath his petty carping he would accord her the awe that she, Daisy Morgan, deserved.

'I might remind you that I am Amy's friend, and I've been your friend, too. If it wasn't for me—'

162

'Uf ut wasn't for you, I'd be having a honeymoon,' Tom cut in. 'But unstead here we are having a cosy chut, just we two. Usn't thus fun?' He stroked her shoulder with a clumsy wiping motion.

'Don't touch me!' She wriggled away but bumped against his other imprisoning arm. 'Excalibur!' she called feebly, wishing that he was a ferocious guard-dog instead of a cuddly young pup.

Tom laughed, an explosion of tobacco odour into her face.

'Tull yer what,' he said. 'Uf yer like, I'll leave yer alone und kull yer dog unstead.'

He said it so sweetly that she was not sure she heard correctly. *'Kill?* Kill Excalibur?'

'Why not?' he parried nonchalantly. 'I was going to unyway whun yer came along thut day.'

Bile rose in her throat. He couldn't be serious.

His voice lilted, as if he was describing something lovely that had happened to him. 'I'll smush hus hud with a rock und thun run the wagon wheels over hum. . . . If yer like.'

Daisy closed her eyes. The bile stung. Her whole body was sweating. 'No . . . of course not. You wouldn't. . . .'

This is power! he was thinking, savouring the moment. This is what Rhys Morgan must have felt when he had absolute control, this intoxicating surge of raw strength, this rushing urge to use it, to crush and humiliate and destroy. Only, Rhys Morgan, now it was Tom who had the whip-hand. He held the power now. The pity of it was that Rhys Morgan wasn't here to see what was happening to his precious daughter.

'Very wull. I'll lut hum live . . . uf you pull your skirts up.'

Her eyes snapped open. 'How dare you!'

He was grinning, showing large uneven teeth. 'Pull your skirts up? Wull, why nut? Ut's nut the first time you've flaunted yoursulf.' When she made no reply but to glare at him he picked up a large rock and weighted it in his hand.

'I'll tell Amy.'

'Tull her whut you like.' He whistled between his teeth, and Excalibur stood up, his tail wagging uncertainly.

'No!' screamed Daisy. Tom paused, stared at her, and in his expression she read that he was capable of doing exactly what he threatened. Still she hesitated.

Tom whistled again. Excalibur toddled towards him over the hot stony ground. As soon as he was within reach Tom pounced, gripping him by the collar.

'No . . . please!' said Daisy.

Whistling a tune now, Tom twisted the collar to restrict the puppy's breathing. Excalibur whined, alarm showing white in his eyes. His paws kicked ineffectually at Tom's forearms. Laughing, Tom sat down, cradling the dog in his lap, making them both comfortable. He stared at Daisy. 'Whut are you waiting for?' he asked.

Ill with fear and shame, Daisy bent down and grasped the hem of her dress.

'Und your petticoat,' encouraged Tom. 'Right up, thut's the way. You cun flaunt yoursulf for me now.'

She was too angry to cry, too ashamed already to give in to weakness that would humiliate her further. In the distance she could see Amy beginning her walk back, a tiny figure almost lost in the dusk and the clutter of the valley floor. Overhead the clouds had darkened. She looked at them, ignoring Tom's gloating grin.

'Und them other thungs,' he was saying. 'Thum pantalettes. Take thum down.'

Cold-eyed, she did as she was told.

Amy arrived back, gasping, laughing and holding a dark purple bottle aloft. 'The old prospector had a whole boxful of these. He wanted us to stop and have supper with him.' She glanced over at Tom, who was whistling as he checked the horses' hoofs. Lowering her voice, she said: 'When I declined he was so annoyed he took every penny of the two shillings I took with me! Don't let Tom know that. He's very thrifty, Tom is. Not that he'd mind in this case, I'm sure. Deep down he's concerned about you, even though he doesn't show it.'

Daisy's teeth chattered against the spoon. A dribble of the syrupy liquid ran down from the corner of her mouth.

'Gracious, he *is* in a cheerful mood! Thank goodness. I was worried that he'd be angry at me for running off like that. I needn't have been. I told you that under all the gruffness he's really very sweet and kind-hearted. Men have to be tough to survive in this hard world, so of course he's got toughness, too. He may seem harsh and unfeeling at times, Daisy, but he's kind to me, and he's got courage and ambition, heaps and heaps of both. That's what you need to get on in the colony, he says. He'll do well for himself, our Tom will.'

'I'm going to be sick,' said Daisy.

SEVENTEEN

'WHEN DID YOU SAY she'd be back?' asked Sir Kenneth, wheeling himself into the drawing-room where Beatrice was sitting with a pillow on her lap, bobbins and thread strung about it.

'She didn't dear. She said that she was going with Amy to visit Mrs Hogg's cousin. Remember, she's been there before. They have a little farm between Sumner and Lyttelton. Daisy had a lovely time when they stayed overnight last summer.'

'She should be back by now. I think I'll send Leopold out with the gig to fetch her.'

'You'll do no such thing,' responded Beatrice in a sharp voice. She sighed. 'I'm sorry, dear. Please go back to your work. This is an ideal opportunity to finish that chapter while Daisy is out of the way.'

When the squeak of his wheels had faded she set the lace aside. In the five years since she began making this collar she had worked on it only when worried to distraction about something, most of it being done when Kiki first became ill. After ringing the bell to summon Albert she took the note from its hiding-place behind a high picture – out of Kiki's reach – and smoothed it out for the fiftieth time.

It was pure invention, of course. Though Beatrice adored Daisy, hers was a clear-sighted adoration, all the more so because so much of Azura was mirrored in Daisy's nature. Even if Beatrice had been deceived in the first reading of the letter, a second scanning revealed the cramped nervousness of the writing, forced and laboured, not Daisy's normal flowing loops and curls that looked as if a breeze had wafted the marks over the paper. This had been written in a mood of high excitement.

First, the excuses about Mrs Hogg's cousin, then at the end a plea for understanding. 'I'm so happy. Please don't fret about me, Kiki; nor you, darling Aunt Bea. I promise you I'll come to no harm, so please, please don't worry.'

She's eloped, Bea decided. It wouldn't be with Doctor Stafford; he'd let Daisy down badly. Jeremy Drake. This unpleasant business with Andrew would have crystallized things between her and Jeremy, made her see that he was the right one for her after all. It was all as Kiki predicted, Bea thought, folding the note and returning it to its hiding-place. Kiki was so wise.

To check out her suspicions she telephoned Georgia, bracing herself against the grating sensation she experienced when Charlotte Drake's Southern drawl twanged from the earpiece. 'Jeremy? Why, no, honey! Jeremy won't be home for days. He's off catching wee baby pigs, of all things. You're inviting him to dinner? How sweet of you, sugar. I'll tell Jeremy when he comes home. He'll be delighted. Give your darling husband a big hug for me, won't you? And Daisy . . . is she still with you? We love her as if she was our own daughter, you know.' Shuddering, Beatrice hung up on the peal of shrill laughter.

Catching wee baby pigs, my eye, thought Beatrice, wondering what Charlotte would say when she found out what her boy was really up to. She'd be delighted, no doubt, as would Rhys, but even though Beatrice was tempted to share her secret she would say nothing, not even to Kiki. If Daisy and Jeremy had run away to marry, then they should be permitted the joy of breaking their news to everybody. Later, when it was all out in the open Beatrice would reveal how *she* knew all along.

Beatrice did not consider it strange that Charlotte had mentioned neither Rhys's accident nor poor Lowell's tragic death, though, thanks to the telephone, both happenings had become widely known about within hours. Charlotte Drake never gossiped, not for any noble reason but simply because she took absolutely no interest in anything but babies and childbearing. The telephone was ringing now, no doubt another gasping acquaintance asking if it was really true that Rhys was beaten and left for dead. Ignoring its summons, Beatrice conceded that Charlotte had her good points after all.

It was incredible how these stories could build out of nothing. The truth about Rhys was boring in its simplicity. He had fallen from his horse. In doing so he bruised his throat, slightly damaging his windpipe, and had also suffered a deep concussion. As yet he was unable to speak, and to be on the safe side Doctor Meakings prescribed complete rest, mental, emotional and physical. But he was in no danger.

Now Beatrice rang again for Albert, and when he still failed to appear she put her lacework on the dresser and went to search for him. Why did he always provoke her when her nerves were on edge? It seemed that ever since she found Daisy's letter everybody had conspired to irritate her – Albert, Leopold and even Kiki, not to mention these stupid people who kept telephoning avid for gossip.

She'd begin planning a reception, she decided as she glanced in the quiet rooms. Even if they eloped, Daisy and Jeremy must have a proper reception, and what better place to have it than here at Benares with the roses in a riot of colour and the lawns a rich summery green? Mists of Heaven was out of the question – Lisabeth was in no condition to organize anything, and Gwynne was incapable of arranging a sandwich. It would have to be here, with a marquee perhaps, and punts to drift on the Avon, a trio to play sentimental music for strings, and champagne, sponge cakes and pyramids of sweet-meats. The invitations – they could be handwritten on pink cards embossed with a rose to echo the floral motif – she could order those right away.

Albert appeared at her elbow, making her start out of her reverie. 'Please be excusing me, but there is coming Mrs Hogg to the door.' His yellow eyes looked malevolent in the dim hall light. 'Mrs Hogg she is being very upset. I was asking her to come in, but she is refusing me. Miss Amy she is going away, and Mrs Hogg she is not knowing where she has gone.'

'Oh, dear Lord,' whispered Beatrice as the significance of this news sank in. 'If Amy is missing, too, then Daisy can't have eloped after all. Oh, Albert, where can she be? Albert, what can we do?'

Albert looked dismayed and enormously surprised. In all his forty years of service this was the first time Lady Launcenolt had ever asked his advice. 'We are waiting,' he said gravely. 'We are waiting to see what will happen. Something, it will happen.'

Beatrice clutched at her pearl choker. 'Yes, but what?'

He did not reply. He felt that somehow she had let him down.

Lisabeth closed the door behind her, leaned on it for a second, then tip-toed over to Rhys's bedside. His eyelids flickered, opened, and his lips curled in the gentle little smile that never failed to move her. 'I love you,' she whispered.

His fingers reached, touched the swell of her waist, then rested there. 'Our baby, Rhys. Soon, very soon,' she said, reassuring him that she was all right, that the child within her was healthy and kicking.

He closed his eyes, resting, and when he opened them again there was a question in them. His lips moved; his head strained to lift off the pillow.

'Hush. Doctor Meakings said you're not allowed to talk.'

Daisy, his lips articulated. *Daisy . . . Daisy?*

'Hush, dear,' soothed Lisabeth. She could guess what he was desperate to know. 'Daisy is still at Benares. She is well and happy, and she sends you her love. She doesn't know anything, Rhys. She doesn't know.'

It was what he wanted to hear. His eyelids drooped in relief, and the tight muscles of his face relaxed as he subsided on to the pillow. *Good*, his lips whispered.

Was it? wondered Lisabeth bitterly as she stood up and pretended to adjust the window-blinds with her back to him so that he could not read her expression. Where was the spoiled little missy when her father was ill and needed her? And what was Lady Launcenolt playing at blithely informing her that Daisy hadn't accompanied them because she had a headache and stayed behind to 'write letters'. Write letters! The only person Daisy ever wrote to in her life was Andrew, and now that he was here in Christchurch there was no call to write to him. She was being selfish, that's what—

Lisabeth stopped, inwardly scolding herself. Daisy probably hadn't come because she was upset, and she had every right to be. From what Kiki said, Daisy had expected Andrew for lunch that day and 'the blighter' hadn't shown up. Distressed the poor lass no end, apparently.

As she measured Rhys's medicine into a glass Lisabeth told herself that Daisy was young and her heart, like her arm, would soon mend. Once Rhys had recovered enough to explain, all would be resolved; Daisy would understand, of course she would.

That night Daisy lay awake listening to the hollow death-rattle of the wind along the rocky hillside. All evening she had said nothing, numbed by the nastiness of what had happened earlier. It would have been preferable if he'd hit her, she thought. That would have been simpler to comprehend, but his loathing of her was so intense, so *sordid* that he had not attempted even to touch her, and when finally he had permitted her to reclothe herself he had flung Excalibur at her in hatred, like a payment from someone who feels cheated.

There were two consolations in this, she told herself. One was that Amy suspected nothing. She assumed that Daisy was withdrawn because of the laudanum. Her father took laudanum for his toothaches, and a single spoonful could turn him from a raging lion into a meek lamb.

The second consolation was that Excalibur was unharmed. He was cuddled against Daisy's side as she lay staring out at the wild darkness, and her fingers stroked incessantly under his chin where the skin was warm and velvety. 'I've still got you, and that's the main thing,' she whispered smiling as his damp tongue striped her hand.

She was still whispering to him, her voice brushing away the snoring that grated from Tom's cocoon in the open, when suddenly the whole valley was illuminated by a dazzling white light that flashed on and was nudged off by a deafening crash that dumped down hard on the wagon. Excalibur yelped, starting up. Daisy grabbed his collar. 'It's only lightning and thunder,' she soothed; but, even as she spoke, the rain began, dashing down so hard that it strummed on the tarpaulin and splashed around the wagon.

Cursing, Tom scrambled into the tiny shelter, pushing Amy close against Daisy so that he could squeeze his own bulk under cover. His soaking-wet bedding was flung in with him. Then, while the storm raged on overhead, he and Amy scuffled and giggled while Daisy lay rigid with loathing, trying desperately to ignore Tom's proximity and the suggestive endearments he was whispering to his wife.

I'll think about Andrew, and how surprised and pleased he'll be to see me, she resolved, but all the shine had gone off the adventure, her plans seemed tarnished, and echoing in her head was Tom's warning that Andrew should be left in peace if that was what he wanted.

In the morning it was still raining. Last night the horses had been tethered to a dead tree in the centre of a small grassy area; now they stood up to their fetlocks in mud. Cloud hung so low that it obliterated the upper half of the waterfall. The stream was swollen, and the waterfall gushed out of its cleft in the mountains like water forced from a pipe.

Now Daisy's silence did worry Amy. As they folded the damp bedroll and stowed it away, she asked what was wrong. 'Is your head still aching? Do you feel ill?'

'Leave her be and hulp me cotch the horses,' Tom ordered curtly. He had not spoken directly to Daisy once since the incident. She had proved herself to be beneath his contempt. Like many folk from poor backgrounds Tom had a casual attitude to animals and was unconcerned about their suffering. In Daisy's place he would have allowed a hundred puppies to die rather than sacrifice the smallest part of his dignity. It was incomprehensible to him that she might genuinely love her pet. Certainly she fussed about him, but Tom could see no difference between that fussing and her dismay when she found a rip near the hem of her gown.

'She's a tart!' he said to Amy as they led the horses back to their dismal camp-site. 'She's rubbish, Amy! Just like thut father of hers. Flauntin' hersulf in public, und running ufter a mun who doesn't want her. She's no butter thun a trollop.'

'Tom!' cried Amy. 'Please don't say such things. It distresses me terribly—'

'Ull right, ull right. I hear you,' he said. He tipped his head back so that the drizzle brushed his face with a slick of wetness. 'We'll huv ter hurry,' he said. 'Ull this rain. The ruvvers wull be bursting their bunks. We've a bug one ter cross before we gut to Shakerville.'

The rain stopped shortly after they crossed the little stream. Amy laughed aloud as the sun came out and a magnificent shimmering rainbow arched over the mountains. 'Look at that! An omen!' she cried, clasping her hands together under her chin. 'When will we get to Shakerville, Tom? Tonight? Tomorrow?'

'Soon enough,' said Tom.

Amy prattled on, now trying to jolly Daisy out of her strangely withdrawn mood. 'Tom says that Shakerville was named for an earthquake. In the gold-rush days of twenty years ago the first buildings put up here were all jolted apart by a severe quake. The town was called Stillwater before that, but some wag said that a place so prone to the jitters couldn't possibly have the word "still" in its name, so Shakerville it became. I can't wait to see it. Tom says it's a large town and very pretty with lots of daffodils in the town square. We're going to set up a stall right there amongst the flowers and sell all our goods. You should see what we've got back there under the tarpaulin, Daisy! There are rugs from Auckland and all manner of bronze and copper utensils, and crates of crockery. Tom says a place that's plagued by earthquakes is bound to be a thriving market for crockery! And everything is so pretty. You know, Father has a theory that even if folks don't need something they'll buy it if it's pretty enough. They can always persuade themselves that they need another tureen if the old one is scratched and faded and the new one has a garland of roses around the rim, isn't that so?' She leaned forward to glance back into Daisy's face. 'Are you still feeling sick? Do you want some more laudanum?'

'Leave her be,' rumbled Tom.

Daisy hugged Excalibur on her lap. He was asleep, his spray of white whiskers quivering with every gentle exhalation of breath.

Amy said: 'I hope you're not nervous about the earthquakes. There haven't been any there for ages. Besides, they never hurt anybody, not really. Just push a few old shanties over – isn't that right, Tom? Tom says there are thousands of old shanties there on the hillsides all around. It's still a thriving gold-town, you see.'

Daisy wasn't listening. She gazed at the rainbow, focusing her mind on it until she could feel the translucent colours absorbing the tiredness, the aches and the loneliness out of her soul. Soon the pain eased; she was refreshed.

Late that afternoon they wound down from the foothills and back on to the plains, having travelled in a wide semicircle north. Daisy drew in a deep breath of plains breeze tangy with the hint of salt. As they rolled along through the tussock she glanced south. In that direction but miles over the horizon lay Mists of Heaven. If she climbed out of the wagon here and began to walk, she would eventually make her way home.

She shivered, pulling the shawl around her shoulders as the wind tugged at her clothing. There would be a full-scale panic by now, with both herself and Amy discovered to be missing. Aunty Gwynne would be clutching her swoon-bottle, Kiki and Aunt Bea would be blaming Albert for not watching her properly, and Lisabeth would be out of her mind with worry. . . . Or would she? She was probably so occupied with tending to Papa that she'd not spare a thought for Daisy. And Papa – was he conscious yet? Would anybody tell him that Daisy had run away?

The rainbow was still arching in the sky, hovering above the mountains, its colours clear as water. Daisy looked at it and smiled. Wouldn't everybody be surprised when she and Andrew arrived back in Christchurch together as man and wife? Papa would be sorry that he'd chased Andrew away, and everybody else would delight in their happiness.

The doubts crept in. Andrew could easily have come to her and explained . . . if he'd wanted to. Had she misread his attentions? Perhaps he had never really wanted to marry her.

Squaring her shoulders, she shoved the doubts firmly away. Of course everything would be all right. After all she'd been through, there had to be a happy ending.

Suddenly Tom dragged on the reins to stop the wagon. 'Lussten!'

Daisy and Amy listened. Faintly, softly, as gentle as the noise of the breeze stirring the greyish wintry tussock came the sound of water. Rushing water.

'Is the big river in flood?' asked Amy timidly.

'I thunk so,' said Tom, grim as he flapped the reins again.

He had explained that they were returning to the plains in order to cross the Clarence river where it fanned out in its wide shingly bed, after which they would follow it back on the other side into the hills until the road branched off for Shakerville. They had make excellent progress, far better than he had originally anticipated.

There have been no stops for dalliance, that's why, he mused sourly. *We'll take our time on the way back, instead.*

'It won't be long now! We're nearly there!' sang Amy, squeezing Daisy around the waist. Daisy smiled in response; Amy's good humour was infectious. Tom see-sawed his voice up into one of his Irish tunes, and with Amy singing 'La-la-la-la' for the words she didn't know they rolled along, their voices trailing like scarves behind them.

As they approached the river the landscape changed, and instead of the snow-bleached tussock clumps they wound through thickets of shiny-bladed flax where the sound of the river rushed at them louder than the wind now, louder than their singing. All three had fallen silent when Tom suddenly cursed with a single shouted exclamation.

Amy didn't rebuke her husband. She and Daisy craned their necks as the horses slowed, then stopped on the stony river-bank. 'Oh, dear me,' said Amy.

Daisy gazed at the river, speechless with dismay. She knew how it should have looked, a braided river intertwining between a myriad of lozenge-shaped islands, the water clear, the islands each a miniature slice of landscape tufted with flax and reeds and *toe-toe* bushes.

But the river was high, a vast tumultuous spread of yellowish brown water chopped into thousands of wavelets that pushed and jostled each other as they churned past. All the islands had disappeared, and only a few clusters of streaming flax and sodden *toe-toe* bushes marked where they should be. There was a smell of stale mud, and apart from the whooshing of the water a strange eerie silence. There were no birds, no animals to be seen, no signs of life at all.

'What can we do, Tom?' wondered Amy. 'It looks frightfully dangerous.'

'We'll wait. Ut's ull we cun do.' He turned the horses' heads, and they began plodding back the way they had come, towards higher ground where they could camp safely for the night.

While Tom went off with his shotgun to find game for their dinner Amy brushed Daisy's hair and dressed it into two bunches of ringlets. This display of tenderness did not reach Daisy's heart; she felt isolated, as if she and her friend had become strangers. Instead of the warmth Daisy usually felt, there rested inside her an icy core. She could not even laugh when Amy called herself a gowk and postured playfully in Siobhan's old clothes. She looked on unsmiling, her soul withering, as Amy threw her arms wide and pirouetted, the shabby black jacket swinging out around her. She looked like a man's umbrella.

'I'm so happy!' she exclaimed, subsiding on to a tussock clump with a laugh. 'Do you realize how few woman actually share their husband's work? I'm going to be right there beside him, helping him. Isn't he the most marvellous man? I *know* we're going to have a wonderful life together.' Catching the expression on Daisy's face, she rushed on defiantly: 'Unfortunately he has this hostility towards your father, but if you knew all the facts of what happened you would understand Tom's point of view. But I'll talk him around. I can soften his attitude. In the mean time, Daisy, don't take anything Tom says as a personal attack on you. He doesn't mean you any harm. He *likes* you. Honestly!'

Daisy could not trust herself to reply.

Next morning Tom was away at daybreak to check the river. He came back as Amy was swinging the billy, hugged her exuberantly and announced that the river was low enough to be safely crossed.

'We'll be un Shakerville by nightfall, und thut's a promise,' he whooped, his broad face pink with excitement.

The river was still brown, still a jostling mass of hurrying wavelets, but

172

he islands had heaved clear of the surface, their shoulders draped with tangled sodden debris.

Ears back, the two huge horses plunged straight into the frilly edge of the stream and as Tom shouted encouragement they waded out up to their bellies in water as the wagon rumbled and crunched over the river stones behind them.

Daisy sat on the upstream side of the wagon with Amy in the middle and Tom on the far side. Careless of his muddy paws, she rested Excalibur in her lap. Hugging him seemed to be the only thing that gave her some respite from the cold that permeated right through her, from her damp skirts to her clammy numb flesh. He wriggled with excitement as the wagon edged into the water, uttering little yips of panic as the stream slurped higher and higher until it was almost licking the sides of the wagon bed.

It was hard work for the horses. The water pushed and shoved at them with such force that it formed a rippling wall all along the upstream horse's side and tugged and gurgled around the wagon wheels and underbracings, like some voracious monster intent on swallowing everything that could be sucked into its maw. To Daisy it seemed incongruous that there was a clear baby-blue sky stretching over them with the serene mountains as pretty as one of Lisabeth's landscape paintings posing on their left. This river was ugly, choked and engorged. It didn't match its surroundings at all.

Their plotted route across took in two of the islands with equal spreads of water between, in the first two river branches and a much wider gap at the far side. Tom rested the horses at the first island. They stood shuddering as water ran off their dark coats in ragged sheets. Tom stood up on the wagon seat, frowning as he studied the next part. The water was deeper than he had expected, dangerously deep, so he studied the surface carefully, searching for clues which would help him decide on the safest place to cross. There, where the water fluttered into narrow chocolate corrugations, that should be the shallowest part, while where the surface had a swirling oily look it should be deepest.

'You look worried,' said Amy, not sure if she should worry, too.

'No need ter fret whun I'm looking ufter you,' grinned Tom, planting a kiss on her cheek as he settled back beside her, but when he clucked the horses forward his features squeezed together in the frown again.

His calculations were exact. This time the horses' bellies were above the swirling surface, and they trod out more confidently, soon gaining the second island. Startled by their arrival, a flock of river birds flung up out of the vegetation and wheeled scolding over their heads before flapping away in a ragged banner across the plains. Tom barely glanced at them. Pausing only for a brief intense study of the stream ahead, he urged the horses on. They'd be in Shakerville soon, and their honeymoon could begin. He could hardly wait.

They were halfway across, some fifty yards beyond the island and fifty yards short of the flax-tufted bank, when things began to go wrong. First the downstream horse stumbled and lurched forward, losing its footing. It splashed and wallowed, its back surging in and out of the water as it struggled for a grip on the riverbed.

'Dumn thung's trod un a hole,' cursed Tom as he wrenched the reins to try to steer the wagon upstream.

The full force of the current was against him, pushing at the other horse and the wagon itself, trying to slew them around the other way. With the sudden extra load thrust against it the other horse panicked, too, whinnying and tossing its head, its glossy flared nostrils scenting its partner's fear.

Unrolling the whip with one hand and straining at the reins with the other, Tom's face was grim with strain. He cracked the heavy stock-whip and loosed a string of spicy curses at the unfortunate beasts.

Glancing up at him in disapproval, Daisy saw at once that they were in trouble, serious trouble. Sweat greased his face, and his eyes were hard with a mixture of fear and determination, as he struggled to gain control of the stricken vehicle.

It was too late. All his panting efforts had not deflected the wagon's inexorable course; and now, at the same moment Daisy realized there was danger, the wagon rolled over the rim of the same hole that had unbalanced the horse only seconds before.

With a single groaning noise the wagon tipped as the right-hand front wheel dropped into the chasm. The whole chassis wrenched as the front corner tilted crazily down. The sudden drag on the reins jerked Tom forward, catapulting him into the foaming tumult churned up by the horses. Amy slithered sideways, shrieking as she splashed into the water, while Excalibur, tipped unceremoniously from Daisy's lap, flailed after her, his claws scrabbling uselessly along the length of the timber slope. He howled, then gurgled, as the current dunked him, whisked him up and brushed him away.

Daisy grabbed the rail in front of her. When the wagon twisted she, too, was thrown from her seat but managed to hang on with her one good hand and one partially useful one. The jolt flung her bodily along the rail, wrenching her shoulder and smashing her bandaged arm as she crushed against it. Gritting her teeth, she bit back a scream as sweet unbearable pain gushed hot and red up her arm.

'Daisy!' gasped Amy who was clinging to the twisted side-rail. Her black jacket fanned out around her, billowing behind her shoulders. She was not in any immediate danger.

Daisy scrabbled with her feet until she managed to brace herself into a

174

standing position, boots planted on what was the side of the wagon. Gingerly she relaxed her grip, closing her eyes in relief as the pain in her arm eased. She cautiously flexed her shoulders and only then dared to look around.

Amy was bobbing in the water, fingers white with strain as she gripped the timber. Her hair was loose, wet and drab, and she had lost the battered black hat that had been jammed on to her head. All around her floated packages that were toppling gradually from the wagon and being twirled and tumbled away in the muddy water.

Daisy looked beyond the flotsam. *Excalibur!* she thought. For a moment her insides turned to freezing mush as she feared for his life, but then beyond the string of bobbing packages she saw his head held bravely above the mass of choppy wavelets. Swimming strongly, he was already almost to the far bank. She laughed aloud with sheer relief. He'd almost died by drowning once; it was plain he had no intention of suffering that fate this time.

'Daisy!' pleaded Amy, and by now Daisy's arm had recovered sufficiently for her to use it for balance while she reached down with her good hand to her friend. Hampered by heavy sodden clothes, Amy panted and struggled, forcing one foot up on to the wagon edge, then a knee, and finally hefting her body up. 'Tom!' she said, her teeth chattering so hard that Daisy couldn't understand her. 'Tom! What's happened to Tom?'

Precariously balanced on the crazily tilting wagon, both girls scanned the river for a sign of him. There was a long stillness, filled with the hollow rushing of the river; and then, with an explosion of disbelief Amy burst out: 'Oh, Daisy, my Tom's drownded! He's nowhere! *Nowhere!*'

'It can't be. . . .'

Amy was choking back sobs. She was oozing with dirty water, flowing with it. Rivulets ran from her rat's tails of hair, puddled around her feet and dripped over Daisy as she leaned against her. Her face was a white grimace; she was freezing cold and ill with apprehension. 'There's not a sign of him!' she wept.

Daisy clung fast to the wagon rail as the horses thrashed about, tugging it this way and that against the implacable force of the relentless current. There was an almighty jolt, and with a triumphant whinny one of the horses broke loose and immediately plunged for the freedom of the shore. The other horse brayed and kicked in panic, desperate to escape, too.

On the pitching wagon Amy grabbed at Daisy as she sobbed hysterically. Her hands were cold and hard as a gate-latch on a frosty morning. 'Tom! Tom!' she shrieked, in a high keening wail that froze Daisy's nerves.

Daisy shivered, pitying her and infected by her terror, but her fear was for themselves. One horse had gone, and the other was bucking and kicking at the traces. It wouldn't be long before she and Amy were alone here in the middle of the pelting flood with no hope of reaching land. Amy couldn't swim – not properly – and Daisy doubted her chances of forging through that tumult with her arm still bandaged in splints. Tom was the least of her worries.

EIGHTEEN

'He can't swim,' Amy bleated. 'Sailors hardly ever can. Father has a theory that if they were swept overboard it would be better to drown at once than to tread water and watch the ship plough on without them. Oh, Daisy, I can't bear the thought of losing my Tom. . . .'

Daisy wasn't listening. She was watching the remaining horse. It was kicking back with its massive hind legs and rearing up with its tree-trunk-sized front ones, tossing its terrified head and uttering frantic snorts of panic. Around it and over its back wound the remains of the broken leather traces. There was something else, too. In the murky water, now beside it, now underneath it and entangled in the reins, was an object. *Something*. While Amy was dithering in mindless fear beside her, Daisy stared at the object. Every time it bobbed to the surface it looked different. First she saw the shape of a boot, then an outflung hand disembodied like a starfish in the gloom, and at last Tom's head broke the surface, but for only a moment, so briefly that she could have imagined she dreamed the painted- down hair and twisted agonised face.

'There he is,' she said. It was quite matter-of-fact; Amy's extravagant outpourings would do for them both.

'Where? Where, Daisy? *Where?*'

'He's caught up in the harness,' said Daisy, tugging her arm free of Amy's freezing grip. As she spoke the boot appeared again, meandering just below the surface, a dark sole-shaped fish. 'Look. There's his foot!' It flashed across the surface, scything up a yard of spray, then disappeared.

Distant barking snagged her attention. Excalibur was trotting along the bank now, pausing every few moments to shake himself. He barked at the wagon, chiding, as if to ask what was causing the delay. In the shallows the first draught horse was stumbling ashore, its every step brisk with panic. Excalibur barked at it, too.

'He'll drown!' screamed Amy. Her eyes were fixed in terror on the place where Tom had disappeared. Daisy thought he well might, but there was nothing she could do about it. In a strange way she felt numbed by what was happening to Tom; if the wagon tipped over, that could be her fate, too, and Amy's yet she felt dispassionate about the prospect.

Tom's head appeared again, and a flailing arm. As the girls watched, he gulped in a hasty breath of air then sank below the surface, his hair a flash of orange water-weed.

'He's tangled up. He can't free himself,' cried Amy, peeling off her sodden jacket. It was so old and tattered that the water had torn it in several places, pushing through it as if it was paper.

'What are you doing?'

'Somebody must help him. I'd never f-f-forgive myself if h-he drowned. I'd never have another clear night's s-s-sleep as long—'

'No, Amy, it's too dangerous.'

Shoving Daisy's hand away, she crawled over the front rail and lowered one foot to the central bar against which the one horse was still thrashing.

Daisy watched, fascinated. What could she do? What did she think she could achieve? There was nothing beyond this rail to hang on to, and only inches from where she was leaning was the very real peril of flailing hoofs.

Before Amy could move the horse reared again, jolting the wagon. A veil of spray flung its net over her as with a final gargantuan struggle the horse plunged free and surged with ears flat and neck arching towards the bank. Still attached to it by the tangle of reins, and dragging in its wake like a log, was Tom. He was struggling, twisting and kicking as the brown water curled over him in a translucent caul.

'Tom!' screamed Amy, reaching uselessly with both arms.

'Be careful! Be careful!' cried Daisy behind her.

It was too late. Freed from the horse, the wagon swung and resettled on the riverbed with a shuddering jerk like an animal rippling its skin to shake off a fly. Squeaking with fright, Daisy clung on in desperation, watching, horrified, as Amy pitched into the tumult. As the wagon subsided, all the water that had been pressing against the upstream side was released in a rush. Daisy stretched out her good hand, urging Amy to grasp it, and for a few seconds Amy bobbed there in the lee of the wagon, her outflung hands touching and sliding away then touching Daisy's fingertips. Then, just as Daisy was crouching lower for a longer reach, the rush of pent-up water surged around the wagon, swirling to Daisy's knees, tucking her skirt around her freezing ankles and lifting Amy upwards in its buoyant swell. Had she been a little closer, it would have hefted her right up beside Daisy, but she was still tantalizingly out of reach.

'We'll do it!' promised Daisy. Wedging her hurt arm under the wagon rail and ignoring the pain that brought an immediate blistering of sweat out on her forehead, Daisy extended her good hand, stretching until every joint burned with tension. 'Here! Grab my hand! You can do it!'

Amy kicked, and the water wafted her closer. Both hands reached up in supplication, fingers spread. The river washed into her mouth, slapping at her cheeks. She swallowed wet gulps with every gasp of breath.

'There! I knew you could!' Daisy's throat ached with sheer relief as her hand touched both of Amy's.

But the river had done with teasing them, bored as a cat when it has finished playing with a mouse. It lifted Amy up one last time so that her fingers brushed the length of Daisy's hands, but when her fingers clawed to grab it suddenly tugged her away so that her hands closed on palmfuls of water.

Daisy screamed. The river was boiling around Amy, pushing her backwards, nudging her sideways, jostling her further and further away from the wagon. She stared with horror into Amy's terrified eyes. Her own screams echoed in her skull, but when Amy opened her mouth to scream, too, the river slopped a wet gag into her mouth, muffling any sounds she made with its own vast hollow roar.

Daisy couldn't believe it was happening. On this clear and sunny day, under the serene gaze of the mountains, Amy was fighting for her life. The notion seemed impossible – not on a perfect day like this when Amy had been, just a moment before, so happy. A trail of soft puffy clouds was basking on the horizon; low across the brown water flew a trio of herons, their necks arched in symmetry. And here Amy was dying. Drowning before her eyes. It was ridiculous, a joke, a terrible, terrible joke.

On the riverbank Excalibur frisked nervously around the first horse while the second approached wallowing through the shallows with Tom lurching behind like a prisoner in chains, hunched and stumbling on hands and one leg, dragging the other. He couldn't see Amy and the distance that was widening between her and the wagon.

Daisy screamed. Already she had been screaming; she didn't know, she hadn't heard herself, but her throat was raw and her screams scraped out of that throat with increasing hoarseness. She called to Amy as if Amy could come back to the wagon of her own free will. She called to her to come back, not to go, please, please, Amy come back!

This was incomprehensible. Amy should be back here on the wagon-seat sitting perkily beside her singing 'Tra-la-la-la' to the trill of Tom's sea-shanties. She should be smiling, she should be happy. She shouldn't be that anonymous bundle of sodden rags that the river was tumbling and slurping over, pawing at and slopping like a contemptuous uncaring crowd.

Daisy screamed on and on, her voice dragged away by the wild hollow rushing just as Amy was being dragged away. Could Amy even hear her?

179

Daisy could no longer see her face, only the thousands of jaunty little wavelets that were pushing and pulling and bearing her along, shrinking her and shrinking her so that soon Daisy couldn't even be sure that she saw her any more, whether that smudged shape was her or was one of the packages shaken like ripe fruit from the wagon or was even a rippled braiding of the current jutting above the other waves.

'Amy!' shrieked Daisy in desperation.

Towards noon a fisherman and his adult son were taking a load of fresh flounder to sell in Shakerville. They stopped, hearing the sound of the river at the junction where the inland track met the road south. The roaring was so loud today that the two men decided to detour with their cart to take a look.

Later both said that the Lord himself must have guided them there.

In the lupins fringing the road two draught horses wandered. Both were dazed, both had dried blood matting the hair over their hoofs and bleeding torn flesh around their mouths. Both trailed ominous shreds of leather harnessing.

Further on a broad shingle bank opened to a view of the rushing muddy torrent. Here a small brown and white dog barked a furious alarm, then dashed over to where fresh flotsam skeined the high water-line. Not until the cart was almost upon him did the fishermen see the body lying face down on the grey pebbles. His few pitiful scraps of clothing were torn almost away from his waist and shoulders, while his back and legs, exposed, had flushed a bright sunburned pink; he had been there for hours. One ankle seemed to be injured, crushed and bleeding.

The dog rushed at the man, harrying him, yipping incessantly until he raised his head, uttered something unintelligible, then flopped his cheek back on to the warm stones.

'Sweet Mary and all her saints,' said the father, pointing so that his son could also see the final piece of the puzzle.

Partially obscured by a clump of flax that speared out of the shingle, and marooned midstream, was the wagon. One front wheel had been torn away, the chassis was twisted and the tray tilted at an angle of defeat. The floodwater had given it quite a battering. Only a few remnants of whatever load it had been carrying still remained, a jumble of boxes and packages tipped into one corner and a ragged tarpaulin streaming out like a lily pad.

Perched on the highest side, on what had been the tray rim, above the visible slice of one of the iron back wheels was a woman. A lady. Even seated as awkwardly as she was on that precarious perch there was something elegant about her. Her chin was up, her gown pulled down over her toes, and her face was shaded by a stylish pink parasol. When she saw the two men she folded the parasol and placed it across her knees, giving a clear sign that she had been waiting to be rescued and that now her wait was over.

Both men admired her cool courage, but when they lifted her to safety she collapsed at a touch, babbling and trembling in a jangle of shattered nerves.

'Amy? Amy? Who's Amy?' asked the father, a wiry man with a full black beard and black hairs on the backs of his hands. He stared into Daisy's blank blue eyes. 'Who's Amy, missus? Is she your little girl, then?'

Daisy shook her head violently. She pointed downstream with an unsteady hand. 'She's there . . . Amy. Amy's there.'

When she was a little girl, lonely and bored with Rhys away as he so often was, Daisy would wander into the gloomy library, pull one of the heavy volumes from the shelves and sit on the window-seat with one foot tucked up under her and the huge book spread open in her lap as she pored over the pages. There was an etching in *The Mediaeval Age* that fascinated her, an illustration of the landscape of Hell, where razor-backed hills reared over haunted valleys and from every fold and crevice on the bleak treeless slopes issued a poisonous-looking vapour that hinted of an inferno raging under the thin crust of earth.

When the trap lurched over the last saddle and down towards the basin where Shakerville lay, Daisy thought immediately of that macabre etching. The sprawling town merged so perfectly with the landscape that most of the shabby canvas dwellings seemed like rocks or portions of the cliffs, and it was only the threads of smoke tugging from their incongruously solid chimneys that betrayed the presence of people living within. There were so many chimneys that the dusty hovels adjoining could have been huge pebbles in a vast smoking crater. The town's centre was not yet in view.

It was evening now, and the whole valley sheltered in deep shade, while the sky was palest gold silk, melting over the snow on the mountain that loomed straight ahead, silhouetted against the diminishing folds of range upon range of endless mountains beyond.

Daisy shifted position as she examined this mountain, and her heart quickened. Yes, this was the place Andrew had described, and there it was, purple and narrow-shouldered with the peak that jutted into four little points like a crown. She hugged Excalibur closer under the salt-stiffened cape that had been draped around her hours ago. Excalibur whined and wriggled, bored with sitting still.

'That be Rainbow Mountain,' said the younger fisherman helpfully, twisting around to give Daisy a gap-toothed grin. He couldn't be more than twenty and had less than a dozen teeth in his head, all of which he displayed when he smiled, as he attempted to entertain her by pointing out places of interest along the route. 'Two wagons went over there last spring when the river were up,' he said cheerfully at a hairpin bend that swung around a cliff-face dizzily high above the raging torrent. 'Smashed to smithereens they both were, kilt seven people.' Orses lived, but.' And at a rickety bridge inches above the dark swirling water: 'This bridge were swept clean away last flood. Three people gone, dashed away while their friends looked on. Never a trace of one poor soul.'

At another time Daisy might have been amused, but she resented these casual allusions to death and guessed that this would be Amy's destiny, too, to be tucked into his repertoire with the countless other grisly casualties. She could hear him: 'Searched the banks for better'n two hours we did, with 'er 'usband lying senseless, poor devil, and 'er friend beside 'erself, crying an' begging us not to give up the search. 'Opeless it were, o' course. The flood so 'igh an' so fierce. Swept 'er clean out to sea, it did.'

Amy, oh, Amy, Daisy kept repeating silently as the fish-cart clipped along at twice the wagon's lumbering pace. She and Tom and Excalibur were more or less comfortable on the folded tarpaulin that was wadded over the willow fish-baskets, bouncing along in a tang of fishy smell with the draught horses jogging behind loaded with what remained of Tom's goods. Daisy had come unwillingly. In the end they forcibly hefted her on to the makeshift seat, thrust the puppy up beside her and then swung Tom's inert body up, too, placing his head in her lap, ignoring her violent protests. 'Look after 'im, Miss. Bathe 'is 'ead with this cloth. 'E's in a bad way, poor wretch.'

I don't care if he dies! Daisy wanted to scream, but there was no room for her opinion and the men had wasted too much time already. Seething with resentment, in an agony of frustration – they *had* to find Amy! – Daisy was forced to endure the added discomfort of having Tommy Nevin's loathsome head weighing down on her, numbing her legs.

When they arrived at the outskirts of town he had still not stirred. His left ankle was badly damaged, still swelling despite her awkward ministrations with the cloth and water-bowl, and was now puffed to the size of his thigh with the toes so distended that his foot looked like a cow's udder. His eyelids flickered constantly but did not open, and when he breathed he made the scraping, whining noise of a gate that had not been unlatched for many years.

Looking down at his battered face, Daisy realized that her animosity had faded. *His hatred towards me caused all this*, she thought with sudden insight. Why, though, did he detest her so intensely that he was driven to humiliate her in the worst way he could imagine? Once he had shamed her he felt shame himself, which was why he was goaded on by anxiety to be rid of her and why he took such blatant risks. If not for Daisy, he would have waited an extra day on the other bank until the river subsided, then crossed in safety. Hatred was what pressed him on. That hatred killed Amy.

But why? she wondered as she wrung the cloth out again and pressed it to his burning forehead. What endless harm had been suffered, and so needlessly! That was the pity of it all.

Dogs rushed out to meet them. Yapping heralded their jolting descent of the steep road. Excalibur was up and straining at once, fangs showing, his shoulders bristling with false confidence. Daisy scolded as she tightened her grip on his collar. 'They'd crunch you in one bite,' she told him.

Progress on this last section of road was slow, interrupted continuously by men hurrying from their huts to bargain for the fish. Daisy was astounded; she had imagined prospectors to be all of a kind, labourers and the like, but from their dress and voices these men had abandoned professions and gentle lifestyles to come here. Dusty top-hats were as common as cloth caps.

In the gloom they peered at her as they bought their fish and a few made jokes about mermaids. The fishermen were too busy to explain her presence there. Daisy waited in vain for a woman customer to appear so that she could ask after Andrew; finally she began to wonder if this town was populated entirely by men.

They reached the town square with two baskets of fish sold and a jostling clamour of potential customers following behind. Here, at last, was the 'pretty' part of the town, a square of shabby grass freckled with daffodils. On the four streets facing this park stood ranks of wooden buildings, some with verandas jutting in front like cap peaks, some with hollow eyes and faded painted façades like raddled tarts' faces. While Daisy waited she counted seven hotels all with customers spilling like loose change on to the dusty street.

'We're in luck,' said the fisherman, emerging from one as he wiped a fluff of froth from his moustache. 'A good fresh brew arrived this morning and they've just tapped the barrel. And good luck to you, too, miss, ah. . . .'

'Pilkington,' Daisy reminded him, supplying the name of an old governess.

'Yes. There's a doctor 'ere in town. 'E's staying over yon at the 'Orse an' 'Ounds. We'll 'ave you over there in a jiffy.'

He didn't see her at first, and she hung back. Her dreams of rushing to him and flinging herself into his arms evaporated in the face of this reality. She was filthy with road-dust and sweat, tired and aching and with a sick depression that was wrapped around her as tightly as the wet bandage encased her arm. And Andrew seemed different now. Gone was the vague romantic image of tragic suffering, and in its place was a brisk efficient man who had not even noticed Daisy but was concentrating immediately on Tommy's injured leg. To rush up and fling her arms around him she would have had to push the fisherman and his son aside – hardly appropriate behaviour!

Glancing around the room, she decided that it must have been the hotel's grand dining-room in the town's gold-rush heyday. Tattered velvet curtains hung from tarnished brass rods, while sooty cobwebs festooned a once-grand ornate plaster ceiling. The embossed scarlet and gold wallpaper peeled from the high walls. Glancing around tiredly, Daisy counted five beds, three occupied by motionless figures, one empty and the last on which Tom had been placed.

Andrew was saying: 'His leg is in bad shape – a triple compound fracture, I'd say – and at least four of his ribs are cracked. Was there any evidence of indulgence in liquor that might have contributed to the accident, did you notice?' He saw Daisy, and his face altered.

'Hello, Andrew,' she ventured timidly.

'What in the—? What are *you* doing here?'

Her hopes, already blighted, shrivelled and died. He wasn't pleased to see her. Tom was right. He'd wanted to be left in peace, but she'd ignored his wishes and chased right after him with as much sense as a dog chases after a farm cart, and now it was plain he didn't want her.

She stared at him, dumb with dismay. How many days ago was it that he held her in his arms and told her that he loved her? Was that just a dream? This was certainly a nightmare.

Raising her chin, she echoed; ' ''What are *you* doing here?'' What kind of a welcome is that?'

'The kind you deserve,' he snapped; then, seeing the tremulous disappointment on her face, he paused. In a gentle voice he said; 'People are looking for you, Daisy. People are terribly concerned about you.'

'Someone important, is she? There wouldn't be a reward out for 'er, by any chance?' asked the fisherman.

Andrew looked into the man's creased face, took a deep breath and exhaled through his nostrils. He couldn't be blamed for asking. He said: 'If there's a reward, it's my thanks. The lady is my sister.'

'That was clever of you,' whispered Daisy. It was more than an hour later, and Andrew had finished bandaging and strapping Tom's leg and ribs. He had washed his hands and was sitting at a desk below a golden-haloed kerosene-lantern, making notes in a book. Daisy gazed at him hungrily. A lock of hair flopped over his brow, reminding her of

Jeremy – but she didn't want to think of Jeremy, not ever again. It was Papa he reminded her of most, now that he had put on his spectacles and was peering at the page like Papa did when the light was poor or the print too small.

'You shouldn't have come,' he said, still writing. The shock of seeing her still hadn't worn off. 'How *did* you get here?'

'With him . . . with Tom Nevin.'

'My God, Tom Nevin, of course it is! What with the sunburn and the bumps and scratches all over his face, I didn't recognize him at all.'

Through her tiredness she noticed he made more of a fuss over that fact than of her being there. In a dull voice she said: 'He and Amy were eloping. I guessed that this was where you might be and I persuaded them to bring me along. Tom was planning to sell a load of goods he'd brought with him.'

'Eloped!' Andrew shook his head. 'Her and Tom Nevin! Who'd have imagined . . .? Where is she?'

Daisy swallowed. 'Amy. . . .' She burst into tears. 'Amy's dead. . . . She's drowned, Andrew, and it's all my fault. It was terrible. She touched my hand . . . she almost reached me . . . I almost grabbed her, but the water swept her away. If it wasn't for me. . . .'

'It sounds as if you tried your best. Don't feel badly—'

'It *is* my fault, though.' Her eyes were wild and blurred with tears, and he could see that she genuinely believed what she was saying. 'If I hadn't been there, the accident wouldn't even have happened.'

Andrew had arrived in Shakerville atop a load of coal, nursing bruised fists and a burning hatred that scorched right through his shaken soul. With no idea of the chaos he was leaving behind, his one thought was to put as much distance as possible between himself and Mists of Heaven. Had a passage been available, he'd have headed straight back to Europe.

He found Shakerville in desperate need of his services, all the doctors in that part of the province having gone north to a small prospecting town where typhoid had broken out. The town's sick and injured were being tended to by the constable's wife, a well-meaning but unschooled woman whose remedies were a choice of two: a purge or a poultice, depending on whether the ailment was visible or not.

She greeted Andrew with enthusiasm, Constable Creely unlocked the medical-supplies cupboard, and friends of the men most urgently needing attention helped willingly to set up the makeshift ward. 'It's not usually like this,' said Mrs Creely apologetically. She was a fussy animated person with nervous hopping movements and an anxious, perpetually frowning face. 'I warned Constable Creely that it were tempting fate to send the doctor off. We had not an accident for months, but the moment the stage had left someone chopped a finger off, someone else fell down the Harburg track and old Wallace Edwards brewed up a stew with heaven knows what ingredients that brought almost a dozen men down with the bloody flux. You don't mind my speaking frankly, do you?' she said, her frown pinching tighter. 'But being a constable's wife . . . I do know more than a lady should of the seamier side of life.'

'But you are mistaken, Mrs Creely,' Andrew corrected her. 'A true lady thinks of others rather than of her own selfish interests. She may know all about the sordid side of life but she is never stained by it. Her good works elevate her above the mire, as they have elevated you, Mrs Creely.'

She flushed and peered doubtfully into his face. *We've got a strange one here*, she thought. She wondered if he drank.

From the moment he began working again Andrew's life was transformed. Gone were the feelings of uselessness that had trapped him in the swamp of self-doubt and dissipation. The remnants of grief were gone, too, seared away by the rage that now began to ebb. One night as he listened to an ill man's fevered ramblings he thought: *Who am I to judge Rhys Morgan for what he's done? He may have given me my life anonymously, but it's mine, and I alone can shape it.* Relief seeped through him as he realized that now his years of antagonism towards Rhys had found a personal focus that antagonism was fading, too. Paradoxically he no longer cared what Rhys and Lisabeth did. He stopped drinking.

About Daisy he was much more disturbed. He had met her when he was in a dazed state, and whatever passion there was between them was ninety per cent on her side. At the time it had puzzled him. Why should an entrancing young woman be so attracted to a defeated, grieving, much older man? Now the reason was obvious. She was responding to the likeness between them. She could see what he in his bemused state could not: that under their surface differences strong currents of similarity flowed. Not knowing the truth, Daisy responded in the only way possible: by falling in love with him.

Until now Andrew had reflected that there was no need to wish vengeance on Rhys for his years of deception. The ordeal of breaking the news to Daisy would be punishment enough for anyone. Rhys had always doted on Daisy, indulged her and, yes, ruined her, twisting an intelligent caring nature into that of a wilful demanding brat. It would kill Rhys to have to confess to her, and Andrew had smiled grimly at the prospect of all Rhys Morgan's chickens coming home to roost.

Now, as he comforted Daisy, he reflected with wry irony that Rhys Morgan had wriggled away from this consequence of his actions, too.

Plainly Daisy didn't know anything: that reference to 'my sister' hadn't elicited the hoped-for response.

She hadn't been told, and he would have to tell her himself.

'She's fast asleep, bless her soul,' whispered Mrs Creely. She sighed. Well past middle age herself, she sometimes wistfully recalled the romantic moments of a youth lived so long ago that it might as well have belonged to someone else. 'She must love you very much, this young lady of yours.'

'Did I forget to mention it? I'm sorry, Mrs Creely. She's my sister, my half-sister.'

The good woman's eyebrows steepled. 'Your *sister*? I didn't realize. . . .'

'A lot of people don't realize,' he assured her gravely.

NINETEEN

'I DON'T KNOW HOW CLEVER this idea of yours is,' said Daisy next morning as she paused at the doorway to loop Excalibur's lead around the leg of an armchair. 'It gave me a real start when Mrs Creely started questioning me about our supposed blood-relationship. I managed to evade her questions by flattering her collection of crockery moustache-cups and teapots, most of them given to the Constable in lieu of fines, she said. It's just as well that she's susceptible to flattery or I'd not have known what to tell her!'

'Where is she?' asked Andrew, looking up from a young man who was groaning in the fifth bed. 'Where is she? I need her to help me.'

'She said to tell you she'd been called to a birthing. It's a relief to know that there are some women in this Godforsaken place after—'

'You'll have to help, then,' interrupted Andrew.

Daisy looked at him askance. He was swabbing a wound, a burn that had eaten deeply into the young man's arm. The poor wretch looked about eighteen and was moaning and twitching, his grey face sheened with sweat as he fought against the pain. There was a sickening stench in the room, sour and rich, that made her stomach tighten.

'Come and hold John's other arm,' Andrew ordered abruptly. 'I can see by that fancy gown that you're not dressed for hospital work, but I need assistance. Just do what you can to calm him while I fix his dressing.'

Daisy was stung. After rising she'd dressed with special care in this apple-green watered silk, hoping to charm Andrew out of that puzzling reserve with which he'd greeted her last night. While she brushed her hair and rolled it around her fingers into ringlets, she assured herself that he hadn't meant to be so cold and rude. He was exhausted. All men were grumpy and unfriendly when they were exhausted. Even Papa – but she didn't want to think about Papa now, nor about the alarm that had gone out about her disappearance, nor about the trouble she was causing. All that mattered was Andrew.

But he still wasn't pleased with her. Her elaborate attempts to make herself beautiful for him had been curtly dismissed without so much as a smile. She wanted to sling her disappointment at him, have it out with him now, but instinctively kept silent. Now, while he was tending the sick, was not an appropriate moment.

Obediently she took her station at the other side of the bed and timidly reached for the young man's hand. It was as rough as bark with blackened broken nails. As soon as he felt her touch he seized on her fingers, crushing them with a desperation that drove the rings into her flesh. She muffled a squeak of pain.

Andrew glanced up at her face. 'Think of what *he's* suffering. He and his partner were modifying part of their mining machinery. He'd heated it up, hammered out the bent parts and was carrying the red-hot metal to the river when he slipped and fell, and the metal jolted out of the tongs and struck him.'

Daisy shuddered. Andrew was picking charred fragments of cloth out of the wound, and each time his tweezers touched raw flesh John convulsed, dragging at Daisy's hand in a paroxysm of agony. His teeth ground together as he swallowed his cries before they could burst out and shame him.

'Sorry about this, old chap. Only a few hours now.'

'*Hours?*' Daisy was aghast.

'There's no laudanum left, and he needs it to ease the pain. We're expecting more on the stage-coach this afternoon.'

As he spoke Constable Creely came in, lifting his boots quietly as he walked across the shabby floor until he was standing at the foot of the bed. Catching the last of what Andrew said, he shook his head. 'It's only Wednesday today. The stage isn't due until Friday.'

'Oh, dear Lord . . .,' hissed John. Daisy could glimpse the pinkish grey of bone in his wound.

'I've got some,' she said.

'Laudanum?'

'Yes. Nearly a whole bottleful. I was ill on the way here with a sunstroke headache, and Amy. . . .' She paused, gulping back a rush of weakness at the mention of Amy's name.

'Hurry . . . please . . .,' gasped John. Huge beads of moisture stood out on his forehead.

'I'm sorry.' Immediately she forgot the horror of that bright blue day, of Amy stretching to grasp her hand and being swirled away slowly and deliberately by the ravenous brown water. The present swamped the past. 'I'll go right now, if you'll let go of my hand.'

'An angel,' muttered John when she had gone. 'Yer wife's an angel.'

'She's my sister,' said Andrew carefully. He was still not sure whether he liked the idea, but there was a rightness about it that was beginning to satisfy some unrealized need inside him.

'Your sister?' Constable Creely was as astonished as his wife had been. 'Then, what is the . . . er, connection to the other fellow they brought in? I'd gathered she was his sister, too.'

'No connection at all, Constable. His wife, the one the party went out to search for this morning, she was Daisy's best friend, and they were chaperoning Daisy on this visit to see me.'

But you've only just arrived here this minute, thought the Constable, leaving that observation unspoken. There was something very odd here. He glanced down the row of high beds to where Tom Nevin dozed in the far-end one next to the door, his freckled face as grey as the pillow on which his head rested. 'He's no relation of yours, then?'

'No,' said Andrew, adding grimly. 'Not so far as I'm aware.'

'Pardon?'

'Nothing, nothing. A private joke. No, I've known Tommy all his life, but we're not related.' He stared into Constable Creely's leathery face. 'In trouble, is he? He always was a tearaway, young Tom.'

Constable Creely tugged at his sparse grey beard. 'I just had a look at the goods that came off the wagon, the ones Jack Ingles and his son brought in with him. There's stolen property amongst the things – a valuable Moorish piece I particularly recognize. Just like one we saw at the Provincial Chambers when the wife and I went down to town on holiday. Soon as I saw it I recognized it from the newspapers. It went missing from a liquor merchant's home in Auckland.'

'Nothing about Tom Nevin would surprise me,' said Andrew, 'but all that concerns me is the condition of his ankle; and that, I don't mind telling you, is giving me serious worry.' He wound the bandage around John's arm and neatly tucked in the edges. John made a sharp squeaking sound, to which Andrew said: 'You're doing splendidly. Your arm will be better than new.'

When he straightened he was puzzled to find Constable Creely staring at him with a hard challenging expression. 'Is something the matter, Constable?'

'Suppose you tell me.'

'I don't understand.'

'Are you planning to stay in Shakerville long?'

'I was, but I may need to escort my sister home. It depends on when the other doctor returns. I'm planning to send off a couple of telegrams when the office opens—'

'Were you now? What about, may I ask?'

Andrew grinned suddenly. 'You think we're some kind of band of thieves, don't you?' He laughed aloud. 'This beats everything. It's quite unthinkable.'

'A lot of unthinkable things happen in this world,' said the Constable heavily. 'Besides, Doctor Stafford, you don't fit in. There's summat odd about you that I can't quite put my finger on. Be best, I'm thinking, if you go back to the big city where you belong. We're not sophisticated here, like them in Christchurch.'

Christchurch! If he hadn't been so angry, he'd have laughed again in pure scorn. 'I'll go when I'm no longer needed,' he informed Creely. 'And it will be to London, or perhaps to continue my studies in Paris. Christchurch, *sophisticated*?' And he laughed again, but Constable Creely's whole tone had angered him and when Daisy returned a red flush was still staining the back of his neck. Wordlessly he took the bottle from her, uncapped it and drizzled a large spoonful into John's grimacing mouth.

John gasped his gratitude, but Daisy didn't hear him; she was plucking at Andrew's sleeve. 'The policeman just handcuffed Tommy Nevin's wrist to the bed-frame. What did he do that for?' she whispered. 'They don't suspect him of killing Amy, do they? Because he didn't! I was there the whole time and I can tell them—'

She was interrupted by a shouted curse from Tom, who woke just as the Constable was clicking the cuffs shut. 'You busstard! Undo thus at once!' he roared to Creely's disappearing back.

Before Andrew could stop her Daisy hurried after the policeman, calling to him that he had made a mistake, please to come back and undo Mr Nevin, please to listen to her. . . . Calling out, she walked past all the beds and around the side of Tom's, where she was jerked to a sudden halt, his free hand fast on her bandaged wrist.

'The foine lady hersulf!' he spat at her. 'Foine Muss Morgan tulling everybody whut to do as usual. Where's Amy, huh? Where are you keeping Amy? She shud be here wuth me.' As he spoke he twisted Daisy's arm. 'Where us she?' he demanded.

Daisy gaped at him, more frightened than hurt. He knew about Amy; Andrew told him last night.

He twisted her arm again. 'Where us she?' And this time Daisy yelped in pain. Raising his head, Andrew saw what was going on and hurried from John's bedside.

'Bitch!' hissed Tom, his battered face puffed, suffused with loathing. 'High and moighty bitch!'

Andrew said nothing. With two extended fingers he jabbed Tom hard and suddenly in the shoulder, striking on a nerve and temporarily disabling that arm. Tom swore. Daisy pulled free, her face very white, her lips twitching. 'Did he hurt you?' asked Andrew, and she nodded.

'It's probably time that wrist of yours was looked at anyway,' said Andrew, ushering her over to the table. Tom's shouts followed them; Andrew walked back, leaned over the bed, said something in a flat cold

191

voice and returned, this time in silence. To Daisy he said grimly: promised I'd jab him in the vocal chords next time. It's how I got aw⟨ay⟩ from your father after he knocked me down, you know.' *Our father*, ⟨I⟩ thought. *My father, and it's a pity that he wasn't knocked down lo⟨ng⟩ ago*.

Now was the chance she'd been waiting for. 'You hurt Papa qui⟨te⟩ badly, you know, though Doctor Meakings said he wasn't in any *re⟨al⟩* danger. You must have had a serious quarrel. Was it over me?' His fa⟨ce⟩ was implacable, unencouraging, as he flicked at the bandages an⟨d⟩ began to unwind the cocoon on her arm. 'What did Papa say to you?'

Andrew didn't reply. Shaken by Tom's insults, by the pain he ha⟨d⟩ inflicted, and by Andrew's continuing rejection of her, Daisy lapse⟨d⟩ into miserable silence.

The bandages were an embarrassment, stinking with mildew and sour body smell, filthy with the journey's dirt. Under the wrappings h⟨er⟩ arm was white, ridged, and clammy as a dead thing. Andrew though⟨t⟩ fully probed her wrist and held it in one hand while he manipulated h⟨er⟩ fingers with the other.

Watching him, Daisy felt as if she was being smothered by a hea⟨vy⟩ clinging blanket that paralysed all her feelings. Everything had go⟨ne⟩ wrong, and she was powerless, unable to put things right because s⟨he⟩ didn't understand. She gazed at Andrew's face thinking how dear ⟨he⟩ was to her, how she felt so comfortable, so *right* with him, and yet ho⟨w⟩ deceived she must be because clearly he didn't feel the same way abo⟨ut⟩ her. He hadn't been pleased to see her, he was putting her on the fir⟨st⟩ stage-coach home, and still the reasons were a mystery to her.

Checking to see if his manipulations were hurting, he glanced up an⟨d⟩ saw the hunger in her eyes, the desolation. 'Daisy, I'm sorry,' he said. ⟨I⟩ truly don't want to harm you.'

'Then, why do you?' she burst out at him. 'I thought we cared abou⟨t⟩ each other! I thought you loved me, but you're so cold and distant th⟨at⟩ it's breaking my heart. I can't bear—'

'I do care about you. I do.' He rubbed her arm; it tingled.

'It doesn't seem like it.'

'I told you!' crowed Tom, who was listening avidly. 'I told you nut ⟨to⟩ chase ufter a mun who doesn't wunt you!'

Tears stung Daisy's eyes.

Andrew was replacing the splints, wrapping fresh bandages aroun⟨d⟩ her arm. 'As soon as Mrs Creely comes in, we'll go for a walk. I'll expla⟨in⟩ everything to you then,' he promised.

'Tell me about it again,' said Daisy like a child demanding a retelling ⟨of⟩ a favourite bed-time story. 'Oh, Andrew, I've made such a fool ⟨of⟩ myself.'

'No, Daisy. Your father – *our* father – has made proper fools of us both.'

Daisy squeezed his hand. *My brother. My brother!* After six hours battling incredulity and a storm of conflicting emotions she was beginning, cautiously, to like the idea.

She and Andrew sat close together on a low stone wall overlooking the square, while Excalibur, puffed from chasing sticks and snarling at other dogs, lay with tongue lolling at their feet. It was evening; the sky was orange and brown, and smoke from wood-fires smudged the bare hills all around the valley. A soft breeze combed the grass in the park, tugging at the knots of yellow daffodils and ruffling the leaves on the one tree, a scraggy oak. There was a malty yeasty smell in the air, lingering since one of yesterday's ale-barrels had lost its bung as it was being loaded outside the Southern Cross.

Andrew again told her what he knew, keeping to the facts as he understood them. 'We can only speculate about the whys and wherefores, but one thing is clear. There's no shame or disgrace for either of us in what happened It's only natural that we should feel strongly about each other. We simply misunderstood our attraction, that's all.'

'The disgrace is all Papa's,' decided Daisy fiercely. 'I can understand why he dreaded our finding out, what we'd think of him, but to keep quiet all these years was despicable. It's so unfair! You're his son, his only son, and he should have acknowledged you. The unfairness of it absolutely galls me!'

'Don't upset yourself on my account. I've thought about this a lot in the past few days. Part of this could be my fault. I never really liked Rhys Morgan. I always resented his attentions to Lisabeth, especially as part of the time he was married to Az—' He stopped.

'He was married to Mamma. It's all right. I do already know about that.' She gazed at the Golden Nugget's sign, swaying as it creaked in the wind. 'How odd. I am jealous of Lisabeth because she comes between me and Papa, and you resented Papa because he came between Lisabeth and you.'

'Rather a waste of time for both of us, wouldn't you say? But I am responsible, in part, for my own ignorance of all this. I condemned Lisabeth and Rhys for years. I used to receive the most shocking printed pamphlets that were apparently circulating in the province – sent anonymously, of course. I won't trouble you with the details of their content—'

'I've seen one,' said Daisy. 'Four years ago.'

He looked shocked. 'You poor child! You've suffered through all of this mess just as I have. I couldn't stand by and keep silent. I had to speak out, and I'd do it all again – even knowing who Rhys Morgan is, I

193

suppose. I wanted to protect Lisabeth and I felt that Rhys was dragging her name in the mud.'

Daisy smiled bitterly. 'While I believed that Lisabeth was leading Papa astray, poisoning his mind against Mamma, subjecting him to gossip instead of going back to her husband where she belonged. As you say, all of our anger and resentment didn't do one speck of good, did it?'

'True.'

'I feel so angry when I think of how we've suffered so needlessly. And think of how it could have been! If I hadn't come running after you, then I might never have known. And if I hadn't flung myself at you in the beginning, then you'd not have had that confrontation with Papa, and neither of us might ever have been told the truth. Just think, Andrew. We could have grown old and died and never known that we are brother and sister. I'm sure they never intended to tell us . . . it's only that you forced the issue.'

'You're probably right.' Andrew recalled how Rhys had prevaricated, offering a plethora of excuses before reluctantly bringing out the truth, and how Lisabeth, instead of showing concern for either him or Daisy, had pleaded only for Rhys.

'It's so selfish . . . so inexcusable! If Papa had acknowledged you, you would be a wealthy man. You could have had all the money you wanted to start off the best hospital. You wouldn't have had to struggle all those years, working long hours to finance your studies.'

'Easy on,' warned Andrew, taking her injured arm and massaging the fingers. Since he had changed the dressing they had taken on a purple tinge and were obviously bothering her because she kept scratching them, savagely when she was agitated as she was now. 'Perhaps it's best for me that I've had to work, not had things too easy.'

She was incredulous. 'But Papa's money *belongs* to you by right! Some of it anyway.'

'But I have no desire for it.' He laughed at her disbelief. 'That might be difficult for you to comprehend, but frankly, Daisy, you have been spoiled. Money and privilege make a comfortable bed to lie in, but there are bars around that bed and those bars prevent you from knowing about the real world.'

'I've had a dose of that in the last few days.'

'Of course you have. A nasty dose, too.'

She smiled at him, studying his face, finding more likenesses, some to Papa, some to Lisabeth, and a few, like the slight widow's peak, the long neck and wide cheekbones, that she, Papa and Andrew all had in common. 'I flung myself at you for selfish reasons,' she admitted. 'I'd adored you all my life without really knowing you, and I hate to be proved wrong, so it was automatic that I'd fall in love with you. But I was desperate to marry you because Amy was marrying Tom and that would make such a hole in my life. . . .' She was silent, sad for a moment. 'Papa and Lisabeth wanted me to marry Jeremy Drake, and I was so angry with them that poor Jeremy had no chance of being considered.'

'So it wasn't all-enduring True Love?' teased Andrew.

'I thought so at the time,' she giggled. 'That's why I felt such a fool when you told me the truth, but now I feel marvellous. It's as if I was hoping for something special, and I haven't got what I was expecting but something even better instead. All along you never seemed passionately interested in me, did you? Not in the way Jeremy—' She broke off, flushing.

'I know what you mean. We're friends, and I'm proud fit to burst to be your brother. You're quite the loveliest young woman I've ever met.'

'And you're the loveliest man. Isn't it marvellous? We've got each other for family now. I no longer care what Lisabeth and Papa do – you're all I want!'

Andrew watched a group of prospectors swaggering across the road to the Prince of Wales. 'Life isn't so simple,' he warned.

'But it's simply resolved. It was the worst day of my life when I learned that Papa had loved Lisabeth since before he even met Mamma. It seemed so terrible that Mamma and I had never been really loved or wanted, yet now I've got you nothing else matters.'

Her sunny optimism saddened him. She was still so naïvely young with such a heartaching amount to learn, and the bitterest part was that he wouldn't be there to support her, to protect her from life's storms and injustices. 'Life's not easy,' he repeated.

'What a gloomy creature you can be at times,' she chided affectionately. 'What can be difficult if we help each other? Just think how wonderful it will be always to have each other to turn to. We can go riding together, and to plays and concerts, and perhaps I could even go with you on your rounds when you're established in Christchurch. I enjoyed helping, and I was of some use, wasn't I? And then when you're married and I'm married we—'

'Daisy, stop.' He agreed that she had been a help to him, for she was quick and intelligent and after the first flinch she didn't recoil, not even when Tom developed a fever early in the afternoon and swore and raged at her again. She'd make a grand nurse. 'My sister,' he said to people who strayed in to seek attention or to visit. 'My sister's helping me today.'

But there wouldn't be the future she was picturing. 'I'm not staying here, Daisy. I'm returning to England as soon as I can. When I put you on Saturday's stage-coach we may not see each other again for years. I may travel directly to Wellington and catch a steamer from there to—'

'You mustn't go! Andrew, you can't leave me now!'

Hearing the distress in her voice, Excalibur whined and jumped up to lick her face. She patted him and tugged at his ears, not daring to look at Andrew's frighteningly sad face. She would have blocked out his voice, too, if she could, but there was no escape from what he was saying.

'When I remarked that there was no shame or disgrace in this for either of us, I wasn't referring to my own personal situation. Being a doctor, it's imperative that I have an impeccable reputation. There's going to be a scandal about this, a vicious maiming scandal with those disgusting gossip-sheets flourishing like leaves in the springtime. Can you imagine what fun people will have with the story? Everywhere I go heads will turn, insults will hiss after me. I'm a bastard, Daisy. A genuine, wrong-side-of-the-blanket, illegitimate bastard. It's an inescapable fact that people will talk!'

'They'll talk about me, too.' The prospect of what they might say crept over her like a live thing. Amy was dead; there would be an inquest and all of the story would be written in the newspapers. When Tom was charged and sent to prison it would all be printed again, and the taint of Tom's stealing would stick to her, perhaps forever.

She thought about that unspeakable incident when Tom had made her take off her drawers so that he could stare at the most secret, intimate part of her body and she shuddered. Tom could shout out about that in court, he could boast about her; he hated Rhys Morgan enough to do anything.

'I wish I'd died instead of Amy,' she said suddenly.

'Daisy! No matter how bleak things seem, they'll always improve. So what if there is gossip? It will die down; it always does, and some new disaster always comes along to replace last year's avid sensation. In the mean time you'll cope, I know you will. You'll set your chin high at its most stubborn angle and stare right back at the gossip-mongers, won't you? You're strong, Daisy, but I . . . I have my work to think of. I'm no use to anyone if I can't work.'

He's weak, thought Daisy with a flash of compassionate insight. *Kiki was right; Andrew does bolt at the first sign of trouble*. At the same time she understood his loathing of scandal. It was fear, she now realized, that provoked him into writing scathing letters to Lisabeth, fear of the gossip that reached out and touched him right the way around the world.

She felt a great emptiness open under her heart. Her shoulders slumped, and her fingers listlessly began to caress Excalibur's velvety ears. A silence deepened between them.

Finally Andrew said; 'Look, it's going to rain.'

Daisy raised her head to see where he was pointing. Against the golden clouds of evening hung a perfect shimmering rainbow, its colours merging in a halo of iridescent light.

196

'A rainbow,' said Daisy in a dull voice. She knew he was trying to cheer her up, but the knowledge that she was losing him was too unutterably depressing to be borne. 'That's what I've been doing – chasing rainbows. This is where the rainbow led me, to the foot of Rainbow Mountain, but when I arrived what did I find? Nothing. The rainbow had moved, like it always does. You think it's going to be there, you can see it so clearly, but when you hurry to the exact spot it's moved away somewhere else. What have I achieved?'

He laughed at that. She was adorable, delectably adorable even in her theatrical despair. 'What you've achieved is progress. You're standing in a different place now. You've gained a new perspective. Different choices.'

'Choices? What choice have I got? My life is ruined, and you're going away and leaving me.'

Impulsively he said: 'Then, come with me. Study at the medical college as I did. Become a doctor. You've the intelligence to pass the exams and the gift for dealing with people. Leave this place. Come with me.'

'But then I'd be running away, too,' she blurted without thinking.

He flinched, and immediately she was sorry. Other people at other times had accused him of the same thing, and it stung. He was quiet for a moment, then said carefully: 'That's a matter of perspective, too, Daisy. If you move forward when everybody else is standing still, then it could look like running away. I prefer to think of a forward movement as progress.'

'You're right,' said Daisy quickly. 'I'd never thought of it that way before.'

'Lots of people don't,' he assured her.

But she had hurt him. Though he continued to be cheerful and friendly, loving even, towards her, he never again mentioned the possibility of taking her back to England with him. What he did do was send his telegram to Rhys, informing him that Daisy was safe and well and would be returning on the stage-coach on Saturday.

Constable Creely was there when the message was sent. 'Daisy *Morgan*? You mean that she's the lass there's rewards and alerts posted out for? Rhys Morgan's daughter? The heiress?'

'That's correct.'

'Daisy Morgan? The lass you introduce everyone to as your sister?'

'The same.'

'And I've been pounding my feet into the ground dashing about asking questions after her! You . . . you're a bastard, Doctor Stafford. A right bastard, that's what!'

Andrew's jaw tightened. Then he smiled. 'Indeed I am,' he said.

'Hurry!' gasped Daisy, sagging against the door-frame and cramping sideways to ease a stitch. She had been running fast, pelting to cover the distance from the hospital room to the Creelys' where she burst in at the kitchen door just as Andrew was sitting down to a bowl of Mrs Creely's mutton-shank soup. 'Hurry, Andrew, you must come quickly. It's Tom Nevin. He's screaming and flinging himself around so much that his bed is in danger of collapsing.'

Constable Creely looked over the top of the week-old newspaper he was reading. He had finished his luncheon and was pointedly ignoring Andrew, for he still simmered about the way these two had made a right donkey's backside out of him. letting him accuse them of complicity in robberies while laughing at him because he couldn't recognize the most famous young lady in the province when she was right under his nose. How was he supposed to guess that an impoverished doctor's 'sister' was really Rhys Morgan's daughter, heiress to Mists of Heaven and one of the wealthiest young women in the whole of New Zealand? Mind you, he'd picked that something was amiss. Given time, he'd have latched on to the truth of the matter.

Now he said nastily: 'If your friend wants you, you'd better hop to it, hadn't you?' As he spoke he surveyed Daisy with well-concealed disgust. Look at her, hair dragged into a scraggy bun, gown stained and her bonnet halfway down her neck. What was a wealthy woman like her doing toiling like a drudge over a sick criminal and a bunch of careless layabouts? Aloud, he blustered with feigned warmth: 'Do sit down, Miss Morgan. Mrs Creely will make you a nice strong cup of tea. You could do with a rest, by the look of you.'

'I can't – but thank you. It's his leg, Andrew. He's in terrible pain, and those scarlet streaks are right up past his knee already.'

Andrew was already putting on his bowler hat and reaching for his jacket, while Mrs Creely fluttered in the background protesting that he'd been up half the night and had no breakfast and he *must eat*. 'Later,' he promised. 'Constable Creely, this looks serious. I'm going to need some assistance. Could you please help? Daisy, you'd better stay here. This won't be at all pleasant.'

'I'm going with you,' Daisy said, turning ahead of him and talking over her shoulder. 'I want to help you, and I shall. Watching Amy die wasn't pleasant, as you put it, and identifying her poor body was harrowing, but I stood that, didn't I?'

'This will be worse,' Andrew warned.

'It couldn't be,' she retorted, quickening her step. A man was in desperate pain and needed urgent care. It didn't even matter that it was Tommy Nevin, someone she'd privately wished over and over again had drowned instead of poor Amy. Her personal antipathy was forgottten now; all she wanted was to ease his suffering.

Nothing could be worse than yesterday, she thought, shuddering as she recalled Amy's face, white as foam and her hair tangled like seaweed.

Daisy had managed to be calm. Her 'Yes, that's her' had been uttered in a voice that barely shook, but then Daisy's downcast eyes fell on the old black dress with the white satin blouse showing underneath where it bunched up around the neck, and she remembered how Amy said: 'I keep it on under the other things so I don't feel drab. It's my little bit of luxury. I feel pretty, having that next to my skin.'

That had been too much. Then she'd bolted out of the police station with her bonnet jerking behind her and dashed on rickety ankles to the old dining-room at the Horse and Hounds where Andrew was working patiently on Tom's already gangrenous leg.

She stood beside him, her breath coming in scalding gasps.

'Was it . . .?'

'Yes,' Daisy replied, realizing as she did so that, shocking and unpleasant though the task had been, it was nothing compared to what Andrew was calling upon all his knowledge and skill to accomplish.

Compared to yesterday's horror, today was a nightmare magnified a thousand times. Over and over in the next hour Daisy wondered how God could permit such a thing.

Tom was woefully under-drugged, numbed with a mixture of laudanum and whisky but sharply aware of the pain, and when Andrew cut into his flesh he bellowed like a dying animal, a noise that scraped at the marrow in Daisy's bones.

Chalk-faced she stayed there, mopping his wide, freckled brow with cool water and murmuring unheard reassurances to him in a terrified voice. A week ago her stomach had heaved at the smell of her own vomit, but now she steadily watched everything Andrew did and only at the end, when he manipulated the bloodied knee to tug away the useless limb, did the sound of bones grating and the flickering of severed cartilage combine to make the gorge rise in her throat.

Tucked about with an oilskin apron now splattered with Tom's blood, Constable Creely held the tourniquets tight and pressed pads of gauze against the spurting arteries. 'That's one foot that'll never trespass on other folk's property again,' he declared as the purpling severed leg dropped into a bucket. Daisy would have gladly slapped the self-satisfied grin off his face. She was relieved when Andrew said: 'We can manage now, thank you, Constable.'

'This will make you feel better.' Andrew thrust a mug of whisky and water into her quivering hands. Her teeth juddered against the rim of the mug. 'You were wonderful. I couldn't have coped without you.'

Her head jerked 'No'. In her ears hung the terrible pleading, the animal moans, the sound like a frog when the leg plopped into the bucket of disinfectant. After a sip and a splutter she said: 'How do *you* feel?'

'As though I've failed. There are far too many amputations, and they shouldn't be necessary; if only there was some way to stop that spread of infection. Once gangrene starts, there's nothing that can be done. You were fortunate, Daisy, to break your wrist on a winter's night and to have medical assistance quickly. Tom lay out in the sun for hours after his injury, and by the time he arrived here the insidious process was well begun.'

'Poor Tommy Nevin, he's suffered a double loss. His wife and now his own life.'

'He won't die.'

'But his dreams will. He was going to be a grand man, a toff, but instead he'll be a dreg, begging and scrounging with no hope of a decent life. I should hate him, Andrew – I've ample cause to – but instead I feel so sad for him.'

'He won't go to gaol, at least.'

'He won't?'

Andrew tipped a little more whisky into her mug. 'I've persuaded Constable Creely to forget the whole thing. There's no firm proof that those goods were stolen, even though you and I know they probably were, but Tom's been punished enough. I hope you don't mind, but I told Constable Creely that he could take the credit for finding you – he can say I gave you refuge here but he recognized you from the description and made us send the telegrams. In return he's agreed to let Tom go free. I hope you don't mind . . . ,' he said uncertainly. 'Tom's a rogue, I know, but harmless enough for all his scheming ways.'

Is he? thought Daisy bleakly. She wondered if Andrew would be so magnanimous if he knew how Tom had bullied and humiliated her in such a perverted way. 'Tom hates Papa,' she said.

'I know,' admitted Andrew, adding: 'I suppose that's why I've so much sympathy for the blighter.'

'I must be tipsy. . . . I think that's very funny.'

'Good. I want you to sleep well tonight and be rested for the coach journey tomorrow. It's a long hard day's run, and you have to be up early. The coach leaves at five.'

She stared into her mug. 'Andrew . . . I'm not going.'

'What do you mean?'

'I'm staying here with you until that other doctor comes back, and then we'll go home together. And then. . . .' She drew a deep breath and raised her eyes to his. 'I'm coming with you to England. I'm going to study to be a doctor, too, as you suggested.'

'Splendid!' He crossed to her chair and stooped to put his arms around her for a quick hug. 'That's really splendid, and I think you'll make an excellent doctor.'

'Will I get into medical school, do you think?'

'I'd like to see them try to refuse you!' He sat down again and stared across at her, his face thoughtful. 'You do realize that your father will very likely withhold permission?'

She grinned. Despite her exhaustion, despite the horror of the afternoon, she felt marvellous, 'I'd like to see them try to refuse me!' she said.

TWENTY

'Suit yourself,' said Tom laconically. 'Uf her dud wunts to brung her buck to have her buried wuth her mam, thun thut's foine by me. I don't care. She never wus a proper wife to me unyway, uf you know whut I mean.' He sneered at Andrew's perplexed expression. 'Oh, we were murried by a priest ull right. We just never . . . you know, spliced ut. Well, we never hud a chance, dud we, nut wuth foine Muss Morgan there every bloddy munnut.'

Andrew winced at the bitterness in the tone, understanding why Tom resented Daisy and why they'd quarrelled.

So, when Daisy declined to say goodbye to Tom, Andrew didn't press the point. Not even when she said: 'He gave me a ride here *and he extracted payment*, and I hope never to see him again.' Daisy was disappointed with his silence; she hoped he'd ask how much she'd paid so she could tell him about the sordid episode and wipe the 'decent enough fellow' image away for ever. She was ready to tell him but not ready to volunteer the subject.

Andrew's like Papa, she thought. *Papa accepts things, lets them lie. Not like me. I have to ferret out every reason. I have to question.*

Amy's body travelled back to Christchurch with them, her lead-lined coffin strapped with trunks and suitcases to the frame behind the coach. Daisy sat inside with two women and four wriggling obstreperous children who grizzled all the way, while Andrew rode on the roof with the other men. Constable Creely and his wife, both all smiles now, got up before daylight to wave them off.

The journey was arduous, covering in one day what Tom had taken three to accomplish. During the infrequent refreshment-stops Daisy and Andrew sat apart from the others, whispering nervously, while during the dusty lurching ride Daisy was subjected to a continuous barrage of chatter from the children's mother, a fat greasy woman with rank body odour, with a loud voice that sounded like ducks quacking, and with a merciless supply of anecdotes about other journeys she had endured, one when a woman sitting opposite had suddenly gone gibberishly insane (Daisy could comprehend *that*) and another where a morose convict sat handcuffed between two soldiers and none of the three had uttered a single word for more than nine hours.

'They probably couldn't get a word in edgeways,' said Daisy pleasantly, wishing that the woman would restrain her children.

As they approached Christchurch in the dark Daisy's heart stilled with apprehension. Lights of the outlying houses seemed to bob and sway as the coach sagged and sprung on the rough road. The roadside fell away in a black ragged blur. Then, after an eternity of endurance, came the gas-lamps with fuzzy gold haloes that merged like a string of soft beads as the road smoothed underneath the wheels.

The coach station was lit and crowded. The fat woman shoved past Daisy, trampling on her foot in her haste to climb out. Over her shoulder Daisy saw Aunt Bea's face. She was glancing down, talking to Kiki, and both were smiling.

Only then, when she saw them, did she acknowledge a cold fear that had gnawed at her since she left, that Kiki's health might have been precipitated into a crisis by the shock of her running away. Obviously both were well; and even Albert, who stood behind Kiki with his yellow eyes slicing disdainful glances at the working-class people around him, even Albert seemed lukewarm about seeing her again.

'Bless you, child, that you're safe,' said Kiki. His hands shook as he placed them on her cheeks when she stooped to kiss him.

'You're not angry with me?'

'We're furious,' admitted Beatrice. 'And of course we were both extremely worried for a while, but then Lisabeth told us that most extraordinary story about you and Andrew.'

'Not here, Bea.'

'I'm not going to *repeat* it, dear! But why didn't you confide in us? It put a completely different complexion on everything.'

'Because neither Andrew nor I knew,' said Daisy.

Kiki tugged at his ropy white beard. 'You mean, nobody ever told you? A thing like that, and nobody *told* you?'

'That's correct, sir,' said Andrew. 'Furthermore, I doubt that anybody really intended to.' He turned away to lift his and Daisy's bags down from the rack and found himself facing Horace Thorne. At first Andrew didn't recognize him; it was with a jolt that he realized this aged, dishevelled and bleary-eyed man was Amy's father.

Horace Thorne had been waiting at the depot since dusk, his insides disintegrating in a morass of unspoken regrets and futile raging against a monstrous Fate. Since learning of Amy's death he had been paralysed with grief, closeted in his room with pictures of Amy and his long-dead wife, ignoring Mrs Hogg's entreaties to come out and spurning the trays of food she left at intervals outside his locked silent room. When finally he emerged to go to the stage depot his appearance shocked her. He had lost an alarming amount of weight and had shrunk and shrivelled inside his once nattily fitting clothes. Without so much as glancing at her he shuffled past, as abject as one of the wretches in the city asylum at Seaview.

And Andrew only realized who he was because Mrs Hogg was hovering anxiously at his elbow. Covering his surprise, he thrust out a gloved hand, saying: 'Please permit me to offer my condolences, sir. It was a tragic loss.'

'It's Doctor Stafford,' murmured Mrs Hogg.

Thorne swung him an unsteady but belligerent glare. 'Accident! You made free with her and then you killed her – murdered her! – and now you tell me it was an accident! You may be that whore Mrs Morgan's brother but that won't protect you in court when I—'

'Sir!' interrupted Andrew in alarm, aware that already a circle of bystanders was thickening around them, faces intent with interest in the yellow gaslight. He spoke loudly and clearly so that the facts could be noted now, while at the same time regretting the necessity for having to do so. Thorne was displaying symptoms of brain disorder: flushed complexion, twitching of facial muscles, laboured breathing and, though he had clearly not been drinking, slurred speech and unsteady movements. It was degrading to be exchanging verbal thrusts with a deranged man in a public place, but Thorne's outrageous accusation simply could not go unchallenged. 'Sir, as the inquest will publicly state, I had nothing whatsoever to do with your daughter's tragic death, and at the time it occurred I was twenty miles away. Your daughter was travelling north with her new husband, Mr Tom Nevin, when their wagon overturned in a flooded stream. Mr Nevin is recuperating in hospital from injuries sustained in the accident.'

Bravo! thought Daisy, hearing the nervousness in Andrew's voice and knowing what it would have cost him in effort to stand up to Mr Thorne's threatening stance. To Mrs Hogg, who seemed unduly apprehensive, Daisy said: 'It's true, Mrs Hogg, and all of it will be substantiated at the inquest.'

'You're liars, both of you.' The words scraped harshly from Thorne's throat, and he reached out to grab Andrew's shoulder as he turned away.

Andrew paused. Light as the touch was, it contained such menace that Andrew felt a shiver of fear.

'Mr Thorne, no!' screamed Mrs Hogg, alarming Daisy now. Someone else screamed, too, and others scattered. A man in the crowd shouted: 'Watchit, guv'nor. 'E's got a popper!'

Andrew froze, his back half-turned. Daisy saw the gold stripe of gaslight on the wavering pistol-barrel and did not even pause to speak, for one glance at Thorne's contorted face confirmed his intentions. While people around them fled and Mrs Hogg cringed with her hands cupping her terrified face, Daisy swung the bag she was holding up and around in a swift solid arc, dashing Thorne's hand upwards with a violent blow. The pistol discharged with a clap audible above the cacophony of shouts and screams, then spun end over end into the darkness and back down into the light. It landed near Andrew's boots.

While two men from the crowd subdued Thorne by pinning his arms behind his back, Andrew picked up the pistol and held it in his hand. It shook. 'He was going to kill me,' he marvelled to Daisy. 'He was actually going to kill me, but you—'

'No,' Daisy said quickly. 'He's upset, that's all. He's not himself, you can see that.'

'Call the police!' someone was shouting.

'No police,' hissed Daisy to Andrew. She wanted him to stop standing there looking dazed, and to take charge. She was so alarmed by what she had done that nothing seemed quite real; it was as if she had shrunk right back inside herself when the gun discharged and now she could not see out properly. 'Please, Andrew. Please tell them what to do.'

With difficulty he rallied. 'No police!' he insisted loudly. 'Nobody's hurt. There's been no trouble.' He shivered. The pistol was heavy and cold. Holding it up, he said; 'My hand-gun accidentally discharged. There's been no harm done.' Then, drawing Mrs Hogg aside, he said: 'Have you any laudanum at home? Good. Then, have these men help take Mr Thorne back to the hotel, and give him thirty millims – no more – of laudanum. Make sure that he swallows it – have the men hold his nose if he won't co-operate. And when he is subdued call a doctor. Is that clear?'

The woman nodded. Andrew studied her with concern.

'Why are you so frightened? Has he threatened you?'

She shook her head. 'Not yet. But he will when it sinks in about Tom Nevin. Right now he doesn't believe it, you see. If it was you Amy married . . . that might not be so bad, but Tom Nevin? How *could* she? How did they meet? How did it happen? I tell you, Doctor Stafford, I have my work carved out for me just to believe one word of it. She was in my care all the time, and I never suspected anything. Her and Tom Nevin? That rascal? I just can't believe it . . . I can't. . . .'

'I'm sorry, Mrs Hogg, but it is the truth,' Andrew told her. When he turned away she stared dumbly after him, her pretty face still blank with fear.

*　　*　　*

'We must try to avoid bitterness if we can,' said Andrew.

'I don't see how we can avoid it,' Daisy countered righteously. 'Papa knew you were his son and yet he kept it a secret. What I'm determined to find out is *why*.'

'Please remember that your father is still recovering from his concussion,' warned Beatrice, with a glance at Kiki who was dozing in the corner, lulled by the motion of the carriage. His whiskers ruffled at the edges of his breath. The trauma of this morning's funeral had proved too much for the poor darling, and halfway through the gloomy service (during which much emphasis was laid on Amy's youthful purity but no mention made of a husband) he had instructed Albert to wheel him from the church and out into the sunshine, down the street to where Andrew waited in a closed carriage, tactfully out of view of any mourners who might have heard about last night's scene at the depot.

Both of them missed seeing Daisy step forward at the graveside to place a white rose on Amy's coffin, only to have her action blocked by Mrs Hogg who sobbed: 'This is all your fault. She would still be alive, if not for you!'

Daisy gaped in disbelief at kindly Mrs Hogg's puffy hostile face. Without a word of protest she turned, still clutching the flower, and stumbled away across the churchyard, blindly pushing through the throngs of curious as Beatrice hurried in her wake.

'Was it very bad?' asked Andrew, helping her into the carriage and touching her damp cheeks with a folded handkerchief.

'Very,' she admitted. 'She blamed me, Andrew, and she was right. Amy would be alive today if it wasn't for me. It *is* all my fault.'

'It's not,' he chided gently. 'But promise me, Daisy, that you'll put aside all thoughts of blame and fault. When I see how much damage it's done to me over the years I'm anxious to protect you from falling into the same trap.'

The carriage rocked as Beatrice climbed in and settled herself with a sigh of satisfaction. 'That's over, thank goodness,' she declared, patting Daisy's wrist with her folded fan. 'Don't pay one speck of attention to what that harridan said to you, dear. Common she is, and her husband was the same. "Hogg by name and hog by nature," Kiki always said, didn't you, Kiki?' She glanced at her husband.

'He's been asleep for at least ten minutes,' Andrew told her as they set off towards Mists of Heaven. Kiki was so deaf there was no need to lower his voice, but to Daisy he murmured: 'Promise me you'll neither place blame nor accept guilt. It's important, Daisy, believe me.'

Raising her chin, Daisy avoided his gaze. Just as she was unable to forgive herself over Amy's death, so, too, was it impossible for her to forgive others.

Beatrice smiled indulgently. Brother and sister were already scrapping, just as her five brothers used to scrap with her, and Daisy was putting on her most mulish face exactly as Beatrice did when her brothers attempted to instruct her. Gazing at Andrew who sat opposite, she wondered why she had never suspected the truth before; his likeness to Rhys was so obvious, like the solution to a puzzle which seems impossible at first then ridiculously simple. How ironic it was that years ago Rhys had taken Azura away from them and now Rhys's own son was the means by which they would claim Azura's daughter.

The prospect made Beatrice dizzy with happy anticipation. Andrew had arranged it all. Together they would sail in the *John Corbett* when it returned from Sydney and set steam for London. By train they would travel to Edinburgh where Andrew was confident Daisy could be enrolled in the Edinburgh medical college where women, under the auspices of Doctor Elsie Inglis, had been training for some time. While Daisy studied, Kiki could be treated by Professor Benedict Cheeseman, a specialist renowned for his advanced studies in vascular heart conditions. When Daisy had been granted her licence Andrew planned to sell his hospital in Kent and then all four would return to Canterbury where, with Kiki's patronage, they would start a small hospital and medical practice of their own.

'I don't think it's possible to avoid blaming Lisabeth and Papa,' Daisy was saying. 'What they've done to us is *unforgivable*.'

'There's no such thing as unforgivable,' Andrew said.

Oh, yes, there is, mused Beatrice as Birdie Nevin's cottage slipped into view behind a white veil of apple blossom. Birdie's black-clad figure was spreading nappies to dry over the gooseberry hedge near the tank-stand. *I can think of a few unforgivable acts*, thought Beatrice. *Rhys carrying on with Lisabeth and breaking poor Azura's heart. That's one.*

'Here they come,' said Lisabeth, straightening the stacks of *Horse and Hound* and *Punch* on the library desk. She moved a vase of apricot roses an inch to the left and twitched at a fold in the bronze velvet curtains.

'Sit down, darling,' croaked Rhys. 'You're making *me* nervous now.'

She picked up a paperweight and polished it on the hem of her concealing wrap. In an unconscious echoing of Andrew's concern she said: 'Please, Rhys, promise me you'll be fair to Andrew. Please, dearest.'

'Fair?'

Lisabeth gazed at him in affectionate exasperation. These past days had been a trial for her, an agony of worry about Rhys and then about Daisy and Andrew. Now she was sure that all her anxieties were almost over; a reconciliation was within easy reach now, the family would be together and everything she wanted for their happiness would be theirs. . . . If only Rhys would co- operate.

'Yes, fair,' repeated Lisabeth.

Rhys made a strangling sound. 'But he knocked me down and left me for dead. It's a miracle I didn't—'

'Don't strain your voice so,' chided Lisabeth, reaching over to take his hand. She said gently: 'You probably knocked Andrew down, too, with what you told him. He must have received quite a shock.' She smiled, making light of it. Oh, she hoped there wouldn't be a quarrel! This morning Rhys had, with characteristic generosity, signed contracts for the building of his freezing works and had given the contract manager his assurances that the wages would be consistently above the basic award rate. If he could be so open-handed in his dealings with his employees, why couldn't he do the same with his family? Where was the warmth for these, his own children? wondered Lisabeth in despair. Why did Rhys think it a sign of strength to be magnanimous to strangers but a sign of weakness to display love to his own family? She had no time to reflect further; there was a knock, and Carthew's voice was saying: 'Sir Kenneth and Lady Launcenolt, sir, and it's Doctor Stafford and Miss Daisy back again' – the last with a nervous giggle of excitement, for it was almost two months since Daisy had been at Mists of Heaven.

'Fine chaperons you two turned out to be,' remarked Rhys without preamble. 'I trusted Daisy to your care, both of you, and you let her go haring off over the countryside.'

Sir Kenneth looked astounded. Beatrice said crisply: 'It's lovely to see you, too, Rhys. I'm so pleased you're feeling better. As for Daisy, I can understand your readiness to accuse us, but it would have made no difference where she—'

Daisy interjected: 'Let me speak for myself, please, Aunt Bea. Papa, she's quite right. If I'd been here at the time, it would have made no difference at all. I was determined to find out the truth of the matter from Andrew, and because of some promise he had made to you two I had to chase after him to get that truth.'

'You had no business to go. . . .' Rhys began to cough.

Lisabeth went to rub his back, between his shoulderblades. 'Your father has been extremely worried about you,' she said. 'Please, Daisy, do try not to upset him.'

'Upset *him*?' said Daisy. 'I'll tell you who is upset, Lisabeth. I'm upset, and Andrew is upset, too. There are certain things we had a right to be told, and I demand to know why those things were kept from us.'

Lisabeth went white. 'Daisy, *please*! Your father didn't know the truth for a long time. I kept it from him.'

Still coughing, Rhys went to the tantalus and poured out a shot of whisky for himself, sipped it, and only after recapping the bottle remembered he had company and poured one each for the men.

'Thank you, Rhys,' said Kiki, relieved.

'Thank you, Father, or would you prefer "Papa"?' Andrew couldn't resist saying. *He'd get out of this if he could*, he noted with grim amusement as Rhys's natural floridity deepened. His father was squirming like a worm stranded on hot asphalt.

Rhys felt helpless. Never before had he been trapped in a situation where he felt less in control. This scene was nothing like the reconciliation he had occasionally given a few scant thoughts to, imagining how he would break the news to Andrew as if he was offering him a gift, and to Daisy with a demand for the understanding that he, as her father, had a right to expect. Instead, both were treating him with scant respect and when he tried to shout them down he was seized in the throat and shaken by a fit of coughing, helpless as an old rug.

Daisy said: 'I didn't come out here today to quarrel or to indulge in petty recriminations, but I insist on knowing why Andrew has been treated so despicably by you both. Lisabeth, you say Papa didn't know the truth himself for a long time, but he *has* known these past ten years or so, hasn't he? Then, that really isn't a valid excuse, is it?'

Rhys couldn't believe what he was hearing. In outrage he found voice. 'Daisy, you forget your place in this house! How dare you speak to Lisabeth like that? She's my wife. . . .' His voice rasped to another scratchy halt.

'And Andrew is your son! That's something you forget, just as you forget *his* place in this house!' She paused to draw breath, noticed the silence and for a moment was horrified. What was she doing, a raw eighteen-year-old, shouting defiance at her own father? Such insolence was unheard of. Fathers were kings in their households, and nobody dared contradict or disobey them.

Andrew watched, amusement showing on his face. What sheer courage she had; it was courage she would need to endure the rigours of medical training where women students were often hissed at, jeered at and made the butt of cruel practical jokes. She'd fly through. She'd stand up to anything. Nobody would try to cross her a second time. Yes, his sister was a winner.

Rhys said: 'This is my house, Daisy. I built it, and I decide what happens here.' He was speaking in a husky murmur, almost a whisper, and his eyes had chilled from blue to grey. Lisabeth knew that he was extremely angry; she had never seen him in such a quiet rage, not even when his best dogs were shot by 'Baron' Windsor for allegedly straying on to his property.

Daisy sensed his fury, too, but having gone so far she was unable to turn back. 'I can remember when I was a little girl, how heartbroken you were when Darius died. Everybody said what a tragic thing it was for a man to lose his only son, and like everybody else I believed that, too, and I felt sad for you. All my life, Papa, I felt sad for you, and the terrible thing is that now I feel even deeper pity for you because you had a son all along and you couldn't bear to acknowledge him. Why not? Is he black? Is he ugly? Is he disabled, or mentally deficient in some way? Is there a reason any of us could understand? No, there's not!'

Rhys looked as if he was being strangled. Kiki and Beatrice were plainly ill-at-ease; Rhys was their friend, and instinctively they feared that later, in the future, Rhys could resent the fact that they had witnessed this scene.

Lisabeth was almost in tears. If only Rhys had listened to her, this would have been settled years ago. Anger jabbed her into saying: 'Your father had his reasons. He was worried about what you would think – and with excellent cause, too, it would seem.'

'Worried about what we would think? Ha! Papa doesn't care what anybody thinks – nor do you, the way you carried on, staying here when you had a husband and scandalizing the entire province. Why, last night at the coach depot Amy's father called you a "whore" in front of the crowd of people. I don't know what "whore" means, but it sounded like an ugly name to me, and I was humiliated.'

'Please, Daisy, stop this,' pleaded Beatrice in and undertone into the terrible silence. Lisabeth had burst into tears, Kiki was wordless; even Andrew thought that she had gone too far – Rhys was turning purple now.

Rhys tried to speak, but his throat was blocked, choking him with his own rage.

Daisy continued, white and frightened but unable to stop. 'Andrew says that you accused him of wanting your money, Papa. He says you tried everything you could think of to avoid telling him the truth. You never intended to tell him at all, did you?'

'It's none of your—' Rhys managed to drag out those words before more coughing overtook him. He bent his head, eyes stinging with moisture as he massaged his throat to ease it. When he looked across at her Daisy was waiting, tapping her foot, looking exactly as Azura did when she taunted and defied him with that smug knowing expression, as if to say she'd weighed him and found him wanting.

'I want an answer, Papa.'

He didn't notice the timidity in his daughter's eyes. All he saw was the arrogant bravado, and it enraged him still further. He tried to speak, gasped and coughed; and then, when she repeated her demand for an answer, he gave her one. A heavy slap across the face that caused her to sway on her feet.

The silence was so palpable that even the echo of the blow tingled in the air, sharp enough for the others to feel. Both Lisabeth and Beatrice raised hands to their cheeks in an involuntary gesture, but Daisy did not move. With the mark of the blow livid across the side of her face she stared at her father, still with the same goading expression. *She wanted him to do that*, thought Andrew. *She taunted him and provoked him until he struck her. But why?*

The door swung open. Gwynne's voice entered ahead of her. 'What in the world is going on? What is going on? Albert tried to stop me from coming in. Really, Sir Kenneth, you must have words with him. I'll not have a blackfellow ordering me about even if he does wear a scarlet turban and gold buttons!' Her gaze swung around the room. Kiki was in his Bath chair, Lisabeth and Beatrice sat quietly, fists in their laps, Andrew was leaning on the mantelpiece, and Rhys and Daisy stood a pace apart, like boxers on the scarlet Afghan rug.

'*What* is going on?'

They ignored her. For a moment Daisy did not speak; she was waiting in vain hopes for an apology. Then she said: 'I'm going now. I'm going to live with Kiki and Aunt Bea, and they've agreed to help me with something I want to do. I'm not coming back here, ever, until—'

'Daisy, no,' interrupted Andrew. 'Don't say anything you'll be sorry for later. Words spoken in anger are notoriously difficult to retract. Please consider what—'

She brushed his suggestion away with a wave of her hand. 'This is for you, Andrew.'

'But I don't need—'

'Papa, I shall not come back to this house until Andrew has been publicly acknowledged as your son and heir. *And heir*. That part is extremely important.' She glanced at Lisabeth, whose billowing dark garments disguised the bulge of the baby soon to be born. 'I hope you understand, Lisabeth, but Andrew is Papa's first-born son and he deserves his rightful place. Especially after all these shameful years of neglect. He has been—'

'Get out!' croaked Rhys. 'Get out! Go! Leave this house at once. Both of you . . . all of you. . . . You—' And again he doubled over in pain.

'What is happening? What is happening?' pleaded Gwynne. 'Won't somebody please talk to me?' She stepped back as Beatrice wheeled Kiki out of the room.

Andrew paused as he walked past her behind Daisy. 'Are you giving him tar for that cough?' he murmured. 'Tar in two-grain pills should help, or two drops of creosote. And try to see that he avoids excitement!'

211

TWENTY-ONE

Daisy remained stubborn. That everybody including Kiki suggested she soften her attitude and that everybody hinted that she should apologize to her father merely cemented her already rigid stance.

'She must have inherited this mulishness from her father,' sighed Beatrice. 'Dear Azura was always so biddable, so reasonable.'

'Nonsense,' snorted Kiki. 'She was as stubborn as an Indian tonga pony when she'd set her mind on something. Andrew and I were discussing that extraordinary business, and we both agreed that Daisy deliberately quarrelled with her father so that he wouldn't stop her from going to Edinburgh. He never would have let her go otherwise, you know.'

Rhys was certainly not stopping her now. Daisy's letter outlining her plans had not been answered by her father – a sign, Daisy declared, that he was not withholding his permission for her to leave New Zealand.

'It appears that I'm to be your dependant, Aunt Bea,' Daisy told her with feigned gaiety. 'Andrew says he'll help pay my fees, and whatever it costs you I'll pay back once I'm a proper working doctor. In the mean time I hope I'm not going to be too onerous a financial burden.'

'Burden? My dear child, this could be the saving of Kiki, you know. He'll be able to consult with heart specialists and the finest doctors in Europe, and it's all thanks to you. All Doctor Meakings could do for him was confine him to that wretched contraption.'

Daisy looked up from the blouse she was hemming, ready for the voyage. 'Did you know that Doctor Meakings isn't even properly trained? When we visited him yesterday, while we walked in the garden I asked him what medical college he had attended, and after much bluster and changing of the subject he finally admitted that he'd never been formally tutored. Old Doctor Jacobsen had taken him on as an apprentice when he was a young man! That's why Andrew suddenly went to look at the swans' nests behind the boathouse. He was laughing so he could hardly contain himself. Andrew says it's a miracle my arm mended as straight as it did when all Doctor Meakings's knowledge has been gleaned from old medical journals!'

'Doctor Meakings is a fine doctor, and you'll do well to remember that,' warned Beatrice. Her frown hid her inner doubts. Why in the world did Daisy persist with this insane idea of wanting to become a doctor? Wasn't life difficult enough for her already, without her setting her sights on an impossible goal? The sooner she gave up this ridiculous notion the better.

On the morning before the *John Corbett* sailed Lisabeth rang Benares. Rhys was away making his postponed journey to Dunedin so that he could be back before their baby was born.

'She has refused to speak to me, too?' asked Lisabeth when Kiki told her that Daisy was out walking.

'I wouldn't lie to you, young woman,' bridled Kiki. 'If I say she's out walking, then you can be confident that she is definitely not here.'

'I'm sorry, Sir Kenneth. I didn't mean—'

Her voice sounded frail and unhappy over the wires; remembering her condition, Kiki was immediately sorry he had spoken so harshly. 'Would you permit me to help you?' he offered. 'I could tell her you called, but I'm afraid I cannot guarantee that she will telephone you in turn. She's extremely distressed, you realize,' he added, unaware that now, so soon after bristling over his assailed honour, he was lying; it was he who was upset, not Daisy.

'We're all distressed,' Lisabeth told him. 'But, yes, Sir Kenneth, if you are amiably disposed towards us, there is something you could do to help. Please try to persuade Daisy – and Andrew, too – to write to their father, could you? I can assure you that I've learned from bitterest experience that silence is the worst thing to follow a quarrel. Feuds feed on silence.'

'You're right there, young lady. In India a spat like the one we witnessed the other day could linger on for centuries, passed down from one generation to another like some kind of heritage, a sacred curse.'

'Yes, well . . . if you could please try to convince them both to write. It will ease the way for later. And in the mean time would you please look after them both? Andrew worries me. He looks so old and ill. I worry that he's letting life defeat him.'

'He's not getting much assistance, is he?' said Kiki bluntly. 'He is entitled to some consideration, you know.'

'I know,' said Lisabeth. Her voice sounded sad and far away. 'Believe me, I know.'

'Just so long as you do what you can, too,' Kiki told her. 'Don't just leave it all to us and expect things to come right of their own accord.'

In the previous three weeks Benares had been a chaos of activity. The sepoys packed clothes and household articles that would be needed abroad, while Sir Kenneth marshalled his notes ready for further study on the voyage and Beatrice organized a massive clean-up of weeds in the garden and interviewed prospective tenants, for the house would be rented 'to a genteel family of means' while they were away, and Beatrice's standards of 'genteelness' were high.

Andrew and Daisy spent a lot of time together sitting in the sun talking about the private practice they would set up together on their return. 'It's a pity Doctor Meakings isn't ready to retire, or we could buy his practice,' said Daisy.

'Lyttelton could be the place to begin,' suggested Andrew. 'All those incoming immigrants, many of them ill after the voyage. Don't wrinkle your nose! You won't just be able to treat rich people; and be warned – some sick people are more disgusting than anything you saw in the Shakerville infirmary!'

Daisy shook her head. 'Nothing could be more horrifying than seeing Tommy Nevin have his leg cut off. If I can endure that, I can endure anything.'

'I like your confidence!'

'And I like your impudence!' she retorted, throwing a twig at him. Excalibur barked and jumped up at once, sensing a game.

Andrew dodged the twig. 'That's no way for a doctor to behave. Dignity always, that's the thing.'

'Never!' cried Daisy, pulling a face, laughing.

At Andrew's insistence she wrote letters of farewell to everyone she knew: the Martins and Westlakes, the Bethkinhalls and Jones-Pattersons, the Thomases and the Updykes. When she protested that they would think her crazed if she revealed her plans, he agreed but insisted she do it. 'At the moment the very notion of a lady doctor is so outlandish as to be unthinkable, but tell them now, anyway, and in five years the idea might have filtered through to their strait-jacketed brains. Tell them that you were privileged to have an excellent education and plan to do what you can for society with your knowledge and abilities.'

'But that sounds boastful. Couldn't I be more . . . modest?'

'How many people will come to consult with you if you present yourself as a feather-brained helpless female? No, Daisy, do it this way . . . and for the moment leave me out of it. It's best if you merely happen to be accompanying Aunt Bea and Kiki.'

Andrew also decided that they should visit the Days and tell them of their plans. To their astonishment Joseph and Emma greeted Andrew with the news that they were aware of his relationship to Rhys and Daisy. 'Lisabeth told us,' Emma said simply. 'She wanted someone to confide in, and knew it would go no further than these walls.'

'She's a good lass, Lisabeth,' said Joseph. Catching Daisy's expression, his voice hardened and he said: 'It was Lisabeth who insisted that you have a proper education, you know. Rhys would have been happy to leave you with Gwynne all week learning how to knit and sew, but Lisabeth always understood the value of a first-class education.'

'That's very true,' Andrew added. 'Lisabeth earned money from the sale of her paintings so that I could go to Christ's College. Uncle Charles was too mean to send me.'

'Ah, but he was a miserable beggar,' agreed Joseph.

'Charles *Stafford*? Gwynne's husband? The man she speaks so highly of?' asked Emma, passing tea-cups and urging them to help themselves to chocolate cake.

'The same. Only he turned into a saint since I last saw him,' said Andrew. 'In life he was considerably less charming than he is now.'

Daisy hoped the subject had been dropped. She was not about to feel grateful to Lisabeth for her education when she knew that her years of schooling were a transparent excuse to get her out of Mists of Heaven so that Lisabeth could have Papa all to herself. When Joseph turned to her she said quickly: 'Show Andrew your gold cup, Mr Day. Do you see it there, Andrew? Isn't it magnificent?'

But Joseph was not to be deflected. 'Lisabeth is extremely proud of both of you, you know, and your father is, too.'

'He doesn't show it!'

Joseph's dark brows bunched, and a smile twitched at the corners of his mouth, under his luxuriant moustache. 'Ah, but he's not only a proud man; he has a certain little streak of intransigence – one he shares with others of his family, I've no doubt.'

Daisy drew a deep breath. It was on the tip of her tongue to utter a rude retort, but she caught herself in time, forced a smile and turned to Emma. 'And how are the girls, Mrs Day? Are they visiting their aunt, Mrs Rule, today? Do tell them I'm sorry to miss them. I saw young Ethel with Mrs Rule in town last Tuesday, and she said she was running errands for you. What a pretty, dainty girl she is!'

Andrew and Joseph laughed.

'You made fun of me,' accused Daisy on the way home. 'You and Mr Day laughed at me!'

'We laughed *with* you.'

'I wasn't laughing.'

'But you should have been. Daisy, this quarrel with Rhys – it's not too late to patch it up before we leave. You said some rather drastic things to him.'

215

'And I meant them! He's been despicable to you.'

'But I don't care.' He pulled the pony-trap over to one side of the road to make way for a scraggly flock of sheep that was meandering towards them, harried by two black dogs.

'I do care.' She waved to the shepherd and wished him 'Good day'. When they were past she said: 'I care, and I'm not going near Mists of Heaven again until he grants you what is rightfully yours. Recognition, money, and a place in the family.'

'That could be a long time, Daisy. It could be never.'

'Then, let it be. He caused the damage. Let him fix it up.'

'That sounds hard, Daisy. It's not worthy of you.'

'You called it ''tough'' before and you told me I needed my toughness, remember?' She pulled a playful face at him, but this time he didn't smile.

One person she didn't write to was Jeremy. Deep down she expected him to turn up on the doorstep at Benares, but when time went by and he failed to appear she was piqued. He should come, he must know she was back in town, she thought; and, later, he should come because he'd have learned from Maurice Andruth or from Arabella Martin that she was going away to study. Daisy couldn't imagine Arabella keeping such a delectable piece of news to herself. She kept thinking of Jeremy and the brutal sensuous way he had kissed her. Every time she walked into the parlour she was reminded anew of how his arms had crushed her against his body, how thrilling and disturbing it had felt to be completely in his power. The recollection was so intense that Daisy alternately avoided going into the parlour and made excuses to be in there, in her mind shunning Jeremy or rushing into his arms.

He should have called, at least. Even just to offer his condolences about Amy. But he didn't.

In those few weeks she missed Amy with surprising fierceness. Andrew was there most of the time, so she had company, but whenever anything interesting happened she filed it away in her mind automatically with the thought, *I'll share that with Amy*, and whenever anything funny occurred her first thought was *Amy would enjoy hearing about that*. Then in the next moment she would realize that Amy wouldn't be able to share her news and jokes, and again would come that sharp cold sense of loss. On the morning before the *John Corbett* was due to sail Daisy woke and lay staring at the ceiling swamped under the knowledge that Amy was gone from her life for ever, that tomorrow she would embark on a new life in which her friend had never played a part, and from now on she was alone without friends of her own sex.

At breakfast she announced her intention of going to the churchyard to visit Amy's grave. 'Good idea. I'll come with you,' said Beatrice at once.

'Do you mind if I go alone?' asked Daisy.

216

'Let her, Bea,' said Kiki. 'She'll come to no harm.'

'At least let me pick some roses for her headstone,' said Beatrice, who prided herself on knowing when people needed to be left alone: heaven knows she'd had enough practice with Kiki and his moods. 'Take an umbrella with you, dear. I hope it doesn't pelt down tomorrow when we're embarking. Remember, Kiki, how we left India during a monsoon storm and the decks of the *Samantha* were swirling with water?' She saw he hadn't heard, took a breath to repeat herself more loudly, then gave up. Nodding to Albert to clear away, she went to find her secateurs.

Jeremy finished his errands at the stock merchant's and paid the Georgia account at Tomken's feed and grain stores, then decided to visit Lowell's grave again. He was in the habit of stopping there on the way home with a bunch of violets purchased from the elderly flower-seller in the theatre arcade. Lowell's death was still painful to him, and like a toothache he sought it out, probing to discover the source of his distress. Could he have prevented such a needless death? Was it his fault? Had he rejected Lowell's sinuous yet clumsy advances too brutally, so roughly that Lowell felt he couldn't face himself or go on living? Again Jeremy wondered whether that same direct roughness in his character had kept Daisy away, too. He knew she cared for him at one point, and with care and delicacy he could have courted her and won, but instead of treating her like a fragile butterfly he had blundered on in his usual way, teasing her and goading her, then grabbing at her as if she was a strong young horse to be broken.

No wonder, then, that she succumbed immediately to the elegant Doctor Stafford. Jeremy saw him one day in the saloon bar of the Lady Margaret and was frankly shocked that Daisy could love someone so old and worn-looking. Tragedy seemed to seep like sweat from his pores, but there was a languid sureness of style in his voice and gestures, the patina of a true gentleman. Gazing at him with loathing, Jeremy could picture him sauntering around the grand cities of Europe and wished heartily that he had remained there, where he so obviously belonged.

Acknowledging that the fellow would doubtless court a lady with sophisticated refinement, Jeremy still marvelled that Daisy would want someone so much older, a mystification that remained until he saw Andrew laugh and the likeness to Rhys was sudden and remarkable. Rhys was tanned and muscular, Andrew pale and slender, but the resemblance was there along with the answer to the puzzle. As jealous and possessive of her father as she was, she had chosen a man as much like him as possible.

The news that Daisy was going to Europe to study medicine was an even greater shock, delivered as it was by Silas along with a diatribe of judgemental remarks and anger. Silas had adored Daisy, and that she turned out to be a 'rum one' rankled in his mind like a personal insult. While Charlotte snuffled away her disappointment and dealt the cards for whist, Silas rearranged his hand, all the while barking at his son. 'She says she wants to be a doctor, of all the lunatic things. I wouldn't be surprised if her mother was a touch crazy, too. That's what *she* is, a crazy woman. She's obsessed with this man – this doctor fellow. Mrs Morgan's brother, isn't he? Have you seen him at all?'

'Looks like death,' said Jeremy.

Silas slapped a red queen on to the table.

'That's a heart, sugar,' said Charlotte, dabbing at her eyes. 'You need a diamond for this one.'

'She's not even going to marry the fellow; that's the really weird part! Rhys said there was no possibility of that. I asked why – thought he might feel better if he got it off his chest – but—'

'Sugar-plum, you need a diamond.'

He replaced the card. 'But he wouldn't say why not. That's the weirdest part. Maybe he has a wife already.'

'Maybe.' Charlotte trumped the trick and collected the cards.

'Strange family that altogether. You had a lucky escape, son,' said Silas. 'Rhys Morgan is a damned fine fellow to do business with; there's something very odd about the lot of them when it comes to moral principles, and we Southerners pride ourselves on our strong moral principles, don't we, sugar?'

'Honey, you need a heart. That's a diamond you played,' replied his wife.

The churchyard was swept with wind and city dust. The flowering shrubs around the cemetery section were as always plucked bare, and the tired-looking flower-beds had been plundered, too. Whistling, Jeremy hitched Angel to the branch of a low-slung tree and, still whistling, he strolled around the side of the building where he stopped, the tune dying on a harsh intake of breath.

Daisy was kneeling at Amy's grave arranging pink and yellow roses in a jam-jar that had been sunk to the rim in the naked earth. She wore a yellow and white striped gown with a high collar and long sleeves and a white straw hat with a yellow band around the crown, while her hair was drawn up into a chignon so high that it tilted the hat forward over her eyes. Her hair looked soft as cornsilk; wisps of it hovered in the breeze that tickled her face. It was the first time Jeremy had seen her since that afternoon at Benares, and he gazed at her, hunger gnawing at his belly and longing floating like oil over his thoughts.

How incredibly beautiful she was! Others didn't agree – Maurice Andruth for one, who thought her pallid and too animated – but in Jeremy's eyes she was perfection. *And perfection all over*, he thought, wistfully remembering that day in the glade when he had surprised her wet and exquisite as a water-nymph.

Daisy's hands moved slowly as she arranged the roses, and she stopped after placing each one to study the effect. Her heart ached. *Amy, what a waste of a life!* she thought, and when a large drop of water fell on the bare ground that covered Amy she thought at first that it was a tear she had shed. Then another fell, and another, round penny-sized spots on the brown soil. 'The sky is crying for you, too,' she murmured and, glancing up at the grey heavens, she smiled.

Jeremy had been about to turn and leave when he saw that smile and thought it was for him. 'Daisy!' he called, smiling in response.

She was startled, but rallied with hope in her voice. 'Jeremy! Did you follow me here?'

He was prevented from replying by the rain. Down it dashed in great sweeping torrents that brushed across the yard and bounced off the gravestones. Daisy fumbled with her umbrella. 'Here, quickly!' shouted Jeremy, holding out his hand to her as he ran for the vestry doorway.

Within the stone porch were two wooden benches against the wall, one on either side. Jeremy took the umbrella from Daisy, closed it and shook it, while she laughed and brushed at her damp skirts. 'Look at my sleeves! They're *soaking*!' she cried. Sitting down opposite him, she leaned forward, her face alight. 'You did follow me, didn't you?' she accused. And before he could deny it she rushed on: 'Oh, Jeremy, I'm so glad! I thought you were going to let me sail off to England and never say one word of farewell.'

He swallowed the denial. 'Why are you going?'

'I'm going to study to be a doctor. Surely you've heard that?'

'I've heard it, but I don't believe it.'

'Whyever not?'

'Because you're a rich man's daughter, that's why. Oh, I don't doubt that you have the intelligence to pass the examinations. You're extremely bright, and everybody says so. I think they're all a bit afraid of you, Arabella and the Westlake girls. You make them feel stupid, did you know that?'

Daisy shrugged. 'Why should being wealthy stop me from doing what I want?'

'I think it's a whim, that's why,' he said, aware as he spoke that what he really meant was he *hoped* it was a whim. 'You've had every one of your wants and needs catered to all your life. You've been adored and pampered since the cradle—'

'That's not how I see it,' Daisy cut in coldly. 'If you ask me, I've been ignored and fobbed off. Oh, I've never known hunger or thirst or real discomfort – not until recently, that is – but now I have a taste of the real world, Jeremy, and I like it. I really do.'

'What's the real attraction in this ridic – I mean this scheme of yours?'

'Pardon?'

'It's this Doctor Stafford, isn't it? You chased him to Shakerville, and he wouldn't marry you, and now you're pursuing him right across the world! Yes, I know he's travelling in the same ship as you are.' His voice grew more bitter as he spoke. 'Your father told my father, and he dished up every last sordid detail to me. Why doesn't this Doctor Stafford marry you, Daisy? Why are you hell-bent on ruining your life for a dried-up old roué like him?'

'You don't know every detail,' said Daisy quietly. Head bent, she was plucking rose thorns from her cotton gloves. The rain scythed past the open archway with grey even strokes. A scattering of drops flung in as it passed. *Damn Papa*, she thought. *He told Mr Drake everything but the truth*. Raising her head, she looked Jeremy right in the eye. 'Papa didn't explain it all, that's obvious. That Andrew is his son, for example.'

'Andrew is your *brother*?'

'Half-brother. I thought it would rock you. It did me.'

'It does, but deep down I wondered. . . . No, I simply saw the likeness and imagined that was your attraction to him.'

Daisy sighed happily. 'Andrew is family, that's what he is! It was his idea that I study in the same medical school that he did, and later we hope to set up in practice together. Isn't that exciting?'

He could see that she clearly expected him to share in the joy of her plans, but instead a fierce anger was building inside him. He didn't think it exciting – he thought it was a stupid idea, and doubly so because it was at Doctor bloody Stafford's instigation. Daisy wasn't suitable to hare off and try to be a doctor. Her life was in the home being pampered and adored, following the lifestyle to which she was ordained. Ever since he met her he had planned to make her his wife, and he was irritated that she would find this idiotic venture more appealing.

Or was she teasing him? he wondered. What would happen if he sank to one knee, put his hand over his damp heart and asked her again to marry him?

When she received no response from Jeremy she glanced away from his glum face and out into the white sky. 'That rain! It's as if it came bucketing down on purpose to trap us here together.' She gave him another glance, flirtatious this time, and why not? He was dear to her, and she was sorry that there wasn't room in her life for everything; but, as Andrew pointed out, she was still extremely young and nowadays there were occasionally women who didn't marry until they were past thirty. There was still plenty of time. 'Will you miss me when I'm away, Jeremy? Will you write to me?' She laughed. 'I thought you didn't care

220

at all, but you followed me! I didn't think you were so romantic. That's encouraging, I must say.'

He reached over and picked a wet rose petal from the hem of her gown. Something horrible had just occurred to him. 'Why didn't you tell me that Doctor Stafford was your brother before? Why couldn't we have got that cleared up the last time we met? Who knows, perhaps I could have acted as a go-between and helped you keep in touch with him, instead of your going off on that tragic journey. Now we've each lost a friend, haven't we? Why didn't you confide in me before?'

'I didn't know before.'

'What?' His smooth open face darkened, and Daisy saw what had not been visible before: the thread-like scars that were a legacy from his beating by 'Baron' Windsor. In a voice she could barely hear above the rain he said: 'Do you mean to say that when you went chasing after Doctor Stafford you didn't know he was your brother?'

Daisy nodded. Something in his face frightened her, but she raised her chin and said: 'I don't see any point in being deceitful to you, Jeremy. You don't want that, do you?'

Oh, I do, thought Jeremy, but he let her go on.

'All I knew was that something very powerful drew me towards Andrew, but I didn't understand what. And I knew he'd had a terrible quarrel with Papa, so terrible that Papa had driven him away. I didn't know what had happened between them but I was determined to find out. I tried to get a message to him, but he had gone. So. . . .'

'So you followed him,' finished Jeremy, feeling that something inside him was finishing, too. His dreams. His hopes. She'd told him in not so many words that he was of no importance to her at all. As he struggled to cover his crushing disappointment with a few rags of dignity he gave silent thanks that he hadn't proposed and made a complete fool of himself.

Wearily he stood up. Her eyes followed him in surprise. Was he going to kiss her? *Was* that what she wanted? He could see expectation in her eyes and he wondered if he was misreading that the way he'd misread all the other signals he'd ever received from her.

'Good luck,' he said bleakly, tugging up his coat-collar and plucking his trilby from the seat beside him. 'I dare say we won't meet again.'

He might as well have struck her. 'No, Jeremy . . . don't go like this! Please don't go. . . .' Her hands reached out, and she half-rose out of her seat, but he ignored her, striding out into the curtain of billowing rain. 'Come back!' she called after him. 'Come back! You'll catch your death!'

He turned and grinned a crooked ironic grimace. 'I already did!' he shouted, then turned and hurried away as if he needed swiftly to put distance between them.

221

Subsiding back on to the seat, Daisy stared at his back, and when he disappeared she stared at the place where he had been. She couldn't understand his coldness. She thought he'd appreciate her honesty and share her plans with interest and be glad for her and tell her to take care and look after herself and come back safely and not fall in love with a dashing Frenchman when she holidayed in Paris, and to write him all her news and remember that he'd miss her. . . .

She couldn't understand him at all.

Of their household, only Gwynne came to see her off. 'Mr Tenks brought me and Birdie and the twins,' she told Andrew; and, while the Launcenolts busied themselves with the boxes and trunks enough to be able to ignore Gwynne's presence entirely, Daisy and Andrew went to the carriage to inspect the babies which Birdie was holding self-consciously, one in the crook of each arm like sheaves of wheat. They were identical, button-faced with skin the colour of burned cream and scalps covered with straight black hair like bread mould. *Half-caste Maori babies!* suspected Andrew, though he couldn't be sure. 'They're both girls, und dark us their mother, poor wee busstards,' said Birdie fondly. *And possibly their father*, thought Andrew. He sympathized with Birdie's words. *Poor little bastards*, he agreed.

Later, in the ship, he asked Daisy if any young Maori men had been seen in Siobhan's company. Yes, she said, there was one; he was in charge of spraying the orchards with Paris Green arsenic for codlin moth, and several times Daisy had seen them together walking on the shoreline below the cliffs and looking into the caves that the sea had hollowed out. 'Are you wondering about the babies' father?' she said. 'Well, it couldn't have been him! He disappeared weeks before any-body knew Siobhan was going to have a baby. *Weeks!*' To which Andrew had smiled. What a lot Daisy had to learn.

Gwynne told them what a marvellous sailor Charles had been, how the captain always consulted him if there were any problems with navigation and so on, while Daisy and Andrew listened solemnly. Then she hugged them both, bursting abruptly into emotions they had no idea she nourished. 'My darling children,' she wept. 'I'm so afraid I'll never see you again.'

'Of course you will,' chided Daisy, holding the downy face between her own and looking through the smudged spectacles to the dull eyes beyond. 'I'm only going to be away five—' Then she realized what Gwynne meant and she was afraid, too. Lamely she said: 'Take care of yourself, won't you?'

'Write to me, please write,' pleaded Gwynne. 'I've not quarrelled with you, have I?'

Daisy looked at her anxious face. Since that day she had resolved to have nothing but the most essential contact with Mists of Heaven; that resolution had given her a cold hard feeling of satisfaction, like an armour strapped about her which protected her but made it impossible for her to bend or stretch. Her impulse was to say 'No', because Gwynne would only share the letters with Papa and Lisabeth. Besides, to agree was to compromise the rigidity of her decision.

'Please promise. Please promise,' said Gwynne.

Reluctantly Daisy nodded. 'I'll write to you.' As she spoke she could feel the shards of her broken armour of resolution falling around her feet. Astonishingly she felt stronger, not weaker, without it. 'Of course I'll write to you,' she said.

TWENTY-TWO

IT WAS FUNNY how life turned out, mused Lisabeth. All her and Rhys's preparations for the baby's birth, their discussions about whether to call in a midwife or Doctor Meakings or both, whether Lisabeth should stay at Mists of Heaven or go into Christchurch to be near medical help just in case; all that fuss and palaver was for nothing. One day right out of the blue, a full three weeks before the baby was due, she slipped on one of the lower steps in the hallway, thumped down hard on the base of her spine – the shooting pains through her skull were worse than any of the labour pains which followed – and before Rhys could be summoned from the back of the estate where he was supervising a new planting of pine forest, before Doctor Meakings's trap had reached the river flats, Lisabeth had herself become a mother. During the astonishingly swift process both Carthew and Mrs Tenks had dashed around in frantic circles – apart from telephoning for help – of little use to anyone, but fortunately Kikorangi, the Maori girl with the rippling waist-length hair, was at the house, come to show Lisabeth an embroidered altar-cloth she had made for the church. She knew exactly what to do. It was she who calmed everybody down, she who helped Lisabeth to the chaise-longue in the library, who found a drawerful of damask tablecloths and spread them out, under and over her, rapidly, for she could see even without a cursory examination that the shock had precipitated Lisabeth full tilt into dilation. By the time Mrs Tenks had fetched scissors and string for the umbilical cord, and Carthew had found a pan for the afterbirth and warmed soft cloths to swaddle the baby, Lisabeth was gripping the chaise-rail sweating and straining, too awed to feel real pain, amazed with the ease with which her daughter was sliding out into the world.

'I never done this before, Miz Nye,' blurted Kikorangi, so nervous that she didn't even hear her own gaffe. Her eyes were huge and dark as a cow's, but her hands were gentle and sure. 'I seen it lots of times, so I know what to do.'

'I've never done it before, either,' Lisabeth told her, astounded that her body instructed her when to push and when to rest and take deep gasping breaths.

'She's beautiful!' cried Kikorangi, beaming as she steadied the narrow blood-slicked shoulders and eased the baby out. So it was that the first words Theodora Morgan was to hear were 'She's a beautiful, beautiful girl. *Wahine kapai!*' Sentiments she would hear echoed all her life.

And Lisabeth? She now understood the deep-centred contentment that moves a cat to purr. Happiness flooded her; it oozed out of every pore of her body. When Rhys arrived home he found her sitting up on the chaise, trying to coax one faintly veined breast into the baby's wailing, wavering mouth and all the while beaming with ridiculous joy.

On a chair near the window sat Gwynne, just aroused and still fuzzy-brained from her afternoon nap. Pouting, she said: 'I never heard a peep all afternoon!'

'Missed it all, did you? It's that tonic wine, I'd say,' teased Rhys, thinking that tonic wine was becoming too central a part of Gwynne's life. He said: 'And what do you think of my clever wife, then?'

'Charles always said childbirthing was easy,' Gwynne told him, at which both Rhys and Lisabeth burst into laughter.

'No,' groaned Lisabeth. 'My stomach . . . I musn't laugh.'

'Let me rub it for you,' said Rhys automatically. He kneeled beside her, gazing at the little pink face. 'Lisabeth, dearest and cleverest wife in the entire world, I am so proud of you.'

'You've offended Gwynne,' whispered Lisabeth.

Rhys kissed her tenderly, then glanced over his shoulder in time to see Gwynne huffily leaving. In the doorway, on his way in, she was greeting Doctor Meakings. Rhys chuckled; laughter was bubbling up in him, relief that Lisabeth had been safely delivered of a healthy baby. He felt like flinging his cap over the moon, so extravagant was his delight. He said: 'Another interruption! Next time you have a baby, Lisabeth, try to have it in a less public place, will you? I've a million things to say to you and none of them can be uttered in front of witnesses. Glory, Lisabeth, I love you!'

'And I love you,' she whispered.

'Our family is complete at last.'

A cloud dulled her eyes. 'Not quite,' she reminded him. 'Perhaps later, when Daisy and Andrew come home.'

'Perhaps.' He straightened up. 'Ah, Doctor Meakings! I'm afraid Mother Nature challenged you to a race today, and won by a good country mile!' he said heartily.

Gwynne wrote to Daisy and Andrew, and received letters in return. These she left lying about the house – as she left her needlework, a sock she might be darning, or her empty tonic-glass – on a desk in the library or on

225

a mantelpiece, where Rhys and Lisabeth could not help but see them. From these letters they learned that Daisy was enjoying her studies and doing well, that Kiki's heart was responding to the treatment and that the sepoys, Albert and Leopold, were a great novelty in Edinburgh. The Launcenolts wrote to Lisabeth, but infrequently, and from them she heard that Kiki was much improved, that Beatrice had joined a garden circle and was occupying herself painting still-life studies of shells found on their excursions to the sea-side, that Daisy was studying hard, pining for New Zealand but enjoying holidays in Paris, Venice and Brussels with properly chaperoned – Beatrice stressed that – lady-friends.

Andrew and Daisy wrote only once to Lisabeth and Rhys, a formal note of congratulations on Theodora's birth. After that, nothing. Lisabeth knew what was needed, an acknowledgement from Rhys, and her heart ached to resolve the conflict; but, if Rhys heard her hints that he make that acknowledgement, he gave no sign.

Outwardly they were happy, so content that this would be one of their seasons of sunniest memories, forever bathed in a golden light. They played with Theodora for hours every day, they took her for rides, on picnics, and even bathing down on the tiny scallop of beach below the house where they dandled her plump toes in the lacy water. It was there, one afternoon that Lisabeth watched, laughing, as Rhys chased a tiny crab along the sand with a stick. Theodora, bending to look at the tiny creature, overbalanced and sat *plop* in the water. Her face creased into the beginnings of a howl, and immediately Rhys scooped her up, careless of the water seeping through his shirt and jodhpurs as he chuckled, coaxing her to exchange the scowl for a smile.

'She's so beautiful!' crowed Rhys in triumph when the dimples coyly appeared. 'Darling, you must have been exactly like her as a child. A beautiful, much-loved baby girl.'

Lisabeth was suddenly sober. Yes, she could see herself at that age – Theodora was almost three – with the same dark tendrils of hair and the slanting green eyes. 'No,' she said. 'There's an important difference. Theodora has two parents who not only love her but also spend time with her, play with her, make her feel special. We're teaching her to be happy, Rhys, in a way we were never shown as children.'

'I never thought of it like that. My parents were poor – which means they were constantly toiling, for other people or in their own stony fields – and they were too old to play, too tired to sit down with me.'

Lisabeth gazed down the beach, narrowing her eyes against the glare that bounced off the water. Out where the sand ran in amongst a low headland of rocks she could see the stooped black-clad figure of Birdie Nevin who was gathering mussels into a flax basket. Nearby, Lisabeth knew, would be Siobhan's half-Maori twin girls, roped together and tethered to a branch for safety. Ever since they were agile enough to climb out of the hand-cart that served as their pram Birdie had led them about like puppies on leashes.

Lisabeth said: 'Those two poor orphaned mites, for all their disadvantages, they're better off than Daisy was.'

Rhys gaped at her. 'Daisy had everything!'

'Did she?' Lisabeth thought of what Daisy's life had been: parents who quarrelled, uncaring governesses, a father who was always away, then the nightmares of seeing her baby brother drown and later being present when Azura choked to death on a crumb of cake. She said: 'Daisy had a grim childhood, Rhys, and so did poor Andrew, being raised by that monstrous Charles who put him to work in the fields as soon as he could hold a hoe.'

He was smiling, chucking Theodora under the chin to make her laugh. 'Don't fret about the past, Lisabeth,' he advised. 'It's too late for regrets.'

'It's never too late, Rhys,' she told him gently. 'We could make up for a lot of things if we wanted to.'

If he heard her, he gave no sign.

'Where are you going?' Lisabeth asked Gwynne one winter morning when she saw her shuffling out to the carriage wrapped in a thick cloak and scarf. Tenks was loading a hamper on to the luggage-rack at the rear. For one insane moment she wondered if Gwynne had ordered a picnic and was going off into the snowy fields to eat it.

Behind her smudged owlish lenses Gwynne's eyes were watery with concern. 'Birdie's sick again.'

'*Again?* She's been poorly all winter.'

'Doctor Meakings doesn't seem to know what it is, either. He treats her first for one thing, then for another. If you ask me, his medicines are making her worse, if anything. My Charles would know what to do. When we were too far from town to call a doctor, Charles—'

'I can hear Rhys calling me,' interrupted Lisabeth hastily. 'Give Birdie my best wishes, will you? I'll try to get down to see her later.'

'You'll do no such thing, 'Rhys told her. 'You've only just got out of bed yourself after losing the baby. I insist that you rest with your feet up and have Carthew bring you cups of tea and hot soup. Then,' he continued, holding up a warning finger as she was about to speak, 'this afternoon when I return from my meeting with Silas Drake, we'll harness up the sled and take Theodora for a skim over the snow before it gets dark. What do you say?'

Her eyes sparkled as she imagined the mountains glowing in the sunset, the crisp whoosh of snow under the rails and the luxury of being swathed to the chin in the warm fur rugs.

'You look like a little girl again,' he told her affectionately.

She said: 'But, Rhys, I am worried about Birdie . . . and those two little girls.'

'From what Mrs Tenks said, Gwynne has been regularly carrying off half the food in our kitchens to that household,' Rhys told her. 'They'll be well fed at the Nevins' at least! Now, you worry about yourself, do you hear me? It was sad to lose that baby boy, but my life would end if I lost you.'

On the way into town he stopped by to see for himself, and found Gwynne scouring the kitchen table while the grimy-looking tots played around its legs on the freshly swept floor. Above the fire hung a big black pot in which water was steaming.

'What in the world is going on?' he demanded.

'I'm going to give the lassies a bath,' Gwynne told him.

'You come down here to *work*? Gwynne, you're my sister! Up at the house I pay servants to look after you so that you don't ever need to do menial tasks like these.'

Her jaw set; her chins quivered. 'Charles said hard work never hurt anyone.'

'Other people maybe, but I noticed that he took care never to try it himself,' snapped Rhys, but was instantly sorry. 'I shouldn't interfere. If it makes you happy to be doing—'

The greasy velvet curtain swung back, and Tom Nevin's voice said: 'So you'll take away my poor mother's only comfort, wull you now, Musster Morgan? Ay, but thut's typical!'

Rhys looked up. Tom blocked the doorway, even larger and bulkier than Rhys remembered. His russet hair was almost shoulder length, and the dappling of freckles on his broad face more pronounced. A wooden crutch was tucked up under his arm. Rhys guessed that Tom expected him to look at his lower legs, to stare at the stump and peg, so he purposely kept his eyes on Tom's face and his voice free of pity. 'I hear you're working for my neighbour now,' he remarked.

'Overseeing hus blackfullows. Not thut ut's any of your bloddy business.'

'Only when my fences get cut and my stock melt away,' said Rhys curtly. 'Then you can be *sure* it's my—'

Gwynne said: 'Tom took the job so that he would be close to his mother, Rhys. He's a great comfort to Birdie, and he's wonderful with the children, too.' She prattled on, determined to fend off what could blow up into a quarrel (and almost had, for the two men were already glaring at each other like pit-terriers). 'I'm going to bath the girls now, Tom, if you'd be so good as to fetch the bath in from the wood-shed. Tom is marvellous to these girls, Rhys. They adore him. Don't you, my angels?'

The girls raised solemn eyes and nodded. Rhys had to smile despite himself. As identical as sixpences, the girls had that appealing dark beauty seen only in Maori children. He said: 'Tell Birdie I'm sorry she's ill.'

On the way out he noticed that Tom was managing the bath with ease. Being maimed had done nothing to diminish his strength and agility. Again despite himself, Rhys felt a prickle of admiration for the way he was conquering his disability. He said: 'I hope your mother's better soon, Tom.'

'She won't be,' Tom told him brusquely. 'Thus winter'll funnush her, I'm pucking.'

'I'm sorry to hear that.' Rhys twisted the brim of his hat in his hands, tried to think of something to say and, having failed, walked on through the bare orchard to where his horse waited.

Eighteen months later a package addressed to Lisabeth arrived at the house. 'A present for you, Mamma!' cried Theodora, hopping from one foot to the other in excitement. She was almost six years old now, but still as slight and small as a three-year-old. All her nourishment seemed to be dissipated in her constant nervous energy. Lisabeth hoped that the next child would be quieter and calmer; Theodora was delightful, but her antics would try the patience of a whole fleet of governesses.

'It's not for me at all,' said Lisabeth, breaking the sealing wax and opening the package. 'It's a surprise for your papa . . . for his birthday. Kiki sent it; and, look, here's a letter from Aunt Bea. Sit beside me, dear, and see if you can help me read it.'

' "Dear Lisabeth," ' piped Theodora, then gave up because the writing, she complained, was 'too woffly'. While she bounced and wriggled on the chaise-longue where she was born, Lisabeth read in silence.

' "There is great exitement here, as we prepare to return home. How I long to see Benares again, and to stroll in the gardens by the river! Doctor Meakings reports that it looked beautiful last summer – his descriptions made me ache with homesickness. Here, at last, is Kiki's *magnum opus*! What agonies he suffered, changing his mind back and forth over the bindings and the gold lettering, but the finished result is, you will agree, splendid. We shall have a reception on our return to launch *Years of Glory*, but Kiki wanted Rhys to have an advance copy presented to him on his birthday, even though we should be home a week later at the most. Daisy and Andrew, together with Andrew's bride Sarah, have been working long hours here to scrape together every penny they can towards the medical practice they hope to establish in Christchurch. With the proceeds from Andrew's little hospital they should be able to make an impressive beginning. If Daisy wrote, she

would have told you that she gained the highest-possible marks in some o
her examinations and has passed with flying colours. You will notice
change in her, Lisabeth. She is so dedicated that it frightens me but she ha
managed to keep her sense of humour, and is longing to be home ever
more keenly than we are. Just between we two, I suspect she is anxious t
renew her acquaintanceship with Jeremy Drake – not that she has con
fessed as much, but his name does crop up in conversation rather fre
quently! She was distressed to hear about Birdie's death. Gwynne said tha
the boy Nevin took himself a wife so that he could give those two poor chil
dren a good home. It goes to show, there is gold lying in the dirtiest puddle
If Daisy has not written, please forgive her. She has been extremely busy
Lisabeth, dear, cannot you please *do* something to ease this situation? I
distresses me so. Love and best wishes to you all. Beatrice." '

Lisabeth folded the letter in silence. *Jeremy Drake!* she thought. *Oh
poor Daisy!*

'What does the letter say, Mamma?'

'It says that Kiki and Aunt Bea will be home soon. They've never me
you, and you have never met them, so this will be such fun for all of you
won't it?'

'Let's tell Papa!' cried Theodora, flinging herself off the chaise as she
heard the clatter of hoofs in the drive.

'No!' Lisabeth reached out and restrained her by tugging at the skirt o
her blue-and-white sprigged dress. 'Let's make it be a surprise, shall we
Papa would love to have a surprise, an extra one for his birthday. We'll tel
him then.'

When Daisy woke in the morning the engines were making a softer, throbbing sound. Up on deck the railings were crowded. Everybody stared at the
mountains that banded like an unbroken frieze across the western horizon, row upon row of snow-etched waves tinted delicate pink with the firs
glow of sunrise. Smothering a yawn, Daisy gazed at them in wonder, while
Excalibur tugged, whining, at his leash.

'I never realized how hungry I was for that sight,' she marvelled to
Andrew, who, arm around Sarah's waist, was telling her the legends of the
mountains.

'The Maori name for them is *Aotearoa*, which is also the Maori name for
the whole of New Zealand and means "The Long White Cloud". Can you
imagine how the Maoris must have felt, after exhausting months at sea in
their precarious open canoes, to glimpse those mountains for the first
time?'

'I know how *I* feel,' Sarah told him. She had a neat clipped voice which
matched her small polished-apple face and her brisk no-nonsense manner. She said: 'I long to feel solid ground under my feet and to taste fresh
fruit and vegetables again.'

Remembering how Joseph Day once said that every new immigrant expressed exactly that same wish, Daisy smiled. Sarah was clever and capable, and an accurate diagnostic doctor, but Daisy had long ago stopped expecting originality from her. Agreeably she said: 'I dream of demons.' *And Jeremy Drake*, she added silently.

Beatrice tugged the fluffy feather boa up to block the chills from the back of her neck. 'If I longed for my garden before . . .,' she began, then said: 'Ah, ladies, you two do look smart in your new costumes. I had worried about these severe new styles, but they suit you admirably.'

Sir Kenneth stood beside his wife. It still amused Daisy to see them standing next to each other, because Kiki seemed no taller than when he was seated in his Bath chair. He was a cuddly toy of a man, with the puggaree flowing down behind his pith helmet and his whiskers flowing over his collar. The cure for his illness had done nothing to improve his temper. 'They're not as severe as Bea's clothes,' he said. 'Her dressmaking accounts are the grimmest things I've ever seen, for all her frills and flounces and furbelows!'

Andrew laughed. He liked the new tailored 'costumes' the younger women wore. Both Daisy and Sarah were garbed in striped silk skirts pleated in a band around the floor-lengths hems, and figured jackets that nipped in at the waist and ballooned at the shoulders into leg-o'-mutton sleeves. To offset the masculine lapels they wore frilly pastel blouses underneath with lace collars that rose up their throats like beer in a glass, brimming like froth under their chins. Their hair was dressed alike, both Sarah's brown hair and Daisy's white-gold drawn into glossy chignons under stiff little flat-brimmed hats circled around the low crown with chains of flowers. Glancing at them approvingly, Andrew said: 'I don't mind what they spend on clothes; they're an investment, Kiki. We need an image, yes, a smart image. We'll find the prettiest horses, the spankingest traps, and rent elegant rooms in the best location in town to hang out our engraved brass shingles.'

'Dazzle the masses, that's right! Just the way a confidence trickster works!' joked Kiki.

Andrew bridled. Kiki often played on the stuffiness in his character, teasing it out of him like horsehair from an old sofa. 'Not a trickster, Kiki,' he explained earnestly, wishing Kiki wouldn't use unfortunate phrases when potential clients might be listening. 'But I do agree about the confidence. That's what we must have – an air of confidence!'

'He's pulling your leg,' said Daisy. 'All I hope is that people accept us, and come to see that a lady doctor is every bit as good as a man. Be *still*, Excalibur!'

'Better than a man for some things,' Sarah corrected her. She tugged at Andrew's arm, interrupting him as he was about to refute her words.

'Look at that magnificent house . . . over there, on the cliffs! Who live; there? The king of the province?'

Andrew swallowed. He saw the headland with its pepperpot light-house and above the cliffs the dark rearing stones that reminded Gwynne of the Ballykelly Circle on her native Isle of Man. His eye travelled along the cliff-path, past the spot where twenty years ago he had rescued Daisy when she fell, on to the house Sarah was gazing at in rapture. Mists of Heaven did look beautiful, he acknowledged. Its white walls were as pink as the mountains beyond in this early sunlight, its mullioned windows sparkled like diamanté clusters, and its crenel-lated walls were sharply etched against the darkness of the distant foothills.

'Who lives there, Andrew?' she was saying. 'Oh, to live in a mansion like that! I do hope those people are sickly old folk who are anxious to try the latest techniques in medical care!'

Both the Launcenolts looked uncomfortable, and Daisy blurted: 'That's my papa's house. He and Lisabeth live there . . . with Aunty Gwynne – remember, she wrote when you were married, and sent you that carved Manx spoon—'

'Dear Charles,' said Sarah. She looked puzzled. 'But that means . . . that's *your* house, Andrew. Your family home.'

'Absolutely not,' cut in Andrew. 'Sarah love, we've explained the situation, and we don't want to discuss—'

'You told me about the feud, but feuds end, and *then* it will be your family home, and Daisy's. This is so exciting, Andrew! Just think! My *father-in-law* lives in a place as grand as Balmoral Castle!'

'Just drop it. Leave it be,' ordered Andrew.

Sarah looked incredulous. 'You're *angry*!'

'I'm not angry,' he said, struggling for control. 'And if I am it's for Daisy's sake, not mine. So please don't raise the subject again.'

'Where are you going?' she called after him.

Daisy smiled. She wasn't listening. Soon, very soon she would see Jeremy again. Had these years altered him? she wondered. Had they altered her? What would he think of her now?

Beatrice murmured: 'Look at those two . . . Albert and Leopold . . . there, by the lifeboat!'

The two elderly sepoys stood shoulder to shoulder, turbans high, chins out. At first glance they looked as if they were standing at atten-tion, but when Daisy leaned forward she saw that their faces were slicked with tears. 'How touching,' she whispered. 'They had such fun being made a fuss of in Edinburgh I didn't think they'd even want to come back, but they're more homesick than any of us.'

'Yes, I suppose so.' Sarah glanced at the sepoys, but her face was blank with lack of interest. It was when her gaze slid back to Mists of

Heaven that her expression changed. Daisy saw a glow creep into her hazel eyes and a flush warm her features.

She's impressed, thought Daisy sympathetically, guessing that this hint of wealth came as something of a shock. She said: 'It's a beautiful house, isn't it?'

'Beautiful? Oh, that's not the word. It's *glorious*!'

'It's just a house.'

'How can you say that?'

'I lived there for eighteen years. Oh, it's grand enough, but it gets cold and draughty in the winter, just like any other. But, anyway, surroundings aren't the only thing that makes a home. It's how you feel inside your heart. I've had some unhappy times there, believe me.'

'I could never be unhappy in a place like that,' declared Sarah loftily.

'If you say so,' said Daisy. When she left to go below with the Launcenolts, Sarah was still standing at the rail, lips parted and eyes aglow, gazing at the house.

'That could be their ship,' Lisabeth said as she rested the spy-glass on the ledge of the casement window. 'There are dozens of people at the rail, and that means a fresh load of immigrants. Daisy and Andrew could be among them.' Putting down the glass, she tightened the Japanese embroidered wrap about her thickening waist and tossed her long single plait over one shoulder as she continued to stare out beyond the Sumner Bar, where strips of cresting waves glinted in the watery light. 'It *is* them, Rhys, I'm convinced of it.'

'You said that yesterday,' Rhys said. He was propped up in the canopied bed reading Kiki's book, while beside him Theodora played with the food remaining on the morning tea-tray, cutting crustless buttered bread into tiny squares and sprinkling sugar grains over them before tossing them into her mouth. A great many sugar grains and buttered squares were landing on the rumpled sheets, but Theodora was enjoying herself hugely, squealing 'Oh!' in exasperation when she missed, and crowing whenever she caught one on her tongue.

Rhys ignored her; his luxury in life was to have fresh sheets every day, so it mattered not what happened to them before they were stripped and replaced. To Lisabeth he said: 'This book is amazing! I've seen some of it in draft form long ago, of course, but to read it like this, its like hearing Kiki talking about his experiences. Eerie, almost.' He closed the book and looked at the words 'SIR KENNETH AVERY LAUNCENOLT' stamped in gold on the spine. 'Good on him! I hope it does well.'

'I wonder what time they'll disembark?' Lisabeth rested interlaced hands on her swollen belly, smiling as she felt life stir within. 'Isn't this a coincidence, Rhys? I was almost ready to welcome Theodora when they left, and now that they're home again—'

'It might not even be them,' Rhys said. 'I say, I wonder what Kiki will have to say about events in the colony since he left? Plural voting established, talk of votes for women – that'll wind him up properly, no doubt – and when he finds out we've elected a newspaper editor as Prime Minister he'll be speechless!'

'Only temporarily, dear,' said Lisabeth, who had never known Kiki to be speechless for long. 'Perhaps we could telephone Joseph Day and see if he has any news. He said he'd keep an eye out, though without the actual name of the ship. . . .' She glanced back at the sea again. 'I have such a *feeling* it's them! It must be! Oh, let's go down to the port and meet them, shall we? Let's be there when they step on to Canterbury soil again!' Seeing that he was looking at the book, pretending to read, she seized her courage firmly by the scruff of the neck and plunged ahead with it. 'If we're there, Rhys, all the past will blow away by itself. There'll be no need for words, no need for apologies. . . . Everybody will be so busy congratulating Andrew, and meeting Sarah, and exclaiming over Theodora, that the whole miserable episode—'

Rhys snapped the book shut. 'Lisabeth, what you're asking is impossible.'

She had gone so far now. 'Why not, darling? Nobody expects you to—'

'I have meetings all morning, and this afternoon I'm addressing a gathering of station-owners about the prices set by our freezing works. "Baron" Windsor's been spreading rumours that he's been unfairly treated. I was going to ignore them, but newcomers to the province who don't know his reputation have been agitated by the reports, so I have to take them seriously.' He tickled Theodora, who was clambering over him and pulling his hair. 'That'll do, lovely. . . . You look after your mamma today, will you?' To Lisabeth he said: 'If you want to drive down to the port, then by all means go. Gwynne would appreciate an outing, I'm sure.'

'I won't go without you,' Lisabeth said quietly.

'Whatever you like.' He swung out of bed and pulled the nightshirt down over his muscular thighs. Putting his arms around Lisabeth, he murmured against her hair: 'Take care of yourself if you do go out.'

Lisabeth sighed. In the night-stand was a bottle of embrocation that she rubbed on to Rhys whenever he had cramp to help the unyielding muscles loosen and relax. If only there was a magic potion that she could rub in to make his rigid nature release him from an equally stubborn grip. He had the most loving and generous nature anybody could hope for, but this hard shell of pride was making everyone miserable. Himself most of all.

Lisabeth kissed him and rumpled his hair, thinking what a sad waste this all was. Then, holding out a hand to Theodora, she said: 'Come on now, you restless monkey. Let's see what Mrs Tenks has prepared for your breakfast.'

'It'll be porridge of course. I *hate* porridge.'

'You do not!' said Lisabeth.

They had so much luggage that three vehicles were needed: one for the Launcenolts, one for Andrew, Sarah and Daisy, and a third for the furniture Sarah had brought with her, having been warned that with so many immigrants flooding into the colony prices of basic tables, chairs and bureaux was astronomical. Riding in the third carriage, Daisy sat up scanning the scenery eagerly, for so much was forgotten and so much was new. 'How *scruffy* the roadsides look after Scotland!' she exclaimed. 'How green and shimmery the pastures look! And don't the buildings look . . . somehow *temporary* after the solid stone Edinburgh houses? These are like pictures of the American Wild West!'

Christchurch itself was bigger than they remembered, with hundreds of large elegant homes having been built and set off with manicured gardens. Sarah was impressed, though she laughed at the funny shop-verandas that stretched out over the pavement. 'You'll be glad of those,' Daisy told her. 'Shade for summer, shelter for winter.' She patted Excalibur, who snuffled, whining at the window. 'I do believe he knows we're home!'

'You could do with those in Kent. It's forever drizzling—'

'Stop the carriage!' urged Daisy suddenly. 'Quickly, oh, quickly!'

Andrew rapped on the ceiling to instruct the driver. 'What's the matter?' he wanted to know.

Daisy picked up her purse and opened the carriage door. Fifty yards ahead, on a bench near the band rotunda, sat Jeremy Drake. He was reading a newspaper, glancing over the top of it from time to time, as if he was watching out for someone. *Perhaps it's for me!* she guessed, marvelling that he didn't look one speck different and she'd recognized him instantly, even at this distance. He even had the same wayward lock of hair falling over his brow.

'She's seen someone,' guessed Sarah.

'Jeremy,' said Daisy in a shaking voice. 'I'll just casually walk up to him as if I've been gone only a few days.' She smiled at them both; the smile seemed to glow through her skin. 'Don't wait for me – I'll take the river path to Benares when we've finished talking. Here, hold Excalibur for me so he doesn't jump out, will you? He was so silly at the wharf. . . .'

By the time she reached the rotunda she was trembling with nervous excitement. He still hadn't suspected her presence; it was a wonder, she thought, that he couldn't hear her heart beating, for it was drumming so loudly in her ears that it almost smothered the laughter of the children playing with a punt on the river. How gorgeous he looked, bronzed and languid, relaxing there on the seat as if he was waiting for her to sit down beside him.

On an impulse she skirted around the rotunda and approached him from the back. She stood only a few inches behind him, breathing deeply to steady herself; and then, when he didn't turn around, she suddenly bent forward and cupped her gloved hands over his face. She could smell the warmth of him, the faint tang of lemon-scented soap, and she thought giddily: *I dreamed of lemons. Of lemons and of Jeremy Drake*.

Expecting him to laugh and to seize her wrists, she was puzzled when instead he said roughly, 'And what are you playing at now?' in such a tone that she dropped her hands at once and said: 'Aren't you pleased to see me?'

'Oh my God! Daisy!' He was on his feet, staring at her in disbelief, all colour draining from his face.

She laughed. 'You *are* pleased to see me! I can tell.' Sitting, she drew him down beside her and scanned his face, her eyes dancing with mischief. 'I'm sorry if I startled you. . . . Jeremy, you should *see* your expression! We've only just this minute practically arrived back from Edinburgh. I'm a doctor now, but I suppose you know; you'd have seen that article in the *Lyttelton Times* about me.'

'Congratulations,' said Jeremy in a strangled voice. 'Yes, I did see that.'

He seemed stilted, formal, but she put that down to shock. 'It was a real struggle,' she told him. 'The studies weren't too difficult, not once I'd learned to find my way around the plethora of strange accents at the University, but there was such a lot of resistance to us women there – there were three of us, Andrew's wife, me and one other – and the male students didn't like us at all. I was shunned socially the entire time I was there, and the teasing was something wicked! Whenever one of we ladies stood up to speak there was the most dreadful storm of coughing. Finally we took to carrying large jars of cough syrup into lectures, which made a joke of it. Oh, Jeremy, I've so much to tell you!'

'A lot has happened while you were away,' he said.

'But now that I'm here everything is the same again, isn't it?' she said brightly. 'You know, before I went away to study I used to feel so disadvantaged when you talked about Canada and America and all the wonderful places you'd seen, but now I feel more *equal* to you somehow. When you talk about Vancouver now, I'll be able to mention Venice, and when you discuss New York I'll be able to tell you about Rome. We'll have twice the fun.' Her eyes were glowing, and she felt so bubbly with happiness that she didn't notice him flinch when she took his hands in hers, as if her touch had burned him. 'It's so *good* to see

236

you! I've thought about you such a lot, Jeremy. I suppose I shouldn't really say that,' she giggled self-consciously, 'but every time I'm introduced to someone I compare them to you, and somehow—'

'Daisy, what did you hear about me while you were away?'

'Nothing. Why? Should I have?' Suddenly it dawned on her that something was terribly the matter. All of the joy and bubbling enthusiasm was on her side; Jeremy shared none of it. She tried, not very successfully, to laugh. 'Why? You haven't gone and got . . . yourself . . . married. . . . Oh.'

'It's a wonder someone didn't tell you.'

'That's why you didn't answer my card.' She was struggling to assimilate this. Married? He couldn't be! Yet she'd seen the answer in his eyes. She said, 'When?' and then: 'No, don't tell me, Jeremy. I don't want to hear. I don't want to know.' Fury and disbelief were seething in her mind. Couldn't he have waited until she got home? Perhaps he thought she wasn't coming back; but, even so, even so, he might have *told* her. Instead he let her go burbling on, making an idiot of herself. . . .

'Daisy, let me explain.'

'No.' She pushed his hand away. Pain, black as tar, was seeping into her mind. It was like having a hand slammed in a door, she thought. There was just a blank shock, disbelief and then this awful incredible pain.

From a long way off he was saying: 'Let's walk together, Daisy. We must discuss this.' Not that he wanted to – that was the last thing he wanted – but he could see the appalled hurt on her face and was horrified. Many, many times he had bitterly counted the cost of losing her, but he had never considered what anguish she might suffer inadvertently at his hands.

'No,' she repeated; then, speaking with difficulty, she said: 'Would you mind leaving me here? I—'

'Of course. Daisy, I'm sorry,'

It took every scrap of strength she had to drag her face into a semblance of a smile. 'Sorry? But congratulations are in order. You . . . you surprised me, that's all.' She didn't mean to ask, for somehow she knew the answer, but she heard herself say: 'Did you marry someone I know?'

He nodded. 'Arabella Martin.'

Daisy closed her eyes.

'Do look at his Lordship. Do come quickly!' laughed Daisy, beckoning to Sarah. She braced herself against the door-jamb, doubled up by the force of her laughter, and Sarah had to push past into the washroom to see what was funny.

Andrew was preparing to make a house call. Because many of the Christchurch houses had nothing that served as a washroom at all,

Andrew decided that they three should scrub up before going out, and again after coming home, donning clean gloves in between. Today he had three bowls on the bench, one with soapy water, one containing a brown liquid and the third that gave off a sharp ammonia smell. While the women watched, Andrew first scrubbed himself to the elbows with soap, then dipped his arms into the coloured liquid, which immediately stained his skin dark brown.

'Why the Condy's Crystals?' asked Sarah. She watched, mystified, as he then plunged his arms into the third basin, whereupon the brown began to fade. 'Doctor Stafford, what are you doing? What's that?'

'That, Doctor Stafford, is an oxalic acid bleach of my own concoction. And doing? I, Doctor Stafford, am preparing for a house call. To a house.'

Daisy laughed harder. 'Yes, a *house*! Mrs Fitzherbert rang. Honoria Fitzherbert, if you please. She wants Doctor Stafford – the *gentleman* one, as she puts it, – to go round to Barbadoes Street right away. For a "professional consultation", she said. Whose profession did she mean?'

'Why is that amusing? I'd have thought you would be annoyed to have someone else ask for the gentleman doctor. Between us, Daisy, we'd have been lucky to see a dozen patients in the past month. If that. Dash it all, Doctor Stafford, I'll take this call. They may have asked for the gentleman but they can have me instead. I'm going to rust up with nothing to do.'

'You won't want this one, believe me,' gasped Daisy.

'It's a cat-house, a brothel,' explained Andrew. He was annoyed that his sister was making such a joke of his thorough preparations. True, for most of his patients he was content to scrub up with mercurial soap, but at the Barbadoes Street brothel he had no idea what diseases he might come in contact with. One could not be too careful.

Sarah still didn't smile. 'It would suit you if you could scrub the whole world with Condy's Crystals and acid bleach, wouldn't it? You'd like to scrub away the dirt and rottenness and immorality and make this world a clean and shining place. Well, you can't, Andrew, and that's the fact of it. You can't just turn your back on your problems and pretend they're not there.'

Uncomfortable, Daisy looked from one to the other. 'I'll leave,' she offered.

'We're not tiffing,' lied Sarah. 'But I'm leaving now. I have to go up to the hospital for more bandages anyway.'

'Damn,' said Andrew when she had gone.

'Is it Papa again?'

Andrew nodded. 'She keeps hounding me to make my peace with him. She says I should. Not that she wants a handout – Sarah has her pride, too – but she has this idea that his patronage would make all the difference to our own business. She says it looks bad that our own family shuns us and patronizes Doctor Meakings instead.'

She, she, she, thought Daisy. *He's taking elaborate care to distance himself from all of this.* Aloud she said: 'Sarah is right, of course.'

'I know, more's the pity.'

Light from the open window shimmered across the white-painted walls, dappling Daisy's face. 'What if I go to Papa and tell him we need him – his support? I could ask; it wouldn't hurt to do that. I know I vowed never to go near until he had properly acknowledged you, but that was *for* you Andrew, so if you like—'

'No!' It was too forceful. Modulating his voice, he added: 'If you want to make your peace with him, then go ahead, but promise you'll never go near him on my behalf. I'd rather be no son at all than a begrudged one.' He saw her hesitating, so added harshly: 'And take no notice of Sarah's moods. She's bored to distraction, that's all. I think she'll accept that job at Seaview if this inactivity continues much longer.'

'Andrew, no! Not the mental hospital.'

'Why not? She has a keen diagnostic mind, and it's going to waste stagnating here. Besides, we do need the money, don't we? And, honestly, Seaview wouldn't be a quarter as bad as what you girls faced in the slums.'

'Then, *I* should do it.'

'Nonsense. Sarah's a married woman; she's more acceptable and, besides, she specialized in mental disorders. No, we'll let her do that if she wants. Cheer *up*, Daisy, will you? We knew it would be tough at first.'

'Not this tough.'

'It's only natural that the good citizens of Christchurch should regard us with initial suspicion. But give them time. We do have a few patients already, so it's hardly unmitigated gloom.'

'We have people too poor to pay, and those notorious for not paying their debts; those are our patients!' But Daisy's spirits never flagged for long, and already a fresh thought was buoying them up. 'Did you know that Doctor Meakings is spying on us? He came over to Benares on Sunday evening when Aunt Bea and I were playing Royal Parcheesi. First he twigged us about entertaining ourselves on the Sabbath and then he made great sport of the fact that Mrs Boswell's carriage was parked outside our rooms half the day on Wednesday. He scoffed that we were falling into a common trap, and she'd end up owing us a fortune in fees, and we'd never see a penny of it.'

'What did you say?' He reached past her for jacket and top-hat that were hanging on the brass rack inside the door.

'I told him that Mrs Boswell pays us for her consultancies in advance, just like all our other clients do. He went so purple that for a moment he looked exactly like a claret-bottle. I asked him then if there was news about Lisabeth's baby, so he puffed up and told me that was privileged information. Silly old toad! Excalibur ran yapping at his heels all the way home, and from the yelp we heard at the gate and the way that the poor dear came limping back I think he must have nipped Doctor Meakings's ankle and received a hearty kick for his enthusiasm.'

'It wouldn't have done him any harm. Excalibur is getting far too aggressive in the way he chases everything. He made my horse shy up the other day. Well, I must go.' Bag in hand, he glanced around the room as if seeking a further excuse to delay.

'Please let me do this visit in your stead,' suggested Daisy, seeing his reluctance. 'If you won't treat Sarah and me as equals, then how can we expect the public to accept us? Honoria's ladies would soon get used to me, and—'

'I can't. I already told Sarah no.' He bent to give her a swift cool kiss on the cheek. 'Cheer up, Daisy. Things will soon improve.'

'They can't get much quieter, and that's the truth,' she said glumly. When he had gone she picked up a duster and began to tidy the already impeccably neat rooms.

The house Andrew chose was a pretty one, with wide bosomy verandas trimmed with white lace and a pleated red bonnet of a roof. Its location, he explained proudly, was excellent, adjacent to the shops in Cashel Street and right on the route all the smartest people would take to do their shopping, yet handy, too, for the teeming lower-class section beyond the railway yards. Daisy admired the huge trees and leafy shade of the front lawn, while Sarah was delighted with the rear section of the house, which would be their first real home. She browsed in Whelan's Furniture Emporium for inexpensive curtainings and floor rugs, while Daisy arranged the expensive leather couches, brass-bound bookshelves and leather-topped desks in the two front rooms which were to be their consulting-rooms. These she decorated in mustard and white with varying shades of blue, colours picked from the tufted silk rugs that patterned these polished floors. Andrew negotiated the purchase of two sleek chestnut horses and a stylish brown trap with brass fittings, ordered a large brass plaque for the front gate and worded a discreet notice for insertion in the Christchurch newspapers, announcing that Doctors Andrew Stafford, Sarah Stafford and Daisy Morgan were opening their medical practice and offered the most up-to-date and highly qualified skills and surgical knowledge. It had been a rushed business, just three weeks from the time they stepped ashore until the date on the issue of the first newspaper to carry their notice.

'You've done marvels,' said Beatrice, who came with Kiki and the sepoys to admire the plaque and to drink vintage champagne, supplied by Kiki, as a toast.

'Good luck to you all,' said Kiki heartily. None of the four thought that the venture would work. In private discussions the Launcenolts agreed that Sarah should be raising babies and that Daisy should marry someone eligible post-haste and forget all this foolishness. After all, she and Sarah had proved they could qualify as doctors, and there was a certain nobility in proving that one could do something worthwhile, though to pen a novel or to paint a picture was a more appropriate ambition for a young lady. The sepoys thought that the fears and prejudices and superstitions of the local people would make them avoid going to women doctors. Though they smiled and bowed and offered flower-symbols of good fortune, they were right.

The local people preferred Doctor Meakings and his ilk. Perhaps he had never been formally trained, and certainly his quaint ideas of revolutionary treatment were scavenged from out-of-date periodicals, but he was so familiar a sight around the streets that he had become like a monument that nobody bothered to read the inscription on. Often his patients took a long time to get well, often there were complications from his treatments, and occasionally a patient died, but his public remained loyal. With him they felt comfortable, and there is nothing a sick person needs quite so desperately as comfort.

So week after week the three waited for customers, and so few came that it could have been a lean and hungry time and would have been frightening if not for the rallying of friends. Daisy was living at Benares, and each day brought a hot dish from Albert's kitchen which they stretched with bread and cheese to share between them for their lunch. Joseph Day stopped by frequently with fish or crayfish or with shrimps he had caught in the harbour, and on his weekly trips to town Jock McFallish delivered a basketful of bounty from Mists of Heaven: apples, peaches, grapes, gooseberries green as ice, succulent golden apricots and always a cut of meat, vegetables, and occasionally eggs or chicken for the pot. 'Mrs Stafford sent them,' Jock explained.

'Why doesn't she come herself?' asked Daisy as she wrote a hasty note of thanks while Jock was shyly accepting a cup of tea and a slice of Sarah's caraway seed cake. 'We're so grateful for these good things, Jock; but, oh, how I'd appreciate a visit!'

Jock looked shifty. 'She's busy, Miss Daisy. Ay, but it's been a right busy summer this 'n!' He thrust it all out in a heap, the words tumbling together, then sat back looking relieved.

Daisy could guess the real reason. Papa had forbidden Aunty Gwynne to come. Lisabeth couldn't, of course, being so close to her time with another baby. What Daisy couldn't know was that Lisabeth and

Gwynne together were indulging in a little subtle pressure on Rhys, making sure that he knew that, though they wanted to visit Daisy, they wouldn't do so without him.

Daisy hungered for her father's approval and for her old life at Mists of Heaven, but every day that went by convinced her more deeply that Rhys didn't love her and never had. She and Andrew were worthless cast-offs in his eyes; all he cared about was Lisabeth and his new family. Sometimes she wondered why they had bothered to return to New Zealand. It was ironic, but far away in Edinburgh with the contact of Gwynne's letters Daisy felt closer to her family than she did here, at the edge of the gulf of hostility that separated them. None of her feelings she shared with Andrew or with Beatrice; with them she was brittle and changeable, swinging easily from sombreness to a bright cheerfulness that deceived all around her into thinking that her despondencies were shallow as puddles and as quickly evaporated. No one guessed her inner despair.

Living in Christchurch heightened her sense of isolation in other ways, too. She missed Amy intensely – a pain that was heightened by disappointment in Andrew's wife. Before she married him, Sarah had been unfailingly sweet and agreeable, the perfect sister, but since the marriage her cordiality had lightened and she seemed at times to resent Daisy and Andrew's closeness, especially when they agreed on something and she did not, most particularly in the matter of Rhys. Sarah was eager to visit Mists of Heaven; she made no effort to disguise the expectation that one day she could possibly live there – perhaps even as its mistress – so she continuously urged Andrew to make peace with his father. Handicapped by the tunnel vision that is the curse of those with grasping souls, she could see no barrier between her and her ambitions and was frustrated by Andrew's obstinate refusal even to discuss the matter. It amazed her that he could be content to be poor and struggling.

Andrew was Daisy's great comfort; his unstinting good humour supported them all. He was least happy of the three about living on handouts, scrupulous in a way that Daisy was not because all her life she had been showered with largess and was easy about receiving things. To Andrew it rankled that they existed on charity. It was he who dug over the back yard, sieved the rich black earth and planted cabbage, cauliflower, Brussels sprouts and carrots for a winter harvesting, readying a plot in which to plant potatoes as soon as the cold had eased its grip and the days warmed with spring. Andrew was the one who went aggressively after work, giving public lectures on health and hygiene in rented halls in the poorest districts and taking Sarah and Daisy along to introduce them so that they could speak briefly about motherhood and child care. And Andrew went after food, setting himself up with a homemade

242

lantern and a spear made of a sharpened stick and a nail which he took out on to the inner harbour mudflats at low tide after dark, spearing flounder which he brought home and gutted, saving the trimmings to fertilize the garden.

'Life is good,' he said to Daisy one afternoon as she watched him nailing wire netting over a frame. 'Emma Day has promised us two sitting hens when we've somewhere to keep them, and that means that by this time next year we will be gathering our own eggs.' He paused to toss a short end of wood so that Excalibur could hurtle after it. 'That is, provided that rascal doesn't slaughter the poor wretches before they have a chance to grow.'

'He *is* naughty,' Daisy giggled, remembering how Andrew had snatched next-door's bantam rooster from his jaws and hidden it just in time, when the woman came bustling over with a full head of steam on looking for it, accusing Excalibur and brushing aside Daisy's protests that he was 'a harmless fun-loving dog'. In defending him Daisy knew nothing of the dead rooster, and wondered why Excalibur was jumping and barking at the tank-stand door. 'I'd leave him tied up, but he cries all day; and I'd leave him at Benares, but Leopold complains that he keeps dashing out on to the road, chasing passing cyclists. He's as excited as we are to be home, that's what it is!'

The back door swung open, and Sarah stepped out on to the veranda carrying a tray with glasses of lemonade and shortbread biscuits just out of the oven. 'Refreshment for the worker,' she said, smiling with affection at Andrew. In her eyes was a possessive glow, and watching the two of them settle with their shoulders and knees carelessly touching Daisy felt a pang of that emotion that disturbed her when she used to see Rhys and Lisabeth together – not jealousy exactly but the feeling of being an outsider, of wondering whether she would ever share that enchanted closeness with another person. At such times she tried very, very hard not to think about Jeremy Drake.

Sipping at her lemonade, she said brightly: 'We were talking about how lucky we are. The weather is glorious, the garden is growing, and we have food on the table, *and* we must be living in one of the prettiest cities in the entire world. Aren't we lucky?'

'We're truly blessed,' said Andrew, his voice drowsy with contentment.

Sarah looked from one to the other. She didn't smile. Then she set her lemonade-glass down on the step beside her and stood up and went inside.

'What did I say?' said Daisy.

Andrew shrugged.

In a moment Sarah returned. Her face was white, the skin pressed to the bone as if she was struggling to hold a flood of feelings down inside her. She was holding a sheaf of papers in her hand. When she spoke her voice shook. 'This is how blessed we are,' she said, and she read out the amount on each of the bills, one at a time. 'Gas, five shillings, due three weeks ago. Dry goods, four shillings and sixpence and another here for ten shillings and threepence, with a comment written, "Your urgent consideration would be appreciated". Coal, seven shillings and sixpence. Tailoring – to have that suit of yours taken in – two shillings and elevenpence. Hay and oats—'

'It's all right,' said Andrew, alarmed. 'Truly, it's all right. I told you not to worry about those accounts. Things will turn the corner soon, and then—'

'When? When will they turn the corner, Andrew? I hate owing people money! I loathe and detest going around giving everyone a shilling and a promise! I'd sooner sell everything I own and clear our debts . . . I. . . .' And her face crumpled.

'Dearest,' said Andrew. 'We've been over all this time and again, Doctor Stafford' – he tickled her under the chin, trying to coax a smile through the tears – 'Doctor Stafford, please don't agitate yourself. It doesn't do any good.'

'That's true.' Head bowed, she groped for a handkerchief and blew her nose, then folded the cloth and dabbed at her eyes.

Daisy said: 'I know we make light of our debts, but things will get better, and in the mean time we have to put on a brave face. . . .'

'I know. . . . You're right.' Sarah appeared to rally, then suddenly she burst into a storm of renewed, untidy crying, burrowing her face into Andrew's shoulder.

Embarrassed, Daisy lowered her eyes and met Excalibur's unblinking gaze. His eyes shone like toffee, and his bristly face wore a pleading expression; she realized that from the moment she took a piece of shortbread he had adopted his station beside her, watching every movement from hand to mouth. She smiled and crumbled a few morsels for him to snuffle and snap for in the grass.

'If only you'd go and see your father,' wept Sarah. 'If only you weren't so stubborn!'

'I'll never do that,' said Andrew. 'You know it's no use asking.'

'I know . . . but I'm in such a *panic*, I don't know. . . .'

Daisy decided to make a tactful exit, but before she could set her glass down Sarah abruptly straightened, smoothed her face with both open hands in a single stroking gesture and put on a crooked smile. 'I've decided,' she said. 'I've decided to accept that post at Seaview. I feel terrible about letting you two down, especially after we'd made all our plans and had the plaque engraved and the cards printed and the notices put in the papers. It seems cowardly to dash off, and I hate to alter arrangements once they've been made. I'm a tidy person, and that's such a messy thing to do, but I want the job, I really do. It's much more along the lines of what interests me, and they're offering an excellent salary, so I do hope you two don't mind. . . .'

'Mind?' Daisy choked back a laugh. 'Sarah dearest, you must do what is right and proper for you, and never matter whether we mind or not, and of course we don't, do we, Andrew?' She realized belatedly that again she had spoken automatically for her brother, too – something that she had resolved to stop doing.

Sarah didn't seemed to notice this time. 'I've been agonizing over this for ages,' she confessed, 'but I hated the feeling that I was letting you down.'

Daisy laughed. She took Sarah's hands and tugged her gently to her feet, then embraced her. Sarah's face was hot, and her whole body quivered. 'What a funny, dear and wonderful friend you are!' exclaimed Daisy. 'Of course you're not letting us down.'

'On the contrary,' drawled Andrew. 'If things don't improve soon, you could well soon be supporting us!'

TWENTY-THREE

I T WAS ONE of the ironies of life, reflected Daisy, that the instant one no longer needed something one received it in abundance. Now that Sarah's salary from her post at Seaview was not only placating the tradesmen but also building a little buffer in the Savings Bank besides, Andrew's practice began immediately to climb out of the doldrums. If there was not a cluster of patients waiting in his outroom, then he was likely to be off somewhere on a house visit.

Initial suspicion towards him seemed to have melted. After all, he was not exactly a 'new chum' even if he did have a posh toff's way of talking. He had lived in Canterbury twice before. And, though he was Mrs Morgan's brother, he was hardly a nob himself; he was, in fact, perfectly sited in society to be a doctor, far enough above the masses to command respect, and yet not in the ranks of the élite, but poised on a step somewhere between.

Though she was chafing at her own enforced idleness, Daisy was pleased for him. 'Once they tried your services they knew they were in safe hands,' she said. 'I hope they'll do the same for me, and then, Andrew, we won't look back. Sarah can give up her hospital job and we'll all be in a thriving practice together, exactly as we dreamed!'

'In the mean time I'm getting paid,' reported Andrew. 'It's not like it was at first, when I flinched from asking for payment in advance. Now I'm blithely callous about it. If a patient says he hasn't any money, I tell him to borrow some or to scratch out something that can be run down to the pop-shop to raise the necessary for my fee. I say: "If I don't eat, then I'll soon be ill, too, and who will look after you then?" I'm no longer shocked that they're inevitably bluffing – the money always seems to be tucked away somewhere – and I've a sneaky feeling that they respect me all the more for demanding it.'

'It's hardly *demanding* when we charge less than half of what Doctor Meakings does,' protested Daisy. '*And* you're twice as good.'

'At least,' he said, grinning.

They were alone in the kitchen, sharing leftover mulligatawny soup that Albert had made for dinner at Benares the previous evening. Daisy spooned some up, hesitated, then laid her spoon down. 'Speaking of Doctor Meakings, there's something worrying me. Do you think he may be deteriorating as he gets older? I hesitate to mention this but, even though I've had only a few patients, most of those have already been to Doctor Meakings, and in one or two instances I've been seriously concerned about the quality of treatment he's given out. That woman I was called to last week, for example. She had a third-degree episiotomy which had not been stitched. The handywoman told me that Doctor Meakings had used forceps to deliver the baby and had hurried the process because his dinner was waiting at home. When she asked him to come back next day because the poor mother was in agony he dismissed her, saying that a small amount of discomfort was to be expected. So that's why she came for me. It's a miracle that the woman hadn't contracted puerperal sepsis.'

'H'm,' said Andrew. She could see he felt ill-at-ease having her discuss these matters with him. 'I don't know what we can do. . . . Medical ethics. . . .'

'And this morning a woman brought in a little boy with an inflamed throat. He was vomiting pus and blood, and he shrieked blue murder when I tried to get him to open his mouth. His mother explained that the "old doctor" had strapped her son into a chair, forced his mouth open with a metal brace and then shoved a long pair of nippers into the boy's mouth to clip the infected tonsils.'

'That was a common enough procedure in the old days,' Andrew said. 'We must be fair—'

'I *am* being fair, dash it! I know it goes against your grain to criticize a fellow-practitioner, but we must discuss this. What happened was the little boy kicked out – fear and pain, probably – and the "old doctor" dropped his guillotine to the floor. He picked it up and *wiped it off on a soiled handkerchief* before finishing the job. I asked the woman if she might not have confused a clean piece of lint with a handkerchief, and she said: "Bless yer, no! I seen 'im blow 'is nose, din't I? Gort ever such a bad cold, 'e 'ad." Oh, Andrew, just thinking of it makes me feel ill.'

'What did you do?'

'I couldn't examine the lad, so I gave her some mild sedative syrup and explained that whatever harm was there had already been done. I asked her to bring him back this afternoon to have his throat swabbed.' She smiled wanly. 'I assured her that there would be no extra fee for the second visit, and she said: "But yer don't want payin' any'ow, do yer, miss? Yer that Rhys Morgan's daughter, in yer? What'd you want my money for?"'

'I trust you explained.'

'I did, and doubt she believed a word of it. But, Andrew, the problem remains. There could easily have been a death after that rough forceps delivery; and, as for the lad's tonsils, they could have been pedunculated, for all we know, and there was no consideration given to an enucleation. No, I must be fair and not speculate. However, we do know that there is a raging infection in what should be a clean operation, so should we warn Lisabeth that Doctor Meakings is losing his touch? I assume she'll be consulting him about the baby.'

Andrew frowned. He ate his soup a quarter-spoonful at a time, all the while thinking and frowning. Finally he said; 'See if Lady Launcenolt can find out when Lisabeth's baby is due, and if she is in good health. Get her to scratch out all the details she can. Then, and only then, will I consider it. I'm reluctant to interfere, especially as I have no idea whether Lisabeth would listen to my advice anyway. And what could I say? ''Make sure Doctor Meakings uses only sterile equipment''? How is she to ascertain that? I'll wager that she chooses chloroform like all the other station-owners' wives, and while she's unconscious she'll not have an inkling of what is going on. The most I could achieve is to alarm her, and that's the worst thing possible – next to risking having a baby at her age!'

His face darkened, and Daisy guessed that he was again brooding over the gamble Rhys was taking with Lisabeth's health. She said gently: 'Lisabeth probably *wants* the baby, you know. I remember her saying once that she'd love to have a romping noisy tribe of children to overflow the house.'

'Dear Lord, surely not! That might have been a fine ambition when she was twenty years younger, but—' He paused, grinning self-consciously. 'It's nothing to do with me, and I'll not – I repeat, *not* – get distressed over it.'

'Splendid!'

'But you will see if Lady Launcenolt can find out anything about how Lisabeth is keeping? I can't help being a little bit anxious.'

'Just a little.' Daisy hid a smile. 'It's only natural that you should.'

Daisy walked home in the mellow autumn evening along footpaths strewn with scarlet and gold, while Excalibur limped and hopped beside her, breaking into a run with no trace of lameness whenever a cat crossed their path. This evening Daisy didn't scoff at him; she was thinking about the little boy's inflamed oozing throat. Only the roughest methods could botch a straightforward tonsillectomy as grossly as the mess she had swabbed with iodine, all the while chatting briskly with the mother in an effort to mask her rage and disgust. Yes, Doctor Meakings was definitely slipping, and the sooner he retired the better.

'How old is Doctor Meakings?' she asked Beatrice as she hung up her hat and scarf and unpinned her boater hat.

'My dear child, what a question!' Beatrice reprimanded her. 'Why do you ask?'

248

'I wondered if he had any thoughts of retiring, that's all.'

'Not today, I should think, dear.' She was smiling and secretive. He's just left for Mists of Heaven.'

'Lisabeth's baby?'

She nodded, her eyes alight. 'Kiki has just come home from there.' She sighed. 'I'm afraid he's been arguing with your father again.'

He was in the morning room. He snapped the newspaper open, folded it back and glared at her over the top of it. 'That Rhys Morgan is as blind as a bat!' he declared, overlooking the fact that he was addressing Rhys's daughter. 'No matter how I point out that this country is driving itself to ruin, he will not see it! This nation needs people of wealth and position to run it, not jumped-up newspapermen and cockatoos – *cockatoos*, if you please! What's the matter with the populace nowadays? If they actually throw away their precious votes on people like that, then they don't deserve to *have* a vote!'

Daisy wanted to ask about Lisabeth, and if he knew anything, but she could see that there was no hope of wresting his favourite subject away from him – not until after dinner, at least.

They were still at dinner when Doctor Meakings came in, rolling full of Rhys's vintage Canary wine and the news that Lisabeth had been delivered of a baby girl that they were naming Anne Elizabeth.

'Isn't it wonderful?' gushed Beatrice, twitching a smile at Daisy, because this meant that Andrew was still Rhys's only son.

Daisy couldn't help herself. 'You've not been away very long, Doctor,' she said coldly. 'I do hope you didn't rush the delivery with forceps so that you could hurry home to your dinner this time, too.'

Doctor Meakings stared at her, his pale eyes hazy with wine. Daisy wondered if he'd even heard her; he certainly didn't know what she was talking about. Daisy supposed that the woman was too unimportant even to be remembered.

Later she pondered how strange it was that now she had two sisters and was unlikely see either of them, it seemed. In demanding Andrew's rights for him, had she merely joined him in exile?

While Rhys and his new family were very much on her mind, she resolutely never thought of Jeremy Drake. His marriage had been a terrible shock, and had brought home the realization that she expected him to be waiting for her when she came home, along with the realization that she had been stupid and selfish ever to expect such a thing. What encouragement had she ever given Jeremy? He was better off without her. Only . . . she did wish that he'd married someone nicer than Arabella Martin. Then she learned (in hushed whispers) from Beatrice that Arabella had given birth to their only child, a boy, less than four months after the wedding, while Kiki had boomed (in his now deafening voice) that the first baby can come at any time and after that it takes nine months! This news shook Daisy; not knowing what to think of it, she tried to put the whole matter from her mind. It was not difficult. Whenever she glanced at the racing news in the paper, or saw a white horse tethered outside one of the offices in town, or whenever she had kisses for afternoon tea or walked into the parlour or rode past the churchyard where Amy was buried, at all of those times she deliberately turned her thoughts away from him.

She congratulated herself that she had forgotten him so easily.

Jeremy had not forgotten *her*. His marriage to Arabella was one of those nightmarish mistakes that should never have happened, and looking back it seemed incredible that it had, incredible that he had willingly participated in events that projected him headlong into such a ludicrous union. Yet he had. It had all taken place so smoothly that he might as well have been under the influence of a drug. At a party at Martinsfield, Arabella had coaxed him into taking her across the lake to the island in the centre, and he had agreed, thinking she was trying to make Maurice Andruth jealous. Since the cricket game that afternoon he had been drinking whisky, and now, in the moonlight with music hovering over the water and the skies ablaze with stars, every gesture was infused with romance. When the punt nudged on the shore Arabella nuzzled against him with a throaty laugh. She tasted of raspberries; he remembered the swift excitement of it and the overwhelming feeling of being at one with the whirling universe. The incident had been so seamlessly perfect that when he woke next morning he wondered if he had dreamed it.

Not until three months later, when she confronted him in her father's study, was there any guilt. They married as speedily as could be arranged and then settled together in a large house near the Addington racetrack. Apart from Maurice Andruth, who was furious, everyone seemed happy – everyone, that is, but Jeremy, who forever afterwards marked that moment in the study as a turning-point in his life. Since then he had moved in a fog of numbed disbelief. He didn't even *like* Arabella; and once she had him he doubted that she liked him, either. Try as he might, he could find no logical explanation for what had occurred between them; without self-pity he felt like someone framed for a crime he knows nothing about.

His father was delighted. 'Well done, of course, son! One with a spout on naturally!' he swaggered when Silas Algernon Drake was born. 'I told you I'd picked that Martin lass as prime breeding stock. Now you've got your boy and you know what to do, let's see a girl next time, hey? Buck your mother up no end, that would. Course, wouldn't matter if it was another boy. A man can't have too many sons.'

Jeremy gritted his teeth. He was already deciding that there would be o 'next time'. Arabella had moved her things to the nursery and locked ne door to keep him out, but it was an empty gesture on her part. He ad done his duty by marrying her, and he'd be damned if he'd do nything further. Her body repelled him, the sight of her face repelled im. Only at night when he remembered that afternoon when Daisy ad emerged from the water, her body glistening and pale, only then id he feel a sweet stirring in his loins. With his wife he was empty, and fter she had failed to stir him on their wedding night she withdrew and vaited for him to come to her.

Which would be never, he resolved.

Rhys noticed that something was wrong. He saw how the lad flinched vhen people asked about Arabella, how he brushed aside congratula-ions. 'Got you good and properly, did she, lad?' he sympathized. Well, you're not the first to be ensnared like that and you'll not be the ast. Fortunately life has other compensations!'

There was one, one marvellous compensation; and, partly to push way that fleeting feeling that Rhys thought him a fool for being rapped by Arabella, Jeremy began eagerly to tell him about that com-ensation. His son, his marvellous, incredible baby son. How advanced ne was for his age, how strong his grip – why, at two weeks it had such ower in it that he could have held a set of reins with no trouble! How lear his gaze was, how. . . . And then he noticed that Rhys was wearing the oddest expression, a cross between pain and tolerance. 'I'm sorry, sir,' stammered Jeremy. 'I must be boring you.'

It was not until later that Jeremy realized his tactlessness. Rhys Morgan had no legal son of his own: no wonder he seemed affronted by Jeremy's enthusiastic ravings.

That had been almost four years ago, and the situation remained the same. He and Arabella lived apart, each in cool isolation. The bond between himself and his son strengthened. Whenever he mentioned young Silas he caught that same queer wistfulness on Rhys's face. And whenever he thought of Daisy he was overcome by the sensation that his life had been jerked from underneath him.

Sometimes when he sat in the grandstand watching the latest horses in the Georgia stud pacing out during training his thoughts drifted and he wondered what might have happened if he had handled things differently. Suppose he had forced himself on Daisy when he had the opportunity; suppose their lives had been linked by the same kind of 'accident' that linked him to Arabella? Would Daisy now hate him as much as he hated his wife? That, he admitted, would be worse than anything he was enduring now. But there was little comfort in the thought.

* * *

The last few years had hit the young colony hard. The poor had bee[n]
blighted by a depression that tightened money and thinned out avai[l-]
able jobs. Many working people had emigrated, fleeing the country [to]
which they had journeyed with hope only a short time before. Mea[n-]
while the prosperous landowners tightened their belts about their stou[t]
girths and economized by trimming jobs still further. It seemed that th[e]
privileged class rode high on the waves of wealth, but at last the tides [of]
fortune were turning against them.

The new Liberal government was, Sir Kenneth feared, proving to b[e]
every bit as dangerous as he had predicted. Not only had it extravagant[ly]
given every adult male of good character a vote, but there was also talk [of]
extending this to women as well – only *talk*, most sensible peopl[e]
hoped! This lot were mad enough to do anything, though, and ha[d]
recently introduced a Land and Income Tax Bill which instead of taxin[g]
everyone equally was aimed at leeching huge amounts of money fro[m]
the wealthy, who had previously enjoyed a protected tax climate.

In the Canterbury Club the gentry were bitter in their attacks on th[e]
new legislation. This would never have happened if men of the righ[t]
calibre sat on the Parliament benches. People who would stand u[p]
fiercely for what was right. People like Rhys Morgan, who knew who hi[s]
friends were.

But when he again proposed to Rhys that he consider standing fo[r]
election Rhys only laughed at the suggestion. 'It's about time some of u[s]
paid our dues,' he said. 'Years ago I thought that the best thing abou[t]
New Zealand was that it was a clean slate on which we could draw up the[]
kind of society we wanted. I believed we'd invent something fresh and
new, and fair for everyone; but, no, we simply transported an old
out-of-date oligarchy here from England with most of the creaky prejudices and snobberies intact. Perhaps now we're having the chance to
remedy our mistakes.'

'What you mean', snapped Sir Kenneth, exasperated, 'is that this
new legislation won't hurt you!'

'Of course it'll hurt me!' roared Rhys. 'Look at the tax I have to pay!
Five times the amount they're demanding from "Baron" Windsor,
though you'd never suspect it by the way he's squealing. The thing is, I
can find the money. I've diversified, expanded, gone into shipping and
processing. It's these blinkered idiots who've stuck only with wool that
are going to be hit badly. Wool's bringing the lowest price ever at the
moment, and this is the third year in a row. I shudder to think how
they're going to cope when their tax demands come in.' He paused and
added soberly; 'The word is that Algie Martin isn't even trying to cope.
The valuers estimated his worth at £200,000 and charged him accordingly. He's protested, insisted through his lawyers that he's worth
only £125,000 and will pay tax only on that figure. He's bluffing, of

252

course. Martinsfield has to be worth well over a quarter of a million pounds, certainly far over the government valuation.'

'So what will happen?'

'I don't know if it's true, but the whisper is that the Government have told him that they're paying him two hundred thousand, *their* estimate, for his land, and he has to pack up and go.'

'But they can't do that!'

'It seems they can, old friend.' While they argued, they strolled in the heated glasshouse that joined the brick stables. Rain drummed on the roof, smearing the sky as Rhys reached up with secateurs and snipped heavy bunches of sweet purple grapes which he laid on a straw-lined tray.

'But you said that Martinsfield is worth far more than that. That makes the seizure robbery, Rhys, utter robbery!' And he banged down his silver-topped cane for emphasis.

'Is it? Do you think so? I've pondered that question long and seriously. I've even wondered whether it would be robbery if they paid him his own valuation – a much lower figure again – and took the property in exchange. Yes, it's an interesting question.'

'You don't sound in the least sympathetic,' accused Sir Kenneth peevishly. 'I thought Algie Martin was a friend of yours.'

'He is, but I've no misplaced sentiments for him. Next to "Baron" Windsor he's a paragon of kindness, of course, but just the same he's been exploiting his fellow New Zealanders for years. He tossed those Maoris off his land, and he's often boasted of the miserably low wages he pays his shearers. No, I'm not sympathetic. Sorry, perhaps, but more for the lost dreams of this country than for individuals who helped sour those dreams.' He paused to concentrate as he snipped the stalk of a higher bunch. 'There. Do you think Beatrice will enjoy those?'

It was Daisy who loved grapes – they gave Beatrice dyspepsia – but the fiction that gifts were for Beatrice was a pretence both men maintained, a face-saving exercise that deceived neither.

Sir Kenneth said: 'We'll all enjoy them, thank you. Our garden was utterly neglected, as you know, but never mind that. Won't you reconsider, Rhys? The Conservatives do need you.'

But, old friend, I neither want nor need them. Their squabbling and favouritism sickened me; funny about that – other people's feuds are so much more tiresome than one's own. Not that this crowd will be any better. We hear whispers of corruption already! No, thank you. Politics was exhilarating when I was younger and less cynical. I'm too busy to be bothered with it now.'

When he protested that he was too busy, Rhys was not exaggerating. These days he seemed to have no time to himself, no time to stroll through the stables of an evening with a pocketful of sugar lumps to coax a nuzzle from his favourite horses, no time to play his beloved Mozart on the spinet, and not as much time as he wanted to spend with Lisabeth and his two daughters. He lived with a constant nagging feeling of unfinished business. Lisabeth and the girls were a joy, but every time he spent an hour with them he was reminded of the missing pieces of his family, and their shadows seemed to fall between himself and the others, darkening his pleasure. With the shine off his life, he worked harder, started more projects that would keep him stepping faster and faster on a treadmill of his own creation, and still happiness eluded him. His response to every request from Lisabeth and his friends was an automatic 'I don't think so. I'm too busy.'

Or else he didn't return calls. One evening he was given a message to telephone 'Baron' Windsor about some sheep that were for sale. He didn't respond, and when 'Baron' Windsor rang next morning, furious at the imagined insult, Rhys was unable to placate him. 'Yes, we've got room on the winter intake, but I can promise nothing. It depends entirely on the condition of your stock. Yes, yes, I'm sure that they're fine animals, but there are certain qualities we're looking for this time – an experiment, if you like. I'll look at them tomorrow.'

'Blast it!' he said to Lisabeth. ' "Baron" Windsor's sheep are certain to be unacceptable; it's bound to be a waste of time my going to look at them.' He bent over her. She had brought Anne in for him to look at, and she held her face up to him, her eyes luminous with love as he stroked his baby daughter's cheek and let her capture his finger, dragging it into her mouth.

'She's a hungry little devil,' Lisabeth told him ruefully. 'She chews away at me with no consideration. I'm raw on both sides.'

'We can't allow that. I'm jealous of her as it is.' Rhys cupped a full firm breast. Responding to his touch, the nipple began to ooze milk through the muslin of her gown. Desire stirred in him, desire sharpened by weeks of abstinence. 'How long now?' he whispered. 'I'm a hungry little devil, too, you know.'

'I know to my peril,' she scolded, moving away. 'And, since it's prudent to change the subject in front of this innocent child, have you forgotten that tomorrow you are meeting those buyers from Paris and Brussels and showing them around the city? You'll not have time to ride up to White Clouds.' Holding Anne's small pink face up to him, she cooed: 'One last kiss for Papa and it's sleepy-time again.'

Rhys rang Jeremy Drake. Though by now Jeremy was wealthy and independent, with a string of his own racehorses and lucrative business interests in the flourishing grass-seed industry, Rhys often imposed on him to cast his eye over a flock for an expert opinion. The quality of meat they processed was of absolute importance. The first meat to arrive frozen on the European markets had been Argentine beef which was

atchy in quality, some shipments acceptable but others tough and
dark, the meat dry and leached of all flavour; its reputation suffered
accordingly, and customers began to avoid it. Rhys was determined that
meat stamped with their interlocking D & M insignia would be always
sweet and tender, and to that end the strictest quality controls were
implemented. At Smithfield specially trained butchers culled the ice-
burned carcasses out along with any damaged meat, trimmed off the
markings then donated it to orphanages. It was still of good eating
quality, but not perfect, and anything less than perfect was not fit to
bear the D & M stamp.

At this end of the process, selection had to be just as stringent. It was a
trick he had, a gift of the eye, but just as Jeremy could assess the quality
of a brood mare and could tell at a glance whether a horse had the lungs
and stamina to be a distance racer or a sprinter, so he could judge cattle
and sheep. He was an obliging lad, too. Rhys was genuinely fond of
him, and often regretted that things between him and Daisy had not
developed as he had hoped. Perhaps he had hoped too much. . . .

'White Clouds, sir?' came Jeremy's voice over the telephone. 'I'm
afraid I can't go up there.'

'Of course you could,' said Rhys, not knowing anything of the long-
ago trouble between Jeremy and the 'Baron'. 'You're bringing those
two mares up anyway, aren't you? It's only half an hour's ride. You
could make a quick trip up there afterwards.'

'I'm sorry, sir, but I don't think I can manage—'

'Of course you can.'

'Well. . . .' He might not even see the 'Baron'. Word had it that the
fellow was wallowing in his cups most of the time, in binges that lasted
up to a week, and that all his business nowadays was being overseen by a
one-legged Irish fellow – a tough rooster, too, from all accounts. 'All
right . . . if you insist.'

Rhys chuckled into the mouthpiece. 'Of course I insist,' he said. 'You
know me. Why make a suggestion when insistence gets the results?'

'Very funny, sir,' said Jeremy in gloom.

As soon as he saw Tommy Nevin, Jeremy realized that he had seen him
often before, when he was tall and swaggering and handsome. Now he
was hunched over the crutch he leaned on, and his broad freckled face
had a sour twisted look. Old Silas would say he was a human crossed
with a crab, thought Jeremy, and there was something crustacean and
menacing in the way he hobbled, the crutch jabbing the ground like a
claw and the carved peg-leg dragging in the dust.

'Wull?' he demanded. 'You cun tull me your price, und we'll come
to un arrangement.'

Jeremy glanced at his glowering face and back at the sheep. They were

255

clean, suspiciously clean for this dry weather when the White Cloud
pasture was thinning and clouds of brown dust were drifting from the
bald patches in the hills. Jeremy guessed they had been run through a
stream several times to wash their wool. 'They need shearing,' he said
'It's difficult to assess their condition when they're so heavy in the
fleece.' He was stalling; the sheep were not up to standard. Several were
limping with foot rot, and he had noticed a couple at first glance with
filmed-over eyes, a sign of ophthalmia, a condition caused by poor
feeding and a weakened immune system. They were definitely not D &
M quality sheep.

Aggressively Tom said: 'Whut's wrong wuth thum?' When Jeremy
hesitated he answered the question himself. 'Nuthun! They've no
coughing, no scouring. . . . It's perfuct animuls they are, und don'
you try tulling me uny different just to brung the price down.'

'I'm not authorized to discuss prices anyway,' Jeremy told him. He
was anxious to get away, but though his mind had already been made
up he sorted out two or three sheep and checked their teeth, then felt
along their spines for signs of the curvature that indicated parasitic
worms. It was as he suspected. Remounting Angel, he nodded at
Tommy to wish him good day then turned towards home.

The track brought him close past the house, a once-fine homestead
now sagging with decay, the verandas heaped with rubbish and the
garden wild and overgrown. Three blackfellows sat on a broken settle
under a tree, smoking a clay-bowled pipe which they passed from
scrawny hand to scrawny hand. 'Hey, Boss!' one cawed as Angel trotted
towards them up the guttered track.

The door of the privy kicked open, and the 'Baron' stumbled out, one
hand clutching his trousers at the waist. 'Rhys? Rhys?' he called. 'Come
in and have a drink and we'll settle—' He squinted into the sunlight
and his brain cleared with shock as he recognized Jeremy.

'Good day, sir,' said Jeremy with cold distaste, noting that the 'Baron'
wore no shirt, just a grey woollen undershirt through which the hairs of
his chest seemed to be growing, though *that* may have been an illusion
He said: 'Mr Morgan will telephone or write to you about the sheep.'

The 'Baron' gasped. He forgot that he needed desperately to make a
sale; all he could think of was Lowell's tender young body gored and
bloody and broken. 'Murderer!' he bellowed, lunging towards Jeremy
and grabbing at the reins. 'You scummy filthy murderer!'

Jabbing Angel with his heels, Jeremy urged her forward and at the
same time slashed down with his riding-crop, whacking 'Baron'
Windsor's forearms away so that he tottered off balance and almost fell
Thirty or forty yards on he glanced back. 'Baron' Windsor was looking
after him with impotent rage, his mouth working silently as the insult
choked in his throat. Under their tree the blackfellows watched calmly

256

without interest, the pipe moving as if by its own accord from one to the other.

Several days later Jeremy and Rhys were riding together in Rhys's landau, having just been out to the racetrack to watch one of Donegal's more promising progeny show his style. Both were feeling well pleased with themselves.

'A bite of lunch at the club, I think, and a glass of Pol Roger to celebrate,' said Rhys. 'Donegal Prince will romp away with the Melbourne Cup this year. You're doing astoundingly well for yourself, young man.'

'Only because Father transferred Donegal's stud rights to me as a wedding present. He asked me to choose between a hunting lodge in any part of the world I preferred, a house in any city, and Donegal's stud rights. It was the easiest choice I ever made.' As he spoke he thought that one of the nicest things about Rhys was his sincere ability to take pleasure in other people's good fortune. Thinking of money reminded him of 'Baron' Windsor's reversal of fortune, and he said: 'How did the news go down at White Clouds?'

'That we weren't buying? Extremely badly, I'm afraid. The "Baron" seems to think we have it in for him – me mainly, but you, too, for some reason. He telephoned me half a dozen times to rage, and finally I asked Carthew not to put him through. *Then* he swore at her. Told her she had icicles up her arse. Apparently he's made advances to her at one of our parties, advances she repulsed by tipping a tureen of soup over his boots. Don't laugh; it caused such a commotion at the time that I almost dismissed the woman – not knowing of course. This time she wouldn't be calmed until I promised to cross the 'Baron' off our guest-list. Doubt that he'll be here much longer anyway. He's trying to borrow money to pay his taxes, I believe.' He paused. 'I hear your father-in-law is in the same sort of trouble.'

'I warned him not to fight it,' said Jeremy. 'But he's determined to drag it through the courts. Arabella's pretty upset about the whole thing.'

'I suppose she is,' said Rhys.

Their mood of elation had dissolved. In silence they sat opposite each other, both gazing out of the window at the houses and pedestrians, at the wide lawns coppered with carpets of autumn leaves. Suddenly Jeremy was aware that they were travelling up Cashel Street towards the shops, a route he scrupulously avoided for fear of accidentally bumping into Daisy. He glanced at Rhys. His face was set like a mask, but there was an alertness in his eyes, a quickening of breath as his gaze leaped from one house to the next. With pity Jeremy realized that Rhys came this way often and for the very same reason that Jeremy avoided the route: in the hope of catching a glimpse of his adult children.

Jeremy watched, too, hating himself for being unable to look away, clinging to the cowardly hope that she would be inside, out of sight, not there.

But she was. He caught his breath when the plaque on the gate flicked into view, and there she was on the veranda: Daisy, dressed in a smartly tailored costume of a soft mustard colour with a high-collared silk blouse. Her hair was drawn back and up into a glossy gold chignon, under a tiny lace house-cap. Jeremy's mouth went dry. He could feel the texture of her skin on his fingertips. The tangy rose scent of the Yardley flower-water she wore filled his head. *Damn her, damn her, damn her!* he thought in a fury, turning savagely away. As he did so his eyes flicked past Rhys's face and caught the unguarded expression of aching regret – an expression, Jeremy knew, that was reflected in his own eyes.

They rode to the club in silence. Along the rest of the way Jeremy wondered why Rhys didn't make his peace with Daisy and Andrew since he so painfully wanted to. Was it fear of fresh scandals? he wondered. If so, Rhys had his head in the sand. For years now it was an open secret in Canterbury that Andrew was Rhys's son, though it was one of those 'fantasy' rumours that everybody had heard yet nobody believed. After all, they said, if Andrew was Rhys Morgan's son, he'd acknowledge him, wouldn't he? There was no earthly reason not to.

There *was* a reason, mused Jeremy, wondering what it was. Either a powerful reason or a powerful stubbornness was keeping Rhys from his family.

TWENTY-FOUR

THE ADDRESS was a new one for them. 'Hagley Avenue,' said
Andrew. 'Right opposite the park, I should think. There's some grand
houses around there. The man who rang asked for you most particularly.
I say, do you think there's something odd about the call? I'd go with you
but—'

'I'm a doctor, aren't I? Will you please remember that and stop
treating me as though I was a delicate flower to be sheltered? If I'd kept
looking over my shoulder for footpads, I'd never have gone into some of
those Edinburgh slums, let alone some of the streets not far from here!
What harm can come to me in a grand house in Hagley Avenue?'

It was an imposing residence, creamy bricks with a broad veranda
roofed with tiles, the roof supported by white fluted pillars. Stone lions
guarded the entrance gate where a forked gravel drive curved one way to
the front door and two more lions, and the other way to large brick
stables smothered with variegated ivy. Hitching the trap at the gate,
Daisy smoothed her skirts and patted the veil of her hat into place with a
gloved hand. Carrying her bag, she strode up the drive, gazing around
with interest. In the distance beyond the stables were grassed fields
divided up into enclosures by post-and-rail fencing, painted white. In
one of these a young man was exercising a horse on a lead, pivoting at
the centre of the circle its hoofs inscribed as it trotted around him, now
faster, now slower. The man saw her and waved; turning away, she
quickened her pace towards the door, hesitating only a moment as she
wondered whether a doctor was meant to use the tradesmen's entrance.
Not this doctor, she decided.

'Daisy!' called someone. Boots clattered on the gravel behind her,
and she heard panting breath. She turned. Jeremy stopped. 'Hello,
Daisy,' he said.

He was dressed in rough twill trousers and a leather jerkin to which
stalks of hay adhered, and he was puffing, having run from the stables

to catch up to her. She stared at him, but before she could speak he said: 'It's my boy . . . my boy. . . .' He stepped closer, and she saw that his face was puffy, his eyes pink, and to her horror saw that he was still crying. 'I've been up all night with him. . . . I'm so worried. Doctor Meakings came last night and again this morning, but he seems to be worse if anything. . . .' He stopped to take a gulp of air. 'I'm at my wit's end. . . . I want another opinion, just in case. . . . Someone who knows all the latest medical developments. And Lisabeth told me how well you'd done with your studies, what high marks you'd achieved, so I thought . . . I hoped. . . .'

Daisy fought down an urge to take him into her arms and smooth down that lick of hair that flopped over his forehead. He'd crumple against her like a little boy; he was as terrified and alone as any sick or injured little boy she'd ever treated.

'I'll look at him,' she said briskly. And: 'I understand how you must feel. Uncertainty is a very lonely thing, isn't it?'

He nodded, grateful. 'Come this way,' he said, leading her around the side of the house and through a set of french doors into a large airy room decorated in shades of pink and cream. Screens partitioned off one corner of the room, partly obscuring a small iron bed on which lay a young boy with dark brown hair and brown eyes. His complexion was tanned, but was a sickly colour under the tan, and his eyes were wide with fright. When he saw Jeremy his mouth curled at the corners; the resemblance was startling. 'Hello, Papa,' he whispered.

'How are you, soldier?' said Jeremy in a too-hearty voice. To the servant sitting at the foot of the bed he said: 'You may go now.' With a sharp look at Daisy, who was stripping off her gloves, she got up from her chair and bustled out.

Daisy strode to the head of the bed. 'I'm Doctor Morgan, but you may call me Daisy if you like.' She took a wrist in one hand and placed her other hand on the child's forehead. 'Now, what's the matter with you? What did Doctor Meakings say, h'm?'

'He said I had too much blood,' whispered Silas.

'Is that so?' said Daisy, pretending to be entertained. Already she had noticed some worrying symptoms; the child's skin was dry and burning, his pupils were dilated, his tongue was coated and furry, and when she leaned close she noticed a peculiar acid smell. 'Do you mind if I look at your chest?' she asked.

Silas shivered. His head shook violently, and he said: 'No! No!'

'Son!' pleaded Jeremy, stepping forward. 'Daisy isn't going to hurt you.'

'Please, Papa . . . please don't let her put those nasty things on me!' He began to sob as Daisy pulled the blankets back and loosened the neck tie of his white flannel nightshirt. She was about to ask what 'nasty things' he meant, wondering how she could listen to his chest without using her stethoscope if that was the 'nasty thing', but then, as she parted the garment to expose his thin white shoulders she saw a slug-like creature the size of her middle toe fastened to the flesh beside his armpit.

'Look at this,' she said to Jeremy. She was astonished herself because, although she had seen leeches in Edinburgh, they had been demonstrated only as an example of antiquated and unhygienic medical practice. The lecturer had produced a jar of water in which half a dozen of these repulsive creatures floated. To illustrate their use he reached into the jar with forceps and captured one, then manoeuvred it tail downwards into a narrow test-tube. Holding up his hand so that all in the class could see, he made a tiny nick just above his wrist with the tip of a scalpel, then (while Daisy's hair stood on end) placed the mouth of the test-tube against the broken skin and inverted it so that the creature slid down the glass. When the test-tube was pulled away the leech stayed, hanging like a moth-case to the wrist. Within minutes it was bloated and maroon in colour, three times its original size. Exactly like this one.

Later Daisy was proud of the way she acted. After her first horrified 'Look at this!' she collected herself and said: 'Jeremy, do you have any salt, please?'

'Are you going to pickle it?' asked Jeremy blankly.

Daisy laughed. She laughed to release the tension and to stop from cursing and crying, and she laughed to relax the frightened little boy in the bed. 'You have a very witty papa. He must keep you enormously amused, all the time.'

Jeremy had gone for the salt, tripping over his feet in his eagerness to help her. Silas gazed up at Daisy solemnly while she counted the tiny cuts on the swollen side of his chest. More than a dozen. In his haste Doctor Meakings must have left this one behind. Silas said: 'He's really quite sad a lot of the time.'

'Huh? Who is?' Daisy was preoccupied, unpacking her stethoscope, diagnosing, checking her equipment.

'Papa is,' repeated Silas. 'He's sad a lot of the time.'

At that moment Jeremy came in and heard him. He glanced at Daisy with an expression of guilt, then looked at his son. Without a word he handed Daisy the silver condiment-dish.

Daisy ignored the undercurrents. 'This will tickle,' she said as she sprinkled salt over the creature's head where it clung to the flesh. The leech broke free and convulsed, flooding the skin around its head with the blood it had sucked in. Unable to see what was happening, Silas giggled. With a pad ready, Daisy scooped the leech into a jar then applied the swab to his chest. 'I think we can safely say there'll be no more nasty things,' she said, capping the jar and placing it in her bag to take back to show the others. She could imagine their reaction.

A distance away from the bed she told Jeremy her findings. Silas had empyaema, a welling of fluid on one side of the chest. She needed to insert a sterile rubber tube to drain the cavity, and to do that needed to administer a very mild dose of chloroform, just enough to render him unconscious for a few minutes.

'Do it,' said Jeremy. 'But do you mean to say that Silas has this build-up of fluid within the chest cavity and Doctor Meakings has been applying leeches to the outside? That must have been as much use as—'

'Please,' interrupted Daisy. 'It's not ethical for me to discuss another doctor's treatment. Please fetch me something to contain the fluid – something large. A pail, perhaps, or . . . wait, that chamberpot under his bed looks clean; it'll do. But could I please wash my hands before I begin? You stay and chatter to Silas. Distract him.' She smiled reassuringly. 'I can promise you he'll be well again very soon.'

The sour-faced maid showed her to a small bathroom next to the dining-room where there was a toilet with a Willow Pattern bowl and a brass cistern, and beside it a Willow Pattern handbasin with brass taps and a brass towel-rail. On the way back from scrubbing up Daisy peeped into several beautiful rooms where mellow light sifted through lace curtains on to rich glossy furniture and deep buttoned-velvet sofas. A profusion of ornaments, knick-knacks and pictures was crammed on every shelf, every table. These were fashionable rooms in the fussy Victorian style that always made Daisy feel stifled. So this is where Jeremy and Arabella entertain their guests, she thought with an odd pang of aching envy. This is the home they share. This is the home that could have been mine, and that little boy is the child I could have borne.

She caught a glimpse of her reflection in a pier-glass in the hall; caught unawares, she looked vulnerable and wistful. The shock of seeing herself so clearly with defences down pulled her up short. *Easy on, girl!* she scolded herself. *You chose not to marry Jeremy. You could have shared his life; he asked you to, and you rejected him. Don't forget that when you're tempted to lapse into self-pity.*

She looked herself straight in the eye. She was living the life she had chosen. Until Andrew was publicly acknowledged and given his rightful place she would live and work at his side. She *liked* this existence. It offered challenge – too much challenge perhaps! she thought wryly – but, even though she was enduring an uphill struggle for acceptance, every small step brought a thrill of achievement, and when she saw what standards of medical attention her patients had been receiving she felt great satisfaction in knowing that she could do better for them. Yes, it was a triumph to succeed where Doctor Meakings, who had treated her since she was born, was failing.

You're doing splendidly, Doctor Morgan, she told herself and, chin up, she strode back into the room.

The shakiness she had felt earlier had gone. 'Where is your wife?' she was now able to ask conversationally. 'It would have been better if I could have discussed this with her, too.'

'She's at the Blue Garden near the square. It's a tea-room. Arabella lunches there every day with her friends.'

'I see.' Something in his voice warned her that further comment would not be welcomed. To Silas she said: 'I'm going to tickle you again, with this funny thing over your face. You'll feel very sleepy and when you wake up again you'll be all better.'

He nodded, his dark brown eyes so like his father's fixed trustingly on her face.

Jeremy watched while she administered the choloroform and checked his pulse and breathing. Then he said: 'Are you sure he's going to be all right? Honestly, Daisy, I've been beside myself. I sat and watched him for hours this morning and then I couldn't stand it any longer. I called you, and then when I came back in here I just filled up with despair and bolted out to the stables. I felt as if there was a heavy weight pressing down on me. . . .'

'I assure you, he'll be all right.' She knew that he was apologizing for his earlier tearfulness and was touched that her opinion should matter to him at a time like this. 'Do you want to stay and watch? Often parents prefer not to see what happens, and—'

'Good Lord, Daisy. I deal with animals all the time. I've used a lancet to relieve a horse with the strangles and have stuck cattle with a trocar when they've been blown with the bloat.'

'Are you sure this won't distress you?'

'Of course.'

She worked quickly, deftly, puncturing the wall between two ribs with a scalpel and inserting the rubber hose. Immediately a stream of thin purulent fluid began running into the chamberpot. Daisy checked the child's breathing and pulse and gave a heartfelt sigh. Only then did she look at Jeremy, and was startled to see that he was gazing at her with stunned admiration. The intensity of his stare embarrassed her. She said: 'There! I told you it would be a simple procedure.'

Wordlessly he put his hands on her shoulders. His lips parted. He was still looking at her with that deep admiring expression. She wrenched her gaze away. 'Daisy,' he said. 'I've dreaded seeing you again. I've avoided you, do you know that?'

A door banged in the distance, and a sharp voice penetrated the muffled silence of the house. 'Whose trap is that?' It was Arabella, harder and more shrill than Daisy remembered. '*Whose* trap? Are you certain?'

Standing up, Jeremy said: 'I'll go and talk to her.'

'It would be best if she didn't come in here,' Daisy warned. 'I'll be finished in three or four minutes, but not until then.'

The door burst open as Jeremy reached it. He hustled his wife back into the hall and shut the door behind them. As she prepared the dressing for the wound Daisy could hear Jeremy's voice murmuring. Arabella cut across what he was saying. Her voice was lower now, and obviously not meant to be heard by Daisy, but because of its shrill penetrating quality it carried plainly into the room. 'You did what? How dare you! She's not laying a finger on my son! She needn't think—'

Jeremy interrupted firmly. '*Our* son. And I sent for Doctor Morgan because I was not satisfied with the treatment Doctor Meakings had given him. That butcher doesn't care what he does! He left a leech sticking to Silas's skin. He—'

'And she *does* care, I suppose.'

'She's professional, and caring, and I'm extremely impressed.'

There was a silence. Daisy noticed that the tube had stopped dripping. Very gently she pressed down on the boy's pale chest, feeling the ridges of rib-cage under her palms. His relaxed face looked beautiful, just as Jeremy's must have been when he was a little boy. *Papa is sad a lot of the time*, he had said.

'You're impressed, now, are you?' Arabella's voice throbbed with resentment. 'Well, I'm not. Let me pass, Jeremy. I'm going to have her out of my house this minute.'

And I'll go gladly, thought Daisy. Not hurrying, she shook the hose, carefully removed it from the metal syringe and drew that from the boy's side. There was a small dribble of clean blood which she wiped away with an antiseptic solution before applying the gauze pad.

In the hall Jeremy and Arabella were glaring at each other, she with belligerent determination, he with shame and humiliation, for he guessed that Daisy could overhear what was being said. 'Please, Arabella, be reasonable. I only did what had to be done.'

Her mouth worked. It was then he realized how extremely angry she was. Up until now he had attributed her outburst to the ingredients that had been slowly poisoning their marriage; his indifference, her frustration and their mutual antipathy, all brought to a seething head by worry about her father's financial woes and now their son's illness. Enough to blight anybody's life, really. But now he saw in a flash of clarity that his wife had another, far deeper rooted resentment.

'How *dare* you!' She spat the words at him. 'Bringing *her* into our home . . . how could you do this to me!'

'Do what?'

'How dare you pretend not to know.'

'I don't know, Arabella. I don't understand what—'

'It's *her*, isn't it? You've loved her from the moment you saw her, haven't you? She's all you think about, all you dream about. You've never cared twopence for me and you never will. You love only her, and this has been just an excuse to you, hasn't it? An excuse to bring her into your life again. Oh, don't bother to protest, Jeremy Drake. I've seen the look on your face whenever her name is mentioned. I've seen it, and I've died inside. Just tell her to go. Get her out of here!' And her footsteps clattered over the marble floor.

Daisy had finished tying the bandage and was packing her bag when Arabella's outburst came. She listened unemotionally; it was only later that she would feel shattered. Snipping the catches shut, she turned back to the bed. She pushed the chamberpot under the bed with her toe and covered it with a starched napkin from the bedside table. That sour-faced servant could have the pleasure of dealing with the slop, she decided grimly.

Silas was stirring, his eyelids fluttering. Already his colour looked healthier. She knew that he would make an uninterrupted recovery.

On an impulse she stooped to kiss his cheek. Straightening, she paused and studied his face for a few moments as if committing it to memory.

She let herself out the same way she'd come in. Nobody heard her leave.

'I'm disappointed,' announced Daisy one afternoon when she was helping Andrew get his files up to date. 'After that notice Jeremy Drake put in the newspaper thanking us and our ''modern techniques'' for saving his son's life, I'd have thought we would be rushed for custom, but it hasn't made much difference at all.'

'These things take time. We have had quite a lot of interest, really.' Andrew tucked another file into his cabinet, started to speak and then stopped.

'What was it? Go on, say what you were going to.'

'I was going to say that there's been a rumour about you. One that has possibly negated the influence of the newspaper notice. Or perhaps the notice triggered it. Who knows?'

'What sort of rumour?'

'Something really stupid. The whisper says you're indulging in a *grande passion*.'

'Really? With Doctor Meakings, I suppose. D'you know that he hasn't spoken to me since that notice was printed. It's so awkward for Aunt Bea. She—'

'With Jeremy Drake.'

'Oh.'

He'd planned to watch her closely for her reaction, but he didn't need to. If there had been nothing in it, she'd have made a great joke of it, remarked that if it only took one visit to his house to evoke such a reaction, then what in the world was Christchurch saying about Andrew's visits to Barbadoes Street? He'd been there at least four times. Had he a 'thing' going with Honoria Fitzherbert perhaps?

Or she'd get angry. Say what an outrageous idea that was. That she and Jeremy were friends long ago, but not now, and such ridiculous malicious talk could only cause pain to innocent people. What would Arabella think when she heard the gossip? And what would Jeremy think? This was an expensive way for him to pay for her medical expertise.

But she said nothing but 'Oh', and coloured slightly, and was very quiet for perhaps an hour. Then she seemed to shrug off what he had told her; the sparkle returned to her cornflower-blue eyes, and she was her old self again.

Almost.

TWENTY-FIVE

'THERE SEEMS TO BE a much larger crowd than usual this evening,' said Daisy. 'I do hope that's an optimistic sign, and that tomorrow *my* outroom will be full of patients, too. Andrew is doing so well, but I'm still not bringing in a fair share of income.'

'And I'm content where I am,' said Sarah, which was true. Since she had taken the position at Seaview she had reverted to being her old self, quiet and good-humoured; and, though she still occasionally mentioned Rhys Morgan, it was with a wry resignation. Her conversation these days was of the exploits of the inmates, always funny little anecdotes about the quaint things they did. An orderly was with her at all times, so she explained that her life was never in any danger; the thing about mental patients was that if they did become violent it was usually a blind lashing out around them, not a planned attack, so if someone did get hurt it was likely to be an unlucky accident. There was a farm at Seaview which provided all the food for the hospital, and Sarah's favourites were the farm workers; Basil who taught the pigs to line up at the trough and kneel down for 'Grace' before he would dump the slops for their dinner; Edward who sometimes got confused and weeded out all the cabbages, leaving docks and thistles behind in tidy rows; and Arthur whose hens were so tame that they would hop up and ride around on his shoulders, clucking contentedly and poking their beaks about in his unkempt hair and beard. Sarah suspected that he rubbed his head with cornmeal to keep them entertained.

She also told of the solitaries, the men and women who sat staring empty-eyed at the barred windows in their doors. Men and women who were people once, with lives and identities. She told them some of their names: Mary Hopper, William Courtwell, Tom Hart, Horace Thorne. . . .

'We've never had a crowd like this before,' marvelled Daisy. While Andrew was bribing a couple of urchins to watch the trap, she and Sarah peeped into the hall. They never came early for their talks because they found they were pestered by people wanting free and instant consultations. 'The hall is full, and there are even crowds standing around at the sides. At least it won't be cold in there.'

'Once we get used to the smell,' joked Sarah.

Outside it was a clear sharp night, the sky afloat with rafts of stars. The air was tainted with the odours of woodsmoke, of overflowing privies and, as more people pushed past, the stench of unwashed clothes and stale perspiration. Sarah giggled. 'Andrew's talk on hygiene will have fertile well-manured ground on which to fall,' she said.

'Here he comes now.'

'Good. The sooner we begin, the sooner it'll be over!'

As he joined them and they moved towards the doorway a woman wriggled through a group who were going in and stood, breathing heavily, in front of Daisy. 'Muss Morgan – Doctor Morgan, Oi mean . . . . Oi must talk to you.'

Daisy couldn't see her face clearly; below a shapeless cloth hat, moonlight glinted on coppery-coloured hair. A sick child or an unwanted pregnancy, guessed Daisy, fumbling in the little purse she carried and withdrawing a card. 'Here, take this. I'm sorry I can't talk now, but if you come to my consulting-rooms tomorrow morning after ten I can—'

'No! Ut's nuthing like thut!' She spoke in a low gabbled urgency and glanced back over her shoulder as if fearful of being pursued. 'Oi hud to warn you, Muss Morgan. Ut's not hus fault, Oi'm tulling you; so, please, Muss Morgan, don't blame hum.'

'*Warn* us?' said Andrew. 'Hey, what's this about?'

She ignored him, addressing herself only to Daisy, talking to her as if she knew her well. Daisy was baffled. She'd not treated this woman as a patient; there had been so few of those that each one could be remembered by name. So where, then? The woman rattled on that Daisy had been 'kind to her once', and she felt 'drudful' about her husband's 'ull manners'.

'He were put up to ut, und thut's God's truth. Ut's hus job he'll be losing uf he don't—' She broke off, glancing nervously around again.

'If he doesn't what?' demanded Andrew, reaching out a hand to restrain her, but he was too late; the woman had slipped back into the hall, insinuating herself into another group who were pushing inside.

'Do you think someone's going to shoot at us?' asked Daisy.

'Of course not,' scoffed Andrew. 'Would he bring his wife along to watch? Would he shoot at us in front of a hall packed with witnesses? Of course not. But if you want to go home I'll understand.'

'I'm not afraid,' said Sarah.

'Nor me,' said Daisy, wondering if she was the only one who was trying to sound braver than she felt.

'Just watch out for flying eggs or rotten fruit,' joked Andrew. 'Though for the life of me I can't think why. I've not had a single failure yet. Not one disgruntled customer that I can think of.'

He couldn't have been more wrong.

It was always the same at these talks, thought Daisy as, from her chair on the dusty stage, she surveyed the hall. There were some seriously interested people stationed in the front rows who arranged themselves in an attitude of receptive attention preparing to learn something. Then there were the curious, who listened to begin with and, if the subject didn't enthrall them, got up noisily and left. Then there were the bulk of the audience, those drawn to the lit hall because they had nothing else to do and nowhere else to go. Daisy saw these homeless when she walked Excalibur in the park each morning; sad hunched figures with newspapers packed under their coats and their belongings tied in old rags. Tonight the hall was packed with them for the simple reason that it was the first really cold winter evening; Daisy wondered what they would gain from Andrew's rather dry lecture on Listerism. The importance of washing their hands before meals and after going to the 'outhouse', as Andrew put it, was wasted on men who scavenged for scraps of food in bins and who relieved themselves in the bushes. But of the audience these were the ones who never stood up and wandered out, never heckled, and if they interrupted it was only with uncontrollable coughing fits.

After his introductory speech where Andrew explained who the three were, and presented Daisy and Sarah to the people, Andrew told them what their surgery hours were, how his fees were lower than other doctors' in the town and how all three were recently trained and, though lacking in experience, they were thoroughly knowledgeable about all the latest medical advances. He was tactful, taking care not to criticize other doctors but merely to point out the advantages their medical practice could offer to the citizens of Christchurch.

While he spoke Daisy and Sarah often had to stifle yawns behind their worn cotton gloves, but tonight both were unsettled by the woman who had warned them, and both scanned the room, searching in the faint yellow gaslight for her face. Daisy was wondering if she had run away, when Sarah pressed her toe with the toe of her boot. 'Fourth row on the far right,' she whispered, gesturing with her eyes.

Sitting even straighter in her hard-backed chair, Daisy waited a few moments and then glanced quickly around. The woman was right on the end of the row, sitting forward on the bench, not watching the stage but staring, frowning, at a man who sat a short distance from her, on the other side of two dark children who were between them. Daisy glanced next at the children because her interest was attracted, as is natural, to twins. These were girls, Maori-looking, with high cheekbones and slightly flattened noses. They sat quietly, gazing sulkily at the stage. Daisy guessed they were six or seven years old, and in that moment, before her eyes moved to Tommy Nevin's broad face, she knew who they were, who the woman was. She had met her briefly on the day the twins were born, on the day of her birthday; she was Colleen, the Irish cook from White Clouds, who had come to help Mrs Tenks with the catering.

Tommy Nevin. Feeling ill, she looked away quickly, missing the smug grin that spread over his face when he saw her glance at him. Every time she thought of him she remembered that day he had made her undress for him; she remembered the ugly leer on his face as he stared at her, and with a sick feeling she pushed the memory away.

'What's the matter?' whispered Sarah. 'You've gone as white as a sheet.'

Daisy shook her head and raised her chin, determined that Tommy would have no indication of the seething dismay that raged inside her. *I'm not a frightened young girl any longer*, she reminded herself. *I won't be bullied by Tommy Nevin. Daisy Morgan may have been helpless and alone, but Doctor Morgan isn't afraid of anyone!*

With that thought fixed in her mind she forced herself to turn her head and regard Tom Nevin with a cold unswerving stare. Grim satisfaction flickered within her as she noticed surprise and then discomfiture in his expression.

Andrew paused in his speech to display a coloured illustration which was hanging, covered by a draped cloth, on the other side of the stage. He was reaching up to jerk away the cloth when Tom's voice bellowed out, filling the silent hall and causing Andrew to turn around, wondering why the disturbance.

Tom was on his feet, his face dark as the cloth cap he wore pulled low over his brow. He shouted at the audience: 'Don't lussen to hum! Don't uny of you lussen to one word thut he says!'

'Mr Nevin, isn't it?' said Andrew, peering at him across the rows of heads – backs of heads, for all had twisted around to see who was heckling so rudely.

'Ay, ut's Muster Nevin!' roared Tom. He was pushing past the other people in his row, moving away from his wife who held out a beseeching hand in a futile effort to change his mind, crying, while the twins still sat exactly as they were, with those sullen implacable expressions. Tom forged his way with his crutch, banging it on the floor, and people moved their knees quickly out of his way. Soon he was standing in the centre aisle glaring up at the three on the stage. For one giddy moment Daisy thought he was going to try to vault up to join them, but instead he swung around to face the body of the hall, thrusting the crutch up under his armpit and leaning on that side while he gesticulated at Andrew.

'Thut mun botchered me!' he declared. 'Ay, he botchered me whun I lay suck and hulpluss un hus care! Before thut, I wus a strong healthy mun. Some of you may remumber me us I once wus. Tall und whole, wuth two gud legs. Until I fell suck und hud the musfortune to come unto *thut mun's care*!'

Andrew was bewildered. 'Tommy Nevin, I charge you to tell the truth. Tell it like it was, if you must, but there's nothing to be gained by insinuating—'

Tom broke him off without a backward glance. 'Ay, but how dud I come to be suck, you wonder? I wus crossing a ruvver in my wagon whun it overturned, flunging me into the water. I was near-drowned, but wus found alive und taken to thus mun's hospital. It wus thun, good people, thut thus so-called "doctor" took my leg off me!'

Unable to believe what he was hearing, Andrew struggled for comprehension. He had not only saved Tom Nevin's life, but had done so without charge, and had furthermore rescued Tom from arrest and certain imprisonment purely out of human compassion. And this was to be his reward – to have the community trust he had built up so far wiped out in a bitter ranting tirade from an obviously twisted and vengeful man. 'It wasn't like that at all,' he protested. The room swung about him as he visualized his patients abandoning him in droves. This could ruin him. What credibility would he have in the town if it was believed that he had – quite unnecessarily – removed someone's leg for, as Tom was now saying, purely personal reasons?

'Always hated me, hus family has!' declared Tom, though as he said this he felt a flicker of real guilt. Andrew Stafford he had always cordially loathed, but his foster-mother Gwynne was different. She'd always been kind to him when he was a boy, and she'd befriended Birdie in her retirement. Birdie would be disgusted if she could hear him now.

Tom swallowed. Taking a deep breath, he fixed his sights and his hatred firmly on Rhys Morgan and all his clan as he forged on. 'Look ut thum! They're toffs! Whut do toffs care about the likes of us?'

Aware of the murmur of agreement that rippled around the hall, Daisy's alarm intensified. She glanced at Andrew, but he looked as if he wished he was somewhere else – *anywhere* else. *He's going to let that scummy lying Tommy Nevin get away with this!* she realized. *Andrew just won't stand and fight. He's going to let him say whatever he wants to, and not cry him down.*

Before she realized what she was doing she was on her feet, fists clenched at her sides, crying: 'Stop that, Tommy Nevin! Stop those wicked shameful lies!'

He twisted then to look at her. Everybody in the room was looking at her, and there was a strange quivering hush as the people held their breath and wondered what would happen next. An old woman down the front with no teeth put down her knitting and stared, open-mouthed. The young couple behind her leaned forward expectantly, and the two men in uniform beside them grinned. ''Ere's a go,' one said, rubbing his hands together.

A broad smile spread itself across Tom's face. In the yellow light his skin had a greasy look, and his teeth were no longer strong and white, she saw, but stained, with gaps at the sides.

'You're a liar, Tommy Nevin,' said Daisy calmly.

He grinned, almost encouragingly, and she guessed he was pleased she had spoken out because it gave him an opportunity to attack her. *Dear Lord, what he could say about her!* The thought made her dizzy with terror. She clenched her fists tighter, willing herself on. She had entered a path in which there was no room to manoeuvre and the only way was to meet this bully head-on.

Again she felt that strange hush, a vibrating silence, and suddenly it came to her that this was what people wanted to see. Public meetings were a diversion, and a popular one, made more entertaining by hecklers and interjectors. Tommy Nevin's wild accusations were far more exciting than any illustrated lecture on cleanliness in the home.

'I was there when Mr Nevin had his lower leg amputated,' she said in a loud ringing voice. 'Mr Nevin had been ill with fever for two days and, though Doctor Stafford had done everything he could to save the limb, Mr Nevin's foot was too badly crushed to be mended. Even so, Doctor Stafford was reluctant—

Tommy laughed, a harsh grating sound that scraped at her words and obliterated the rest of what she was saying. Daisy paused until he stopped, then began to speak again, but again her words were erased by his loud gritty laughter.

When he paused to draw breath one of the men in uniform shouted: 'Shut up, Tommy Nevin, and let the lady speak.'

'Yes!' cried another voice from the back of the hall. 'H'it's emancipation comin' now, 'aven't you 'eard? The ladies 'ave ter 'ave their say!'

More joined in, with hoots and laughter. It was Tom's turn to look bewildered. 'You mean to say, you *wunt* to lussen to her lies?'

'We've heard *your* lies, now let's hear *hers*!' cried the man in uniform to another round of applause and laughter.

Andrew was furious. He grabbed Daisy's arm. 'This isn't a side-show! Don't let him provoke you, Daisy! Don't sink to his level. Be dignified. Don't—'

She shook his hand away. 'We've got no choice but to answer his allegations.'

'We can answer with dignified silence,' hissed her brother. 'This isn't a political meeting, and it's not a votes-for-women gathering, either.'

Poor Andrew, she thought, sensing that his pride was wounded, but realizing that she was only being made way for because she was a woman, and she would be a fool not to take advantage of that. She stepped forward and in the lull addressed the hall again. 'We came here this evening because we are professional, highly trained and skilful doctors who have qualities this community needs. I gave up six years of my life to study full-time in Edinburgh, as did Doctor Sarah Stafford, while Doctor Andrew Stafford who had trained some years before was employed at the medical college as a lecturer, so greatly esteemed is his knowledge. Medicine is a developing science, ladies and gentlemen. Every year new skills are learned, and new developments made. We undertake to keep ourselves constantly refreshed by reading and studying, solely in order to benefit you, the citizens of our beautiful city. Tonight my brother's talk was interrupted by Mr Nevin here, who unfortunately bears a grudge for something that is nobody's fault. We deeply regret the fact that he has lost a limb, and we understand his bitterness, but—'

'You'll never understund my butterness!' roared Tom. He was shaking his fist at her and stamping his crutch on the floor. 'You're just flaunting yoursulf, that's whut you're doing. Ay, flaunting yoursulf, and we ull know how you like to do thut, don't we?'

'Please let me finish,' said Daisy quietly.

'You heard the lady,' said the man in uniform. He and his friend had risen from their places and were now flanking Tom, their attitude quietly threatening.

'Thank you,' said Daisy. 'As I said, we sympathize with Mr Nevin's bitterness, but the fact is that his limb was lost because he lay out in a hot sun for the best part of a day before he could get treatment, and in that time the wound was open to dust and infection. By the time Doctor Stafford saw him it was too late. He did everything he could, but the gangrene was already there. This is why Doctor Stafford's lectures are so important, ladies and gentlemen. All of us know someone like the unfortunate Mr Nevin who has lost a hand or a foot. In many cases of a break or a deep wound the limb could have been saved if the prompt attention described in detail here to you tonight had been given to the injured person. Please, if you are hurt or sick, come to us *promptly*. We want you to have a better life, where your illnesses are cured quickly and your accidents made better. Thank you.'

When she sat down she discovered that she was shaking so much that she had to capture her hands, one with the other, and grip them tightly.

Sarah leaned towards her. 'Why, you were magnificent! Listen to them clapping! You turned that horrible man's allegations upside down

273

and furthered our cause no end. Look at their faces! They like us, and admire us now. Oh, Daisy, you were magnificent!'

Even Andrew thought so. Though he was irritated that Daisy had captured the limelight, he was gratified that afterwards as many people stepped forward to shake his hand as they did to shake hers. On the way home he said – rather gruffly: 'It turned out well after all, didn't it? If I say so myself, that was one of our better evenings.'

Sarah said; 'I don't know about you, but I could murder a good strong cup of tea, and never mind if it is late at night! I'll risk the nightmares.' She bent to scratch her ankle. 'Is either of you two itching?'

'Yes, I am,' said Daisy. 'I noticed something earlier.'

'Bedbugs!'

'Fleas!'

'Shades of Edinburgh!' groaned Sarah. 'We'd better go back to our place first. The Launcenolts won't appreciate it if Daisy infests Benares.'

While Andrew stoked the fire and pulled the kettle over to the hottest part of the stove, in the washroom the women stripped down and each with a bar of damp soap caught the creatures that were sticking to their bodies.

'Ugh,' shuddered Daisy. 'That stage must be a regular sleeping-place for tramps. I've never seen so many bedbugs. Ugh. This takes me right back to those appalling filthy slum buildings we used to have to go into.' She stabbed the soap at a creature that was crawling at the back of her knee. When she straightened she glanced at Sarah. She had seen her naked only once before, in the ship when she had bathed Sarah with cool water to alleviate her sea-sickness, and had envied her slim waist, but now her waist had thickened and her breasts were full and heavy-looking with dark aureoles around her nipples.

'Sarah . . .,' she said, then stopped.

Sarah flushed. 'Yes, a baby. Isn't it wonderful?' She was whispering and glancing towards the door that connected to the kitchen.

Daisy said; 'Why the secret?'

Sarah began to laugh. 'I've not said anything because I'm wondering how long it will be before Andrew notices! You know the saying: "The cobbler wears the holeyest boots"? Well, I'm waiting to see how long it will take my doctor husband to notice what you've seen in a second.'

Daisy laughed, too, but she wondered whether this 'secret' was Sarah's small revenge for Andrew keeping secrets of his own.

She arrived home very late. Beatrice was still up, sitting in the morning room reading a slim book with a luridly bright cover.

'Another twopenny horrible?' asked Daisy, collapsing opposite her with a sigh of gratitude. 'Dear Aunt Bea, I hope you're not sitting up for me.'

'I couldn't sleep,' said Beatrice, folding a marker into the book as she closed it, then placing her lorgnette on top of the cover. 'What a day! We've had the votes-for-women group here this evening with a petition. They told us they've collected three thousand signatures in just two weeks of canvassing. Kiki was very naughty, and argued with them about how they should be at home looking after their husbands and raising families. You know how he runs on once something has wound him up. A regular clockwork mouse! Oh, my dear, if only you'd been here. You've missed all the excitement!'

Daisy thought of the meeting, of Tommy Nevin's interjections, of the bedbugs, and of Sarah's secret. She smiled. 'Yes, I'm afraid I have,' she said.

TWENTY-SIX

'STOP IT, EXCALIBUR. Oh, you are naughty,' scolded Daisy, dragging at the plaited leather leash.

Excalibur ignored her. Back bristling, ears flattened, he strained at the lead, tugging her arms almost from their sockets until, as he knew she would, she gave in and unsnapped the lead. As soon as that happened he behaved perfectly, trotting along beside Daisy, sniffling and snuffling at interesting scents and carrying his lame back leg, only touching it to the ground every third or fourth step so that he seemed to be skipping along like a stone skimming over the water.

It was dusk, gusty and cold, and they were on their way home, taking the long way round to Benares so that Excalibur would arrive tired and ready to settle down for the night. Daisy pulled her collar up round her ears and thrust her hands into her woollen muff as she strode along the damp footpath. It had rained earlier in the day, and the air was still unpleasantly moist.

At this time of evening the streets were busy, clogged with folk returning from work in the industrial section of town where there were shoe factories, tanneries, a baking-powder factory, a dozen machine shops where clothing was made to supply the town shops, and further beyond the Drake & Morgan meat-packing plant. Quite a few of the people on foot or riding on bicycles recognized her and called a cheerful good evening. If she was addressed as 'Doctor Morgan', she guessed they had been to one of the lectures, and if it was 'Miss Morgan' she supposed they worked for her father in one of his factories. Some she recognized as patients, for since that landmark meeting of a month ago the practice had grown until now Andrew was extending his surgery hours to three evenings a week and Saturday afternoons. Unfortunately, for Daisy business was still a slow trickle. The prejudice against women doctors was a strong one to defeat, and she hadn't managed it yet. Despite her certificate in its heavy silver frame, and despite the initials engraved after her name on the plaque, she resigned herself to the knowledge that in many folk's eyes she was nothing but a glorified 'handywoman' fit only to assist at difficult childbirthings and to cure sick children. Like Sarah before her, she was beginning to get frustrated, a frustration that chafed more each day when the queue outside Andrew's door lengthened while hers was often dismally the same.

'Never mind, Excalibur, as long as we can afford to buy you scrag ends from the butcher, eh, boy?' she said to him. When he didn't look up she added, 'or a tasty *bone*, eh?' then laughed at his reaction, for he recognized the word 'bone' and always pricked up his ears when he heard it.

They were at the end of Cashel Street; she clipped the lead to his collar while they threaded through the traffic as they crossed the road, and had unsnipped it again when she heard Tommy Nevin's laughter. Her steps faltered. That night he had been hustled out by the two men in uniform; and afterwards, when belatedly she thought to look out for Colleen and the twins, they had already vanished.

Now he stood with his back to her in the middle of the footpath, his stocky wife holding his arm while they both watched the girls playing tag around the bare winter trees on the grassy verge. Animated and laughing, the twins looked almost pretty.

Daisy hesitated, then decided to cross the road and avoid them. Not because she was afraid of him, she assured herself quickly, for hadn't she stood up to him in public and won? No, she would walk out of her way because she wanted to spare Colleen and the girls the nastiness of a scene.

'Come, Excalibur,' she murmured, stooping to snip the lead to his collar again. He looked over his shoulder at what she was doing and before she could engage the catch slipped from under and ran quickly over to the girls, barking with excitement.

'Ooh, look, Mother! Look, Father! A funny little dog!' cried one, crouching to scruffle his ears. He jumped up at her, his tail switching.

Tommy turned and saw her standing there uncertainly with the leash in her hand. 'Wull, wull,' he said. 'I thought I'd seen thut ugly mutt before.'

'Tom, please,' said Colleen in a flat hopeless voice as if she knew there was no point in saying anything but she said it anyway.

'Excalibur! Come here at *once*!' snapped Daisy.

He looked at Daisy and back at the girls. One cried: 'He's a lovely dog! He's much nicer than the horrid dogs at White Clouds.'

Daisy thought that he was anything but nice right now. 'At once!' she repeated. 'Come here at once!'

With a backward glance at the girls he reluctantly obeyed, and trotted down from the verge and on to the footpath. His route took him close to where Tommy stood.

'Ugly brute! I should huve kulled hum whun I hud the chance,' said Tom in a voice meant to be jovial, but as he spoke he reached out with his crutch and whacked Excalibur on the hindquarters.

There was an instant reaction, so fast that nobody saw the dog move. One moment he was yelping, lifted from up and under by the metal-tipped crutch and the next he was snarling, attached by the jaws to Tommy's good ankle.

'Look! He's playing with Father now.' And the girls came running to join in the game, while Tom swore hissing oaths and flailed with his crutch, trying to balance, and whack the dog and shake him off all at once.

'Excalibur!' shrieked Daisy.

Tom's arms windmilled; he lashed out with the crutch, and at the same moment jerked his leg, flopping Excalibur over like a gaffed fish being tipped into a boat. Then his crutch connected and the dog was propelled sideways.

Daisy screamed. Rumbling by was a long cart heaped with sacks of grain. Excalibur hurtled through the muddy gauze of spray thrown up by the front wheels and landed in a puddle behind them. 'No!' screamed Daisy, but nothing could be done. The rear wheels revolved as the cart kept moving forward and Excalibur's shoulders were pressed into the mud under their weight. He made no sound. The cart rolled on, and the driver, who was singing lustily to himself, did not even know what had happened.

All five stood in silence, a still tableau in the busy street, all gaping at the body in the roadway. Then Colleen wailed: 'Oh, Tom! Oh, Tom! What huv you done? Thut's Doctor Morgun's pet dog, an' now ut's kulled stone dead!' The girls began to cry in loud frightened voices.

Daisy was too shocked to cry, too stunned to move. She felt as if her limbs were wrapped in wet bandages. This was ridiculous! Her heart couldn't believe that if she called him – *if* she could get her paralysed throat to move – he wouldn't get up and come trotting towards her with his funny three-legged gait. But her brain knew he was dead. His limbs lay at odd angles, and his neck was twisted and broken. His eyes, looking at the sky, were glazed like ice over a pond.

'It wus un accident,' blurted Tom, shamefaced, then again, but defiantly this time: 'Ut wus un accident, I tull you. Thut's all. Un accident!' And, irritable now, he stumped off down the street, pausing after a dozen yards to turn and roar back at his family: 'Come on, wull you? We're late enough ulready!'

'Oi'm sorry, Oi'm so sorry,' gabbled Colleen, her face and neck scarlet with embarrassment. 'Ut seems heartless, Oi know, but there's nuthin' we cun do, us there? Oi mean, whut's done is done, unnut?' Ducking her head, she scurried away to join her husband, her long shapeless coat flapping about her ankles.

Dumbly Daisy watched them go. She was so shocked that she couldn't feel the tears on her cheeks, didn't notice that a carriage had stopped and the driver was getting down. She swung her head, saw the two horses right there at the pavement edge and cried out, 'No! Don't run over my dog!' and didn't realize until she was digging her fingers into the mud around the body that the horses had already stopped moving.

She lifted him in her arms – he was so heavy – and as she did so she remembered that day when she had staggered home with him, with freezing water streaming from her clothes and his tiny body warmly wrapped in her shawl. Now he sagged in her arms, and she sagged with him, bowing her head and sobbing as if her heart would break.

'Give him to me,' said a gentle voice.

It was Jeremy, as he was the last time, as she knew he would be. She said: 'You s-saved his life when I brought him home the first time. You s-said you'd saved puppies that had been found in a s- s-snow bank. But you c-can't save him now.'

'No, Daisy. I can't save him now.'

He helped her into the carriage, sat opposite her and gave her a handkerchief, while his driver wrapped Excalibur's body in a piece of canvas and placed it in the small luggage-compartment at the rear. Daisy stopped crying, took several deep gulps of air and looked bleakly out of the window. They were soon overtaking the family group; the two girls ran on shrieking like gulls, and Tom and Colleen followed together, he lurching and leaning while she hung patiently to his arm.

'It's that Nevin fellow, isn't it?' said Jeremy. 'I had a set-to with him the other day.' He saw the expression on Daisy's face and said; 'I say, he didn't have anything to do with this, did he?'

Daisy shook her head. 'It was an accident, that's all,' she said, knowing it to be the truth. 'Excalibur was always chasing after wagons. It was bound to happen sooner or later.' And she knew in her heart and mind that that was true as well. She looked at him, careless of her swollen eyes and tear-twisted face. 'Why are you here, Jeremy? Were you following me?'

He was taken aback by her directness. 'Yes, I was.'

'Do you follow me often?'

'If I happen to be in town, yes.'

She looked away. They were past the street turning to Benares now. Houses floated by, their windows faintly lit, and around them trees held stiff arms to the lowering sky. The ache inside her chest threatened to rip apart into more crying, but she said softly: 'You mustn't follow me, you know. Andrew said there's gossip about us.'

'Is there?'

'You know there is.'

'I did know. It's been started by Arabella, I'm afraid.'

'I guessed. I'm glad your lad is better. Thank you for your kind letter, and for the money. It was far too much—'

'It wasn't nearly enough. Oh, Daisy—'

'No, Jeremy. No.' She stared stubbornly out the window. They rolled past the Catholic school, dark and shadowy and deserted within its severe stone walls.

'I love you, Daisy.'

And I love you, she cried silently, biting her lip, pushing down on the hurtful emptiness inside her. *It was an accident. . . . It was only an accident*, her mind kept repeating.

'I know you love me, too,' he said. His voice sounded tentative, hurt somehow. She couldn't bear it. It was endurable if she was hurt, but not if he was suffering. There was a tearing, a rupturing inside her, and she thrust his handkerchief into her face to staunch the flow.

'Please . . . Daisy, please don't cry.'

She shook her head. 'Jeremy, this . . . this is pointless. You know it is.'

'It isn't,' he said eagerly. 'My marriage to Arabella was a mistake. A terrible mistake. We both realize that.'

An accident. A terrible accident, echoed Daisy's brain.

'Her father is in financial difficulties. The taxation department valued his land highly, and he argued, and now they're forcing him to sell at a lower price than it's worth. It's going to auction, and Arabella wants me to help him to buy it back again. It would take almost everything I own, and up until now I've refused to entertain the idea. I mean, he brought his misfortunes entirely on his own head. . . . But now, Daisy, I can see a way clear. Arabella would agree to divorce me for a price. I could gain my freedom, Daisy. It wouldn't take long and—'

'No! I won't listen to you. I *can't* listen to this.' She saw the little boy with Jeremy's intense dark eyes and his open vulnerable face. *Papa is sad a lot of the time*. 'Jeremy, it's unthinkable. You have a son. Think of the effect—'

'Arabella doesn't care about him. She neglects him shamefully. Even when he was born she hired a wet-nurse for him. She never went near the nursery from one week to the next, and now it's no different—'

'No! I won't listen. Jeremy, you have no right—'

'Couldn't you love him, too?'

She closed her eyes in pain. Of course she could love him; she already did. The boy was starved for love, just as Jeremy was; she could see that now, but she didn't want to know about it. She had her own emptiness to contend with. 'You're not being fair to me, Jeremy. You've no right to talk to me like this.'

'Needs have rights of their own,' he said harshly. When she drew a

280

deep shuddering breath but did not reply to that he leaned over and took her hands in his. They were bare, for she had stripped off her wet muddy gloves when she entered the carriage. Her hands were freezing, and he rubbed them between his fingers as he said: 'Why didn't you marry me before – when I asked you? You did love me then, didn't you?'

She couldn't answer. The reasons seemed so trite now; she was resentful because she thought Papa and Lisabeth wanted to marry her off to be rid of her. . . . How could she tell him that? She said: 'I was drawn to Andrew, but I didn't understand why, not at the time. He's still a very important part of my life, Jeremy. I've vowed that I'll never go near Mists of Heaven until Papa has made a proper acknowledgement of Andrew. Did you know that?'

He nodded, thinking that the lot of them wanted their heads banging together. All making themselves miserable because of stupid pride; at least he wasn't that stiff-necked.

Daisy said: 'But the real reason I refused you was far more complex than that. I knew in my soul that I hungered to make something of myself. In an odd way I've Lisabeth to thank for that. She's never let being a woman stop her from doing the things she wants. She's become an artist and she's studied papers on history and geology at university – all with Papa's encouragement, of course. If it wasn't for her, I'd have stayed at home with a governess and learned to sew pretty embroidery like most other young women of my class. As it was, I studied properly, at a fine girls' school, *and* I did so well that I had no trouble being accepted for the medical college in Edinburgh. But learning does that to you, doesn't it? It pushes a void in front of itself so that there is a hunger created, and the more you learn the more you crave. That's why I wouldn't marry you, Jeremy. I had this void in me, and I had to study to satisfy it.'

'And now? Is your life full and rich and satisfied now?' His eyes searched hers, finding the answer he sought. 'It's not, is it?' When she hesitated he said: 'Since you came back to Christchurch I've avoided you. I wouldn't go anywhere we might meet and I drove out of my way to keep clear of your part of town, but since you came to the house and I saw you it's been different. I haunt places I might see you. I drive past your medical rooms and I follow you to work and home again, and I've observed you. So don't lie to me, Daisy. I know you don't feel happy and fulfilled.'

How had he guessed she was planning to lie? She said: 'I have problems, that's all. I've got challenges and difficulties to solve, and you're quite right, I'm *not* happy and fulfilled, but please don't be angry about this, Jeremy, because I did what I had to do, what was right for me at the time. I wasn't ready to be married; I knew nothing of life. I'd have

281

been a terrible wife . . . we'd have been wretchedly unhappy together'

'Would we?' he said, but he was beginning to look at his own situation in a different way. Arabella probably wasn't ready for marriage and nor was he, when circumstances thrust them into it. She wanted giddy social life; he was only happy with his horses; neither of them was suitable marriage material.

'I'm more mature now, more certain of what I want.'

'Then, think about what I told you. We can have a wonderful future together if only you agree.' She began to argue, but he silenced her by leaning over and kissing her swiftly on the mouth. When he drew back his eyes were alight. 'There! Things haven't changed at all, have they?'

She looked down at her lap, where his hands still imprisoned hers, and she hoped he could not feel how she was trembling. She felt so foolish, weak and vulnerable. One swift kiss and her stout defence crumbled. She whispered: 'You'd better take me home.'

'Where to?' asked Jeremy. 'Would you like to be taken back to your Cashel Street rooms?'

'Yes, please,' said Daisy, thinking that she would prefer to wash her face and compose herself before facing Kiki and Aunt Bea with this distressing news, but then she remembered that Sarah and Andrew had gone to the Canterbury Hotel this evening for a special dinner to celebrate their coming baby. She didn't want to be alone there, and she didn't dare be alone with Jeremy.

When he rapped on the roof and the hatch was opened by the coachman, Daisy said: 'Please, I've just remembered Aunt Bea want me home early this evening. Could we go directly to Benares, please?'

Jeremy smiled. His face flushed with pleasure like a little boy's when he smiled. 'Good,' he said. 'Benares is much further away. I'll have you to myself for a little longer.'

She didn't reply. It was idiotic but, thinking how they could have been completely alone together for as long as they pleased, she felt as if she was deceiving him.

The sepoys dug Excalibur a grave under the apricot rose bush, where he used to lie in wait to dash out and chase the peacocks when they were strolling across the lawn. They enjoyed this chore; neither of them was fond of the dog. Kiki, who had grumbled incessantly over his bad habits, was surprisingly lachrymose and gulped a large whisky while Daisy read the service over Excalibur. There were no roses, so Beatrice threw a bunch of early jonquils into the grave.

Daisy missed him. It was weeks before she stopped calling him in the mornings to walk with her to work. Whenever a wagon-driver let fly with a mouthful of curses she looked around instinctively, ready to scold and order him out of the way, and then with an ache under her heart she remembered that it was already too late. At the butcher's she had to remind herself not to order scrag ends and bones yet still forgot, and slumped down on a kitchen chair and wept bitterly when Sarah, who had forgotten Excalibur at once, asked what these were doing with her order.

She missed him most of all when she was lonely. In the past he would snuffle at her hands and raise his toffee eyes to hers as if to console her, but now her pain had to be borne alone.

'Daisy's little dog was killed,' said Lisabeth. She had Anne propped up in a soft chair while she and Gwynne held some of Theodora's old clothes against her, deciding what to keep and what to discard. Rhys was watching. He was drawn to this plump little girl; she was blonde and rosy-cheeked with a pointed wilful chin like Daisy's, and she had a way of turning her round blue eyes on him that was exactly the way Daisy looked when she was trying to wangle his approval.

'Her little dog? That little dog she saved?' said Gwynne. 'Oh, what a shame!' She peered through her thick lenses at the maroon smock she was holding up to the child. 'This one's too dark, don't you think? Too dark. Charles had an eye for colour, and he always said that dark colours were unsuitable for little children. Pastel shades, that's what he favoured. Clear pastels.'

Lisabeth said: 'It was a ghastly accident, apparently. The poor creature was run over right in front of her eyes.' She paused and slid a glance at her husband. 'Andrew told me about it when I telephoned him yesterday.' There was not a flicker of expression from Rhys, so Lisabeth continued. 'He said they're doing quite well with their medical practice, but Daisy has been very restless since poor Excalibur was killed. Daisy is quite a character in town, you know. The votes-for-women groups are trying to get her to address meetings on their behalf, and she's been helping organize their petitions. Apparently she has an excellent public-speaking manner.'

Rhys pushed himself forward from the door-post where he was leaning. In a dry voice he said: 'She must get that from her mother. Azura always said far more than was good for her.' With that he left the room.

Daisy's restlessness increased. Meeting Jeremy and discovering that they still wanted each other had set up dark currents in her life. She was gnawed at by vague feelings she couldn't define. Sometimes it was like the sensation of a particularly difficult monthly period when her stomach cramped and a harsh dragging feeling pulled at her insides. She tried to define her feelings for Jeremy and could not; she was angry with him, furious that he had messed his life up and was now wanting to drag her into it, but at the same time she was wildly, exultantly glad. But her health suffered; she couldn't sleep. Her exuberant sense of fun withered. She grew thin.

'I say, Daisy,' teased Andrew, a smile failing to mask the concern in his voice. 'If I didn't know better, I'd say you were in love!'

To his horror she turned and pressed her face into the shoulder of his white jacket, her body heaving with sobs. He was stunned. Absently patting her shoulder, he said: 'You've had a rough time of things lately, Excalibur copping it right in front of you like that.'

'Yes! Yes!' she grasped the excuse gratefully. 'I didn't know how much I cared about him. I loved him, I really did, and now it's too late. I can't bear knowing that, Andrew. Why don't we realize at the time? Why does the truth only come home to us when it's too late?'

He raised his eyebrows. He helped her to a chair, thinking: *He was only a mangy old dog after all. Too late for what, for heaven's sake? She was always saying he'd be run over one of these days.*

'I loved him all along and I didn't know it,' she was sobbing. 'Oh, Andrew, why does life have to be so cruel?'

'Easy on there, girl,' said her brother. 'Tell you what. Your birthday's coming up in a couple of weeks. What say Sarah and I buy you another one as a gift?'

'What?' She raised her head, startled.

'Another puppy. We'll get you—'

'Oh.' Their eyes met then, and a prickle of understanding crawled up Andrew's back. Whatever Daisy had been sobbing her heart out for, it certainly wasn't Excalibur.

TWENTY-SEVEN

THE NOTICE IN THE NEWSPAPER was small and was tucked into a column between advertisements for Symonds Coachbuilders and Wilkie's Sparkling Mineral Waters. Daisy's attention skimmed over it without registering. It was not until later in the day when, with nothing better to do, she was filling in time by scrubbing Sarah's kitchen shelves for her that she remembered the notice with a sudden clarity.

Removing her apron and straightening her lace house-cap, she strode out of her door and along the veranda into Andrew's waiting-room where, as usual, every chair was occupied. That sight usually rankled, but she forced a pleasant smile and knocked on the consulting-room door.

He was peering down an old man's throat. 'Yes, you may take it. I'm too busy to read it today anyway,' he said.

'I can see that,' she said, snatching up the newspaper from the rack behind his desk, returning through the waiting-room with her head held high.

Back in the kitchen she permitted herself the luxury of a few hissing curses. 'Damn them, damn them all. Just because I'm a woman they stay away. What is it?' she railed. 'Don't they trust me? Do they think I'm not intelligent enough to read their miserable symptoms? Are they shy of a woman – a young unmarried woman – looking perhaps at intimate parts of their bodies? Do they think I'm a pervert? Do they think I'm a freak for wanting an honest working life? Oh, damn them all! I've got all this wealth of knowledge and skill to offer, and they're too blind and stupid to take advantage.' Scowling with utter frustration, she considered marching into that waiting-room and voicing her opinions out loud. *That would pin their ears back!* she thought grimly.

Shrugging at her irritable mood, she scanned the columns again, but her anger was such that her eyes skipped over the notice twice before she found it again. She read it slowly.

Applications are invited for the post of Inspector of Factories for the Wellington District. This post is eminently suitable for a Doctor of Medicine, or for someone with a partially completed Medical Degree. Applicants should in the first instance apply in writing and then be prepared to travel to Wellington for an Interview.

Donning her apron again, Daisy resumed her self-appointed task, all the while pondering over her future. Then she tipped out the soapy water, left the up-ended bucket and scrubbing-brush by the back steps to dry and removed her apron, hanging it neatly on a peg beside the coal range before going into her own office. There she took out a white pad, uncapped her inkwell and began writing the letter that was already composed in her head.

'But you can't go!' cried Sarah. 'We need you here.'

'Rubbish! It's sweet of you to say so, but you *don't* need me here, and you certainly won't in two months when you give up your job. You'll be able to do Andrew's bookwork then. I'll only be in the way. As it's going, the practice can't support the three of us.'

Andrew was watching calmly. She had come an hour early this morning to join them at breakfast – a simple meal of porridge sweetened with honey. While she spoke Andrew watched carefully, observing rather than listening, noting her agitated manner, her restless gestures, the way she scooped up porridge with her spoon and then put it down in the plate again, untasted. When she paused he said: 'What do the Launcenolts think of this plan of yours?'

'They support me,' she said quickly. 'Of course they do! I mean, Wellington's not far, and I'll be able to come home four or five times a year. It's not the other side of the world, for heaven's sake! But, of course, all this is premature. I may not even be granted the post.'

'But to go away!' protested Sarah, tears in her eyes. 'If you're worried about employment, Daisy, why not take over my position when I leave? Seaview is an interesting place to work, and the salary is good. Please don't go so far away. Consider Seaview, at least.'

Daisy toyed with her spoon. 'You like it there, Sarah, but it's not for me. I really—'

'There's something else, isn't there?' said Andrew quietly. 'There's some other reason, something that's driving you away.'

'What? No, of course not!' She laughed to show what a ridiculous notion that was. Sarah believed her, but Andrew noticed the panic in her voice, the sudden flare of colour in her cheeks, and the fact that she wouldn't meet his eyes.

He let the silence grow, then said carefully: 'Whenever I've had problems in my life I've taken the easy way out. I've run away. It's—'

'Oh, Andrew, don't be hard on yourself,' protested Sarah.

'Please, dear, let me finish. At the time, Daisy, running away seemed like the only thing to do. It was you who made me look at that differently. It's been difficult for me, coming back here and establishing myself right under Rhys Morgan's nose. You've no idea how I dread meeting him again, yet one day it's going to happen and I don't know whether I'll step forward to shake his hand or whether I'll knock him to the ground. In Edinburgh I forgot my origins. I was simply Doctor Andrew Stafford, self-made if you like, but the day we arrived home it all came rushing back to me that I'm a rich man's unacknowledged bastard son, and here in Canterbury that's what I'll always be, it seems. It's a tough one to live with, but thanks to you, Daisy, I'm learning there's immense satisfaction in staring one's problems in the face and not being defeated by them.' He paused. Daisy was fiddling with her spoon, her face and neck scarlet. Very gently he said: 'Daisy, we love you, and your place is here with us. We'll fight this prejudice together, and if there is something else that's frightening you and driving you away, then we can help you if you let—'

'No!' Her smile was wide, but she looked neither of them in the eye. 'Andrew, you are a darling but you couldn't be more wrong! Truly! Besides, this is all terribly premature, as I said. There may be a score of other applicants for the post. I may not even stand a chance of getting it.'

She arrived on board the *Waimana* early and sent Andrew away. She would be gone only three days, so there was no point in fussing with goodbyes, she said. Andrew accepted that, knowing that there was no point in pressing her. She had her reasons and was determined to keep them to herself.

'I'll wave to you now, from my porthole window,' she said. 'Look, I'm about a dozen places along from the gang-plank.'

Leaving her bag on the bunk, he gave her a swift fierce hug, said, 'I hope you find what you're looking for,' and left.

I've hurt him, she realized. *I've hurt him and Sarah both, but I can't confide in them. I can't tell them why I have to leave.*

She stood at the porthole, smiled and waved when Andrew clattered down through the boarding crowd and stood on the wharf, searching for her framed face. 'Here I am!' she cried. When he blew her a kiss she blew one back. Then he was gone.

For a long while she stayed where she was simply because she lacked the energy to move. People struggled on board weighted with profusions of packages, porters humped trunks up the steep ridged ramp and mothers harried their children with 'Take care with that parcel!' and

'Don't let go of little Mary's hand' and 'Hurry up, Samuel! They'll no
wait the ship for the likes of us!'

The gangway was being unbolted, and people were still arriving or
the wharf, rushing now, stumbling to be there on time. *Waimana*'s horr
sounded, a low single note that reverberated through the ship, tingling
her hands where they rested on the porthole rim and vibrating through
the soles of her buttoned ankle-boots.

Another vehicle arrived late, driving right on to the wharf itself. It wa:
a hansom, with the driver sitting up on the back behind the cab. The
moment it stopped a passenger emerged and thrust a banknote up to the
driver, then leaned into the cab for his carpet bag. He turned, laughing
at the dockers who were yelling abuse at him for driving in past the gates
and, seeing that the gangway was already moving, broke into a run
shouting at the men to wait for him.

Daisy stared in disbelief, willing it to be someone else, not Jeremy,
who was loping up the swinging ramp. She ducked away from the opening and slumped on to her narrow bunk, clenching her hands over her
ears to block out the sound of his voice as he shouted his thanks to the
dockers. This was unbelievable!

The last thing she had done when he left her at Benares was to extract
from him a promise that he would stop following her. He was reluctant,
but she insisted, stressing that if he was seen loitering outside her place of
work the gossip would be cruel and many people would be hurt. In the
end he had agreed; obviously with no intention of keeping his word, she
thought furiously. How dare he do this to her? And how had he found
out where she was going? Was she to have no privacy at all?

The journey was a mercifully brief one, from late afternoon one day to
late afternoon the next, but for the entire time Daisy remained in her
tiny cabin, furious, claustrophobic and hungry, for strong righteous
anger had given her the first hearty appetite she'd known in weeks. Several times during the voyage someone tapped on the door, announced
he was the steward, and asked if she needed anything, but though she
was desperate for a cup of tea she replied that she was all right thank you.
To open the door was to risk finding Jeremy leaning against the jamb, a
prospect that made her tremble with apprehension. If he was so obsessed
that he would go to these lengths, it would be nothing to station himself
outside her door as well.

In her bag was half an orange and a piece of dry bread, slipped in by
Sarah in case Daisy felt nauseous. Those made her dinner. Unable to risk
emerging to visit the bathroom, she relieved herself into the sea-sickness
receptacle beside her bunk and, when the *Waimana* was lurching the
right way, dashed the contents from the porthole into the sea. Next day
she watched the coastline of the South Island disappear and the rocky
crags of Wellington Heads slip into view. She longed to be on deck with

288

the breeze in her face and the majestic scenery sprawled around for her enjoyment. To the depths of her soul she hated Jeremy Drake.

Disembarking presented the greatest problem. If he had followed her, he would wait for her now, and she was determined to outsit him, to return to Lyttelton in this very cabin if she must. Hovering out of view, she watched the disembarking passengers; though she was perishing with thirst and had a foul taste in her mouth, she dared not risk a trip to wash and refresh herself until *he* was off the ship. 'Come on! Come on!' she hissed impatiently. 'What's keeping you? Why the delay?'

At length he strolled ashore, taking his time and joking with one of the ship's officers who walked down the gangway with him, seeing him off. The moment she saw him Daisy dashed to the bathroom and, putting her face to the tap marked 'Fresh', took a long gulping draught. Then, bolting the door behind her, she took a hasty 'Calcutta bath' as Beatrice called it, soaping and rinsing her face, neck, underarms, crotch and feet, while stripped down to her camisole and open drawers. After she had brushed her teeth and smoothed her hair she felt immeasurably better. The view from her porthole lightened her spirits still further. The crowd had thinned, and Jeremy had gone.

'Are you all right, miss?' called the steward, who was checking the corridor making sure all the cabins were empty. 'You're the last one aboard. Can you manage your luggage, then?' He stared at her suspiciously; he met all kinds in his line of work.

Over her protests he insisted on carrying her bag up on deck and escorting her to the gangway, where he left her and went to watch the unloading of a pair of racehorses. Half a dozen stable-hands and a trainer supervised as the sleek dark animals were coaxed down another walkway. The animals skittered. Their eyes flashed as white as the bandages that bound their tender fetlocks. On the wharf Daisy paused to watch them. One of the beasts was a truly magnificent fellow, reminiscent of Donegal. He shied up when he reached the wharf, and the stable-hand holding his halter had to leap out of the way. The stable-hand laughed aloud, calming the horse by reaching up and stroking its neck. As he did so, he looked across the few yards that lay between them, and she saw that he was not a stable-hand at all.

'Daisy!' he cried. When she turned quickly and walked away he tossed the reins to one of the others and dashed after her, catching up to her as she neared the office, grabbing her elbow so that she whirled around to face him. 'Daisy, what are you doing here? Are *you* following *me* now?'

She looked at his face, saw the wild hope in his eyes and realized that her nightmare voyage had been unnecessary. 'I thought you were . . . I thought . . .,' she said stupidly.

'Following you?' He frowned. Someone called: 'Mr Drake, sir!' He glanced around then back, searching her face with a deep intense look.

'Don't go away. They need me. . . . One or two details. . . . I'll be back in a moment.' He let go of her arm, paused, then suddenly reached over and snatched her bag out of her grasp.

'Jeremy! That's got all my papers—'

'I won't be a moment,' he promised, and hurried away, carrying his hostage with him.

She had no choice. Arranging herself on the wooden bench outside the office, gazing morosely across at the city, she resigned herself to wait. Without her bag and the money and professional documents it contained, she could do nothing. As a prisoner on the ship she had been a victim of her own imagination but she was his prisoner now.

It was a long wait, and after a time she began to study Wellington with interest. The city was nothing like Christchurch, which had long streets and spacious tree-lined squares, but it had a distinct and attractive personality of its own, a pretty town with abrupt hills rising almost from the water and a jostle of buildings crowding the foreshore, a crammed vital place, still busy at dusk when Christchurch would be emptying for the night. Idly she counted fifteen hotels and had picked out a place that surely must be parliament buildings, a long three-storeyed wooden structure, which she fancied she recognized from an old engraving.

The hotel windows were lit and sparks of light were beginning to freckle the dark blue hills behind the town when Jeremy finally rescued her. His horses were gone, the staff had disappeared and she had not noticed them leave. He handed her up into a closed carriage and sat opposite her. 'I'm sorry to keep you waiting,' he said as if it had been five minutes instead of almost an hour. 'We had a few problems with Donegal Prince. He's racing in the Wellington Cup next week. That's what I was doing on board – why you wouldn't have seen me. I was down in the hold all night, sitting up with him. He hates ships. The engines drive him frantic.'

So I stayed in my cabin for nothing, thought Daisy, wryly amused. *I could have enjoyed a leisurely meal, sipped coffee in the lounge, and could have been on deck this morning admiring the scenery. Instead I starved and imprisoned myself, and all because I assumed that Jeremy was so obsessed with me that he couldn't leave me alone. Such vanity! And such an ignominious fall!*

'Why are you smiling?'

She didn't reply. 'Do you come to Wellington often?' she asked, looking at him directly and clearly for the first time in years. When she'd gone to the house he was in distress, and when Excalibur was killed she was distraught; it was only now in the mellow evening light that she was able to study his face and notice the changes in him, the leaner lines to his face, the faint creases around his eyes and across his brow. As always, there was a lock of soft brown hair flopping on to his forehead; and, as always, her fingers imagined smoothing it away.

'I do, actually,' he was saying. 'Often enough to keep a house here, in the Kandallah district. I'm here one week a month at least in the racing season. What about you? What brings you here alone?'

She told him, and noticed how his eyes gleamed with interest. *If I'm going to run away from him, it's no use coming here*, she thought, and asked aloud: 'Do you ever go to Auckland? To Dunedin? I don't suppose you'd have any call to go there?'

'You'd be surprised. What about tonight? Are you booked in anywhere?'

She was prepared for that answer, and produced a name she had read while waiting for him at the wharf. 'As a matter of fact I've a room reserved at the Barrett's Hotel,' she replied promptly, and wondered why he tipped back his head, choking with laughter. She added sharply: 'I'd appreciate it if you'd take me directly there. They'll wonder why I'm so late.'

He said, still laughing: 'If you stay there, you'll be the first lady in fifty years to do so. The place is a rough house.' He leaned forward and took both her hands in his. 'Daisy, you're staying with me tonight, and tomorrow night, at my house.' When she opened her mouth to speak he said: 'No arguments. It's settled. There's nobody there. We'll be quite alone.'

The implications of what he was saying escaped her. All she could think of was that she was hungry and desperate for a meal. 'I must go to an hotel,' she insisted.

'I told you; you're coming with me.' They were rattling through town now, past lighted windows and people thronging on the footpaths, their faces black and yellow in the lamps. Daisy saw one sign, *Steak and Oysters, Bob-a-Nob*, and another, *Roast Dinners Now Available only 1/6*. Her stomach cramped.

'You don't understand,' she pleaded. 'I haven't had anything to eat since yesterday, nothing but an orange. I'm longing for a good square meal.'

'Were you ill on the voyage?'

'No. . . .' And she began to laugh, then stopped and, while he lounged back idly listening, she confessed what had happened on the journey.

'Oh, Daisy, I love you,' he exclaimed, leaning forward to kiss her on the mouth.

She closed her eyes. The cramped feeling in her stomach spread lower. *Why not? Why not?* she thought.

'Oi! Lookit them lovebirds!' screamed a voice close by.

They sprang apart. The carriage had slowed to a crawl in a knot of traffic, and on the pavement adjacent stood a group of grubby urchins pointing bony fingers and shrieking like monkeys. 'Lookit that! Ooh, lookit that!'

Daisy hung her head and shrank back into the shadows. This intrusion of the real world was timely. She said: 'Jeremy, we've absolutely no right to talk like this, or to behave. . . .' She faltered and then said unhappily: 'I'd better go to an hotel. Truly it would be best.'

'There's no argument. I mean it. There'll be plenty of food at the house. The people who look after it are expecting me and they air it, put out fresh linen and stock the larder whenever I'm due in. So don't worry – your hunger will be assuaged.' He paused and lounged back again, immensely sure of himself. 'Make your mind up to it, Doctor Morgan, I'm not letting you go. The only regrets in my life – with one horrendous exception – concern you, and if I took you to an hotel I'd have another regret to add to that list. You're staying with me, Daisy, and I'm going to make love to you. And never mind about rights, either. Needs have rights of their own.' He paused again. 'And I, Doctor Morgan, need you.'

She could hardly believe she was hearing this. She knew about sex and hymens and erections from her lectures at Edinburgh, and (she learned from the notes) the lectures had touched on subjects like Arousal, Foreplay and Preparing the Female to Be Receptive. She and the other girls had giggled over the notes when Andrew gave them to her, and later she had even, in a clinical way, wondered what it would feel like to have someone (and her 'someone' was always Jeremy) do those interesting things to her. Would her nipples harden and would her sex moisten? Was there a recipe for sexual intercourse where you did *this* and *this* to achieve *that* result? Rather cold-blooded, they had decided. Highly unlikely that such reactions could be coaxed from their educated bodies. Not them!

Jeremy had not done any of the absurd things outlined in the lecture notes. He had not even touched her for several minutes, and no gesture of an intimate nature had happened between them. All he had done was tell her in a matter-of-fact way that he was going to seduce her, and, incredibly, her treacherous body was Preparing to Be Receptive. This was not the response of an educated person, she thought, wondering if she was hallucinating because of hunger, wondering if something strange had happened to her on the voyage and if Doctor Morgan had been left behind somewhere, to be supplanted by this tense sexual creature Daisy didn't recognize.

I'm going to make love to you, he said, and that was all it took. Immediately there was an intense fluttery feeling that spread from the insides of her thighs and up over her belly, such a peculiar strong feeling that it was all she could do to sit still. Normally she was unaware of her breasts from one month to the next, but suddenly she felt them tingling, too, hurting at the tips where they rubbed against the cotton fabric of her camisole. She felt ashamed of herself for being so weak. What if he could tell that she was aroused? Suppose it showed on her face? The light was fading fast, but there was still enough to see quite clearly by. She turned her head and pretended to look out of the window, at the hills and trees, for they were out of town now and travelling up a steep road; when she glanced quickly back at him she saw that he was still lounging back negligently watching her with that confident little smile playing about his mouth, and she felt her face grow hot. He *knew*. He must be able to tell. Was he silently laughing at her? In her awkward inexperience Daisy had no idea what he might be thinking, and she dreaded the answer.

Near the crest of the hill Jeremy rapped on the ceiling of the carriage, and the driver stopped at a pair of iron gates flanked by brick posts. 'We're here,' Jeremy said.

At the top of a curving driveway a low house crouched, unlit in the dusk. Huge trees flanked the drive, overhanging it to form a high-vaulted tunnel. It was freezing cold on the road; a cutting wind was racing up the hill, its breath sharp with frost. While Jeremy paid the driver Daisy hugged her cape tightly around her and thought: *I shouldn't be standing here. I should be climbing back into the carriage and instructing the driver to take me down to the town. I shouldn't be letting this happen.* But she stood there silent and immobile until Jeremy had unfastened the gate and meek as a lamb she walked ahead of him up the gravel drive.

Nothing will happen, she told herself. *We will have something to eat, and then we'll sit beside a fire and talk – we are old friends after all – and for one evening we'll recapture some of the carefree happiness of long ago. Then we'll go to bed in separate rooms. Yes, that's how it will be.*

While Jeremy unlocked the front door Daisy stood on the veranda, marvelling at the view. The house was built on a ledge overlooking the harbour, the bays and hills opposite and the town directly below. This soft light lent everything the texture of cloth: the water was a spread sheet of golden silk mirroring the muted flame colours of the sky, while the hills were a rich brown velvet studded with pearls of light. At her feet the town was a cutout of black and yellow felt, all the edges ragged with spills of light. There was shouting, clanging sounds, and music, all faint and blended, stirred by the wind that tingled her face and brought the earthy scents of the bush mingled with the salt tang of the sea.

Jeremy stood at her shoulder. 'It's beautiful, isn't it? I sit here in the evenings and all the cares of the day seem to dissolve of their own accord. This is where I think about you,' he added, and before she could speak he had gone into the house. A moment later windows behind her glowed with light and Jeremy was back again. 'Come in. It's cold out here. I've lit all the fires so the house will be cosy in a few minutes. Come and look around. I'm rather proud of this place. It's my very own, and apart from a few fellow horse-breeders you're my first guest.'

It was a simple settler's cottage, four rooms on one floor which Jeremy had arranged to suit himself. From the central passage a door opened to the bedroom on the left – she glimpsed a single-sized bed covered with a tapestry spread and a fire flickering behind a pierced bronze screen. On the right he led her into the parlour, a small room simply furnished in exquisite good taste with such starkness of style that she realized that the mansion in Hagley Avenue was entirely to Arabella's taste. Jeremy preferred an uncluttered look, with polished floors, panelling and rich dark curtains. An antique roll-top desk stood in one corner under a brass wall-lamp and on either side of a hand-knotted silk carpet stretched two deeply buttoned tobacco-leather sofas with low backs and rolled arms, arranged so that whoever sat on them could enjoy the fire on one side and the magnificent spread of view through the wide french doors on the other.

Jeremy poured them each a crystal glass of Spanish sherry and urged Daisy to sit down and make herself comfortable while he raided the larder. He was fussy, preening, beaming with pleasure as she complimented him on the room and on the awesome array of gold and silver cups won by his horses and displayed in a locked glass-fronted display-case beside the cream marble fireplace.

'I love beautiful things,' he said. 'There are usually flowers in here for me, bowls of them. I can't understand how the Watkinses could have forgotten. They've a lovely garden and they usually keep me well stocked with blooms.'

'I'll imagine the room with flowers,' she reassured him.

'Only now . . .,' he said, his smile fading as he gazed at her. 'Tonight it doesn't need flowers.'

Alone, she cradled the sherry-glass in chilled fingers and took tiny sips of the fruity pale liquid which, instead of relaxing her as she had hoped, only exacerbated her gnawing restlessness. She stood up, sat down and stood up again. She seethed with a strumming tension and could no longer tell whether it was hunger, nervousness or the sheer electric excitement of being catapulted into this adventure.

That's what it was, an adventure, a dream. Through the wall she could hear Jeremy stoking the kitchen range and suddenly she was overcome by a compulsion to be with him, to watch whatever he was doing. Only then did she discover the truth that was gradually emerging in her mind, uncovering like a sandbank rising from a receding tide of self-deception and half-truths. She loved Jeremy and she wanted this to happen.

TWENTY-EIGHT

SHE ALREADY KNEW that she loved him, of course; that truth had been evident for a long time. But the rest was a surprise. All this time she had been practising an elaborate self-deception, going to great lengths to put a 'safe' distance between herself and Jeremy, congratulating herself on her clever idea of applying for work in Wellington so that she could easily avoid him in the future. She understood why: her moral nature was outraged by her true self. Her problem was, what should she do now?

Jeremy stood in the doorway. 'I have a confession to make. I don't quite know how to tell you. . . .'

'What's happened?'

'Come and have a look.' He held out his hand to her.

Beyond the door at the end of the corridor was a brightly lit kitchen, cheerfully tiled in blue and white with a huge scrubbed wooden table bracketed by only two ladder-backed chairs. Blue crockery was arranged in rows on shelves above the sink bench next to copper pots and frying-pans which were hanging on wooden pegs.

He saw her glance at a door to her left and said: 'I'm sorry, I should have mentioned . . . there's a bathroom in there, and the . . . ah . . . if you need it . . . through there, too. There'll be plenty of hot water soon, if you want a bath.'

His embarrassment amused her. She said: 'All I want is something to eat, and soon. Jeremy, I'm famished!'

'That's what I wanted to show you. I'm afraid my arrangements have gone terribly awry. The Watkinses can't have received my message. Usually there's fresh-baked pies and a cold joint, soup, bread, eggs and fruit of some sort. . . . But look!' He opened the larder door to reveal a stack of spotless empty shelves. Hanging from a hook in the ceiling was a ham swathed in muslin, and on one of the high shelves a red-coated wheel of cheese and a row of pickle jars, but otherwise nothing. 'I'm sorry,' Jeremy said. 'I've a cellar full of wine and a larder empty of food. You're hungry—'

'Starving,' said Daisy.

'You're starving, and I'd planned to show off by whipping together an absolutely splendid repast. Instead all I can offer you is some cold ham, some hard cheese and pickles on dry cracker biscuits. I am sorry, Daisy, I shouldn't have brought you here. I should have guessed when there were no flowers. . . .'

She began to laugh.

'What's so amusing?'

'You are! This is hilarious, isn't it?'

He saw that incredibly she wasn't in the least angry, and began to laugh, too, but with relief rather than with amusement. Then their eyes met and the laughing stopped.

He placed his hands on her waist, one on either side. 'You're thinner than I imagined you'd be.'

'It's because I'm underfed,' she said, amusement still bubbling inside her.

'Oh, Daisy, I *am*—'

'Hush,' she said, her eyes alight as she gazed into his. She could taste freedom. Whatever happened now would be because she wanted it to, and not because she was being pursued or manipulated or coerced into doing something against her will. The knowledge thrilled her with a wild pure joy. 'Kiss me, Jeremy,' she whispered and smiled at the astonishment in his eyes.

He tilted his head slightly, for they were almost the same height. Her lips parted under his, and she gave a little sipping gasp as if she couldn't wait; their teeth clicked together, and when his tongue slid into her mouth she was ready to meet it. He tasted of sherry, tobacco and something else, a comforting, solid, warm taste that was familiar yet unidentifiable.

His astonishment was still palpable, and it entertained her, for she was giving him a surprise gift and his pleasure was all hers. At the back of her mind she wondered what he would do when he was certain that she was giving herself and was not tantalizing, planning to pull away. Would he sweep her off her feet and carry her down to the bedroom? Of course he would; that was how she and the other two girls had decided all seductions were properly conducted.

She was surprised, then, when Jeremy backed her the two paces to the wooden table, until she felt the edge of it bump against the tops of her thighs. Then, somehow, his hands were under her long woollen skirts, under the petticoat beneath, and she felt a flicker of his fingers as his hands tugged at the buttoned waistband of her drawers. *Of course*, she thought. *He's married. Feminine undergarments would hold no mysteries for him.*

That small thought jabbed in her mind, briefly spoiling the moment for her, but then he slid the cotton garment down over her hips and in the next moment his hands were warm and smooth on the globes of her buttocks, cupping, caressing, and then parting the flesh and probing the place between.

When he lifted her she clung to his shoulders and for a few seconds buried her face in the nape of his neck, breathing in the warm tobaccoey, horsey, human smell of his skin, before he whispered, 'Daisy,' again and sought her mouth with his. Against the inside of her thighs the tweed trousers rubbed harshly, and she could feel, quite distinctly, the urgent bulge of his penis. Years ago, in the parlour at Benares, she had felt it and was faintly shocked, wondering if his erection was something deliberate he was using as a weapon against her sensibilities, but now with her odd accumulation of education and naïvety she welcomed the feel of the hard, rough ridge with a panic of nervous anticipation.

He didn't touch her breasts, not even on the outside of her clothes, and that surprised her, too. This was nothing like the 'recipe' in the lecture notes, girls! Instead his fingers delicately stroked the melting place between her legs, then cupped and pressed and stroked and pressed on the moist folds of flesh until her back arched and in an involuntary movement she thrust her hips towards him.

He was fumbling at his trousers with his free hand; shucking them from about his waist. She felt the ridge of his waistband on the tender skin of one inner thigh and then a whisper of silk and then at last heat, the satiny hardness of his penis shaft and a sticky moistness like a snail slick where he slid against her.

'I'll be careful not to hurt you,' he murmured.

'Be careful . . . be careful not . . .,' she gasped, suddenly remembering other things she had learned: about sperm and fertility and unwanted pregnancy. It was ludicrous, but this was the first moment all evening that those very important details had entered her head.

'Daisy, I'll never hurt you,' he said.

It was enough. She closed her eyes in grateful surrender. The light drummed on her eyelids, and her cheek pressed against his face, while his desperate breathing sighed roughly in her ear. He slipped into her so neatly at first that she wondered if what she had learned at medical school about hymens was inapplicable in her case, but then suddenly there was a tight burning sensation and she realized that she was normal after all.

He felt her flinch in pain and stopped at once, easing back, throbbing softly inside her as he fought against every instinct not to ram brutally home. In the end it was she who wrapped her legs around his waist and pulled him into the mass of skirts and petticoats and at the centre herself, nudging him deeper, coaxing him until with a cry he plunged forward with a single deep thrust, cupped palms on her buttocks pulling her against him at the same time.

Now there was no need to flinch. The pain was fierce but astonishingly brief, over as quickly as the hot flaring of a match that is instantly extinguished. She groaned and arched her back so that she was lying almost on the table with Jeremy supporting them both on his elbows, while her legs, still wound about his waist, cradled their hips as they thrust together in a loose rocking knot.

When she caught her breath Daisy marvelled at the sheer perfection of the act. Lovemaking she had imagined would be an awkward business with knees and elbows needing to be arranged in certain positions so that they would not get in the way; she never could quite visualize how it could be comfortably, let alone enjoyably, managed. But, oh, the reality was so simple. He tucked inside her, and she folded around him, and their sweet friction enclosed the centres of their bodies, building such delicious sensations. It was frantic, it was seismic – shuddering deep below the surface. She could feel herself being wound up tighter and tighter with a kind of desperate anticipation, trembling on some steep mysterious brink, every thrust inching her closer to a vast soaring abyss beyond.

Abruptly, unexpectedly, it was over. Jeremy tugged out of her, leaving an invasive emptiness and a bewildering sense of unexplained loss. He was heavy and gasping at her side; against the outside of her thigh she felt his penis jerking and pulsing like a creature convulsed in death-throes.

'Oh, Daisy,' he said. 'Daisy . . . that was wonderful, and terrible, too. I'm sorry to have to stop right then, but—'

'But you had to,' she whispered. She was struggling not to cry. A story had been interrupted at its most exciting part and the ending ripped away, gone. She would never know it. What had seemed like perfect comfort only moments before now was cramping and uncomfortable. She was aware of her naked legs and pushed one hand at her skirts to cover herself.

'Wait.' He stopped her and lifted her skirt away, to wipe her thigh with his handkerchief. His face was sombre, serious, and she wondered what he was thinking. Was he wishing that this moment of impulse had never happened? She wished it, fervently wished it. Still dangling on that brink with the loss of mysterious promised riches, she felt so miserable and alone that her emotions coiled inside her in a knot, so cold and hard that she was unaware of her welling tears.

Jeremy was shocked. 'Darling . . . darling Daisy,' he crooned, sitting on the table-edge and cradling her in his arms as inwardly he cursed his clumsiness. 'Please don't cry. I didn't mean to take you so abruptly. Quite honestly I didn't know whether that would happen at all. I didn't plan to seduce you – certainly not like that – but I wanted you so overwhelmingly that once I started to kiss you I simply couldn't stop. It's a problem I've had ever since I met you,' he joked, trying to make light of the situation.

She shook her head. Her hair grated against his neck. 'It's not that. I wanted you, too. I think I always have. It's just that right now I feel so . . . so let down. It was lovely, Jeremy, really lovely, and then all of a sudden everything collapsed.'

His heart swelled. Suddenly everything was all right. Her whispered confession that she had always wanted him made him happier than anything had ever done before. Even when he first held Silas in his arms the flood of joy had not equalled this moment. He promised: 'It won't be like that next time. I'll make love to you properly, not rushed like this.'

She shook her head again, glad that he couldn't see her face. 'But you can't. It's too dangerous. We might . . . I might. . . .'

His impulse was to say: 'So what? You're mine now, and I don't care if the whole world knows it. We'll make love and take the risks. In fact I *hope* you get pregnant because then there's no escape, no turning back for either of us.' Aware of the genuine fear in her voice, however, he wisely stilled his words. He loved Daisy. He wanted her to have only good feelings about him and, above all, he wanted her to feel wooed, not trapped. For a moment he fumbled, cursing his unpreparedness, then he remembered his emergency cupboard which was stocked with not only headache powders and tonics but also supplies for other contingencies, too. Watkins had stocked it for him, and at the time Jeremy had laughed at some of the items he had included. Now he was thankful.

He said: 'You're not to worry. No harm will come to you. When we have babies they'll be because you want them as much as I do.'

His confidence and bold assurances about their future made her shiver with apprehension. *No*, she told herself firmly. *Don't even think about tomorrow*. Tonight was a magic interlude, isolated from both the past and the future; she would seize it with joy and not allow reality to seep in and stain its enchantment.

'You're shivering,' said Jeremy. 'Poor darling girl. I'll run a bath for you.'

While she undressed in the steamy bathroom, Jeremy went into the parlour and telephoned Jack Watkins who was apologetic and flustered, even though no message had been received.

'It's not your fault. Never mind,' said Jeremy, brushing his stammered apologies aside. 'What has Mrs Watkins made for your supper?'

'A lovely 'otpot, sir.'

'Is there enough to ladle some out into a dish and bring it over? Enough for two? And some bread and eggs?'

'For two, sir?'

'I have a gentleman friend with me,' said Jeremy, remembering what an avid gossip Mrs Watkins was. 'Can the hotpot accommodate two hearty appetites?'

'Why, certainly, sir. 'Ester, she always cooks enough for Napoleon's troops, you know 'er.'

'And divine it will taste, too, no doubt. Could you bring it over as soon as you can?'

'Right away, sir. A pleasure. And I'm sorry about the mix-up, sir. I can't think what must 'ave 'appened—'

'Think no more of it,' said Jeremy.

He bathed her like he bathed little Silas, soaping a soft cloth and smoothing it over her limbs, all the while talking to her while keeping an ear attuned to noises from outside.

She was shy. It was one thing to examine other people's bodies – she could do that now without embarrassment, no matter how intimate the examination – but it was quite another matter to have Jeremy gazing at her nakedness, even if there was a reverential tenderness about the way he cradled her breasts with soap-slicked fingers and admiration when he outlined the curve of her hips with his palms. But she conceded reluctantly. When he first tapped on the door and came in she had to fight an urge to grab a towel to cover herself.

'Don't forget I've seen you like that before,' he said, seeing the nervousness in her eyes. 'Dear Lord, Daisy, but you're beautiful. Do you realize that I fell in love with you that day when you were swimming in the woods?' He laughed as she blushed, delighted to see the pinkness spread over her breasts and shoulders, too. He said: 'Falling in love is supposed to be a cerebral thing, an ethereal experience; but for me it was carnal, I'm afraid. I fell profoundly in love with your entire body the moment I first saw you. I can still recall every detail of how you looked, you know. Your hair was dripping wet, all hanging down like wet ribbons, and this hair – here – was plastered down, and water was running over your body here, and here, and—'

'That's quite enough,' she chided, dabbing a smudge of soap-suds on to his nose. 'I can see through this story. You're fabricating excuses to touch intimate parts of my body.' But there was another reason, one that she understood and was grateful for. By joking with her, by combining frankness with light-hearted touching, he was helping her overcome an agony of shyness.

She laughed, relaxing as he agreed, as he smothered her body greedily with his hands. She joined in the game by dashing a spray of water in his face, gasping as he cupped her chin in his hands and bent to kiss her, so that the water now ran over her face.

'We're both all wet now,' he murmured, flicking his tongue against her lips. Then, to her astonishment he scooped his palms under her hips and drew her up out of the water, pressing his mouth on to the firm warmth of her belly.

Her mouth went dry as she watched him. Her fingers tightened convulsively in the hair at the nape of his neck. When she spoke her voice was a husky rasping. 'I love you. . . . I can't bear to be away from you another minute. Please. . . .'

He raised his head and met her gaze, humbled by the depth of love he saw in her eyes. She tried to smile. 'Come on,' she whispered. Her fingers tugged at his cream silk cravat, struggling with the ruby-headed pin that kept it in place.

'No, Daisy.' He stood up.

Her hands fell away from him. Her smile wavered, then she said: 'You're shy, too. Go on, admit it.'

'I admit it,' he conceded, dodging the droplets of water she splashed over him. 'But that's not the problem. Listen.'

She paused and heard wheels crunching on the gravel driveway.

'It's Watkins with our supper. Shush now while I answer the door to him. He thinks I've got a man staying with me.'

Her laugh was a gurgle of relief. 'You're not rejecting me, then?'

Her intention was to stay where she was until Watkins had gone, but when he brought the casserole of hotpot into the kitchen and the delectable fragrance wafted through to where she lay languidly in the water sharp pangs of hunger assailed her. By the time Watkins had finished fussing with the tablecloth and had set out the food Daisy was dried and dressed and impatient to begin the meal. As soon as the door snipped shut behind him she emerged from the bathroom, smiling at Jeremy's crestfallen expression.

'This smells delicious,' she breathed, lifting the lid. 'It looks good, too. And fresh-baked bread! Butter and peach preserves. And look at this fruit cake! She spoils you, this Mrs Watkins.'

He watched her eat, enjoying that more than the food itself. Arabella ate with tiny nipping motions, pleating up her lips as she chewed as if everything was distasteful, but Daisy set to with gusto, exclaiming over the flavours, laughing and talking, dabbing at her mouth with the napkin between bites, feeding him morsels with her fork.

Jeremy couldn't believe how much he loved her. His heart swelled and swelled until he no longer could contain his feelings. Getting up from his place, he walked around to her side, kneeled beside her chair and with his arms about her waist buried his face in her lap.

She hesitated, then very gently stroked the back of his head. He seemed so vulnerable and so dear to her that she felt weak tears prickling her eyelids again. When he raised his face she saw that he, too, was overcome by emotion. 'I could die of happiness,' she told him, but as

301

she spoke an inner voice warned her that this wasn't real, Jeremy was Arabella's husband and she, Daisy Morgan, was supposed to have been running away from him today, not getting herself trapped in a quagmire from which there would be no escape.

He said: 'You look like a little girl. You look as if something absolutely wonderful is happening to you but you don't quite believe it's true.'

His perception startled her. She said: 'I'm not a little girl. I'm a respectable lady doctor.'

'Not too respectable for this, I hope,' he said wickedly, sliding a hand up her calf and between her thighs.

Reality was looming again; she could feel its cold shadow on her back. In an effort to thrust it away she smiled coquettishly at Jeremy and teased: 'There's a lot to be said for respectability, you know. To be honest, I found sex rather disappointing. Unsatisfying, you might say.' She squealed as he grabbed her and dragged her down on to the floor beside him, twisting in his arms as he tried to kiss her, breaking free and scrambling to her feet, thinking as she dashed around the table that he could have caught her easily but was joining in the game. She needed the game, she needed to keep the mood light, fearing that if she gave in to common sense, gave in to thinking about what was happening, then she was doomed.

They stood panting, facing each other with the table between them, feinting to move one way and then another. A panicky feeling cramped Daisy's chest; she snatched up a piece or bread and threw it at Jeremy's head, but before he could fling it back at her she had seized the distraction as an opportunity to escape and fled up the corridor, banging the door like a challenge behind her.

She was in the bedroom, her eyes alight with mischief as she struggled unsuccessfully to shove the dresser across to barricade the door against him. He pushed in easily and lunged. She darted around the bed, but he caught her around the waist and pulled her down on to the coverlet, pinning her wrists in his grip, eerily reminded of that party when she had hidden from him in Rhys's room and he had tussled with her on the bed. 'Remember that night? I wanted you then – my God, how I wanted you. There was something so unbelievably erotic about that fur rug and you. . . . One day, I promise, we'll have a fur bedcover exactly like that one and I'll make love to you on it until you're begging me to stop. It'll be like making love on a huge sleeping animal.'

'Speaking of huge animals,' said Daisy, 'I thought we were discussing how unsatisfying lovemaking can be. What makes you think I'd even let you begin?'

'You'll change your mind very soon,' he vowed. 'I can read your future, respectable lady doctor, and I can tell you right now that it's filled with lovemaking. Extremely satisfying, gorgeous lovemaking. Passionate, beautiful, exciting—'

'You're sure of yourself, aren't you?' she said in voice that was not quite steady.

He gazed into her eyes. Her face was still flushed from the heat of the bath, and tendrils of hair, still damp from the steam, clung to her brow. Her eyes were lustrous and huge, the expression in them unreadable. He said quietly: 'I'm sure of *us*. I love you, Daisy, and I want to be with you. No,' he said as she closed her eyes, 'don't shut me out. I need you.'

'I'm afraid,' confessed Daisy.

'So am I,' he told her. 'I want you so much, and I love you so desperately that the power of it terrifies me.' Very slowly he began to undress her.

She was unbuttoned to the waist. He held his breath as his hand slipped over her silky shoulder and down under the lacy-edged camisole to cup her breast. His thumb caressed her nipple, making it tingle. She smiled drowsily at him. He said: 'When I was about five years old Pa gave Mom a valuable porcelain statue of a shepherd in a blue suit. He had a crook in one hand and a lamb cradled in the curve of his arm. She put it on the piano in the front room and, do you know, that statue fascinated me. I had to touch it. Sure, I knew I wasn't supposed to, but I couldn't resist getting up on the piano-stool and reaching out for it, and time after time Mom or one of the servants caught me just as I was on the point of toppling over. Finally it was Pa who caught me gazing at it. "Pretty, ain't it, son?" he said. "It's worth a fine heap of gold, too, I can tell you." And with that he set me on the floor and lifted the statue down and put it in my hands. You'd think that this was what I'd been wanting. Sure, I had, but the moment I found myself holding the thing I was terrified of it. Terrified I'd drop it, that somehow I would be the cause of its ultimate destruction.'

'And you're afraid of hurting me, too?'

He nodded.

She smiled at him. His closeness, the suffused adoration on his face and the eroticism of his touch had banished the future for her. There was only Now. . . . Now was all that mattered. She was dizzy, light-headed from the excitement of what was happening to her, and in her belly was packed a smouldering tension. With a faint flush of shame she realized that she was greedily hungry for what was about to happen. 'You talk too much,' she heard herself say with harshness. 'Let's make love.'

It was much better this time, as they both knew it would be. In bed, between sheets so cold that they made her gasp and cling to Jeremy's warm body, she gave herself utterly up to him. It was so much more luxurious with all her skin sensually against all his skin. She marvelled at how silky masculine skin could feel. She knotted her hands behind his shoulderblades and tucked her feet around the backs of his knees, warmer now and relaxing, as unashamed as a cat stretching and purring in front of a fire. He clasped her buttocks, and his hands were cushions of warmth between her and the sheets as he tilted her hips so that their bodies fitted snugly together, jolting in a movement that was easy, almost friendly at first, but then gradually grew more frantic and then more intense still until instead of lying back and enjoying the experience in a self-centred way Daisy was clinging to him and thrusting up against him and uttering ragged scraps of meaningless sound, forward and upward and soaring into uncharted space and finally tumbling over into a vast melting, throbbing silence.

After a long time Jeremy stirred, propping himself up on to one elbow while he gazed down into her face. Her cheeks shone in the lamplight with a moisture that might have been perspiration or tears. He kissed her brow and smoothed her cheek with a fingertip, feeling the muscles under the skin move as she smiled. 'You're happy now, aren't you?' he whispered, and he smiled, too, when she said: 'Happy? Oh, Jeremy, *happy* is such a weak frail word for what I'm feeling now. Is it always like this?'

'It will be for us,' he told her.

She woke to hear water gurgling in the pipes and the splash of the bath-taps through the wall, and her first thought was irritation at herself for drifting off to sleep when she had resolved to stay awake all night so as not to miss one single minute of this precious interlude. The room was cosy, warmed by the still-burning fire. Outside birds were scratching and twittering in the trees. The closed curtains were dappled with sunshine. It was late. The splashing stopped, and Daisy heard Jeremy murmuring to himself as he stepped into the water. He began to sing. Daisy wanted to go in to him but she was too happy to move. She closed her eyes, feeling drowsy with contentment, his voice lapping at her like warm water.

When she opened her eyes again it was to see him standing beside the bed, a milk-coloured towel bunched around his waist, his chest and shoulders bare. He looked so wholesome and strong that her heart gave a little lurch, already aching for the night that had gone. He was in a good mood, laughing aloud as he grabbed the bedclothes with his free hand and tried to strip them from her while she clung to them, squealing with pretended alarm.

He succeeded, of course, then his hands were on her body and his mouth tracing a cool breathy path from her neck down to her breasts and beyond. He smelt of floral-scented soap, his hair was crisp-clean and damp between her fingers as she tried to restrain him.

'No, please,' she insisted, embarrassed by the contrast between her own stale body and his fresh skin. When he paused to remark that she was utterly delectable the way she was she tugged his towel free and laughed because he made an instinctive gesture, reaching to cover himself with both hands. Pulling at his fingers, she said: 'Let me . . . let me do this.' The enormity of her boldness startled her. Her fingers tingled on the warm flatness of his belly as she traced the stripe of crisp black curls that crested like waves around the root of his penis. Cold reality had no place here, she thought as she drew the fingers of one hand along the shaft and massaged them gently over the rounded tip. He stood very still, so still that she wondered what he was thinking as he stared down at the top of her head.

Suddenly she did something that tangled the breath in the back of his throat and made his heart teeter crazily. In an almost casual fashion she opened her lips and took the tip into her mouth. He could feel her tongue flickering on the sensitive ridge beneath while her hand crept between his legs and gently cupped his testicles. Then, when he thought his lungs would rupture from the pressure of held breath she lay back against the pillow and gazed up artlessly into his face. 'It's not real, you see?' she said. 'This is all something that never should have happened. Perhaps in a few days or a few weeks it will seem as if it never did.'

Her words stunned him more than her actions had done. 'Oh God, Daisy,' he whispered, and slumped against her, his face in her neck. 'Daisy, you're wrong. You're not the most important thing in the world to me – you *are* the world to me. If you think even for a minute that I'm going to let you escape from me now, you're wrong.'

She was silent. Presently what felt like a long sigh trembled through her body, then another. When Jeremy raised his head to look into her face he saw that she was crying. He shook her by the shoulders.'Stop this, Daisy. We should be overjoyed. We should be celebrating a lifetime of ecstatic happiness together. Yes, that's what we should be doing.' He grabbed the towel and whipped it around his waist before leaving the room. When he returned he was carrying a bottle of champagne and two tulip goblets. By now Daisy's tears were flowing steadily. Panicking, Jeremy tried to cheer her by making a great show of opening the bottle. 'It's not a proper celebration without champagne. Now, sit up,' he instructed, handing her a foaming glass. As she shakily accepted it a dribble of champagne trickled down on to one breast. Jeremy bent his head to lick it up, and only then did she laugh. He gazed up at her, relief in his eyes. 'I can't bear it, you know. That frightened me, to see you crying when we should be so happy. And', he added sternly, 'I can't bear to listen to gloomy nonsense, either, about this not being real. Of course it's real! The fulfilment of a dream, sure, but don't hold that against it.' She was shaking her head at him over the bubbled rim of her glass, so he persisted: 'Furthermore, this is our future, Daisy. You and me, together for always now.' He rocked back on his heels and took a sip of champagne, grinning as he tried to evoke her response.

If they had drunk this toast last night, she could easily have joined in with enthusiasm to equal his, but by now the coldness of reality had settled over her. She stared into the flickering grate and shook her head. 'If only that could be so. But it can't. It's—'

He said eagerly: 'But you want me, don't you? You want to be with me, and for us to build a life together?'

'Of course I do. But don't you see—?'

'Then we'll have each other! We'll have our life together!' Placing his glass on the bedside table, he cupped her face in his hands and gazed earnestly into her eyes. 'Don't you understand, Daisy? You and I, we're the lucky ones! We know what we want out of life, and that's why we'll get it. Knowing what you want is the secret.'

She failed to be cheered. 'How can you talk like that, Jeremy? You've got other people to consider . . . a wife and family. You can't simply pretend they don't exist!'

'Why not? She's been pretending I don't exist for years,' Jeremy flung back with uncharacteristic bitterness. Immediately he was remorseful. 'I'm sorry. That was untrue, and unkind.'

'I'm sorry, too,' said Daisy, seeing that her words had stung him. 'I know things haven't been easy for you and Arabella.'

'They're ending easily, though.' He chose his words with care, not at all certain how she would react to talk of divorce. 'You'd have heard how Mr Martin bought his house back at the tax auction? Well, I helped him do that – at considerable sacrifice, might I add. I've had to sell almost everything I own to bail him out, but it was worth it. I did it for Arabella, you see.'

'I don't see.'

'It was in return for an amicable divorce. She's giving me grounds – desertion, abandonment. . . . It'll take five or six years to be made final, but the marvellous thing is, everybody is happy about it. We've had a full discussion with the lawyers, Arabella, her folks and my folks. Look, nobody was ever happy about this marriage, and Arabella's breaking her neck to get out of it, too. She's promised to make no demands of any kind. I tell you, she's happy.'

'There's one very important person you haven't mentioned yet,' said Daisy slowly, thinking of the sick little boy who said: 'Papa is sad a lot of the time.'

'That's because he's being kept well out of things,' Jeremy told her. 'I wish I could report that Arabella and I fought for possession of Silas, but I'm afraid that isn't so. I hoped that when she was faced with the prospect of losing him she'd suddenly realize that the boy meant somehing to her after all, but she agreed so readily to give him up that the lawyer was shocked. When he made some comment she shrugged and said that she was never meant to be a mother and it was hypocritical to pretend otherwise.'

'In a way, I admire her honesty,' said Daisy, who was too appalled to trust herself to say anything else. Seeing Jeremy's expression, she added: 'She may grow more attached to him when he's older.' But inwardly she was weeping. Poor boy! Poor darling little boy! How could anyone turn her back on a delightful child like Silas? Cautiously she ventured: 'How is Silas taking all this?'

Jeremy poured himself more champagne. 'Fortunately, very well. He's never had a lot to do with Arabella, and he's content with the notion of seeing her once a month for a few days in the country. He's over the moon, though, about moving to Georgia, and my mom is equally ecstatic. She's always spoiled him rotten, so I'm going to have to be stern with her, I can see that. Hagley Avenue is being sold, of course, so I'll be back at Georgia, too. So you see? Happy families again. Let me top up your glass . . . and let's have that toast. . . . To us, and a wonderful future.'

She tried to smile at him, marvelling at the way he sought to tidy everything away with a few deft decisions. He made it all sound so smooth and easy – everybody smiling, everybody happy. Only it wasn't as simple as he argued. Her heart ached. If only they could stay here for ever, shut the world out and be content with each other. 'I love you so,' she whispered. 'Oh Jeremy, I do love you.'

'There's my girl,' he smiled, clicking the rim of his glass against hers.

'That's the trouble,' said Daisy soberly. 'I'm not your girl, Jeremy. I'm a respectable, eminent lady physician with a position in the community to maintain.'

'Which is why this job application of yours is a stroke of good fortune. If you move to Wellington, it means we can see each other regularly. We can be together here whenever I come up to Wellington. I know that five years is a long time, dearest, but knowing that we have each other will help the days pass quickly.'

The ache in her chest intensified. How beautifully easy he made it sound, and how tempting. Idyllic trysts, the spice of secrecy and ecstatic reunions, their passions always whetted by hunger and the pain of separation. But could she live what would be, in effect, a double life?

Placing the glass beside his, she drew him down so that they lay together. She stroked his dear face as she said: 'If only we could. . . . If only.'

'Of course we can!' Propping himself up on his elbows, he searched her face. 'I still haven't convinced you, have I?'

'You weren't living in Canterbury when I was young, but you may be

307

aware that for years there was scandal, terrible scandal, about Papa and Lisabeth.'

'Sure. Who hasn't heard about that?' He shrugged. 'But they're married now, and—'

'Please, darling.' She placed a finger on his lips. 'I knew about that scandal when I was very young. I read one of those filthy pamphlets that they sell in the Canfield Street market. I know there are always people willing to write such vile things and people willing to buy them, and most of their targets are big enough and broad-shouldered enough to ignore the spiteful lies; but I was only a little girl, and it distressed me terribly to read that Rhys Morgan was a wicked adulterer and that he and his whore would burn in hell's fires for eternity. It wasn't so much seeing those words that distressed me; it was the thought of half the province reading them and sniggering at Papa behind his back. And laughing at me, too.'

'They wouldn't have been laughing at you.'

'I realize that now, but at the time I imagined that they were. Things seem so intense to children, don't they? For years I actually hated Papa and Lisabeth for bringing shame on us all, and when they married I hated them all the more for openly flaunting what they'd been doing. It seemed to give validity to all the accusations. They harmed themselves, they hurt Lisabeth's husband and made him a laughing-stock, too, and they certainly hurt me.'

'But surely now you can understand that Rhys and Lisabeth were only human. Surely now you can't condemn them for loving each other.'

'How could I, in view of what we've done? No, I don't condemn them, but I do bear the scars of that time. Hatred is a very corrosive thing. Sometimes I even wonder if those early feelings have stopped me from trying to effect a reconcilation between Papa and Andrew. Maybe by standing back I'm punishing Papa for all the anguish he caused me. You see? It's not a straightforward situation, Jeremy. I've had enough gossip in my life, and I dread the prospect of any more. I'm not prepared to take that risk.'

He looked stricken. 'You can't be saying no to me! I'll be discreet. I'll protect you, Daisy. I promise you on my life that there won't be a breath of scandal about us.' But as he spoke he recalled Watkins's quickening of interest when a companion was mentioned, and wondered how long it would be before news of this past night leaked out. Unless he smuggled Daisy out very carefully, someone would be sure to see her and it would be all over town by this evening.

She said: 'There already has been gossip about us. Fortunately nothing much, but talk just the same.'

'So what? We love each other. Darling, let's face up to them, then. Ride it out. We can—'

'Oh, darling. . . . What about Silas? In a year or so he'll be old enough to understand if people gossip about his papa. He'll be distraught when he hears things like I did: "What's the difference between Lisabeth Nye and an old mattress? You can get more sleep on an old mattress but it's not half as much fun!" That kind of thing.'

'Oh God,' groaned Jeremy, nuzzling into her neck. 'Please don't talk like this, Daisy. When I think of the alternative, not to see you at all, it scares the wits out of me.' He drew her hand up to his mouth and placed a kiss in her palm. 'I can't lose you now. I can't even bear the thought.'

She closed her eyes. Her lips trembled. Jeremy closed her fingers over the kiss and said: 'We could go away together until everything is settled. We could go to America and live there as man and wife. Nobody would know the truth, nobody would care. Or to Canada. You'd love Canada. The plains are dizzying, the sky is so deep it makes your head spin, and at night the stars are so bright you could reach up and pluck one down. Silas would love Canada, too,' he added in answer to her unspoken question.

There must be a way, she thought, and for the first time that morning a glow of optimism melted some of the gloom. But there were still so many obstacles. Could she practise medicine in Canada? How would Arabella react to having Silas taken out of New Zealand? They couldn't hope to avoid a scandal here simply by running away – or could they? Opening her eyes, she met Jeremy's gaze, so tender and full of hope that her heart swelled and the painful ache vanished.

'You will?' asked Jeremy. 'You will come abroad with me?'

'Let me think about it,' Daisy pleaded. 'And, in the mean time, if I'm not to be late for this appointment—'

'There's plenty of time,' Jeremy said, his hand cupping a breast, his thumb teasing the nipple. 'I have to make love to you again first.'

'You *have* to?'

'My life depends on it,' he said gravely, but with a twinkle of repressed humour in his eyes.

'How so?' She reached out and smoothed the straying lock of hair from his brow.

'I'd kill myself if I didn't,' he said, laughing as he poised to kiss her. 'Call me an opportunist if you must, but I can't pass up a chance like this. I love you, Daisy. Have you any idea how much I love you?'

'I have a faint suspicion,' she told him.

TWENTY-NINE

'I THINK SHE'S INVOLVED with a man,' mused Beatrice as she watched Daisy wandering in the garden. 'Look at her! She can't keep still, and she seems to be fretting.' At that moment Daisy turned, saw she was being observed and started guiltily. 'Mmm,' said Beatrice, fingering her triple strand of pearls. 'I wonder who he could be?'

'What nonsense, Bea!' grumped Kiki, who was puzzling over an ancient *Times* editorial about the state of the River Thames. 'What utter rot you dredge up at times. After that obnoxious dog of hers was killed she mooched about with a face as long as a maharaja's elephant's earring, and you were sure then she was pining over some man. If you ask me, she's wondering whether to accept that post in Wellington; and, if *she* asks me, she's a fool to take it. This is her home, and this is where she belongs.' He rapped his cane on the parquet floor to show that the problem, in his opinion, was solved.

'When does she have to make her decision?' asked Bea with a frown. 'Oh, I do hope she decides against it.'

'Of course she will,' Kiki said. 'Lot of fuss about nothing.'

'Mmm,' said Bea anxiously, still stroking her pearls. She had never seen Daisy like this before, so on edge, so deeply worried. 'I'm sure it's a man,' she repeated, but quietly so that her husband wouldn't hear her. Whoever he was, it was obvious he wasn't making her angel happy. She wondered if there was anything she could do.

Andrew and Sarah noticed her preoccupation, too. 'It could be anything,' she said, speaking with listless indifference, for her own sparkle had been swamped in the petty malaises of pregnancy. She held her stockinged feet up to the grate, examining her puffy ankles. Only five more weeks and no Seaview, no more hours of walking the stone corridors.

'Do you think she'll take that Wellington position?'

310

'Ask her, why don't you?' snapped Sarah, sick of the subject. Relenting, she said: 'I'm sorry. I know how much it means to you if she stays and, frankly, I'll benefit, too. If we women are to succeed in carving out careers, it won't be by running away; and if Daisy makes a fist of it, then it's easier for any woman coming along behind her. We're trail-blazers, like the early American pioneers.' She hugged his arm. 'Now, are you and Daisy coming to the Seaview picnic on Saturday? Basil has promised to wait the porkers' luncheon especially so that you can watch them say Grace. A special command performance for you and Daisy.'

'I wouldn't miss it.' He kissed the top of her head. 'Now, what do you want for Christmas? I know it's some way off, but in your delicate condition you're entitled to a double gift this year. What do you say?'

'You know what I want,' said Sarah, staring at the flames.

'Not that again.'

'Yes, *that* again!' Spoken with a pleading upward glance. 'You're all so stubborn, Andrew! You and Daisy and him, too, because I'm sure he'd be delighted to know he's about to become a grandfather. Blood tells, Andrew, so please do it for the baby. Just a short friendly note. It wouldn't hurt.'

Andrew imagined Rhys's snort of scorn, the crumpled paper being tossed into the fire. Rhys would think he was trying to worm his way into the family to see what he could get out of it. 'I can't do it.'

'You mean you won't!'

Wearily, 'All right, then, I won't. Not yet, Sarah. Not while we're so poor. Once we're established, and so firmly on our feet that there can be no question in anybody's mind about us wanting something . . . then we'll see.'

'That could be never.' Suddenly Sarah saw the drawbacks of pregnancy: her lost position, their lost income. 'Oh, please, Andrew, won't you reconsider—?'

'For once and for all,' expostulated Andrew. Getting up, he stalked off to bed, leaving her staring cold-eyed into the fire.

'Daisy, it's me,' came Jeremy's voice over the wires. And after a pause: 'Daisy, are you there?'

She nodded, Leopold's footsteps stilled, then pattered away towards the morning room. He had ears as sensitive as an antelope's. 'Yes, I'm here,' said Daisy in response to the repeated question. 'You promised you wouldn't do this.'

'You sound angry.'

A helpless laugh. Angry? How could she be when she was so starving for a glimpse of him, for a single spoken word, that every minute away from him was agony. 'I'm not angry.' Her voice shook. Looking down at where her free hand rested on a chair-back, she saw that her whole body was trembling like a tree under an axe.

'Have you been thinking about your decision?'

'About nothing else.' Her initial shock over, she was eager for details. Where was he standing while he made this call? Was he at Georgia? In the Hagley Avenue house? Or even out at Mists of Heaven where he was spending the night before tomorrow's big race meeting? What was he wearing? Was that lock of hair flopping over his brow? Was he smiling as he spoke to her? *Jeremy, I want you*, she cried silently. *I want to see you, to be with you. I can't bear this separation.* But, mindful that anything uttered on the telephone could be overheard by the operator or by anyone else sharing the line, she said: 'I haven't yet come to a firm decision.'

'You're tormenting me,' came his voice, low and insistent. 'Sunday. Remember what you promised.'

'Yes, Sunday.' Replacing the receiver with an unsteady hand, she hurried out into the garden where she sat hunched on a bench under the willow tree, facing but not seeing the river, not noticing the ducks which floated hopefully in her direction. What should she do? It was almost three weeks since Wellington, a week since she had been offered the post, but she was no closer to tidying the confusion in her mind. Obstacles littered every path at the crossroads; the future was obscured and dark. To accept the Wellington offer seemed the most obvious solution, but the job itself threatened to be a dismal one with none of the daily contact with families that made being a doctor so rewarding. Five years of that could seem like a prison sentence, and how often could she see Jeremy before scandal erupted, scandal that could cost her her job? Canada was the most tempting prospect, but could she work there and, if not, would they survive? Jeremy had breezily talked of 'finding employment', but times there were hard with tens of thousands out of work. Besides, they had no resources to fall back on. Arabella had literally cost Jeremy every penny he owned. The idea of being together was bliss – she ached at the thought of waking up beside him every morning – but would poverty sour their love? Jeremy thought not, but Daisy wasn't so sure. 'All that matters is us,' he told her. 'The only aim is for us to be together . . . for always.'

'A penny for your thoughts,' came Kiki's voice beside her, and she glanced up guiltily to see him leaning on his cane. 'An unoriginal challenge, my dear, but pertinent nevertheless, hey? May I sit down?' He took his place next to her and whacked at a withered daffodil with his cane. 'Fact is, Bea thinks you're troubled about something. I wondered if you might like to talk it over with me. Being an old magistrate means that a little of the world's wisdom has rubbed off on me, though Bea would say precious little, hey?'

Daisy smiled at him, touched by the effort he was making. 'I'm fine . . truly. A little anxious about whether I should accept this Inspector of Factories job, that's all.'

'Rubbish!' he declared, reverting to his true self at once. 'You don't want a twopenny-halfpenny position like that. The insulting salary they offer, I'm surprised that you entertained the notion for one day, let alone this long. You're a sensible lass, and sensible folk know where they belong. You belong right here, hey? Mind you, one day a suitable fellow will come along and then nobody will be prouder and happier than me and Bea, seeing you happily married.'

Daisy said nothing. Without looking at him she was aware of his analytical gaze as he stared at her from under his snow-white eyebrows. She hoped her calm demeanour was giving nothing away.

Satisfied that romance wasn't at the base of her problems, Kiki said, 'Then, it's settled,' and stood up to leave.

Daisy didn't know whether to laugh or cry.

'Sarah said that the inmates are particularly fond of sweets, so I've brought a huge boxful of chocolate fudge and another of peanut brittle,' exclaimed Daisy next morning when Andrew collected her at the front gate of Benares. She giggled. 'I didn't have the faintest notion of how to go about brewing the wretched stuff, so I borrowed one of Aunt Bea's old *Women in the Colonies* books – you should read the medical section! Leeches for *absolutely everything*! – found some recipes and set out all the ingredients on the bench. When Albert saw me donning an apron in his spotless domain he clasped his turban with both hands in horror.' She grinned. 'He'd never have made the sweets for me if I'd asked him outright, but this way he was only too glad to shoo me out of his kitchen. He makes delicious fudge, too. Careful with that box; it's our picnic lunch,' she said, climbing up into the trap. 'This should be fun – if it doesn't rain.' She glanced over to where the mountains were screened behind a sold grey hedge. 'I sound like Mrs Tenks! She could always be relied on for gloomy forecasts for any event.'

'It'll be fine out at the asylum,' speculated Andrew, glad to see that she was so cheerful. 'Before she left this morning Sarah reminded me that I'm to be your partner for the three-legged race. She's excused, of course, and she's afraid one of the less docile of the inmates might claim you as his partner.'

'Thanks! That was thoughtful of her.'

'She cares about you,' Andrew said, flapping up the reins. 'She told me that when she stopped to buy some oranges at a stall in the market the other day she heard two women discussing you. One said: "She's ever so nice, that Doctor Morgan. Don't speak down to yer, like, for all that she's a toff." And the other one said: "Not like that Doctor

Meakings 'oo makes yer think yer scum. An' the way 'e pokes an' prods wif 'is cold 'ands!'' ' Andrew rolled his eyes. 'So, you see, you're gaining quite a following. It's been slow, but you'll get there.'

'I don't know why you're telling me this,' said Daisy, though she knew very well. Neither Andrew nor Sarah had mentioned the Wellington position – and she appreciated their tact – but it was plain that neither wanted her to go. That knowledge sat heavily on her determinedly cheerful spirits. Today was picnic day, she had declared when she woke. The decision had to be made tomorrow, but for today she would clear her mind, resolve not to think of it, and hope that the complete rest from worry might make her situation seem clearer.

Andrew was saying, 'I thought you'd like to know you're highly thought of around town,' a remark which caused another pang of guilt. *I won't think of it*, she told herself again. *Now is not the time to reflect on people's opinions, and how they would alter if they knew the truth.*

'That's nice,' she said absently, pretending indifference. They drove in companionable silence through town, the only sound being the hollow clopping of hoofs on the cobblestones. As by now it was Saturday mid-morning the shops were shuttered and the streets almost empty, with only a few clusters of children playing marbles on the dirt footpaths and an occasional stray dog snuffling through the rubbish in the gutters.

'I've never seen the town so deserted,' remarked Daisy. 'Surely everybody isn't going to the asylum's picnic!'

Andrew laughed. 'Much more prosaic than that. The races, they're the big attraction. Surely you haven't forgotten.'

'It slipped my mind.'

'It's being heralded as a rivalry between Rhys and Jeremy Drake. The newspapers are full of it. For the big race they're both entering offspring from that Donegal. Mists of Donegal has the edge; it's being tipped as favourite, but I hope that Jeremy's Donegal Prince trounces it. After all, Donegal was the Drakes' horse to begin with, but they've never had quite the same luck as Rhys with its offspring. Maybe today will be a turning-point in Jeremy's luck. He's—'

She had to stop him. Mention of Jeremy was filling her head with suffocating, aching thoughts. Quickly she said: 'Do you mind very much? Do you mind missing out?'

'Missing out?' He reined in to give way to a wagon that was coming out of the grain and farm supplies store and on to the narrow bridge ahead of them.

'Mists of Donegal is Papa's horse. It's a big day for him today, and by rights you should be there to share it with him. You should be in the owners' stand, you should be checking the horse over beforehand and opening the champagne afterwards.'

'Easy on, Daisy! I know nothing about horses and I've no interest in racing.'

Normally she would have let that claim pass unchallenged, but a fresh idea was rising in her mind. Andrew and Sarah were letting no opportunity pass without subtly letting her know that they needed her and wanted her to stay, and if she did leave it would be with the added burden of knowing that she was letting them down; but should by some miracle a reconciliation be forged with Rhys, then she would no longer be so desperately needed. Mists of Heaven would fill a gap in their lives. She said: 'You read all about the race in the paper, didn't you? You must have been interested. Andrew, it's time that something was done to jolt Papa out of his obstinacy. Wouldn't it be lovely for Sarah if, when the baby arrived—'

'You sound exactly like she does,' said Andrew in a huffy tone. 'If Rhys Morgan wants to be aloof and arrogant, then that's perfectly fine with me.'

You're as stubborn as each other, thought Daisy in exasperation. Refraining from comment, she watched the approaching wagon, which seemed to be taking forever to cross the bridge. Under the span the Avon was almost a solid mass of watercress. Two Maori children in men's jackets with rolled-up sleeves crouched on the far bank with flax baskets while a man waded to his waist in the greed sward, harvesting bunches with sweeps of a huge black cutlass. Daisy wondered if he was cold. The wind was freshening, and there was a decided nip in the air.

'It's that bastard Tommy Nevin,' exclaimed Andrew suddenly.

'He wouldn't go in the water, not with that peg-leg,' said Daisy, then she realized that he meant the driver of the wagon which was right abreast of them now as he lumbered off the bridge.

He must have heard Andrew's comment, for his scowl deepened. Flat cap pulled low over his narrow brow, he snapped his whip over the backs of two listless-looking horses. He must have seen Daisy and Andrew but he stared straight ahead.

'He's not getting a day off anyway,' remarked Andrew.

'No,' said Daisy, who felt sorry for Tom despite the nastiness he'd displayed towards her. He'd been such a fine young man once, big and strong, the world before him on a platter, and look at him now, grubbing for menial wages at White Clouds. She said: 'I believe that things are seriously wrong with the "Baron". The Government has put a lien on his property, and he'll lose everything unless he can pay his taxes. I do hope the rumours aren't true. "Baron" Windsor has been at White Clouds as long as I can remember. If he goes, part of the history of the province will disappear for ever.'

'Not the most illustrious part,' said Andrew drily. He, too, had heard the rumours, how 'Baron' Windsor and Rhys had almost come to blows outside the Bank of New Zealand in Cashel Street. He said: 'I believe that his problems could be solved overnight if Rhys Morgan would buy his sheep for process through his freezing works. The "Baron" i putting it about that Rhys won't buy them because he wants to se White Clouds bankrupted, so that then he can pick up the entire estat for a pittance and add it to Mists of Heaven.'

'That can't be true!' scoffed Daisy.

'It's harsh, but it's what people are saying,' Andrew told her.

She swivelled her head to watch Tom Nevin's disappearing figure 'It's utter nonsense! Not only would Papa refuse to buy that land – it' not a patch on his own place – but there's a far more practical reaso why he wouldn't buy the "Baron" Windsor's sheep for meat. His flock are so riddled by disease and so neglected that the Maoris won't eve *steal* them! Kikorangi once told me that when they need meat for hangi* they pay Papa for a couple of his sheep rather than help them selves to the strays that are always wandering through the broken fence from White Clouds. His sheep are so tough as to be inedible!'

Andrew shrugged, and said: 'We have half an hour to spare. Let' stop by at Joseph and Emma Day's place on the way over, shall we?'

'Good idea,' agreed Daisy. They were already within sight of the littl cottage – it looked very white under the dark lowering sky – but as the approached they saw that traps, carts and gigs were lined up along bot sides of the street, while people hurried on foot towards the gate carrying baskets covered with starched dish-towels. 'We forgot th date!' exclaimed Daisy. 'I don't believe we could be so remiss! It' Joseph Day's presentation day . . . it must be! Someone told me tha he's been serving the community for thirty years now, so all of Sumner i giving a party to celebrate. Isn't that lovely? We must pop in to wis him well and offer congratulations—' She broke off, clutching Andrew's arm. 'Drive on quickly,' she hissed. 'I just saw Lisabeth at the window. If she's there, Papa is certain to be there, too.'

'No,' said Andrew. 'You should just go in and pretend you don' know they're there; just meet them accidentally, as it were, and see wha happens. I know you've vowed not to set foot on Mists of Heaven unti I'm acknowledged, but surely this is different?'

'It *is* neutral ground,' allowed Daisy, but she shook her head. 'No. Our father is perfectly capable of stopping by the offices if he ever wants to see us. He hasn't written to us once, in all this time.'

Andrew gaped at her. 'But not ten minutes ago you were saying that something should be done to jolt Rhys Morgan out of his complacency.'

I'm a coward, thought Daisy miserably. *A coward and too cowardly to admit it.* She wanted reconciliation, but the prospect of facing her

*Feast

316

father – and the certainty of his scorn or wrath – made her shiver with apprehension. Lamely she said: 'I know I said that, and I'm sorry, but it hurts me, Andrew, that he hasn't telephoned or sent a card to wish us luck . . . . He didn't even congratulate me when I graduated from medical college. If he cared the tiniest jot about either of us, he'd. . . . he'd. . . .'

Andrew was shocked. 'I had no idea you felt so upset.'

Daisy shook her head, dashing the tears away with the backs of her hands. 'I didn't know, either,' she said frankly. 'It's strain, I suppose.' And then in a deliberate diversion she said: 'Look at that beautiful clematis, there, up in the hills. Isn't it spectacular? Do promise me you'll stop on the way home so that I can dig up a root of it. Wouldn't it look heavenly twining around our veranda?'

'Yes, it would,' agreed Andrew, but he looked at her with concern as the wagon climbed the winding road up to the high saddle between the hills. He wished he could give that arrogant Rhys Morgan a piece of his mind.

Inside the house Emma Day was cuddling baby Anne while she showed Lisabeth the gigantic cake that had been iced for the occasion with symbols illustrating Joseph's many accomplishments. There was a life-buoy, a policeman's helmet, a fishing net, a depiction of the signals used to inform shipping of the condition of the bar, and an iced picture of the gold and silver cup Joe and his brother Alf had won with their racing cutter *Red Jacket*.

'And there's even a picture of your cottage with the family lined up beside it,' enthused Lisabeth. 'Look, Theodora, isn't this just the prettiest cake you ever saw?'

'When are we going home?' asked Theodora.

Lisabeth rolled her eyes in helpless exasperation, for her older girl had been deliberately awkward ever since Anne arrived and took the spotlight of attention away from her. Seeing the predicament, Emma said, 'Josephine!' and her third daughter, a pale fourteen-year-old with tendrils of dark blonde hair, came over to answer the summons. 'Where is Nina, dear? She might like to play with Theodora.'

'Of course, Mamma,' said Josephine dutifully, though Theodora was not liked by the gently bred Day girls. Theodora was used to getting her own way at all times; she snatched things rather than asking politely, and if she couldn't get her own way she bellowed until, to quieten her, the others gave in. Josephine said: 'We were going to go up the creek to catch *koura*.* Is that all right, Mamma?'

'Who else is going with you?'

'The Morris children are coming. And Arthur Saley. He wants to know if we can take two buckets, please, Mamma.'

*Yabbies, freshwater crayfish

317

'*Two* buckets! There's optimism for you!' smiled Emma. 'They'll be quite safe,' she reassured Lisabeth. 'Arthur is a sensible fellow, and Bella Morris is almost sixteen. Yes, you may take the buckets.' She cooed and chuckled at Anne when they had gone. 'I do envy you, Lisabeth! Sometimes I long for another baby. It would have been so satisfying to give Joseph a son, but I fear the Lord has deemed otherwise. Still, Joseph maintains he's happy to be surrounded by women.'

'Rhys never complains, either,' Lisabeth told her. 'I forgot to ask you. Is it convenient if Jeremy Drake comes with Rhys after their race? Jeremy was particularly anxious to come and congratulate our honoured citizen today.'

'Of course! I'll be delighted to welcome him.' She bit her lip. 'Is it true what people are whispering about him and his wife?'

'He's charging her with desertion in order to get a divorce? Yes, it's true. The papers have been served.'

'How tragic. They're such a lovely couple. I'm so sad for them both.'

'Then, don't be,' retorted Lisabeth crisply. 'Look at the predicament I was in because Athol Nye refused to grant me a divorce; I deserted him, and I pleaded with him to initiate the process, but he always refused, and not until that nasty accident. . . .'

'*You* couldn't divorce him?' Emma was fascinated. This was a subject the two friends had never touched on in their quiet moments together; and now, with the house full of people, she was suddenly opening up with details Emma had never heard before.

'That was impossible. I consulted several lawyers, but they all gave the same answer. To obtain a divorce myself I had to prove' – she glanced around, then lowered her voice because old Mrs Rule, seated on a hassock nearby, was training her ear-trumpet in their direction – 'I would have had to stand in court and swear that Athol and performed bestial acts upon me.'

'*What?*'

'It's vile, isn't it? But it's true. I couldn't have perjured myself like that, and in any case Rhys forbade it. If only Athol had agreed to sue me for desertion, Rhys and I could have been married years ago – we could have had half a dozen children by now.'

Emma said: 'I wonder if our dashing Jeremy Drake is wanting to marry someone else?' She looked calculatingly at Lisabeth's face. 'He was keen on Daisy, wasn't he?'

'Oh that was years ago. Long forgotten, I'd say. No, it's Arabella who wants the marriage to end, or so we've been told. Already Maurice Andruth is calling at Martinsfield several times a week.' She wrinkled her nose. 'It's hardly romantic. Who'd prefer pudgy dour Maurice Andruth to Jeremy Drake? Still, there's no accounting for taste, and just as well, otherwise all the ladies of the province would be setting their bonnets at Rhys Morgan!'

'No, it's Joseph Day they'd all be wanting!' Emma corrected her, and they laughed together.

The arthritis in her hands was worse today. Gwyne sat alone with her tonic wine on the enclosed porch beside her room gently massaging her fingers. The mauve of her skirt acted like a bowl, catching the sunshine in a puddle in which her sore hands bathed. Around her ankles twined one of the stable-cats. His purring strummed against her legs.

Gwynne said, 'Just you and me here today, cat,' and reached down to stroke it, sighing as she remembered Charles. He was fond of cats . . . well, he was wonderful with all animals really. He had a way with him, Charles did, and all creatures responded to his sympathetic nature.

When she saw the cart Gwynne was puzzled. It was a large flat-topped wagon carrying what looked like a few pieces of canvas and it was rolling down the road towards the wool-shed. As Gwynne watched, it stopped by the main entrance into the yards and the driver jumped down to open the gate. Gwynne frowned. Nobody would come to collect anything today, not with the biggest race-meeting of the year already under way. The whole province knew that Mists of Heaven would be deserted, for Rhys shared his interest in racehorses generously and gave all his workers time off to watch the big race and a shilling apiece to bet on the outcome.

Gwynne sipped her tonic wine while she turned this over in her mind. The wool-shed was sited where it was because of the valuable machinery and implements that were stored there. Nobody could come and go without being observed from the house, and from her favourite nook here at her window Gwynne witnessed most of the traffic that flowed to and from the large red shed. The wagon was not delivering anything; therefore it must be picking something up, and Rhys was extremely strict about the rule that nothing went out of that barn without being checked with someone in authority. So what was going on?

'Dratted nuisance,' grumbled Gwynne. 'Someone's come to borrow something, and there's nobody here but me. Dratted nuisance, I say.' Setting down her half-empty tumbler, Gwynne tugged her shawl around her shoulders and, leaving the cat settling down on her just-vacated chair, she set off, hobbling down across the path and past the mansion's huge vegetable gardens.

Tom Nevin was sweating as he wrestled with the bolts on the huge doors to the wool-store, and as he wrestled with them he swore under his breath. There was no sign of the 'Baron' yet, and if he wanted the Mists of Heaven wool-clip stolen, then at least he could show up, as agreed, with his team of blackfellows, to help load the stuff on to the wagon. How was Tom supposed to manhandle these enormously heavy bales of wool by himself?

The doors groaned open. Panting, Tom stared at the towering stack of bales. Each was stamped with the distinctive Mists of Heaven logo – mountain peaks piercing a fleecy cloud – and each contained prime long stapled wool worth upwards of a hundred pounds.

The plan, concocted by Tom and the 'Baron' together, was simple and effective. The wool-clip would be taken and rebaled at White Clouds then shipped quickly to Wellington by coastal barge, where its sale had already been arranged through one of Tom's old contacts. As soon as the shed was empty it would be torched so that when Rhys arrived home he would find only a spread of charred embers. He wouldn't suffer: insurance would cover the loss of the great red barn and all its contents including the wool, while 'Baron' Windsor's predicament at White Clouds would be over. Proceeds from the sale of the stolen wool would be enough to pay his taxes and to buy new breeding rams and ewes to upgrade the condition of his flocks.

But where was the 'Baron'? According to the plan, he and half a dozen blackfellows were supposed to be already here with another wagon which should by rights have been loaded by now. Tom, meanwhile, had set off for town with the twins, and at every house along the way had sent them in with a letter announcing firewood for sale, a pretext to see who was home and who was not. Having found all the shepherds' huts empty and the farmworkers' cottages similarly deserted, he sent the two girls home to report that the countryside was deserted while alone he hurried into town to purchase two large tarpaulin covers and three drums of fuel, to accelerate the wool-shed fire, for it was important that the building went up quickly, consuming all evidence of the theft before anybody could get close enough to put it out.

Wondering what could have delayed his employer, Tom manoeuvred the horses around so that the wagon tray was close to the loading-dock. The ground here sloped away slightly, so that when the props were removed from under the wagon shafts the vehicle would move forward slowly, thus giving the horses a helping boost with that initial heavy drag.

Shaft-props were something Tom hadn't thought to bring with him. He looked around for suitable timber, and noticed that the horses were restless; even the weight of the fuel-drums pressing on the shafts was pushing them forward. He would have to get those drums off first.

It was when he was tilting the first one over the side that he heard his name called. He froze, frowning. His brow was greased with perspiration and the blood drummed in his ears as he strained against the weight, trying to balance the drum so that it would slide to the ground within the circle of his arms.

320

'Tom! Tommy Nevin! It *is* you, isn't it?' Gwynne was calling as she approached the outer webbing of sheep-pens. The sky was tumbling with dark clouds that made it difficult to see. She hoped the rain would hold off until she got back to the house. Who would think that the lovely sunshine would vanish so quickly?

Tom tensed in shock. A glance around confirmed the horrible truth, and he swore, a savage spitting with frustration. What was that dense old bat doing here? Her Charles was against gambling, he supposed, which was why she was staying back instead going off with the others.

'Tommy Nevin! What a lovely surprise! And are your two delightful girls with you today? I haven't seen them in such a long while!'

Tom felt the drum move. Too late he twisted back to deflect its course, too late he tried to step out of the way. With a crunch he could hear as well as feel the drum's lower rim landed with full force on the instep of his only foot.

He screamed, shoving the drum over, doubling up with pain as he crouched, rocking over his ankle. His crutch fell into the dirt beside him.

'Oh dear, oh dear!' cried Gwynne, hobbling closer. 'You've hurt yourself. You've *hurt* yourself! Come over to the steps and sit down, and we'll take a look at that.'

She bent to help him up, but Tom reacted furiously. What in *hell* was she doing here? If they wanted to proceed with the job now, they'd have to kill Gwynne; and, though the 'Baron' might stoop to something like murder when backed into this hopeless situation, Tom couldn't let a thing like that happen. His hatred of the Morgans didn't reach as far as Gwynne, who was a harmless old stick who, furthermore, had been kindness itself to Birdie, especially during that final illness. But right now Tom was angry with Gwynne, simply for being here, for complicating everything and for putting her stupid life in danger. As she reached towards him he struck back to push her away but, in agony and off balance as he was, he missed and struck the drum, causing it to roll slowly under the wagon.

'Don't you be a silly boy,' scolded Gwynne. 'Birdie would want me to look after you. You know she would! So come over here, and we'll sit you down and take that boot off, and—'

One of the horses whinnied in alarm and plunged forward, jostling the other horse and jolting the cart into motion. As he straightened Tom saw through the hot blur of pain that the rolling drum was nudging against the horse's back legs. Tom cursed again. Swiftly grappling to hoist the crutch under his arm, and grabbing at the wagon tray, he half-dragged, half-scrambled around to the driver's seat where he swiftly unknotted the reins and dragged on them with all his strength.

The panicked horse wouldn't be calmed, not while that drum

bumped against its legs, forcing it along. Thinking quickly, Tom decided to abort the whole scheme. Even with Gwynne's feeble help he would never be able to hoist that drum back on to the tray, not with his one foot throbbing like the furies, and should the 'Baron' arrive now Gwynne's life could be at real risk. There was nothing for it but to leave, and fast.

Gwynne's hands flapped like agitated chickens. 'Tommy! Tommy, wait! You've left something behind!'

Tom screwed his head around. 'Tull Musster Morgan thut's a guft from the ''Baron''!'

And why not? he thought as he flicked the reins. Perhaps this was one way of salvaging the situation. 'Baron' Windsor could tell Rhys he had come by some fuel, and having no use for it himself had sent it down to Rhys as a goodwill gesture. All Tom was doing was delivering the stuff, and he'd opened the wool-store doors to put it away in there.

He glanced back. The fuel-drum was resting against a post, and Gwynne stared after him, her thick spectacles dots of light on her shadowed face. As he turned back on to the road he saw, in the distance, 'Baron' Windsor's other wagon come trundling into view. If he hurried, he could head them off before Gwynne saw them, too.

It was as he snapped the reins again that the first huge drops of rain dashed into his face.

THIRTY

A FEW MINUTES LATER the rain moved across the Sumner foreshore, hissing over the Days' tin roof. Crowded into the parlour, guests listened to Joseph Day recount some of his amusing experiences as a police constable. The rain drowned his words, and he paused, waiting for it to quieten before continuing.

In the kitchen Lisabeth was pouring tea from an enormous enamel pot, while Ethel and May – elegant young ladies now – placed the cups and saucers on a tray to carry around. Lisabeth glanced up at the window when she heard the noise. 'You can't see a thing out there!' she exclaimed. Then a thought gripped her. 'Where are the children? They'll be caught in this downpour.'

Ethel had a quiet but positive voice. 'Please don't worry, Mrs Morgan. They came back some time ago. I think they're playing in the stables. We have three darling kittens nesting in the feed-box.'

Lisabeth continued pouring, but the thought that gripped her wouldn't go away; it clung with prickly little claws when she tried to brush it off. When the cups were filled she set the tea-pot down on the table and topped it up with water from the kettle on the stove, then went to stand at the window, gazing across at the grey blur of the stables.

'We were so hoping it would be a fine day, too,' said May at her elbow. She shuddered delicately. 'I do so detest the rain!'

'There you are, Lisabeth,' said Emma. 'Do come and hear this! Joseph is going to tell how he rescued Rhys and Jock McFallish on that fishing trip years ago. Remember that? I'm afraid that Joseph has taken poetic licence to make the story more amusing, but you'll love it! Do come. Mrs Rule is saving a place for you on the sofa.'

Ethel pushed her head around her mother's shoulder. 'Mrs Morgan, Anne is awake. May I pick her up, please?'

Lisabeth looked from one to the other. She seemed distracted, as if

she hadn't heard. Then she blurted: 'I'm worried about Theodora. I've
a really frightful premonition. . . .'

It was not like Lisabeth to be alarmist. Calmly Emma instructed May
to take her father's oilskin coat and put on her rubber boots, then hurry
out to the stables and check that Theodora was all right.

Seeing May's face, Lisabeth said: 'I don't want to be any trouble. I
don't want to send you out in that deluge. Emma, I'm sure everything's
all right. . . . It's just . . . I've got this nasty *feeling*, and—'

'May doesn't mind, do you, May dear?' replied Emma. Taking
Lisabeth's arm, she said: 'Joseph and the others are waiting for us. We'd
better not keep them.'

Lisabeth allowed herself to be shepherded up the corridor and obediently settled herself beside the bosomy Mrs Rule. She smiled and
clasped her hands together as Joseph began but she knew the story well
and didn't hear it this time, not really. Inside she was waiting for May,
waiting for the moment when she burst into the parlour, interrupted
her father's anecdote just as Rhys was bending over the side to bait his
hook, and announced in a breathless gasp that Theodora was missing
and that nobody knew where she was.

'May, this is not an appropriate moment for one of your jokes,' scolded
her father, brows bunched together in his sternest expression, one
usually reserved for youngsters behaving dangerously in their boats.

'It's not a joke, honest, Papa,' squeaked May.

Josephine appeared beside her, hair painted to her forehead and the
shoulders of her dress dark with wetness. 'We don't know what's happened to her. Nina and I came back from collecting *koura*, and
Theodora came with us a little way – just as far as that fallen log. Then
we heard Arthur laughing and laughing and we wondered what was so
funny. Theodora said she wanted to go back with the others, then. We
told her not to, but she wouldn't listen to us.'

'You let her go back on her own?'

'It was only a little way, truly, Papa. We thought she'd be all right,'
quavered Josephine.

'Arthur says that when he was laughing, that's because they were
setting off to play hidey-go-seek and he was the It to begin with. He was
laughing because it was going to be so easy to find the others, only he
says he never saw Theodora at all. She must have turned around to go
back and lost her way.'

Lisabeth listened with a sense of dull inevitability, and all the while
panic flooded inside her, rising higher and higher like water, floating
everything else up and spilling it out of her until the panic was all that
remained.

Joseph said: 'Tush, May! Don't be dramatic! It's perfectly likely that

324

Theodora is somewhere in the house, or even in the stable. She may be hiding somewhere right under your noses just to tease you.'

Lisabeth said in a strange voice: 'No. She *is* lost. I know it. I have this feeling, this exact same feeling. . . .' Every face in the room turned towards her. The atmosphere was electric with expectation. 'It's exactly like the time Rhys lay near death in the midst of that fire. I knew that something terrible had happened to him then . . . and I know that something has happened to Theodora now.' Her face was bone-white; there were no tears in her eyes, and her voice was steady, but those sitting near her observed that her hands were gripping each other so tightly that her nails were driven right into the flesh. She said: 'Please send for Rhys. Please. He'll know what to do.'

The picnic ended with dancing. While an accordionist played a lively reel the inmates stood in a circle clapping time while staff and invited guests moved in a circle within, taking the inmates each in turn into the centre to dance. It was exhilarating fun spiced with a sense of the unexpected. As Daisy said later, one couldn't lay wagers on whether one's partner would skip, stamp, shuffle or simply trample one's feet and not always in time to the music, either.

In between dances Daisy retreated to the comparative safety of the lemonade-stall where she sat on a wooden bench behind the two middle-aged women (both mothers of manic depressives) who were dispensing home-made, rather sticky drink in thick china cups. From there Daisy could see out across the sports-field beyond the huge bare elm trees to the ocean beyond. The sea was slate-grey, dark as the sky, yet here the sun shone and the colours seemed unnaturally bright, the grass an acid green, the inmates' clothes such vivid red stripes that they seemed Christmassy, gloriously festive.

'It's going to rain,' the women said to each other as they dipped their ladles into the lemonade-crocks. 'It's going to be a wild and miserable night.'

It was already growing chill. When Daisy, rested, rejoined the dancers she noticed that her hands were numb. She wished they could leave now, and start for home, instead of waiting for Sarah to finish her duties.

While Sarah disappeared into the grey stone building with the inmates Andrew harnessed the horses and he and Daisy sat in the trap outside the doors. Sarah was helping shut the inmates in for the night, giving them mugs of warm cocoa.

'I could do with some cocoa myself,' said Andrew. 'I'm freezing! There's snow in that wind, I wouldn't be surprised.' The observation decided him. Climbing down, he opened the shallow rear compartment and brought out the weather gear: padded covers for the horses and a buckle-on canvas screen to fit across the front of the trap. Behind that, tucked up with their lap-rugs, they should travel in dry comfort.

While he was fastening the first horse-coat the rain began, large penny-dark drops that pelted like flecks of gravel, stinging where they struck bare skin. The horses nickered and tossed their heads. Andrew said: 'Strike me pink! It's trying to hail. . . . Hold on there, my beauties, and we'll shelter in against the wall.'

By the time Sarah finally emerged the sky was so low it was like a sagging dark hammock. Sarah skipped over the puddles, her head ducked, rain beating her shoulders like a whip. Wetness ran in slicks off her coat, and she tried to wriggle into the warm between the two without bringing too much of it with her.

'What a day it's been!' she cried. 'But this rain!'

'Reminds me of Scotland,' said Andrew.

'It's *much* too violent for that! Scottish rain is like heavy mist. This is hammer-blows, sudden and slopping. Look at the sports-field. It's already a lake.' She patted Daisy's knee. 'You made a conquest today. When Brian found out that I was your sister-in-law he pleaded to be allowed to come home with me.' She laughed with faint malice. 'I'm envious. Brian has adored me unconditionally until now, but today he didn't even want to dance with me!'

She recalled Brian, tall, lumbering and fair with a lisping voice. She said: 'He kept saying: "Are you a spinster lady? I'm a bachelor, I am." He was the only one who could really dance.'

'There you are, then! A match.'

'What's wrong with him? Apart from his pathetic taste in women, that is,' teased Andrew.

'He cut his mother up with a tomahawk,' said Sarah airily.

Daisy was not sure if she was serious. When Sarah was in one of her brittle moods she often said things for effect. Tugging the rug up around her shoulders, she leaned against the damp canvas hood and closed her eyes against the peppering of fractured raindrops. There would be a fire in the drawing-room at Benares, and Albert would make her hot milk, pungent with Indian spices, and a cinnamon stick for stirring.

Rain sleeted across their path. Rain tore at the roadside bushes and battered the horses into lowering their heads. When they turned out of the Seaview gates and faced west rain drove straight in above the canvas screen. Within seconds Daisy's lips were numb and icy water was dribbling underneath her collar.

'Our bonnets will be ruined!' wailed Sarah.

Already the road was blotted with huge puddles. Above the din of rain on the hood they could hear the ghostly whoosh of running drains on either side of the road. Andrew's face was grim under its beading

326

of cold drops. 'I hope we can get across the stream,' he worried.

Daisy shivered, but Sarah snorted: 'That tiny little brook? Of course we will! No matter how rainy it is, I've never had the smallest spot of bother with any of the crossings, except perhaps the lowest one, just above Sumner.' As she spoke she became more and more thoughtful. The rainiest days had been nothing compared with this. Never before had she seen the road lying in inches of water, so that the horses had to wade. Never before had the drains boiled to overflowing. Never before had the force of the raindrops stripped leaves from the trees and flung them into the torrents below.

They rode in silence through the gathering darkness, until Andrew said; 'Well, here we are. This is our first crossing.'

It was a stony ford in the lee of steep rugged banks atop which *ponga* ferns bowed and whipped in the sheeting downpour. On the way up the hill six hours earlier the ford had been barely discernible, a sheen of greenish moisture seeping over the cemented stretch of roadway. Now it was knee-deep and raging, braided into dozens of rippled currents as it gushed, brown as treacle, from the gash in the hills above. The horses laid their ears back and twisted their necks, but Andrew forced them through. Sarah gabbled a prayer, and Daisy watched Andrew's profile; she could tell that he was seriously concerned.

There were five more crossings to come, for in its wending down from the crest of the Port Hills the road crossed and recrossed the same stream half a dozen times, four times in fords and twice, where the gully dropped away steeply, by narrow straight-sided bridges. A bridge came next; they rattled on and off that at a spanking pace, then crossed the next ford as easily as the first. Sarah began to sing an old Gaelic song they had learned in Edinburgh; and, teeth chattering, Daisy grafted her own shaking voice to the melody. They were halfway there! Sumner lay only a mile away through the gorge.

In the middle of the next ford the trap suddenly lurched sideways with a full gush of released water. Daisy screamed. She had been determined not to show fear, not to think of that other river in flood, of that beautiful clear blue day when Amy had drowned before her eyes. Her singing and her determined faith in Andrew's judgement had managed – only just – to keep the spectres at bay, but now her scream snapped the release on her terrors and when the trap rolled out on the other side of the ford she was a helpless quivering mess.

'Easy on there, Daisy,' protested Andrew. 'I can understand your nervousness, but we have to remember Sarah's condition, don't we, dearest?'

'I'm sorry,' gabbled Daisy. 'Truly I am; but, Andrew, I don't think you fully appreciate the danger. When we had our accident it happened so suddenly that—'

'Daisy, please!'

She lapsed into jittery silence. Nobody else spoke, either. It was a degree or two darker now, though not quite dark enough for carriage-lamps. Andrew hoped to leave putting those on until Sumner, and then it might not even be necessary, for it always seemed lighter out in the open than here, with the hills pressing in on both sides.

It was light enough still to see the second bridge, or what was visible of it: two spindly rails jutting only an inch or two clear of the turmoil.

'Oh, damn,' said Andrew in a hollow voice. He brought his fists up, jerking the reins to halt the horses. Bowing his forehead on to his fists, he said: 'I'm sorry, ladies, but damn, damn, *damn*!'

'We can turn back,' Sarah suggested. 'Perhaps we can carry on down to Lyttelton. There are several hotels there. We'd find beds and stabling for the horses, I'm sure.'

'Good idea,' approved Andrew.

Daisy thought about the Lyttelton road, about the river crossings down that flank of the hills. What made them think that the going would be any easier that way? She rubbed her numb face with gloved bloodless fingers. In this almost-darkness the hollow roar of the stream had a predatory starving sound that chilled her right through. Why weren't the others frightened? Surely they could see the danger, and would realize the fool-hardiness of pressing on? Daisy was afraid to keep silent and yet reluctant to speak out for fear of Andrew's rebuke.

In the end it did not matter whether she spoke or not. By the time Andrew had performed the difficult manoeuvre of turning the trap and horses on the narrow road at least ten minutes had elapsed, then five more minutes was spent travelling back to the ford where Daisy had received such a fright. In this time the darkness had pulled down tight and the stream had risen appreciably; they could hear its savage roar as they approached the last bend in the pale wet road.

Sarah plucked at Andrew's sleeve. 'Dearest, please don't take any risks . . .,' she begged. 'I'm really frightened. That flood sounds so *fierce*. . . .'

Andrew was piqued. He liked his creature comforts and had already planned to have a good roast-beef dinner at the hotel and, as a treat, a wedge of Stilton and a glass of porter. He said: 'It's all that alarmist talk; that's why you're a little hesitant. Trust me, Sarah. I know—'

'Please, Andrew. It's nothing to do with what Daisy said before. The water is higher by a long way than when we were here a few minutes ago. The roaring is much louder, and you can even feel the vibrations from it. I'm so afraid, dearest, that if we drove in at this side we might not drive out the other.' In the darkness she could feel him sulking, and she coaxed: 'Let's stop at that wide place by the bridge, where we turned around before. There are trees overhanging where the horses can shelter, and it's high enough above the flood to be safe. Please, dearest. It'll only be until first light.'

Daisy said nothing. She was careful not to, for she sensed Andrew's frustration and guessed he would funnel an outpouring of anger against her if she gave him the smallest cause. But inwardly she felt like cheering.

Joseph Day telephoned the racetrack as soon as Lisabeth asked. Unable to speak to Rhys personally, he composed a message that would convey the situation without being unduly dramatic, for despite Lisabeth's proclaimed premonition he suspected that the child would be found right here on the premises, in one of the outbuildings if not in the house itself. It wouldn't be the first time Theodora had resorted to colourful tactics to draw attention to herself, and hadn't Emma reported that Theodora felt resentful and left out since baby Anne arrived to usurp her place in the Mists of Heaven nursery?

His calm, therefore, was unfeigned. 'We're searching the house and grounds now,' he told Lisabeth as he handed her a glass of medicinal brandy.

Lisabeth turned a white terrified face up to him. She shook her head. 'She's out there in the bush, Joe. I just *know* she is.'

'Tush, now. We have to be certain of that, don't we?'

'But I *am*. . . .' She could see it was futile. Joseph Day would do everything by the book, and since he had led dozens of searches and rescues she couldn't argue with his methods even though she knew in her heart he was wrong. 'When will Rhys be here?' she asked. She sounded like a prisoner awaiting parole.

Rhys arrived in less than an hour, with Jeremy Drake. Both were drenched. Rhys's face was so cold and clammy that when he clutched Lisabeth to him and pressed his cheek against hers she felt in his chilled dead-seeming skin a vivid illustration of how it must be right now for Theodora, lost out in the weather without so much as a warm jacket to insulate her frail thin body. Clinging to Rhys, she at last began to weep, her fears spilling out of her.

He tried consolation. 'There, now, we mustn't imagine the worst. We don't really know what has happened, do we? Relax, darling, I'm sure she will be perfectly safe wherever she is.'

His voice sounded soothing, but when she drew back to search his face Lisabeth saw a terror in his eyes that matched her own.

At around midnight the rain stopped. Daisy woke, startled by the diminished noise, and saw that the cloud bank overhead was rent in places so that a cobwebby glow of moonlight showed through, enough to illuminate the others in the trap. Sarah was sound asleep, her head flung back against Andrew's shoulder and her mouth open. Her breath smelt of the coconut ice they had nibbled several hours ago. Andrew sat upright, staring straight ahead. Daisy patted his hand, and he turned to her, smiled and shook his head to indicate that she shouldn't wake Sarah. Any talking would have to be loud anyway; the roar of the river was still there, as vociferous and threatening as it had sounded when they last stood on its edge.

Andrew jerked his head in the direction of the valley below, and she turned to see what he had been staring at. The canopy of tree-tops was a black mass, but intermittently pierced by lights shining up from underneath so that branches and clumps of leaves were illuminated as silhouettes. Daisy was surprised to see signs of habitation tucked into the depths of that forest. Then she saw that the lights were moving. First one tree-top was flung into relief, then the light swung away, beamed on to another tree and painted that one yellow before moving away again. After watching for a few minutes Daisy wondered if the lights were carried by a strung-out party of road-maintenance people, searching to see if anybody was stranded, like them, on the roadway, but soon she decided that the lights were too dispersed for that. Someone must be lost in the woods.

The realization gave her a thrill of horror. To be out, and lost, in the torrential rain they had experienced would be a nightmare. Daisy and the others had suffered torments of freezing damp discomfort and they had the shelter of the trap hood and screen to shield them from the worst of it. Whoever was out there would be soaked to the skin, for the natural shelter the bushes offered would be hopelessly inadequate under the force of that lashing rain. Daisy hoped that the lost person would soon be found; she didn't like his chances of survival otherwise.

THIRTY-ONE

'SHE'LL BE ALL RIGHT,' CALLED RHYS, splashing through the downpour towards the house. 'Lovey, I'm sure she'll be safe.'

The wavering hoop of light from his lantern illuminated Jeremy's rain-slicked features as he, too, approached the doorway where Lisabeth stood gazing out through the curtain of rain. Like Rhys, Jeremy was clad in borrowed fisherman's gear: long oilskin coat, boots and a floppy-brimmed rain-hood that draped over his shoulders. Seeing the panic on Lisabeth's face, he knew that he and Rhys were right to come here to reassure her instead of going back with the other searchers to the Sumner Community Hall where first-light strategy was being planned. He said: 'Mrs Morgan, please don't alarm yourself. Theodora will have found some cosy dry shelter somewhere and she'll be curled up snug as—'

Lisabeth began to cry. She had been waiting for hours to hear positive news, occupying herself with simple preparations to welcome Theodora: setting out dry clothes beside the fire, warming towels to chafe her cold limbs, preparing a milk drink and placing it in a saucepan at one side of the embers. Now frustration and anger came bubbling up from within.

'Darling, don't cry,' exclaimed Rhys. Handing the lantern to Jeremy, he loped up the steps and reached to seize her upper arms. She shoved him away, backing into the kitchen with a look of horror on her face, as if, thought Rhys, he was some kind of criminal, a housebreaker intent on assaulting her.

'You promised me, you promised you'd stay there until she was found,' screamed Lisabeth, her voice shredded by the din of rain on the tin roof.

Jeremy followed Rhys into the kitchen and began stripping off his sodden coat. His face was sore from the slapping of wet leaves, icy fingers of rain reached to his waist. He said: 'Mr Day called the search off. He said there was no hope of finding anything and with the roar of the river you could shout yourself hoarse and not be heard. We could walk within a yard of her and not—'

331

Lisabeth didn't notice his presence. She was gripped with a fierce anger, the pressure of old grievances and resentments that had been lulled over the years by the soothing ointment of her love for Rhys but now erupted like festering boils, ugly and demanding attention. 'Don't touch me!' she shouted, words she had never uttered before. 'You care nothing for your children, so don't tell me that you gave your all to find poor Theodora! Look at how you drove your other children away! Look at how you've treated Andrew all these years, and Daisy, too. Should I be surprised if you care nothing for Theodora, either?'

I shouldn't have heard that, thought Jeremy, swiftly leaving through the door into the corridor beyond the kitchen. In the dimness he almost collided with Emma Day, who was hurrying to investigate the shouting. Her face was puckered in alarm. 'Is it bad news?'

In the kitchen, Rhys was stricken, stunned, the breath knocked out of his lungs by the ferocity of these accusations. Of course he loved Andrew, and Daisy, too, but none of what had happened was his fault, was it? Hadn't he tried to broach the truth to his son in the only way possible – bluntly – and hadn't Andrew turned on him, his own father, like a mad dog in response? He couldn't help it if things had turned out badly. He could hardly be blamed. And, then, wasn't his heart broken when Daisy flew to her brother's side, choosing him above her own father, then going off with the Launcenolts and uttering high-handed demands that only a spineless weakling with not an ounce of pride would accept? He was distraught, but he hid his feelings, reasoning that it was Daisy's place to be the obedient daughter, to come back to him and apologize. Certainly not to issue ultimatums in a hard voice with her eyes cold as stone. He'd borne his distress stoically over the years, taken comfort with Lisabeth, pushed aside hurtful mention of Daisy's name, left the room when Lisabeth tried to bring the subject up because of the pain those two syllables smote into his heart; and now, to his utter astonishment Lisabeth was blaming him. Accusing with as much venom as Daisy had done. As if he didn't care!

As abruptly as it had swelled, her anger subsided, and she was in tears, sharing his anguish instead of dumping her own on to him. 'I'm sorry, dearest, I truly am, but I can't bear it. Losing Andrew and Daisy has been such bitterness, such misery, and if we lose Theodora, too, I don't know . . . I don't know what I'll do.'

'Hush, darling,' soothed Rhys, folding her in the arms of his dripping coat, helpless to answer. He didn't know, either.

When Joseph Day returned from escorting some of the searchers home he reassured the distraught parents by telling them that children are hardy creatures and Theodora in particular was sturdy and strong. 'We'll find her tomorrow at first light, not a jot the worse for wear,' he said heartily. 'Just imagine how ecstatic you'll be to see her. A perfect family reunion, all of you together again.'

'Not quite all of us,' Rhys heard himself say. Stung by Lisabeth's earlier words, he had found himself musing over the whole situation. For the first time since Daisy had stormed out of Mists of Heaven, Rhys considered the mechanics of her terms. All she had demanded was Andrew's acknowledgement and public inclusion in the family. These were things he had years ago accepted as inevitable; so, he grudgingly conceded, all that stood in the way was that hard tone of Daisy's, the coldness of her eyes when she made her demands. The solution now seemed so simple, like a puzzle suddenly explained, one piece moved into position and all the others falling so easily – so obviously – into place. To Jeremy, Rhys said: 'I suppose you heard what my wife said earlier, when she mentioned . . . ah, Doctor Stafford?'

Jeremy was astounded to see that Rhys was so embarrassed that he couldn't utter his own son's name. What a tangled mesh of pride the man had wound around himself, and look at it now, tripping him up at every turn. He said, with pity: 'I was not surprised by what she said, sir. About Andrew being your son. For years it has been common belief in the province that for some reason you were reluctant to recognize him, and unfortunately there has been a great deal of speculation as to the reason.'

For a moment Jeremy wondered if he had been too bold. Rhys reared up in his chair by the fire. With his nostrils flaring, his blond-grey hair wild and wet, and with steam rising from his clothing, he looked for a moment like a *taniwha*, a Maori sea-monster. Then, when Jeremy braced himself for a blast of rage, Rhys froze into an attitude of stiffness and turned to Emma for corroboration. 'Well, is this true? I've heard no gossip, but you'll know what's being said. Please, Mrs Day, tell us, do. What are the wagging tongues saying?'

Emma's thin cheeks went pink. Though she enjoyed savouring juicy morsels of scandal, she indulged in secret, listening to whispers behind closed doors. With extreme reluctance she conceded that she might have overheard a chance remark or two, but no more than that.

'Do share them,' urged Rhys, not letting her off the hook.

'It's just that you and Doctor Stafford are so alike in appearance, I think,' said poor Emma. 'And the fact that Daisy and he are so close . . . working together and so on. It's taken for granted that he's your illegitimate—'

'Right,' said Rhys. The word seemed to cost him a real effort. 'He is my son, and it's high time I said so publicly. On Monday there'll be a notice on the front page of the *Lyttleton Times* announcing that Rhys Morgan has made a new will leaving his estate in five equal shares, one-fifth to his wife and the other shares to his four children. And I'll make

333

immediate cash settlements of ten thousand pounds each. Do you think that'll silence the gossips?'

Lisabeth laughed. 'It will stir up a hornet's nest of talk.'

'And I'll have the satisfaction of knowing I started it intentionally, which will make all the difference. Ay, that it will. I'll dare them openly to say what they like.'

'They'll admire you for your courage, sir,' said Jeremy, who was thinking: *Ten thousand pounds!* He and Daisy need have no worries about an impoverished future now. Ten thousand pounds would give them a fresh start anywhere in the world.

Lisabeth was kneeling in front of her husband. There was an abrasion below his jawline where a branch had whipped sharply against his face in the wild wetness. Gently she touched the place with her fingertips. 'I hate it when you talk about wills, but I love you for what you've done this evening. I know what it cost you to speak out, because saying all those terrible things to you cost me dearly, too. I love you, Rhys, and I've never been so proud of you as I am now.'

'It was nothing,' said Rhys, not noticing that Lisabeth ducked her head to hide an affectionate indulgent smile.

The rain stopped shortly before dawn. As the sky lightened Daisy noticed that the noise of rushing water had faded, too. The sky was pale overhead, smudged with pink, grey and blue like one of Lisabeth's watercolours. To the north a sprawl of soft grey cloud was tinted pink in the sunrise.

When Sarah stirred, noisily yawning, Daisy gave silent thanks, for at last she could move from her own stiff cramped position. All that rain and hurtling water had worked an insidious effect on her, and she was so desperate to relieve the pressure that a tight ache spread like a band right around her abdomen. Unbuckling the canvas screen, she pushed her way out of their shelter.

Sarah blinked rapidly, then rubbed her grit-rimmed eyes, complaining: 'What a terrible night! I've not slept a wink in the entire time! I say, can't you keep still, Daisy? Give a person a chance to grab a little bit of rest without being trampled.'

'Rest!' snorted Daisy impatiently. 'You were snoring so loudly that it's a miracle your throat isn't rubbed raw.'

Sarah ran her tongue around the inside of her mouth, grimacing. 'You're right. It is sore, and my mouth all dry.' She giggled and said unrepentantly: 'I hope I didn't keep you awake.'

'The river kept us awake,' Daisy told her. Picking her way down the slope, she gazed around for an accessible yet screened place to stop and squat down, where Andrew wouldn't see her. He was a prim prudish fellow still, and Daisy shrank from contemplating his shock and dismay (inevitable, she feared) when he found out about Jeremy. They would have to face him together, try to make him understand their desperation; but, though she hoped for his blessing, she feared that all they would get from Andrew would be a lecture about moral issues.

Pushing the prospect from her mind, Daisy picked her way down the slope over the stony ground. The Port Hills were extinct volcanoes, pitted with numerous tiny ridges and crevices on their slopes, so Daisy had to take extreme care as she descended until enough shrubbery had screened her from the road above. When she could no longer see the horses or the trap she lifted her skirts and squatted, sighing in blessed relief.

As she straightened – feeling enormously better – she noticed perhaps twenty yards further on a young clematis vine. In the night's battering it had been partially torn away from the young tree it was clinging to, and what remained of the crown of starry white flowers were shredded and limp, but even from here Daisy could see that the scour of water around its stem had unearthed some surface roots. Daisy hoped that the deeper roots would be loosened, too, enough for her to ease them out with a sharp twig and wrap them in some of the stripped leaves that were lying about. She felt that she had discovered treasure, for when she expressed a desire for one of these beautiful plants she knew how difficult it would be to find one small enough successfully to transplant. Scrambling down over the mossy rock-slope, Daisy paused to snap herself a stick from a *manuka* bush.

She had completed the delicate task of freeing the roots together with a sizeable ball of wet leaf-mould, and was looking about for material to plaster around the clump, when she heard the sound, a ragged mewing noise. Daisy stopped to listen carefully. In the trees below birds were scuffling and twittering, making scratching noises which were barely audible above the rushing of the hidden stream, but this was no bird; Daisy was sure of that. Having lived in the province almost her entire life, she knew and recognized by name every birdsong, and this was definitely neither of the two likelier ones: the weka, which could sound like a baby crying; or the greenish native parrot, adept at mimicking others' songs. This was definitely an animal – a wild cat, perhaps – marooned in a tree by the subsiding floodwaters. There it came again, faint but close, guessed Daisy. The poor thing sounded distressed, and no wonder. Even in last night's relative shelter Daisy had suffered enough dampness to catch a chill; she could feel it in the sudden flushes of warmth and just-as-sudden cold chills that swept through her.

'I'm coming to help you, little one,' she called. Putting aside her precious plant, she grabbed at *manuka* branches to impede her progress down the steeper slippery incline until she reached a point where she could go no further. Here she leaned forward until she was gazing down over the rim of a fifteen-foot escarpment.

At the foot of the drop, huddled against a flattened flax bush, was a young girl.

It was difficult to tell what age she was – only four or five, thought Daisy, and delicately built. She was wearing a gown which was originally of some warm cream-coloured fabric but which was now sodden and so plastered with mud that only by the lace collar and the embroidered smocking on the shoulders could Daisy tell it was expensive – the kind of dress she used to wear at that age.

Her face was raised towards the sound of Daisy's voice. Such a sad tear-ravaged face, paper-white, framed with rags of wet dark hair. 'Mamma!' she cried. 'Want Mamma!'

'Are you hurt?' asked Daisy, speaking her first thought, but in reply the girl began to wail that helpless yowling noise again. *Stupid question!* thought Daisy, for even if nothing was broken the night's exposure would have made the poor child ill at the very least. Her voice had a harsh cracked sound to it. *Bronchitis,* thought Daisy.

'Wait there,' ordered Daisy. Another stupid thing to say, which prompted more pathetic cries. Daisy hesitated, then fled back to the others for help.

'I've found her!' she cried. Andrew was down the road surveying the half-exposed bridge, and Sarah was holding the horses while they grazed at the sodden clover at the roadside. 'I've found her!' She called to Andrew. 'Those searchers last night – they must have been looking for a lost little girl, and she's down there, beside the river. It's an absolute miracle that she wasn't swept away.'

'There really were searchers?' asked Sarah.

'Quickly!' cried Daisy. 'Come and help me bring her up, Andrew. No, you stay here, Sarah. The ground is so slippery, you could fall.'

'Yes, darling. You look after yourself,' Andrew told her as he followed Daisy. Pausing only to grab a picnic-rug from the trap, he hurried after Daisy.

The girl had not moved. She was huddled, hugging her chest, crying quietly, but when they approached she stopped whimpering to watch them and, looking at the small face with the slanting green eyes, Daisy felt an odd stir of recognition which she didn't understand until she glanced at Andrew's intent face and realized that the child vaguely resembled him. Andrew and Sarah's baby could look very like this child, she thought with a rush of auntly warmth.

She was quiet until Daisy began unbuttoning the collar of her gown, whereupon she shrieked in protest. 'It's all right, dear. We're both doctors and we're going to check you over and make sure that everything is all right, before we take you home. If you've a bone broken, we would have to make a stretcher before we could move you.' But her explanation was lost in wails which Daisy was forced to ignore as she stripped the sodden clothes from the child's thin shoulders.

'Nanny said I mustn't take my dress off,' sobbed the girl.

'Nanny didn't know you were going to get all wet and cold, did she now?' replied Daisy, thinking that she had guessed right, that this was a child from a wealthy family. She said, 'And what does Nanny call you, pet?' but the child mulishly clamped her mouth shut, shivering in frightened discomfort as Daisy gently checked her over for injuries.

'She's absolutely uninjured,' Daisy reported, lifting her skirts so that she could strip off a petticoat to drape over the child's bare shoulders like a tent. 'Here, little one, this will keep you dry while we take off those nasty wet stockings and shoes. Doctor Stafford, would you wrap her in the blanket now, please? He'll rub your shoulders and arms so that soon you'll stop that shivering and feel snug and warm again. All right?' She smiled, and chatted, to distract from what she was doing under the petticoat. 'Don't you feel like telling us your name? You had lots and lots of people looking for you, right on into the middle of the night. They had lanterns and they looked everywhere, but they didn't find you. My goodness, pet, won't they be pleased to see you safe and well?'

But still the child, sullen and mistrustful, refused to speak to them.

On the way up to the trap Daisy, who was carrying the wet clothes, stopped to collect her clematis plant. She would treasure this as a souvenir of last night: a storm, an adventure and the strange events of this morning.

Andrew, puffing under the load, was wondering if there might be a reward for finding the child. Lord knows, they could do with every scrap of extra they could find right now, with Sarah's income about to cease. To cheer himself up he talked about what would happen in the next few hours, how he'd have a hot bath, a glass of brandy to warm away this chill, and a huge platter of bacon, eggs and crumpets.

'I suppose you'd like some of that, too,' said Daisy as they settled the girl on the trap seat. She was going to help Andrew with the horses when, as she moved away, the girl suddenly wriggled her arms free of the petticoat waistband and flung them around Daisy's neck, snuggling her freezing-cold face into Daisy's neck. Daisy was so moved by this unexpected gesture that tears came into her own eyes. It gave her such a delicious sensation of strength and protectiveness, yet at the same time set up a keen yearning in her, too.

'Am I going to get some help here?' asked Andrew from behind her. 'The river might be down far enough for us to cross now.'

'I'll help you,' said Sarah, 'though I think you're being optimistic. That water is still very high.' She climbed down to hold the horses while Andrew harnessed them. Daisy, meanwhile, took her place in the trap and was delighted when the little girl immediately climbed on to her lap and snuggled against her again. Sarah tossed them a glance. 'You're supposed to be treating the child, not adopting her,' she commented.

Daisy said: 'Whoever she is, they're not over-feeding her. She feels as light as one of the Benares peacocks, and you could play a xylophone on these ribs, as Papa used to say.'

'My papa says that, too.' The child's neck twisted. 'Are you taking me to meet my papa?'

'If you tell us who he is,' Andrew assured her as he helped Sarah up into the wagon then climbed in beside her.

The girl began to cough, so Daisy rubbed her back. Sarah, who was feeling decidedly left out, said: 'A child suits you, Daisy. I think we should find you a nice prosperous rancher so that you can settle down and raise a family of your own.' Then, knowing that Andrew would point out that Daisy couldn't be spared and Sarah mustn't put ideas into her head, she interrupted herself quickly to say: 'Look up the coast, will you! Look at that rainbow in the sea mist! It's moving over on to the land. Isn't that the most beautiful thing?'

She felt even more excluded when immediately Daisy and Andrew said, together, 'That's our rainbow!' and both laughed.

'Your rainbow? Both of you?'

'Yes, ours,' said Daisy, gazing at the perfect shimmering arch that now poised between mountains and ocean far into the distance. The clear bands of colour seemed to be painted on the mist that floated behind it. 'Tell Sarah about it, Andrew. You tell the story so well.' She adjusted the weight of the child in her lap. 'Our little girl would like to hear it, too, I'm sure.' She waited for him to begin, but instead he whistled between his teeth at what lay before them.

From the observation-place where they had spent the night it had appeared that the way was clear, but now that they were down level with the bridge they saw what had been screened from above. On their side of the structure a gaping rent had been scoured out of the road by the raging water which still swirled through it and poured back into the riverbed in a gushing brown waterfall a dozen or so yards downstream.

'I wonder how deep it is,' mused Andrew.

Probably too deep to negotiate, for the decking of the bridge was still awash with a dark flood. Branches, swards of grass and matted vegetation were draped along the sides, showing how high the water had been in the night. Immediately beyond the bridge stood a dark brown brougham with matched bay horses. The driver was standing down at the bridge approach, sizing up its condition. Beside him was another man.

'Jeremy!' piped the girl on Daisy's lap. 'Look, there's Jeremy!'

He looked as scruffy as she felt, his velvet jacket torn at the elbow, jodhpurs streaked with mud, his boots black with moisture. Seeing his unslept stubbly face brought back poignant recollections of how he had looked after their exhausting night of passion – just like this, bleary-eyed and unshaven, that lock of hair flopping on to his forehead. He was staring at Daisy and at the child in her arms. They heard him whoop with exhultation, and Andrew said: 'He must have been out with the search party, too.'

'Jeremy!' called the child, but he had turned away. It was only when he went loping back down the road that those in the trap noticed a couple standing at the roadside, gazing down into the gully.

'Of course she won't be swept out to sea,' Rhys was saying, trying to sound more confident than he felt, for that was the essence of his night-mare: that Theodora had been washed away in the floodwaters, perhaps never to be found. As Lisabeth began to quake again he put a reassuring arm around her and drew her against him. 'Darling, most of our fears are our own imaginings. Please promise me that you'll—'

Her eyes were as dark as the swirling river below. 'I've been expecting something terrible to happen to us,' she said with sudden violence. 'This is our punishment, Rhys. This is what we've brought down on ourselves for all the years we flouted society. We went against everything that was decent and acceptable, and now God—'

'No,' he said harshly, his fingers digging into the soft flesh of her shoulders so hard that the pain made her wince. 'I won't have you saying such things. You're not even to think them! If there's a God, He under-stands our feelings for each other. He made us, didn't He? Lisabeth darling, please—'

'Sir!' interrupted Jeremy, thudding along the road towards them, his boots shearing through puddles and sending up wings of water. His voice was shrill with excitement. 'Sir! She's been found and she's safe. It's incredible, it's wonderful.' Whooping, he swung Lisabeth up in his arms, then immediately realized what he was doing and set her down, blushing furiously and stammering apologies.

Lisabeth barely noticed his confusion. 'Where is she?' she demanded, but Rhys, speechless at the news, grabbed her hand and dragged her after him as he sped back to the bridge. Jeremy ran alongside.

'Who found her?' Rhys wanted to know.

'You're not going to believe this,' panted Jeremy, smiling. He couldn't contain the joy he felt. Laughter surged through his veins like foam. This was Fate, a sign that the future would be everything he hoped, and from today onwards he and Daisy would be sharing their lives. She had to say Yes. Anything else was inconceivable now. This was an omen, after a black night of anxiety a glorious morning with all fears gone, all uncertainties melted away.

From where she sat Daisy saw what was happening and at once she understood. The realization struck Andrew at the same time, and he, too, gaped at Theodora in astonishment. 'Great Heavens! This is incredible!' he muttered.

'What? What's incredible?' snapped Sarah, her patience exhausted. Would nobody ever explain anything to her?

'We've found our own sister. This is Theodora,' Daisy told her. She was thrilling with a queer shock; all the hairs on her arms and legs rose up as if a charged silk scarf had been passed over her body. 'Oh, Theodora! I'm your—'

But Theodora didn't hear her hesitant introduction. As soon as she sighted her mamma and papa she began to wail, and nothing Daisy could do would calm her. Wriggling free of Daisy's embrace, she flung out her thin white arms imploringly and screamed, all the terror and misery of the past night bellowing out of her frail body.

'Hush, darling. You're safe now,' begged Daisy ineffectually. 'Sarah, help me. The poor lass will rupture herself. Who would have thought such a tiny creature had so much noise in her?'

Sarah didn't reply. Her gaze swung from Theodora across the chasm to where the three people stood. Jeremy looked so pleased with himself that he might have arranged this whole thing, and beside him the older couple clung together laughing in relief. As the significance of it all dawned on her a great swelling of satisfaction rose inside her and she folded her hands in gratitude over her belly. Here, upon them, was the reconciliation she had longed for, had prayed for and dreamed about.

'I'm coming over!' shouted Rhys.

'It's too dangerous!' protested Andrew, but Rhys was already plunging into the torrent, gripping the bridge-rail and pulling himself along hand-over-hand as the murky water swirled around his waist.

'Papa!' shrieked Theodora in terror. 'Papa, don't get dwownded!'

'Hush,' pleaded Daisy, though fear froze her and she had to force herself to look away. This was too reminiscent of other horrors, and a sick feeling of inevitability clogged her mind and she hugged Theodora despite the child's frantic struggles to be free.

But Rhys forged easily through the flood, brushing debris aside and wrenching a jammed branch out of his way as easily as if it was a tangle of spider-web. Andrew had jumped down from the trap and hurried to help him, but there was no need. Ignoring his son's out-thrust hand, he scrambled up the bank with a hoarse 'Thank God'; but then, at the top, instead of rushing to snatch Theodora in his arms, he stood for a moment staring Andrew in the face. 'Son,' he said simply. 'I don't know what to say. I can't tell you how I feel for the way I've treated you. I'm sorry . . . I'm sorry, son.'

Andrew gaped at his father, at the shamed face, the hopefully extended arms and, with a gasp, walked into his embrace. Daisy, daring to look now, saw the bemused expression on Andrew's face. When her father turned she saw that he was openly weeping. Moved, she felt the scratchy budding of tears in her own eyes. He raised his arms to encompass both her and Theodora, crushing them together and against his shoulders, his head thrust between them and his wet face kissing first one then the other as over and over he said: 'Thank God, thank God for you all. Thank God you're all safe.'

'It's a miracle, isn't it?' said Daisy ecstatically. 'When I found . . . when *we* found Theodora down by the river we marvelled that she was perfectly unharmed.'

Rhys stood back a pace, disentangling himself from Theodora's thin clinging arms so that he could stare at his eldest daughter. 'Don't you know?' he said. 'You were reported missing, too. All three of you. The Superintendent at Seaview was worried when the storm blew up and telephoned to make certain that you'd arrived home safely. When it was discovered you hadn't, Joseph Day was contacted and asked to look out for you. He told me, but I've kept the news from Lisabeth. She was already beside herself over Theodora. Daisy, child, I've been pacing the floor all night out of my mind with grief and worry thinking I'd lost all of you. Thinking that I'd left it too late to tell you how much I love you all and how stubborn I've been. I . . . I just. . . .' His voice cracked, and his jaw worked to free the words that were jammed in his throat.

Daisy's own emotions erupted in a rush. Standing up, she leaned forward, falling against him and out of the trap in the one movement. Her arms wound around his neck. 'Papa, I'm so very proud of you,' she told him, laughing and sobbing as she tugged a damp handkerchief from her fob pocket and tenderly blotted his face with it. 'Here,' she said. 'You haven't met Andrew's wife, Sarah.'

'Welcome to the family . . . daughter,' said Rhys.

'Thank you,' said Sarah with a sly smile. 'And might there be room in that family for a grandchild?' She extended a hand in greeting. 'We're both delighted to meet you.'

Daisy's attention swung back to where Jeremy and Lisabeth were waiting across the stream. Both were smiling and waving. Lisabeth was crying in sheer relief at the same time, while Jeremy jollied her with one arm about her shoulders. Even at this distance Daisy could sense his frustration; longing to be beside her, he was staying with Lisabeth out of politeness.

He's doing the right thing, thought Daisy suddenly. It was a tiny stray thought, but it gave her a jolt.

It was Lisabeth who insisted that they all squeeze into the brougham and return together to Mists of Heaven for a celebration breakfast. Jeremy drove the trap, waiting until the waters had subsided, then catching up to them at Sumner where the search had been called off and where Andrew and Rhys were thanking the volunteer searchers. Inside the Days' cottage Daisy was telephoning Kiki and Beatrice to assure them that she was safe. 'Come out to Mists of Heaven for the festivities,' she urged. 'Lisabeth has rung the cook and ordered an enormous hot lunch with iced champagne. Please won't you come, too?'

Beatrice hesitated. Daisy could sense her apprehension. 'If you're sure we won't be in the way,' she finally said.

Daisy laughed. 'Of course not,' she chided. But as she rejoined the others she looked thoughtful.

Jeremy was just arriving. She could see from the tension on his face that he was aching to talk to her, to be alone with her, and as soon as he could he touched her elbow, drawing her away from where Emma was leaning into the brougham, fussing over the baby. 'Ride back to the house with me,' he urged.

Daisy shrugged unhappily. She felt as if a great surging ocean of indecision lay between her and the answer he was waiting for. 'I wish . . . I wish life could be straightforward.'

'It can be,' Jeremy told her.

'I wonder. I wanted to stay behind with you, and ride down with you in the trap, but I didn't. I couldn't, Jeremy. It would scandalize the whole town if you and I were seen together alone, especially at that hour of the day, wouldn't it? I want to be strong, and stare the world down and tell them I don't care a fig for their opinions, but I do care, Jeremy. I didn't even have the courage to stay behind with you, and I'm appalled with myself. I'm a coward, Jeremy, and I—'

'Hush. . . . Never mind,' soothed Jeremy, for Rhys was approaching. 'I'll talk to you out at the house. Ask me to show you Donegal's latest little filly, will you?' And with that arranged he climbed back into the trap.

Morning mist still floated on the harbour. A cluster of gannets perched on a rocky promontory, holding drying wings up to the early sun. It was Sunday, a fact which jolted Daisy when, as they passed the Ferrymead church, the bells suddenly began to peal. She stared at the grey stone fence and the tidy serried gravestones and thought: *I have to give Jeremy my answer today.*

'The world is fast asleep!' exclaimed Lisabeth as they rolled past quiet cottages, still tucked behind quilts of shore mist. 'Isn't it astounding that we've had a night of absolute agony and the rest of the world is sleeping blissfully, quite unperturbed. Don't you think so, Daisy?'

'Sorry!' Daisy flushed. 'I didn't hear the question. I was miles away.'

'In Wellington, perhaps?' insinuated Sarah archly. She was sitting beside Rhys, her face alight with excitement as she gave him sideways glances of admiring awe. The enormity of what was happening was too much for her to contemplate at once. Here they were, reconciled and good friends again (for Andrew and Rhys were talking like old friends, moving easily from one subject to another) and on their way to Mists of Heaven, the mansion of Sarah's dreams and aspirations. And it had all fallen into place because the river rose too quickly for them to cross. It made Sarah shiver to think of how delicately their fate had hung in the balance. Had they stopped for the night a quarter of a mile in either direction, they'd never have discovered Theodora, none of this would be happening now.

Lisabeth was joggling Anne on her lap, trying to subdue Theodora's whining bids for attention with quick cuddles while attempting to subdue the baby's fractious wails by consoling her with a rag-twist dipped in sugar-water. When she heard Sarah's remark she picked it up, glad of a distraction. 'In Wellington? Does this mean a young man, Daisy?'

Daisy's discomfiture deepened. Sarah, her tongue loosened by her high spirits, said: 'Andrew and I were wondering the exact same thing! Daisy has been very mysterious lately and—'

'Mamma, my feet are still sore,' complained Theodora. Seeing an escape, Daisy quickly offered to chafe them for her and get the circulation going.

'That's good of you,' accepted Lisabeth. 'You know, Daisy,' she confided, 'these two cause me so much anxiety between them, yet nothing in the world has given me more pleasure than they have.'

'Nothing?' teased Rhys, reaching over to pat her knee.

'Nothing,' repeated Lisabeth firmly. She wrinkled her nose at him and slid him an affectionate smile. 'Last night when Theodora was lost I thought it would be the end of the world if anything happened to her. Suddenly I remembered all the things I'd been planning to tell her, things I'd been hoping to do. It came upon me that hers is a fresh new life through which I can gain a different insight on to the world . . . and of course, I realized for the first time what mother love really means. I think it takes a crisis like that to awaken the full depths of a mother's feeling.'

Listening, Daisy experienced another jolt of recognition. It was as if Lisabeth's confidences were opening a window for her, too, one she had never glanced into before. *Supposing we do go to Canada or somewhere and take Silas with us*, she was thinking. *And supposing some crisis happens to him. It's bound to – children invariably get sick or hurt. I know that Arabella didn't show much concern when Silas was ill before, but that doesn't mean she wouldn't next time. She is his mother. It's her right to be with him when she needs to be. We can't take him away.*

Dismay seeped through her like a stain. She glanced up, and her eyes met Andrew's for a second before she glanced away. She hoped he couldn't read her thoughts. The brougham was rounding a long slow corner. From where she sat she could see Jeremy following in the trap, keeping well back to avoid breathing in the dust swirled up by their wheels. *How symbolic*, she thought bleakly. *I'm whisking along with Jeremy following just too far behind, while between us the issue is this great ugly cloud, this turmoil of doubts.*

At lunch she was quiet. Sitting opposite her, Jeremy tried to coax a smile by describing his floundering and wallowing in the dark wet bush the night before. She listened to him with the same leaden attention she gave to Andrew's umpteenth (and beginning to sound pompous) recital of how they had discovered Theodora.

Finally Jeremy said, 'Would you like to see Donegal's latest filly?' and Daisy started, belatedly remembering that she was supposed to have used that pretext herself.

Andrew glanced over as she pushed her chair back. 'Try to talk her out of this Wellington business, would you, old chap?' he said, his tongue thickened by the champagne he had drunk. 'Sarah and I have kept quiet, let her make up her own mind and all that, but dash it all, to be honest we need her.'

'We certainly do,' piped up Sarah. 'Can't *you* persuade her to stay, Mr Morgan? After all, you'll want her to come home to live *here* now, won't you?' she added, taking a sip from her crystal goblet.

Beatrice bridled, tucking her chin down and breathing in through flared nostrils. 'Her home', she enunciated clearly, 'is with us!' And, so saying, she stabbed a piece of bacon with her fork and sawed into it.

Sarah said artlessly: 'Benares is very nice, of course, but this house is a *mansion*.' She sighed. 'Wouldn't it be heavenly to wake up in the morning and come floating down to breakfast down the wide marble staircase. And the views!'

'One gets used to it remarkably quickly, I believe,' said Daisy, trying to keep the peace and deflect attention from herself so that she could leave unobtrusively. 'After all, home is where the heart is, don't you agree, Lisabeth?' As she spoke she glanced at Jeremy. He was gazing at her with an undisguised expression of longing that she felt certain was being observed by everyone else in the room. Nobody, however, was taking any notice: Beatrice and Sarah were exchanging haughty glances; Lisabeth and Gwynne were fussing over Theodora, coaxing the exhausted child to eat; while Rhys was gazing out through the french doors across the wide sweep of lawn to the rose garden, beyond which the ridge of the huge red shed was just visible. He said, suddenly and loudly: 'We might have lost everything we owned today, if not for Gwynne. And she could have been killed, too. I'd have not valued her life at twopence if she'd come along once the fire was under way.'

All looked startled. Gwynne, flushed with importance, said: 'You're exaggerating, Rhys. Exaggerating! Tommy Nevin is a good lad at heart. He'd not have let harm come to me.'

'I'm not so sure.' Looking at the puzzled faces, Rhys quickly explained yesterday afternoon's events, then told how he had been warned that something like this might happen. There was a rumour amongst the wool-buyers that the 'Baron' was offering a first-class clip for sale and much speculation about where he was planning to get it.

'What are you going to do?' asked Lisabeth. 'I don't think I could sleep an easy night in my bed now, for fear he's planning to torch the place.' She interrupted herself to glare at Gwynne. 'And don't you dare make remarks about white stone being unlucky, and how we've brought this down upon our own heads.'

Rhys laughed. 'Nothing like that will happen. I'm buying the "Baron" out. He's not been happy at White Clouds since that nephew of his was killed. I'll give him a fair price and send him on his way home to England. Tommy Nevin can stay on as manager; but if he puts a foot wrong – sorry, unfortunate pun – he'll be sent packing, too.' He glanced at Daisy, who was standing behind her chair; having got up to go with Jeremy, she was wondering whether she should sit down again. 'I thought you two wanted to inspect the filly?' Rhys said. 'She's in that pen on the cliff-top by the old cottage. McFallish thought the sea air would be good for her, I think. Go on, then,' he said. 'Don't be long. Jeremy and I have a wager to settle from yesterday's race.' He yawned. 'Yesterday! It seems a million miles away and half an age in another universe.'

'Who won the race, then?' murmured Daisy at the doorway. She'd forgotten yesterday's excitement, the town empty, everybody at the races for the big meeting.

'Who won? *I* did . . . at last!' he said, pulling the door shut behind them. 'I warn you, Daisy. I always do win in the end.' One hand holding the door fast, he grabbed her arm with the other and jerked her hard against him. His breath was hot against her neck, and his lips were moist as he whispered harshly: 'Last night was the longest of my life. When Rhys told me that you hadn't arrived home from that wretched picnic I imagined all manner of terrible things might have happened. Your trap could have overturned . . . you could have so easily been killed.' He shuddered. 'Mom always told me I had an over-active imagination, and last night it put me through torments.'

'And nothing did happen,' she murmured, twining her hands behind his neck. In the corridor's dim light her eyes were liquid, glowing with an inner radiance. He reminded her of the time when Silas was so alarmingly ill, and his vulnerability moved her.

From somewhere further along the corridor a door shut with a clap. Daisy moved away from him at once. 'Let's go outside before Mrs Tenks

345

discovers us here,' she said, dodging out of his embrace as he tried to kiss her again. As she walked towards the front door she glanced back with a theatrical shudder. 'You see, Jeremy? I *am* a coward.'

'A coward? You're wrong,' he hissed, overtaking her in the cavernous cool hallway and gripping her shoulders so that she had no option but to face him. 'You're one of the bravest people I know. You've plunged out into the world and made something solid and worthwhile out of your life, when you could have done what all the other young ladies do: frittered your time away on tea-mornings and at-homes and stitching needlepoint in front of the fire. Last night I did a lot of thinking about that, and I realized for the first time what an important person you are not just to me, but to the province. You're a true pioneer, aren't you? You've forged a path where other women might follow. I don't mind telling you, Daisy, that I'm humbled to think that you'd chuck it all and go galloping off halfway around the world with me.'

'Please Jeremy, I . . .,' she began, but he stilled her with a kiss which he transferred with his fingertips from his lips to hers. 'And you're wrong about something else, too,' he told her softly. 'Last night something did happen. Last night I came face to face with the realization that you are the centre of my existence, the well-spring of my joy, the focus of my hopes and ambitions. In other words, young lady, I cannot live without you.' With that he opened the door and escorted her out into the sunlight.

Confusion swamped Daisy. How could she give Jeremy his answer when there seemed to be no practical solution to their dilemma? He seemed to be taking it for granted that she'd turn her back on everything and stroll off with him, but she was still assailed by doubts. They couldn't take Silas away from New Zealand, which meant Daisy would have to accept the Wellington post, and the more she contemplated that the less happy she felt. There would be a certain adventure, a piquancy in carrying on a long-term affair with Jeremy, but how soon would their love pall if their encounters were all secretive, behind closed bedroom doors? They wouldn't even be able to stroll through the Botanical Gardens for fear of arousing scandal. And five years. . . . She sighed and glanced up at Jeremy, her heart contracting with that familiar ache of yearning. Surely the prospect of being with him eventually would make the long years worthwhile? They'd have their moments to treasure, and anticipation would sharpen those moments. She loved just being beside him like this, to curl her fingers around the fine linen of his sleeve, to be able to breathe in the warm soapy smell of his skin when she leaned closer, and to smile at the frown that had gathered between his eyes as he squinted in the harsh sunlight. There was a tiny cut under his jawline where he had nicked it while hastily shaving before the meal. She wanted to kiss it, she wanted to be able to kiss him here, out in the

346

sunshine without a care of who might see or what they might think. *If only Canada wasn't so far away*, she thought. *If only life was simpler, if only problems could come with neatly packaged solutions.*

In silence they walked past the orangery where the dark foliage dripped on to slicked paving stones. There was a sharp sweet tang in the air until they emerged beyond the clipped hedges to the cliff-path where rose a waft of salt air from the ocean. The sky was a pale washed blue and the sea grey and cold and so loud today that they could hear the waves' gravelly breath as they raked over the beach far below. Daisy paused to pluck a blue wild flower from a bank. Its petals were soggy and bruised. It steamed faintly. Gazing towards the sweep of mountains beyond the plain, Daisy said: 'Look, there's another rainbow, in the mist over by the mountains. How innocent it seems! Who could imagine last night's storm?'

Jeremy was looking at her, studying her face. 'I love you.'

She shivered. 'And I love you.' The words burst out of her like birdsong in a spontaneous rush. 'I love you, Jeremy Drake!'

He sat down on a rock and drew her down beside him. She waited, expecting him to ask for her answer, but instead he surprised her by saying: 'How does it feel to be here at Mists of Heaven again?'

'Marvellous! I didn't realize how much I'd missed the place. I—' She stopped, confused. 'That wasn't what you want to hear, was it?'

He shook his head. 'I want the truth. I've been the romantic impetuous one, making grand plans to sweep you away to a new life in another country, but last night I realized that I had no right to uproot you from everything you've built up so carefully. Today has confirmed that decision. I overheard Sarah telling Emma Day that she wants you to bring her baby into the world, that she hopes you'll be the baby's godmother. Rhys is already planning a fireworks display to mark his grandchild's arrival. If I took you away. . . .'

She gaped at him. Only a few moments ago he was saying that he couldn't live without her, and she had been struggling with the anguish of her decision; but now, calmly, he was telling her he had made up his mind in quite the opposite direction. There would be no elopement, no new life, no future together. Interrupting, she cried: 'Don't you think I'd rather be with you than be a godmother a hundred times over? I love you, Jeremy. *Us* – isn't that what's important? Us!'

'What about your career? It's more significant than you realize. Sure, you and Sarah have already proved a point, but Sarah is out of it now, and she's looking to you to carry the torch for her, too. Women everywhere are talking about you, you know. They're thinking: "If she can march out and establish herself in a man's world, then maybe I can, too!" Dash it all, Daisy, you're an inspiration, and you've a responsibility not to let your image down. If a scandal does break over your head, people will gleefully say: ''There, that proves it! Women are too flighty and unreliable to be doctors.'' '

He was right, and the recognition winded her. This was so unfair! All along she had known that Canada and Wellington were makeshift solutions to their problems, but now that he had dismissed them, and her too, she was desolate. He was rejecting her for all the things about her that he most admired. Indignantly she protested: 'You make me sound noble and good and strong, but I'm not like that at all.' Tears choked her. 'I don't want to think of a future without you, Jeremy. I can't bear to face the thought of losing you.'

'Losing me? That's not going to happen.' He put an arm about her shoulders and drew her close to him. When she didn't pull away he said: 'You're not afraid that someone might see us sitting here together? You're not worried that people would gossip if they saw us walking along the path?'

She stared at him oddly. 'Of course not. You come here often, don't you? And this is my father's property, after all. Why should—?'

'Exactly. I'm here so often that Lisabeth has threatened to give me my own room. I've already a closetful of clothes here and a set of toiletries in one of the bathrooms. Silas is at home here, too – he's one of the few children Theodora can play with peaceably.' His grin widened as he saw a flicker of comprehension in her eyes. 'You'll be spending a lot of time out here now, and I'll simply go on as before.' He lowered his head and whispered in her ear. 'I sleepwalk, you know.'

Daisy pulled away. 'No! Absolutely not! After all the misery I suffered over the years because of Papa's relationship with Lisabeth I couldn't possibly consider doing the same thing. And under their roof, too? No, Jeremy . . . if you knew a fraction of what I'd endured, the shame, the humiliation, you'd never suggest such a thing.'

Jeremy kneeled in front of her. 'But I *am* suggesting it, and seriously, too,' he said, unclenching her knotted hands and taking them in his. Gently he said: '*Is* it such a shocking idea? You said yourself that nobody would think anything of it if they saw us together here, and it's true. We'll have to exercise some discretion of course, but out here we can go for rides, take walks, bring Silas and Theodora down to the beach for picnics, go out in that little rowboat. We can have *fun* together . . . get to know each other, and all in an open atmosphere with no fear of scandal. And, if we're very daring, we could go swimming at the old dam.'

Her lips twitched. She was resolutely staring down at their twined fingers, but he knew she was listening, considering his proposal. He continued eagerly: 'I often go to concerts and to the ballet with Lisabeth and Rhys. You'll come, too. And if I was a member of your party at a dance who would raise their eyebrows if we enjoyed a waltz or two together? We could do none of those things in Wellington.'

Daisy bit her lips, then said doubtfully: 'It still seems so terribly wrong. After all the nasty things I thought about Papa and Lisabeth. . . .'

'Then, look on this as your reward. They exposed you to the pain of gossip once; now they'll be shielding you from it. And, once my divorce is through, then what more natural than we get married? Our families are old friends after all.'

Slowly she met his eyes. 'You make it all sound so easy.'

'It will be.'

'It may not be so easy to treat that sleepwalking, though. Even for an eminent lady physician like myself.'

'Treat it? You want to *cure* me?'

Only then did he see the mischief in her expression. 'I'll have to find a way to make certain that it keeps recurring.'

Hugging her, he laughed in an eruption of delight. 'You'll think of something, sure you will! Next Saturday, perhaps? Lisabeth and Rhys are hosting an Italian dinner-party, and I know they'll invite you to stay over. I'll be counting the hours. But be warned: Italians can be excessively passionate people!' He stared up into her face, his smile fading as a warm surge of emotion welled through him. 'Daisy, I adore you.'

'So you keep saying.' She tried to be light-hearted, but her voice shook, too. She wondered how she could endure a whole week of empty waiting until Saturday night when they would be in each other's arms, but then immediately she knew, for Jeremy had given her the answer. Instead of marking time from one stolen moment to the next, her life would be full and rich and open, filled with love and laughter and good things. The best of everything. 'Come,' she said. 'You have a filly to show me, and then we'd better rejoin the others. Oh, Jeremy, I'm so perfectly happy!'

'You deserve to be,' he told her. '*We* deserve to be. And so we shall. For all of our lives.'

'For ever,' she agreed.

Arm in arm like old friends, they walked along the cliff-path. The sun warmed their faces. From the distance rose the rasp and slap of waves and a haunting cry of gulls wheeling like kites above the surf. The last of the rain-cloud had dissolved, erasing the rainbow and leaving the mountains standing in a clean line from one end of the horizon to the other. Daisy thought they had never been so beautiful as they were at this moment. Just looking at them filled her with a wild strange joy.

475